# Ligurian Mission

## The Ninth Carlisle & Holbrooke Naval Adventure

## Chris Durbin

Chris Durbin

To

Louise

Our daughter-in-law

Ligurian Mission

Editor: Lucia Durbin

Cover Artwork: Bob Payne

Cover Design: Book Beaver

First Edition: March 2021

Chris Durbin

# CONTENTS

Chris Durbin

# LIST OF CHARTS

# NAUTICAL TERMS

Throughout the centuries, sailors have created their own language to describe the highly technical equipment and processes that they use to live and work at sea. This holds true in the twenty-first century.

While counting the number of nautical terms that I've used in this series of novels, it became evident that a printed book wasn't the best place for them. I've therefore created a glossary of nautical terms on my website:

https://chris-durbin.com/glossary/

My glossary of nautical terms is limited to those that I've mentioned in this series of novels as they were used in the middle of the eighteenth century. It's intended as a work of reference to accompany the Carlisle & Holbrooke series of naval adventure novels.

Some of the usages of these terms have changed over the years, so this glossary should be used with caution when referring to periods before 1740 or after 1780.

The glossary isn't exhaustive; Falconer's Universal Dictionary of the Marine, first published in 1769, contains a more comprehensive list. I haven't counted the number of terms that Falconer has defined, but he fills 328 pages with English language terms, followed by an additional eighty-three pages of French translations. It is a monumental work.

There is an online version of the 1780 edition of The Universal Dictionary (which unfortunately does not include all the excellent diagrams that are in the print version) at this website:

https://archive.org/details/universaldiction00falc/

# PRINCIPAL CHARACTERS

## Fictional

**Captain Edward Carlisle**: Commanding Officer, *Dartmouth*

**Robert Mackenzie:** *British Envoy to the Kingdom of Sardinia*

**Matthew Gresham**: First Lieutenant, *Dartmouth*

**John Halsey:** Second Lieutenant, *Dartmouth*

**David Wishart**: Third Lieutenant, *Dartmouth*

**Arthur Beazley**: Sailing Master, *Dartmouth*

**Enrico Angelini**: Midshipman, *Dartmouth*. Cousin to Lady Chiara

**Able Seaman Whittle**: a follower of Captain Carlisle's from his home in Virginia

**Lady Chiara Angelini**: Captain Carlisle's wife

**Viscountess Angelini**: Lady Chiara's aunt

**Black Rod**: Chief-of-Household of the Angelini family

## Historical

**William Pitt:** Leader of the House of Commons

**Lord George Anson:** First Lord of the Admiralty

**Vice-Admiral Sir Charles Saunders:** Commander-in-Chief Mediterranean Squadron

**Lieutenant-General James Paterson**: Governor of the Sardinian province of Nice

Chris Durbin

# The Western Mediterranean

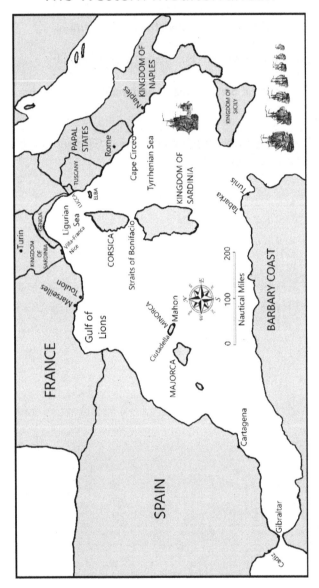

x

# Southern Approaches to Port Mahon

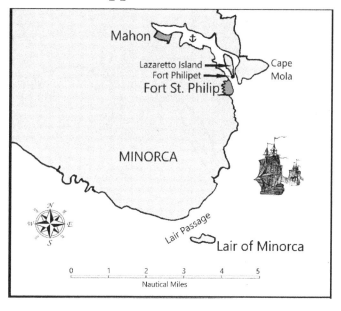

Mahon

Lazaretto Island
Fort Philipet
Fort St. Philip

Cape
Mola

MINORCA

N
W E
S

Lair Passage

Lair of Minorca

0   1   2   3   4   5
Nautical Miles

# Ligurian Sea

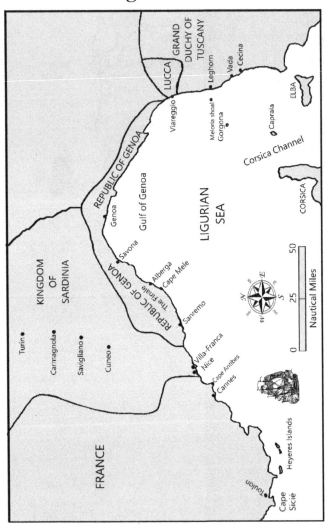

# Nice & Villa-Franca

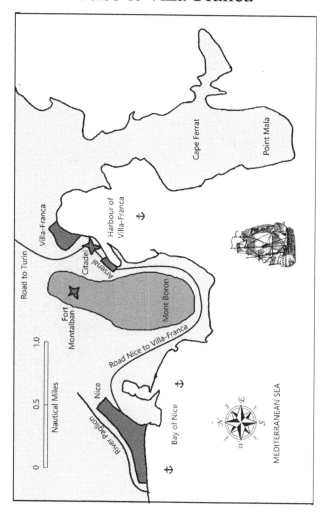

# Cecina & Vada

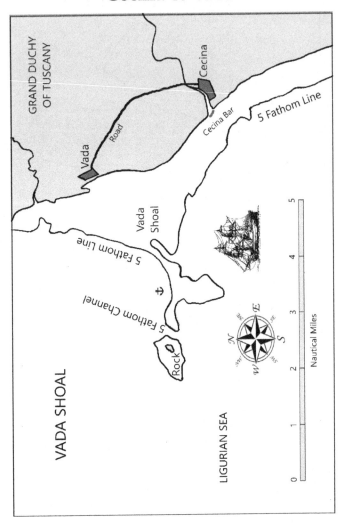

# '*A house divided against itself, cannot stand.*'

*Abraham Lincoln, later President of the United States, on
June 16, 1858
at the Illinois State Capitol in Springfield.*

*Paraphrasing Saint Matthew's Gospel.*

Chris Durbin

# INTRODUCTION

## The Seven Years War at the end of 1759

The end of 1759 was the turning point for Britain's fortunes in the war. In Europe, the allied forces had won at Minden, and Frederick of Prussia had turned the defeat at Kunersdorf into a strategic victory, as the Austrian and Prussian armies failed to follow up and withdrew to preserve their lines of communication. In America, the three-pronged attack on New France was nearing its crushing finale, with Quebec and Fort Niagara both in British hands and Montreal poised to fall in the following year. In India, the French had failed to take Pondicherry and Madras, and it looked like they had lost their last chance of securing the continent. In the West Indies, the French were just about holding onto their sugar islands, but at sea their fleet had been soundly beaten at Lagos and Quiberon Bay. The British navy was the master of the world's trade routes.

It was the year of victories, a second *Annus Mirabilis,* and the church bells were worn thin with ringing. It was commemorated in song by David Garrick when he penned the lyrics to *Hearts of Oak*, and such was the mood of national confidence that the massive keel of a first rate ship-of-the-line was laid down in Chatham's No. 2 dock. The building of a first rate was a monumental undertaking in the eighteenth century, and a year later she would be named *Victory* in commemoration of the *Annus Mirabilis*. *HMS Victory* is now the oldest commissioned ship in the world. It can be visited in Portsmouth, preserved from the breaker's yard by a near-miraculous series of interventions.

# Carlisle and Holbrooke

Carlisle spent the year of 1759 at the siege of Quebec. His frigate *Medina* was so severely damaged by French shore batteries that she was sent home for repair, and Carlisle was given command of *Dartmouth,* a fourth rate ship-of-the-line. When Quebec fell, he returned to home waters in time to join Admiral Hawke's squadron at the Battle of Quiberon Bay, where the menace of a French invasion was laid to rest in one of the most daring fleet actions in naval history. In early 1760, Carlisle escorted a convoy to the American colonies and found time to visit his home in Virginia. On his return to England, he joined Admiral Saunders' squadron bound for the Mediterranean.

Carlisle's friend and protégé, George Holbrooke, also spent the year of 1759 in the Americas. He was without a ship and seconded to the British Army for the expedition against Fort Niagara. He organised the vast fleet of boats to carry the army up rivers and across lakes and in a series of brilliant strokes, dealt with the French vessels that dominated Lake Ontario and threatened to prevent the army from arriving before the fort's walls. Holbrooke returned to England to be advanced in rank to post-captain and was given command of a frigate. His promotion broke down the last barrier that his sweetheart Ann's father had built against their relationship, and the end of 1759 saw them together at last.

# PROLOGUE

## The Middle Sea

*Tuesday, Nineteenth of February 1760.*
*Hayes Place, Kent.*

The coach-and-four bumped and squelched its way south and east, out of London and into the frozen Kent countryside. The man in the forward-facing seat looked cold and miserable. He was wrapped in a huge, grey blanket with a red woollen cap in place of his wig so that only his eyes and nose were visible, and with every draught of cold air, he sneezed. Anybody who didn't know him could hardly be blamed for imagining him an aged rustic – a minor country squire at best – rather than the highly respected First Lord of the Admiralty. After William Pitt himself, Anson was the chief architect of Britain's burgeoning success in the present war. He carried on his shoulders the weight of over a hundred ships-of-the-line, deployed across the world's oceans in support of this the first truly global conflict. He would never, ever have submitted to sharing his coach under such conditions if he didn't know the other passenger so intimately.

Vice-Admiral Charles Saunders, by contrast, looked fresh and eager, twisting this way and that to look out of the windows. He had returned in triumph from the Quebec campaign only three months before and had spent the winter in the bosom of his family. Now he was ready for a fresh challenge and some warmer weather. He'd been given the Mediterranean command; it was hardly the focus of the war, but he knew it of old and was aware that it had its challenges, and he would soon know what was expected of him.

Anson's muffled voice came from deep within his protective blanket.

'Have you marked the significance of the date, eh?'

Saunders started from his reverie. Lord Anson had not been inclined to talk and they had spent the last hour in silence, so this abrupt question caught him by surprise.

'I beg your pardon, my Lord.'

'D'ye mark the anniversary, Saunders?' he repeated with the first gleam of animation in his eye.

'Oh. Yes, I do Milord,' Saunders replied. He'd been thinking of it as they passed through the last village. 'Nineteen years ago, this very day, although it was touch-and-go whether I ever took up my command.'

Anson smiled beneath his blanket, but all that could be seen was an upturn in the lines that radiated from the corners of his eyes. St. Julian's Harbour, that remote and forbidding haven on the coast of Brazil, was a place of death and despair. In 1520 Magellan had hanged a mutineer at St. Julian's, and Drake in 1578 had executed his friend for a similar crime. Yet in 1741 it was the scene of a minor revolution in the fates of the officers that had followed Anson on his quest for glory in the far Pacific. The death of one of his captains had created the opportunity for a series of promotions, and Saunders had been plucked from obscurity to the glorious position of master and commander in the sloop *Tryall*. A sudden illness prevented him from taking immediate command, but it was from that date that his seniority as a commander was measured.

There was a special bond between Anson and those officers that had survived his circumnavigation, and he looked after them for the rest of his career. Saunders knew that he owed this new command to that special relationship, aye, and all the commissions that came before.

That brought on a flood of memories, and they fell to talking of old times and old shipmates. Gradually the look of age and decrepitude fell from Anson's face; he cast off the blanket, donned his wig and started to prepare himself for the forthcoming meeting.

'I do believe this is Hayes Place now,' said Saunders, wiping the condensation from the window.

The coach swayed as it left the highway and turned into the long drive leading to the house. There was a short pause as the keeper was summoned to open the gates, and then they were on a smooth gravel path lined on either side by young trees, their bare branches not yet grown to their eventual meeting overhead.

The man they had come to see – William Pitt – held the innocuous-sounding positions of secretary of state for the southern department and leader of the House of Commons. In reality, he led the British war effort and managed the national economy, leaving the Duke of Newcastle, with the nominal title of prime minister, to manage the House of Lords. Pitt was at the very height of his power and prestige with the French on the retreat in America, the West Indies and India, and stalemated in Germany. At sea, the British navy was triumphant, and only in the Mediterranean – the *Middle Sea* of antiquity – could the French sail with any measure of impunity.

***

Pitt was dressed in country browns. Silhouetted against the library windows, his long face and massive nose gave no hint of the consummate statesman. They had spoken for two hours; it was almost time for dinner, and he was ready to conclude the meeting.

'I don't mean this as a lesson in recent history, gentlemen,' said Pitt, rubbing his hands to keep the chill off. 'Damn this library! I won't have a fire in here, it damages the books, but on days like today I regret my obstinacy.'

Anson and Saunders exchanged rueful glances. They hadn't recovered yet from the coach ride and had hoped for a roaring log fire.

'However, it is important that you understand how we've come to this pass, because you'll have an interesting role to play, Admiral Saunders.'

Pitt paused, mustering his thoughts; he wasn't a man to resist the opportunity to deliver an oration.

'The realignment of alliances at the start of this war was

nothing short of a diplomatic revolution. Now that Austria and Russia are allied with France, we have only Prussia and a few German states to stem the attacks on Hanover. That seems to be working for now, but only because you gentlemen are bleeding King Louis' treasury to pay for his navy. If he could divert that gold to his army, he could launch an overwhelming attack on the continent. Frederick would be hard pressed, and Hanover would inevitably fall. I don't need to remind you of the consequences; everything you have gained so far would have to be surrendered at the peace to reclaim Hanover.'

'The King will never give up his ancestral home,' said Anson. 'He'd offer all of New France and the lands beyond the Ohio to keep it.'

'Just so, just so,' said Pitt, irritated at the interjection.

'Now, the greatest threat that we face is a resumption of the Bourbon family alliance. If Spain joins France this year, there'll be an extra fifty or sixty of the line ranged against us. That will allow Louis to concentrate on his army. In a year or two we'll be so strong that it will make little difference, but not this year, not in 1760!'

Saunders looked thoughtful. None of this was news to him, but it appeared that he would have an active part to play in this diplomatic *quadrille*. Anson looked bored but Saunders knew that with the French navy reduced to a shadow of its former self after their disasters at Quiberon, Lagos and the Saint Lawrence, the Mediterranean offered perhaps the best chance of a fleet action in 1760. He longed to round off his career with a great victory at sea.

'You must watch Cadiz to remind this new King Charles of Spain of the immediate consequences to his fleet if he should be so careless as to make an alliance with France. In addition, as soon as you arrive on station you must make contact with my Lord Bristol in Madrid so that you can concert your actions.'

Saunders bowed cautiously. Keeping in contact with the ambassador in Madrid was no easy task, with the Spanish capital deep in the heart of the country, hundreds of miles from the sea.

'And there is another matter of high diplomacy, the Kingdom of Sardinia.'

Pitt strode over to a map on one of the few spaces of wall that was not covered by bookcases.

'It's not just the island of Sardinia of course. The kingdom encompasses most of Piedmont, Savoy and Aosta, and the King keeps his court at Turin. It would be ah – *inconvenient* – if Charles Emmanuel should join France. Robert Mackenzie, the Earl of Bute's cousin, is our envoy. I've summoned him to London for a few weeks and you'll take him back to Turin, or at least as far as Nice or Villa-Franca. I have it in mind that King Charles Emmanuel should be reminded of the reach of our sea-power, but I'll need to consult Mackenzie as to how that can be achieved. Now, I understand you'll have *Dartmouth* under your command.' He glanced at Anson for confirmation and received a short nod in reply.

'Do you know Captain Carlisle, Saunders?' Pitt asked.

'I do, sir. He was with me at Quebec last year.'

'Yes, of course he was, I was forgetting.' Pitt tapped his finger thoughtfully on the map. 'Carlisle has family connections in Nice, and he may be the most suitable person to convey Mackenzie at least that far; what do you think, Milord?'

'He's a sound captain,' Anson replied, 'and detaching *Dartmouth* won't deplete Saunders' force. The days of the fourth rates standing in the line of battle are long gone. Minorca proved that, and my admirals won't have them, they'd rather shorten their lines.'

'Yes, indeed,' Pitt replied impatiently. He didn't want to be reminded of that appalling start to the war when Minorca was lost, Byng was executed, and he had briefly been cast into the political wilderness. The awkward pause was interrupted by Pitt's butler.

'It appears that our dinner is ready, gentlemen. I'll finish by saying that you have three tasks in the Mediterranean, Admiral Saunders,' he said watching the rooks whirling and cawing above the tall elm trees beyond the formal garden. 'Your priority is to ensure that the French ships in Toulon cause no mischief. There's little that they can do to hurt us unless they break out through the straits, and you must ensure that they don't do that. They're building in Toulon by all accounts, two or three seventy-fours, and the Duc de Choiseul is trying to scrape together enough gold to pay for some ships-of-the-line building in Genoa. The place isn't what it used to be when Genoa built half of Spain's navy, but they still have a thriving trade in turning out ships for paying customers. With the Genoa ships, Toulon could muster a respectable squadron by the summer, and they'll need watching.'

Saunders kept the expression of glee from his face. If the French should come out while he was there…

'Your second task is to keep Spain and Sardinia out of the war, and your third is to disrupt the French trade. That should keep you busy for this year, don't you think?'

\*\*\*

# CHAPTER ONE

## A Prize for the Taking

*Tuesday, Twenty-Seventh of May 1760.*
*Dartmouth, at Sea. Lair of Minorca northeast by east two leagues.*

'The brig's hauling her wind, sir. She doesn't fancy the Lair Passage. Ah, now the corvette's following her.'

Carlisle nodded distractedly, his mind already on the next move.

'Thank you, Mister Beazley. Steady as you are, keep her hard on the wind.'

'They'll shave the tail of the island on their new course, sir. There's deep water right up to the cape, but they'll have to put in a few tacks before they can fetch Mahon,' the sailing master continued. 'Still, they're a good three miles ahead.'

Beazley had served with Carlisle for nine months now, and he knew better than to point out that it would take a miracle for *Dartmouth* – one of the notoriously slow fourth rate fifty-gun ships – to catch the brig and her escort before they reached safety under the guns of Fort St. Philip.

Carlisle looked up at the commissioning pennant, streaming away on their starboard quarter, then stared hard at the chase through his telescope. The master was right. The corvette and the brig had been watching this gusty tramontana as it veered further to the north, and concluded that the Lair Passage, just five cables wide and subject to unpredictable flukes of wind from the cliffs to the north, was too risky. They'd been complacent, of course. With few British men-of-war patrolling the Western Mediterranean over the winter and spring, they had taken the easy, comfortable course, sailing a few points off the wind rather than squeezing every yard of northing that they could. There must have been some harsh words on the quarterdecks when they'd sighted the obviously British pursuer and they'd found themselves unable to take the shortcut to Mahon. Nevertheless, as Beazley pointed out, they were three miles ahead and barring accidents they'd make the entrance to Mahon without any difficulty.

And yet this brisk northerly wind with its hint of summer warmth was stimulating; it spoke of adventure, of profitable endeavour. Surely something could be achieved on a day such as this. It went against Carlisle's every instinct to tamely let this prize escape; the brig must be carrying a valuable cargo to have its own corvette escort.

'Let me see that chart again, Mister Angelini.'

Enrico Angelini was Carlisle's cousin by marriage. He held an ensign's commission in a Sardinian cavalry regiment, but for now, disgusted at his King's refusal to take sides in this present war, he was serving as a master's mate in *Dartmouth*. Enrico hurried back with the precious chart and spread it on top of the binnacle.

Carlisle had commanded a frigate in these waters before the war and had been at the Battle of Minorca just a few leagues north. He knew the area well but wanted to refresh his memory. What he absolutely didn't want was any interference from his passenger, and yet he could feel the presence of His Britannic Majesty's Envoy to the court of King Charles Emmanuel close at his elbow. He steeled himself for what he knew would be another carping criticism of his conduct. It wasn't long in coming.

'Captain Carlisle. I trust you do not intend any action that could delay my arrival at Nice.'

Mackenzie was a dour Scotsman with a profound sense of his own importance. He was the cousin of the Earl of Bute and a member of parliament for various Scottish constituencies, and he had married well. He carried his birth and position ponderously, insistent upon the full rigour of protocol, quick to take offense and sharp with his tongue.

Carlisle composed his face into a look of the utmost respect. He'd perhaps act differently if he merely had to deliver Mackenzie to Nice, but his orders were to accompany him to Turin, to the court of the King of Sardinia itself. William Pitt had insisted upon it; he was determined to emphasise the reach of British sea-power. They had already had a difference of opinion when Carlisle declared that he would take *Dartmouth* into the protected anchorage at Villa-Franca, the roadstead at Nice being too open for a prolonged stay. It would be as well to humour this awkward guest.

'My duty, sir,' he said bowing to the envoy. 'I'm ordered to annoy the French trade during our passage and as you can see, we have the enemy in sight to windward.'

Mackenzie glanced contemptuously at the corvette and the brig, both now clearly visible in the sparkling sunlight.

'You'll see that nothing imperils my arrival at Turin, Captain Carlisle. My mission, as you know, is of the utmost importance.'

'It will be the work of a few hours, sir, no more, and we may gain valuable information from a look into Mahon.'

Carlisle bowed again and turned back to the chart, banishing the tedious envoy from his mind.

'Mister Beazley; take a look at this chart with me, if you please. I have a mind to cut through the Lair Passage.'

Beazley pulled a disapproving face as he traced his finger along the lines of soundings – the very few lines of discouragingly shallow soundings.

'I've not sailed through here before, sir. I understand ships normally take the seaward route.'

He measured the distance with his outstretched thumb and little finger.

'Only five cables wide and just two lines of soundings.'

Beazley's whole body expressed his misgivings.

'Well, I sailed through here in *Fury* in 'fifty-five and 'fifty-six. If we clear that western point by two cables, we'll have at least five fathoms under our keel. Can you weather that point, Mister Beazley?'

The master looked forrard at the fore tops'l. The luff was lifting rhythmically each time the bows rose to meet the swell, a most satisfying testimony to the quartermaster's skill and vigilance. He glanced at the steersman who was watching the sail intently, hardly looking at the compass at all. That was as it should be, the compass course was largely irrelevant when they were sailing on a bowline, straining to win every extra yard to windward. He looked over the lee bow to where the iron-bound shore of the Lair of Minorca grew steadily closer. The steersman shifted his quid to his other cheek and winked at his mate.

'Maybe, sir,' Beazley said reluctantly. 'In any case, we can bear away if it looks like we won't weather the point,' he added, brightening.

'We can indeed,' Carlisle replied briskly.

Privately he'd be damned if he didn't take that passage. He knew very well that he could take his ship within a cable of the point if he had to. That line of soundings on the chart had been run by one of his own boats and recorded under his own supervision, and he was confident of its accuracy. And this was his only chance of catching the little convoy that was now committed to the southern – and longer – route into Mahon. With any luck he'd be through the passage and to windward of them, between them and their safe haven, if only this wind would hold. If it veered by even half a point *Dartmouth* would be headed and forced to follow around the Lair, and that would be the end of the chase.

Matthew Gresham, the first lieutenant, rubbed his hands, which was his usual gesture at the prospect of a prize. He'd served in this same ship under the previous, unenterprising captain, and as far as his own ambitions were concerned, they'd achieved nothing. This captain was different. Last year they'd taken a French fourth rate off Quiberon Bay, and earlier in the year they'd pounced upon a French West Indiaman, outbound to Martinique with a general cargo of household wares, though sadly of little value. Nevertheless, he was amassing a modest personal fortune and a few more captures would allow him to throw up the service and buy a decent cottage. That was all he wanted, a cottage and of course a wife. He wasn't interested in being made post, or even master and commander – he knew that the chances were slim in any case – and he had no love for the sea, but he was zealous to a fault and in many ways the perfect second-in-command.

'You've been here before then?' Gresham asked Charles Wishart, the third lieutenant.

'Aye, I was here with Captain Carlisle when Minorca was lost. I was the midshipman of the boat when that line of soundings was taken. Mister Seaforth was the master's mate, now second master of *Monarch*, and he'll be a master of his own frigate soon, no doubt. Those are good soundings, and we went closer to the north shore of the Lair too. The captain knows that there's deep water well inshore of those soundings.'

Wishart was enjoying being the man with the true knowledge. He was the most junior lieutenant in the ship and in fact he'd only passed his examination for the rank during their last spell at Spithead, having spent some months in the acting rank. He may have been the most junior of the three lieutenants, but he was the only one to have taken part in a major sea battle and the only one who knew these waters intimately. He was a genuine follower of Carlisle, having been taken onto the quarterdeck of *Fury* as a volunteer when his uncle was the first lieutenant. After his uncle was killed in action against a French frigate, he followed Carlisle into the larger frigate *Medina* and now into his first ship-of-the-line, *Dartmouth*. He couldn't imagine serving under any other captain.

'We'll make it. By a whisker, but we'll make it,' he added with more confidence than he felt. 'Then we'll show those Frenchies!'

Carlisle turned to the group of lieutenants.

'Without tempting fate, Mister Gresham, I'd be obliged if you would beat to quarters. I do believe we may be in action shortly.'

Wishart spared a second to watch his captain before he

ran to his quarters on the lower gundeck. To his intense satisfaction he saw him covertly touch the wood of the quarterdeck rail. It was a private superstition, but Wishart had served with him too long for there to be many secrets left. He'd seen that same almost unconscious gesture in these very waters, aye, and in the warm Caribbean and the frozen Saint Lawrence.

The marine sergeant had also served many years with Carlisle and he'd seen the warning signs half an hour ago. The drummer had been hiding under the break of the quarterdeck this past thirty minutes, and his sticks descended on the drum skin before the first lieutenant's order had left his mouth. The deck was instantly alive with hurrying figures as the men ran to their quarters.

Carlisle paid no conscious attention to the frenetic activity all around him. That was the first lieutenant's business, and he could rely on Gresham to see it done well. It was second nature to most of the crew and in only a few minutes he received the report that the men were at their quarters and that the ship was ready for action.

'May I suggest that we run out the larboard battery and haul the starboard train tackles up close, sir?' asked Gresham, his hat clasped across his chest.

'Certainly, make it so. We'll need every yard we can steal.'

A volley of orders followed, and the ship noticeably straightened as some hundred tons of cast iron and solid oak were moved six feet or so to windward. That was around a tenth part of *Dartmouth's* displacement, as Carlisle well knew. And now the waves were subsiding as they came closer under the lee of this south-eastern extremity of Minorca. He glanced questioningly at the quartermaster as the steersman eased the wheel a few spokes.

'Maybe a mort better, sir,' the quartermaster said after studying the dog-vane streaming from its staff on the weather gunwale.

Carlisle nodded. *Dartmouth* was perceptibly stiffer, standing up to the breeze and not heeling so far to leeward.

As a result, she was steering perhaps a quarter point higher. It wasn't a measurable amount, no compass needle was steady enough to record such a small graduation, but it could make the difference between weathering the Lair and having to bear away and abandon the chase.

'Squeeze everything you can out of her, Eli,' he said to the quartermaster.

'Aye-aye sir.'

Carlisle had never addressed his people by their Christian names, except for old Eli, who claimed to know neither his surname nor his age. He had happily wandered from ship to ship agreeing to any name that the purser or the captain's secretary proposed, and now that he was a settled follower of Carlisle's, he saw no need to concern himself further.

*****

Nobody could call the British fifty-gun ships beautiful. They were the ugly ducklings of the fleet, too small to share the dangerous majesty of the first, second and third rates, yet too large to be classed among the sleek, predatory frigates and sloops. They were utilitarian craft, the cheapest hulls that boasted two proper gundecks and quarters for a flag officer and they came into their own in times of peace, when money was tight and fleet actions unknown. Nevertheless, on this sparkling spring afternoon, *Dartmouth* contrived to borrow some of the grace of her more glamorous cousins. Her prow cut through the deep, deep blue of the Mediterranean and she left a pure white wake that stretched far astern to the sou'west. Here in the lee of Minorca the tiny waves were hardly noticeable and only an occasional capful of spray burst over the fo'c'sle sending a glistening shower across her decks to refresh the gun crews.

'Mister Angelini, a bearing of that nearest point of the Lair, if you please.'

Beazley wished, not for the first time, that his captain would be a little less zealous in his obedience to his orders. Nine out of ten captains wouldn't have dreamed of risking their ship in the Lair Passage with a northerly wind, even with the possibility of a prize on the other side. However, he had to admit that the actual risk to the ship wasn't great, at least not until they had crossed the invisible line that marked their last chance of bearing away to the south. Once they were committed to the passage, a sudden wind shift could leave them distinctly embarrassed. Still, so long as the bearing of that point of land was moving to the right, they were safe.

'East-by-north, a half east, sir, drawing right slowly.'

'Very well. Keep reporting Mister Angelini.'

Carlisle glanced aloft at the commissioning pennant flying gallantly from the main truck. He knew these tramontanas of old and he'd decided that this one had a day or two of life before it would blow itself out. It may back or it may veer, but the likelihood was that it would stay true from the north. It was only the effect of the high ground to windward that concerned him.

Carlisle picked up the speaking trumpet and pointed it towards the fo'c'sle.

'Bosun, have the larboard bower anchor made ready for letting go.'

Beazley nodded his agreement. It wasn't good holding ground inside the passage, but it would be sufficient in an emergency, and in extremis an anchor may be their only chance of avoiding being cast ashore.

'Sou'east-by-east,' Enrico reported, still crouching behind the binnacle and sighting along the cat-gut line stretched taut across the index bar.

Beazley turned to Carlisle and removed his hat.

'I must formally report that in ten minutes we will no longer have the option of bearing away, we'll be committed to the passage, sir.'

'Very good, Mister Beazley.'

Carlisle didn't want to discuss the matter. He'd decided to take the Lair Passage and only a decided wind shift would change his mind.

'Sou'east-by-south.'

'You may cease reporting now, Mister Angelini,' said Carlisle. 'I can see that we'll weather the point.'

The sea was almost flat now with only a long, steady swell coming round from Point Mola and running uninterrupted between the island of Minorca and its outlying rock. Carlisle picked up the speaking trumpet again and tilted his head upwards.

'Masthead! What can you see of the chase?'

There was a short pause.

'Nothing, sir, they're hidden behind the rock.'

Carlisle strode a few paces along the weather side of the quarterdeck, trying not to show his nervousness. He was almost certain that the corvette and brig were making for Mahon, in which case it would be a race to catch them before the guns of Fort St. Philip could intervene. But he could be wrong. They could be heading for Marseilles or Toulon or any of the French ports on that part of the coast. In that case he would have given them a head start and it would be a long chase with no great chance of success. The corvette was certainly faster than *Dartmouth* sailing both by and large, and the brig would be fast enough to keep away until dark. If he had guessed wrong then he would probably have to bear away for Villa-Franca and forget the chase, and he didn't want to do that. However, when they first saw that they were being pursued, the corvette had initially hauled her wind as if trying for the Lair Passage. That was the immediate reaction of a man heading for Mahon and seeking a shortcut before he realised that he was already too far to leeward. Well, *Dartmouth* was committed now.

'Wind's holding steady, sir,' said Beazley.

They were at the mid-point of the passage now and two cables clear of the perilous leeward shore. The immediate danger was over but the atmosphere on the quarterdeck was strained. It was quite evident to all the officers that if they didn't sight the chase in the next few minutes, their captain had made an error of judgment.

'Deck there! Chase in sight, sir, just coming clear around the island.'

Carlisle trained his telescope on the left-hand edge of the rock. At first he saw nothing, the lookout had the advantage of height and could see further over the rocky ridge at the eastern end of the Lair. Then suddenly a ship's t'gallant appeared in his telescope, then another. Soon it was clear that he'd been correct, and the corvette and brig were making for Mahon. He breathed an unconscious sigh of relief.

'A bearing of the corvette, Mister Angelini.'

It was a race to windward now. *Dartmouth* had the weather gage, but the Frenchmen were ahead. The corvette could certainly escape if her captain chose to abandon her charge, but the brig was in a more precarious position. She had to stand well out to seaward before she could fetch the entrance to Mahon's long, deep harbour, and all the time *Dartmouth* was coming up to windward of her.

Carlisle looked appraisingly at the sails.

'We could bear away a point I believe, Mister Beazley.'

'That we could, sir.'

The slight increase in speed was immediately evident although they were sacrificing some of their precious windward advantage.

Carlisle looked across the deck. The guns were all manned and the crews looked eager. It would be a shame now if their prize should escape.

\*\*\*

'There she goes, sir.'

Beazley pointed as first the corvette and then the brig came about onto the starboard tack. They'd fetch Mahon now, but *Dartmouth* still had a chance of bringing them to action.

'Stand on, Mister Beazley, we'll tack before we fetch their wake.'

Carlisle watched the brig carefully. He'd already decided that the corvette was irrelevant.

'Now, Mister Beazley.'

*Dartmouth* came about in a flurry of billowing canvas and settled down onto her new course. The corvette had gained on the brig when they tacked and was now leading the way to safety. Carlisle could guess what was going through her captain's mind. There was nothing he could do to protect the brig once *Dartmouth* had brought her broadsides into range. If he persisted in attempting to protect the merchantman, it would mean the certain loss of his command and the brig would be taken anyway. He'd already demonstrated his intention; he would leave the brig to its fate and save his corvette.

'Mister Gresham. You may try the range of the brig.'

'Aye-aye sir.'

Gresham shouted his orders down through the hatch, and with only a few seconds delay the first of the twenty-four pounders fired.

'Short, sir.'

'Keep trying, Mister Gresham.'

'Numbers one and three guns should bear, and number five soon,' he replied.

Bang! That would be number three gun, the second gun from the bow on the starboard side. It too fell short.

Bang! Number one gun again. That was better, the barrel had warmed up and the range had closed. The master of the brig must have been wetted by that shot.

'The fort's firing, sir.'

A waterspout rose a mile ahead. It was a warning shot from a thirty-two pounder, probably a British gun left behind when the fort was surrendered in 'fifty-six. Carlisle knew the power of those big guns firing from behind solid masonry, and he knew he couldn't justify risking his ship within range of them. *Dartmouth* had perhaps ten minutes to stop the brig making her escape.

'Mister Gresham, fire off the larboard battery immediately and reload with chain shot. Keep firing with the starboard guns. You'll have one broadside to larboard before we have to disengage.'

*Dartmouth* staggered as the larboard battery discharged its load of ball into the empty sea. If Carlisle had the leisure to draw it out on a chart, it would be a nice exercise in geometry. The brig was almost within range of the fort's guns and she was already within long range of *Dartmouth's* guns. Reloading the larboard battery would take a finite time, say three minutes, and the tack that would be required to bring the battery to bear would also take about three minutes, all the time losing ground to the brig. There would be only one opportunity and using chain shot would maximise the chance of bringing down a mast. It was worth the waste of a whole broadside of powder and shot.

'Bring her about, Mister Beazley.'

*Dartmouth's* bow swung through the wind.

'Larboard battery ready with chain shot, sir.'

That was good, but the brig was almost out of range.

'Fire as you bear, Mister Gresham.'

The larboard battery fired in ones and twos. The howling of the chain shot was an eery sound and must be terrifying on the brig's deck. At first there was no sign of any damage, then it looked as though the brig's main topmast swayed a little. As Carlisle watched it fell forward, dropping over the starboard side. Deprived of its leverage aft, the brig's bow immediately swung to starboard. There was a cheer from *Dartmouth's* main deck.

'Cease firing!' Carlisle shouted. 'Get Mister Wishart up here. He's to take the longboat with a prize crew and tow the brig out from under those damned guns. At least the wind will help him. I wish you joy of our prize, Mister Gresham, another few minutes and we'd have missed her!'

***

# CHAPTER TWO

## A Close-Run Thing

*Tuesday, Twenty-Seventh of May 1760.*
*Dartmouth, at Sea. Off Port Mahon.*

Only the blessed tramontana made it possible for *Dartmouth* to claim the prize. The disabled brig lay at the very edge of the arc of sea that was commanded by Fort St. Philip's thirty-two pounders, and each minute the north wind pushed her further out of range of the French guns. The corvette lay off the fort, backing and filling, apparently hesitating whether to attempt to intervene; she looked the image of paralysed indecision.

'You may have to suffer a few balls from the fort, Mister Wishart, but don't worry about that. Board her with the prize crew and the longboat will pull you out of range in no time. Don't take any nonsense from the brig's people. She's a fair prize and I don't see any colours showing; you may take it that she's struck.'

'Aye-aye sir. Shall I take her to Gib?'

Wishart was visibly restraining himself and the effort to prevent his feet doing an involuntary jig on the holy quarterdeck caused his thighs to jerk with muscle spasms. Only yesterday the first lieutenant had pointed out that excitement and enthusiasm were beneath the dignity of an officer holding a King's commission.

'Let's see what she's carrying. If her cargo's not worth much I may send her into Leghorn, then we can stay in company for a few days and you'll find it easier to rejoin us at Villa-Franca. Do you remember Horace Mann? He was the consul in Leghorn in 'fifty-six and he's still there. He'll see us right.'

Wishart bowed solemnly – a difficult manoeuvre when one's whole body craved immediate movement – and turned away, calling his prize crew together and urging the bosun to bring the longboat alongside. Soon they were skimming across the calm, silvery-grey sea towards the brig as the sun inched lower towards the dark, forbidding battlements of Fort St. Philip.

*\*\**

Carlisle watched the longboat pull away. He was glad that there had been no real danger to his ship; the envoy's inevitable complaint would carry more moral force if there had been. It looked very much as though they would be on their way in half an hour, and there was nothing that the French commander on Fort St. Philip could do about it. Through his telescope he saw Wishart leap onto the deck of the brig brandishing his sword, with his prize crew following with bared cutlasses and primed pistols. It was as well to make a show of force to subdue any resistance before it started. A few shots from the fort fell short, and then the French artillerymen seemed to accept that the north wind had carried the brig beyond the range of their guns. Wishart had a simple task of cutting away the wreckage of the brig's main topmast and setting her mainsail. It would be an awkward, slow rig, but if this wind held it would suffice to take them sou'west to Gibraltar or northeast to Leghorn.

'It looks like Mister Wishart has decided not to take a tow, sir. The longboat is standing by her quarter, and I can see the main tops'l coming down already.'

The master's report was unnecessary – Carlisle could see the situation with his own eyes – but all his officers knew that Carlisle wanted to be informed of every event of note, whether or not it was likely that he'd already seen it. That way nothing would slip through the seams.

'Very well, Mister Beazley. Get underway as soon as the brig has a mainsail set and bring the longboat to our stern. What's the course for Villa-Franca after we clear Cape Mola?'

'Nor'east-by-north a half north, sir.'

Carlisle nodded. That course was carved into his heart and even after the passage of four years he could recall it instantly. He looked speculatively at the thin, high cloud that the tramontana had brought from the Gulf of Lions and glanced at the compass.

'We can perhaps make east-by-north, but the brig won't lie that close. In any case, the wind will back in a day or two, when this wind has done with us.'

Carlisle followed the master's gaze. Perhaps he'd been wrong about the duration of the tramontana. Those lofty streams of cloud generally came as the north wind started to fade. A west wind was highly likely; it could be a fair passage to Villa-Franca after all.

'Well, let's see what that brig is carrying, it may be best to send her to Gib, although I'm reluctant to lose a lieutenant and a prize crew so early, and God knows when we'll see them again.'

'Ah, the fore tops'ls filling,' said Beazley, 'and they're getting that main topmast under control. There it goes!'

The mass of spars, canvas and cordage above the mainmast of the brig came down with a rush and a minute later the mainsail filled. It was fascinating to watch and every telescope on the quarterdeck was fixed on the prize as, in the last rays of the setting sun, it was transformed from a disconsolate wreck to a living, moving vessel. If all went well Wishart could make a passage to Gibraltar or Leghorn unaided. Carlisle was starting to relax, the tension of his confrontation with the envoy was easing.

'Deck there! There's a ship coming down the harbour. Can't make out what it is yet.'

Carlisle started out of his reverie. He'd been inattentive, too interested in the technical work of getting the prize underway. He swung his telescope to the harbour entrance, to the right of the fort. He could still see the stark silhouette of the corvette, now lying-to in the narrows below the fort, but the angle was wrong to see further up the harbour, and the glare of the setting sun wasn't helping.

'Mister Angelini,' he snapped, 'take a telescope to the masthead and tell me what you see.'

Beazley offered his telescope and Enrico ran up the main shrouds like a born seaman. Carlisle spared a moment to wonder, and not for the first time, how his cousin would take to a Sardinian cavalry regiment after his taste of life at sea. Perhaps he'd know soon enough; it was quite possible that he'd be recalled to the colours when his regiment heard that *Dartmouth* was at Villa-Franca.

The prize was safe now unless this newcomer should be of sufficient weight to turn the balance of forces in this enclosed patch of sea. It was unlikely to be a merchantman, rumour of a British man-o'-war in the offing would keep them all safely at the wharves or at their anchors, and Carlisle knew how fast news spread around the harbour at Mahon. Probably it was a French man-o'-war, a frigate or corvette, a ship-of-the-line could hardly get underway so fast. There had been just enough time for a frigate to make a hurried departure from the anchorages to the east of the town, and this north wind was ideal for a fast run down the harbour. If that was the case, then he'd place himself to windward of the prize and escort her towards Villa-Franca; a solo passage to Gibraltar was out of the question now. It would be dark soon, but he was confident that he could protect his prize through the night against anything smaller than a third rate.

'Two days to the full,' said Beazley, apparently reading his thoughts. He pointed to the enormous, bright orb creeping above the sou'eastern horizon. 'and the moon doesn't set until six bells in the middle watch.' He studied the sky to the north, over Cape Mola. 'That cloud won't hide it; we've eight hours before it'll be truly dark.'

'Well, let's see what we're up against. Can you fetch the brig without tacking?'

'Aye sir, I'll bring her head round, just in case.'

'Very well. Mister Gresham, run out the guns.'

*Dartmouth's* bows swung around to the west and her tops'ls filled as she moved closer to the brig.

'Captain, sir!' Enrico's voice was clear and loud to the

officers on the quarterdeck. 'It's a ship-of-the-line. A third rate, I believe, possibly a seventy-four.'

Carlisle froze. He could immediately sense the eyes of Beazley and Gresham upon him. What cursed bad luck; the French third rate must have been in the very act of leaving harbour when the alarm was raised. It was no light matter to pit a fifty-gun fourth rate against one of the superb French seventy-fours; the enemy would have twice *Dartmouth's* weight of broadside and her massive scantlings would provide more than twice the protection against shot. It could be done, of course, and under other circumstances Carlisle might consider giving battle, but the presence of the envoy hung like a lead weight upon him. While he could indulge in a little risk-free prize-taking, he was specifically forbidden to endanger his ship until Mackenzie was safely ashore, and there was no way of finessing this, an encounter with a French third rate certainly constituted a grave risk.

His decision took no more than a few seconds; but in in truth, he had no alternative.

'A gun to windward, Mister Gresham. Hoist the recall flag, Mister Beazley, they may just be able to see it. Let's get the prize crew back onboard.'

Bang! The gun's crew had been ready and waiting and there was less than ten seconds between Carlisle's order and the sharp crack of the quarterdeck six-pounder. Wishart may not be aware of his imminent danger, but the gun would draw his attention to the recall, and he'd know that something was amiss.

In the gathering gloom it was difficult to see what was happening on the prize's deck. However, the longboat knew that something was wrong, and pulled urgently over to the brig.

'I can see her now,' said Gresham. 'A ship-of-the-line for sure, and she's bringing the wind down with her, just passing Lazaretto Island.'

'Another gun, Mister Gresham.'

Carlisle was now certain of his duty. He had to

concentrate on keeping *Dartmouth* clear of this Frenchman, and the prize must be abandoned. If it was one of the new seventy-fours, it could easily be faster on the wind than *Dartmouth*. But he was damned if he'd leave Wishart, the prize crew and his longboat to be snapped up by that corvette.

'May I ask, Captain, why we are not heading out to sea? It is imperative, as you well know, that I should be delivered to Nice in a timely manner. I doubt whether the captain of that French ship will be inclined to give me safe conduct.'

He'd concede one point to the envoy, he didn't miss a trick. Few landsmen would have been able to grasp so quickly the implication of this westerly course. He'd heard Enrico's hail as everyone on deck had, and he could make a fair estimate of the danger that they now faced.

Carlisle tried to sound calm, as though there was no danger, no French seventy-four to windward.

'I must recover my boat and my prize crew, sir, then we'll be away for Villa-Franca.'

Mackenzie scowled. In the growing darkness he looked old, ugly and spiteful.

'If you'd taken my advice in the first place we wouldn't be in this position. No prize is worth risking my mission, and now I must insist that you leave your lieutenant to fend for himself. That is the consequence of your ill-judged action, sir. I repeat, I must insist that you withdraw from this position immediately.'

Carlisle stood rooted to the spot. He could take the constant carping criticism, the assumption of superiority and the grumbling, but he would not be given orders on his own quarterdeck. He glanced at Mackenzie; the man looked wholly unabashed.

'Mister Simmonds,' he said in a stiff, harsh voice, not even looking at his clerk who would surely be at his station beside the binnacle, 'kindly escort Mister Mackenzie to the great cabin. He will find it convenient to remain there until the morning watch.'

The envoy glared about him but found no sympathy, no possibility of assistance, from the officers on the quarterdeck. With a face as dark as thunder he strode rigidly ahead of Simmonds, staring fixedly to his front and looking neither right nor left until he disappeared into the suite of cabins that were normally reserved for an embarked flag officer.

Carlisle's face showed nothing, it was an immobile mask. He knew that his action would cause trouble for him in the future. Once ashore in Villa-Franca, Mackenzie would be in his own element and Carlisle would be dependent upon his now vanished goodwill. He didn't fear a complaint to Admiral Saunders or to the Admiralty; neither of them would uphold a protest that had its origin in such a severe breach of protocol. Carlisle was safe in the knowledge that King George himself had commissioned him into *Dartmouth*, and no diplomat could usurp his right to command. No, it was the taking of a prize right under the guns of Fort St. Philip – a clear stretch to his orders – that would be difficult to explain.

The quarterdeck was stilled for the space of a few heartbeats, then Eli's voice, harsh as an old frog in a mire broke the silence with a private aside to the helmsman that could be heard right across the quarterdeck.

'It's damned lucky, I would say, that this 'ere ship ain't a frigate. If 'is nibs had found a ladder in his way, we'd be picking up his parts for the rest of the watch.'

\*\*\*

'The longboat's pulling back to us now, sir.'

Gresham cared even less for envoys and their foibles than Carlisle did, and the unfolding drama on the prize had claimed all his attention. The longboat had quickly grasped the meaning of *Dartmouth's* guns and even though he couldn't make out the recall flag, the coxswain, Jack Souter, had wasted no time in pulling back to the brig. It took just one look up the harbour, and the sight of the enormous two-decker spreading her canvas as she crept beneath the massive walls of Fort St. Philip persuaded Wishart that this was no time for dawdling on the deck of a disabled prize. He and his crew had jumped into the longboat from the brig's main chains before ever the two vessels had touched.

'What's the corvette doing?' Carlisle asked.

'Waiting for the seventy-four,' Gresham replied, 'I don't doubt that he'll leave the brig to its own devices and snap at our heels. Ah, here he comes. He's too late to catch the longboat though.'

'Mister Beazley. Get underway as soon as Mister Wishart and his men are onboard. You can tow the longboat alongside the starboard main chains for now.'

'I'll shift the aftermost guns into the stern-chaser ports, sir,' said Gresham, recognising why Carlisle didn't want the longboat towing astern. With a long night's chase ahead of them they'd need their two aft-facing guns, and those ports were normally empty.

Carlisle nodded distractedly. He could safely leave those things to his first lieutenant and concentrate on getting underway as soon as possible.

'The French ship is passing Fort Philipet now, sir,' Enrico shouted from his high perch.

That was useful information. It was difficult to see how far the seventy-four had come down the channel, but the fort on the end of Lazaretto Island – the little brother to Fort St. Philip – was a familiar reference point. Perhaps three miles separated the two ships.

Carlisle watched the longboat and studied the uncertain wind. It was inclined to be fluky as it dropped down from the high land of Cape Mola and became mixed up with the growing land breeze. The longboat was two cables away and pulling hard for *Dartmouth*. He could see the enormous effort of the oarsmen, double-banked now that they had been joined by the prize crew.

'The fort's joined in, sir,' said Gresham as a vast spout of water from a thirty-two pounder sprang briefly into existence a few cables beyond the longboat.

'Wear ship, Mister Beazley. Keep her a point free, all plain sail. I don't believe this gentleman knows where we're heading so let's keep him guessing and make as much ground to windward as we can.'

Beazley grunted his approval. This was no time to risk tacking, with the wind all over the place and a French third rate bearing down on them. It would have been severely embarrassing to be caught in irons; wearing, although slower, was more certain.

*Dartmouth's* stern passed through the wind and the bosun waved the longboat onto the starboard side. As the ship gathered way the crew came rushing on deck, leaving oars and rig in the boat. It was neatly done, not a moment had been lost and the seventy-four was still making its stately progress out of the harbour. Carlisle knew well how little the wind could be relied upon in that narrow passage, particularly as the land breeze started to set in. Even with a chase in sight, the French captain would be cautious.

'The corvette's almost in range, sir, and our stern chasers will be ready in a moment,' Gresham reported quietly.

'Then commence firing as soon as you're sure, Mister Gresham. That will persuade her to keep her distance. Ah, Mister Wishart, welcome back. What have we lost with that prize?'

Wishart grinned through his laboured breath. He'd pulled along with everyone else and had just scrambled up the side of the ship.

'Wine, sir, and brandy. It appears the French garrison doesn't care for the Minorcan variety. The brig loaded at Marseilles and touched at Ciutadella before sailing around to Mahon. The corvette has been her escort all the way.'

'Then I hope the commandant of Fort St. Philip enjoys his bottles, but it's a sad loss to us.'

'That it is, sir,' added Gresham, 'that it is.'

The Frenchman was five miles astern by the time she cleared Cape Mola, and the sun had already slid below the island. The tramontana had reasserted itself now that they were clear of the land and both ships sped to the northeast, full and by, their tight-stretched canvas illuminated by a waxing gibbous moon that mocked the night with its ghastly, pale illumination.

\*\*\*

# CHAPTER THREE

## A Moonlight Chase

*Wednesday, Twenty-Eighth of May 1760.*
*Dartmouth, at Sea. Cape Mola southwest-by-south 9 leagues.*

Two days to Villa-Franca sailing on a bowline, that was what Beazley estimated. Two days so long as they could keep the Frenchman at arm's length.

Carlisle paced the deck impatiently as Beazley balanced against the taffrail, minutely adjusting his quadrant while a midshipman stood beside him with a darkened lantern.

'Show a glim, there, Mister Young.'

The midshipman allowed the smallest sliver of light to escape through the shutter and the master studied the scale in its meagre beam. It was a good quadrant, the best that could be bought, and it boasted a vernier scale fashioned from elephant's tooth. Nevertheless, the master was working at the very limit of its capability, measuring the tiny change in the angle between the three-decker's masthead and its waterline. With nothing more than the light of the moon to illuminate the two points, it was little more than a guess, but it was all they had.

'What's the verdict, Mister Beazley?'

It was a measure of Carlisle's anxiety that he should be moved to anticipate the master's report. It wasn't his normal style; since taking command of *Dartmouth*, he'd cultivated an air of detached indifference, awaiting reports with a stoicism that was not always easy to maintain. There was something different tonight and a part of Carlisle's brain was busy analysing what was making him so nervous. It wasn't the fear of an engagement with the great ship bearing down upon him, of that he was certain. He knew that *Dartmouth* would give a good account of herself if she was forced to fight; win or lose, it was all part of life on active service. No, it was the envoy's presence on board that was unsettling him. Carlisle knew that he had been wrong to chase that brig right into the mouth of Mahon harbour, it was against his orders and Mackenzie's protest had been justified. And now the envoy was proved correct, and there was an even chance that he wouldn't make it to Nice.

'She's not overhauling us, sir, or not by anything significant,' Beazley replied tentatively. 'She may have come up a cable this last half-glass, but I can't be sure. I would say that she's keeping station on us, sir.'

Carlisle looked astern. The third rate was clearly visible in the moonlight, about three miles distant and perhaps pointing a little higher than his own ship. Even without the help of a vernier quadrant he could see that the range hadn't altered. It was strange. Those French seventy-fours were superbly designed and built and should certainly sail faster than a British fourth rate, particularly close-hauled.

'What do you think, Mister Gresham?' Carlisle asked without taking his eyes from his adversary astern.

Gresham wasn't a talkative man, and he had a maddening tendency to long pauses before answering questions. Carlisle had been watching him this last quarter hour and it was clear that he had formed an opinion.

'There's something wrong, sir,' he replied after his customary silence. 'She should be overhauling us hand over hand. Maybe she has a foul bottom, but then so have we. Do you think that French captain is waiting for daylight?'

'That was my own thought. I would have allowed her a good knot over us and by rights we should be engaged in the middle watch. Why's he waiting? Is he reluctant to have a night engagement?'

'If he's been cruising around the western Med these last years, then his crew may be raw. Perhaps he's been laid up in Toulon over the winter and the men are fresh from the fishing fleets. It'll be twilight before the moon sets,' he added. 'There'll be no real dark this night.'

Carlisle nodded. Gresham knew as well as he how strapped for men and cash the French navy was after five years of war. With no British presence east of Gibraltar since last year, the inner harbour at Toulon would have been stuffed with men-o'-war gently snubbing their moorings. It was an intriguing hypothesis: a French third rate that was too unsure of itself to engage a ship of half its force at night. Carlisle paced restlessly once up and once back the length of the quarterdeck. He was aware of his own impulsive nature, and his tendency to a dangerous level of optimism, and he was suspicious of this hypothesis, it sounded too good to be true. But if it *was* true, then surely with the dawn the third rate would pile on its sail and come surging up alongside. Then it would be a straight fight, seventy-four guns against fifty, thirty-two pounders against twenty-fours. A slugging match with those odds held no attraction for Carlisle.

'The wind's backed half a point, sir,' said Beazley, 'I don't doubt we'll get a few squalls overnight.'

A nudge from the quartermaster drew his attention to windward.

'Here comes the first one, sir.'

Carlisle looked over the larboard bow. A black line of cloud coming down on the northerly wind. It wasn't a powerful squall, those would come later as the tramontana started to fade, and it would only hide *Dartmouth* for perhaps fifteen minutes. Not long enough for his plan.

Beazley was one step ahead of him.

'It'll be a short squall, I don't doubt, but then it'll blank out the moon for a while,' he said, jerking his head to the south where the moon was still hung there, low in the sky. 'We may have half an hour of dark, sir.'

'The men are at quarters, Mister Gresham?'

'They are, sir, larboard guns run out, starboard bowsed tight inboard.'

Carlisle took another quick look astern. The French ship appeared not to have moved, its massive shape outlined in silver with its smaller consort under its lee.

'Then if he doesn't want a night engagement, that's what

we must give him. However, there'll be another squall soon, don't you think?'

Beazley nodded judiciously. Undoubtedly this would be just the first of a sequence of squalls that would increase in strength as the wind backed.

'Then we'll let this one pass. That may persuade him that we're an unenterprising crew.'

Carlisle saw the agreement on his officers' faces.

'Mister Gresham. You have perhaps half an hour to draw the guns and reload with chain.'

\*\*\*

The approaching squall ate up the stars as it rushed down towards the three ships. Beazley felt the first gusts tugging at his coat. The wind was veering a touch.

'Let her fall off a point, quartermaster.'

The steersman let a few spokes pass through his fingers and the bows paid off to starboard. The squall was a modest affair, just a slight increase in the wind, a few drops of rain and an impenetrable darkness made deeper by the contrast with the moonlit night of a few minutes before. It passed quickly but its passing brought no end to the darkness and the Frenchmen were lost in the blackness astern. If the squall had lasted longer, Carlisle would have been tempted to alter course and try to lose his pursuer in the dark of the night, but with only half an hour it was futile and would only delay their progress towards Villa-Franca.

Then, with startling suddenness, the dark line of the squall passed under the moon and sea was once again illuminated by its silvery glow. There was the seventy-four and its attendant corvette, still three miles astern and looking unperturbed by the weather.

On they sailed. Carlisle wasn't concerned with speed anymore; he was satisfied that the Frenchman wasn't trying to catch him. At dawn it would be a different matter and those three miles that separated them would be eaten up before the end of the morning watch. If he did nothing, he'd be fighting on the Frenchman's terms in broad daylight.

'Here comes the next one, sir,' said Beazley.

Carlisle looked to windward. At first, he could see nothing, then he saw the lower stars disappearing one by one. The squall wasn't visible yet, but its effect was.

'Both batteries loaded with chain, sir,' said Gresham, holding his hat across his chest.

'Very well. We'll be engaging with the starboard battery first, then the larboard, Mister Gresham, dispose your men accordingly. After the first broadside you may reload with ball. If we disable her with the chain then we'll leave her be, if not then we'll be toe-to-toe.'

'You'll be wearing ship then, sir,' said Beazley, who'd been listening attentively and decided that his captain planned to reverse his course and pass between the two French ships.

'No, Master, I plan to tack across the seventy-four's bows and then pass between him and the corvette.'

Beazley pulled a long face and looked dubiously astern.

'We'll have to be right smart in stays, sir.'

'That we will, Master, and I'll leave that to you. The first lieutenant will let you have sail trimmers from the guns.'

He turned away as the master hailed the bosun to go through the details of how they would get *Dartmouth's* bows through the wind without delay and without the horror of being caught in irons. That would be a disaster under the circumstances.

Carlisle watched the stars being extinguished to larboard. He could see the black outline of the squall now; it was bigger, more powerful than the previous one. He shrugged. That would make everything just that little more difficult, but he was committed now.

'Mister Young. Nip below and tell Mister Mackenzie, with my compliments, that we will be engaging the enemy soon. If he wishes to come on deck Captain Carlisle would be pleased to see him. Make sure you've got that right. Repeat it if you please.'

There was no room for mistakes in the wording of this

olive branch. He mustn't appear condescending, nor must he appear contrite. He had less than two days – if all went well – to mend his relationship with the envoy. Should he relent and address him as *your excellency*? It was technically incorrect of course, the man was an envoy, not an ambassador; only the emissaries sent to the great powers such as France, Austria, Prussia and Russia rated an ambassador. Yet the man clearly yearned for that mark of distinction. Carlisle banished the line of thought, that was no way to be going into a life-and-death engagement.

The squall hit them with greater ferocity this time. Carlisle looked astern. He could see nothing of the Frenchmen, it was as though a ship-of-the-line had been swallowed whole by the darkness. He had a strange sensation that *Dartmouth* was engulfed in a huge dark blanket, a blanket that pushed furiously against anything in its way and snapped at the sheets and halyards.

'Bring her about, Mister Beazley.'

He had to shout even though the master was only a few feet away from him. It was as well that the sail trimmers were at their stations and all was prepared because communication on the deck had suddenly become nigh-on impossible.

*Dartmouth's* bows swung fast to larboard. A volley of orders from the master brought the great square sails around and in moments her head was through the wind. Carlisle staggered as the wind caught the near-stationary ship and laid her far over on her beam. Then she started to move through the water on the starboard tack and the wind's force was now urging her forward rather than laying her over. It seemed like only minutes and then the squall was gone, leaving behind a starlit sky to starboard and a deep inky blackness on the leeward bow.

Carlisle scanned the sea ahead. Nothing could be seen in the impenetrable gloom. There was no sign of the French ships. Had they outwitted him? Were they even now on the same tack as him, leading the way sou'west? That was unlikely. The French captain would want to keep his quarry in sight, and he was confident that *Dartmouth's* tack couldn't have been predicted. Carlisle held his breath. He was aware of the envoy standing near the taffrail, looking aloof and severe.

'Sail ho!' the lookout shouted excitedly, 'two sails right on the bow.'

Carlisle breathed again.

'Stand by the starboard battery,' he roared. 'Take us across his bows, Mister Beazley, as close as you like.'

The seventy-four was close, very close indeed, and Beazley only had moments to bear away to avoid a collision.

The French ship looked enormous as it bore down upon them. Her captain had no options. His consort was too close to leeward to allow him to bear away, and in any case that would have risked a collision with the British ship. He couldn't tack, not without having prepared in advance, and every indication suggested that he had been caught unawares. He would have to accept that *Dartmouth* would fire an unopposed broadside into his bows, but then he would get his chance to reply as the British ship passed down his starboard side, for that was surely his intention. That was the danger, Carlisle knew, the payback for the easy shots at the Frenchman's bow. They would be lucky to escape without significant damage.

Then he saw it, his golden chance. The corvette had dropped back a little onto the seventy-four's quarter. Was she giving her larger consort room to bear away? If so, she hadn't given enough, but she had opened an opportunity for Carlisle. Perhaps there was no need to pass between them after all.

'Mister Beazley,' he shouted, pointing at the corvette, 'can you cross her hawse?'

Beazley looked for a long second, then nodded.

'Let her off two points, Eli,' he said. 'Check away the mizzen sheets,' he added in a roar calculated to reach the poop deck sail trimmers.

Carlisle had time for a quick look. He could see that it would be close, but *Dartmouth* could just pass the corvette's bows without wearing. He left the ship handling to the master.

'Fire as your guns bear, Mister Gresham!'

The seventy-four's jib boom was only yards away when the first guns roared. Gresham was firing by divisions, with each group of four lower deck twenty-fours and four upper deck twelves firing together. It would have been hard to miss at that range and the chain shot howled as it spun across the moonlit sea and slammed into the Frenchman's bows or screamed across the fo'c'sle, carrying away stays and shrouds as they passed. That was what Carlisle had hoped for, a chance to disable his opponent by weakening his foremast.

The quarterdeck six-pounders were the last to fire. There was no allowance of chain shot for them, so they were loaded with grape and Carlisle caught a glimpse of a group of French seamen on the fo'c'sle that melted away as the grapeshot cut through them.

Now the French guns fired in return. It was a difficult angle for them, and their muzzles were hauled as far forrard as they would go. Nevertheless, it was an impressive response from the French gunners who must have had only a few minutes warning before they were ordered to fire. Carlisle felt the shots slam into his ship's hull and one or two passed overhead with a sound like ripping canvas. He was curiously indifferent. Was he becoming callous, he wondered? Men were suffering and dying below his feet, but that was preferable to his ship being disabled by shots to his masts and sails. Then the seventy-four was gone, no longer able to bring her guns to bear and unable to reload before *Dartmouth* was out of range.

'*Le Bourbon*, sir.'

'What's that, Mister Angelini?'

'The ship's name, sir. It's painted under her fo'c'sle rail. *Le Bourbon*.'

He'd heard of her, of course. Launched at Toulon three years ago, one of the best of the seventy-fours and, so far, un-blooded. What a prize she would make. Anson was eager to bring these ultimate manifestations of the shipbuilder's art into the British navy. But not today.

Now for the corvette. It would be close again, but not so close as the seventy-four, and this time *Dartmouth* had no guns loaded on her starboard side. The corvette passed in a flash, suffering no more than a few musket balls from the marines ranged along the poop deck.

'Bring her hard on the wind, master.'

Carlisle looked to starboard. He couldn't see any damage on the French ship, it was too dark, and in any case he was looking across his adversary's larboard quarter. He could see that the Frenchman's bows were swinging slowly to windward. Was that a deliberate tack or had she lost her staysail and jib? They'd know in a moment.

Her bows turned slowly, almost reluctantly, as though there was another force trying to prevent them turning. Carlisle could imagine the scene on the quarterdeck, the steersmen fighting to bring the bows off the wind, the mizzen being desperately brailed to relieve the pressure aft, for it was evident now that there was an imbalance in the rig.

'Her forestay, for a guinea,' Beazley exclaimed, 'or at least her fore topmast stay. She won't be following us this night!'

'Forestay or bowsprit gammoning, or anything else on her bows. It hardly matters, Master. Now where's that corvette, we may make some good of this night. We may yet take a prize!'

With the seventy-four temporarily disabled, the corvette would be easy prey for a fifty-gun ship, if only she could be separated from her larger, disabled consort. He looked hungrily at the smaller vessel and as he did so his gaze lighted upon the envoy, standing at the taffrail, staring at him. It was as though his thoughts were being read, and what the envoy gleaned from Carlisle's thoughts he clearly didn't like.

Enrico saw the little wordless dialogue and moved close to Carlisle.

'Perhaps the corvette may wait for another day, sir,' he said softly.

'Eh, what's that Mister Angelini?'

It was so startling a break of protocol that Carlisle was left speechless for a moment. He bit off a sharp rebuke to his master's mate as his common sense and discretion got the better of him. Enrico was right, of course. He'd been brought up in the Sardinian court and knew the power and influence of an envoy from one of the great powers. Carlisle was lucky to have come away so lightly from his first breach of his orders, he may not be so fortunate the second time. And of course, if he was to attempt a rapprochement with the envoy, this would be the best time to start, by making for their destination as swiftly as possible and foregoing any other temptations.

'Perhaps it may, Mister Angelini, perhaps it may.'

He turned back to the sailing master. 'Bring us about if you please and shape a course for Villa-Franca.'

*Get thee behind me, Satan*, Carlisle thought as *Dartmouth* tacked handily in the now-steady wind and passed well to leeward of the two stricken French ships.

There was Enrico, laying off the course and making a note in the log as though nothing unusual had happened. Carlisle walked over to him and made a pretence of studying the traverse board. He spoke quietly without raising his head.

'Thank you for your wise words of counsel, Mister Angelini.'

\*\*\*

# CHAPTER FOUR

## Lessons in Diplomacy

*Wednesday, Twenty-Eighth of May 1760.*
*Dartmouth, at Sea. Cape Mola southwest-by-south 20 leagues.*

Away on the starboard bow, far below the horizon, the eastern slopes of Corsica's mountains were already bathed in the light of a new day. On *Dartmouth's* quarterdeck the sailing master and all the young gentlemen of both the middle and morning watches were preparing to take the sun's bearing at the very moment of its rising. Both sets of young men were displeased; those of the middle because the action against the Frenchman had meant that they had been on deck all night and now they were being held back a full ten minutes when they should already be cocooned in their hammocks, and those of the morning watch because the same action had allowed them only an hour in their hammocks before they'd been shaken ten minutes early to take part in this semi-religious ceremony. It was hard luck on both groups that the immutable laws of the universe dictated that the sun should rise at just three minutes past the change of the middle and morning watches at this particular spot on the globe.

'Observe the very first showing of the sun, gentlemen. Now, why do we not take the bearing at this moment, or even when the centre of the sun reaches the visible horizon?'

Beazley turned his unsmiling gaze on the nearest young gentleman, a small boy not yet fourteen. He was a volunteer, absurdly rated able seaman on the ship's books, and it would be more than two years before he could aspire to the lofty hights of midshipman. He was a late addition to the complement, the son of a dockyard officer who had begged the place most humbly, and the ridiculous fiction of his rating was a result of Carlisle's allowance of servants having been used up. Nevertheless, it was the first step on a career as a sea officer and he had to learn his trade.

The boy looked shy, but he had listened to the master's mates and he had read his textbooks and the answer came out confidently.

'It's because of refraction, sir. The rays of the sun are bent around the earth's atmosphere so that when we see the sun break the horizon, it is truly still below the horizon. We wait until it is one semi-diameter clear of the horizon before declaring sunrise and taking the bearing.'

Beazley's craggy face cracked a reluctant smile. He wasn't naturally a harsh man, but the responsibility of imparting the fundamentals of navigation to a horde of indifferently educated boys wore on his soul. There was a noticeable shuffling as the young gentlemen shifted closer to the object of the sailing master's pleasure, to partake in some small measure in the glory of the occasion. *Beastly* – as the young gentlemen privately called him – had never before smiled at an answer to one of his infamously difficult questions.

'An excellent answer, young man, perfect in every respect. Of course, the semi-diameter is only an approximation...'

He would have expounded on the minute differences that the ambient temperature made to the calculation of refraction, were it not for the sun itself that was rising inexorably, paying no heed to the master's pedantry.

'Now, each of you look through the stiles and turn the azimuth index until the sun is bisected by the cat-gut and note the compass reading. You must make sure that the cat-gut is aligned with the very centre of the sun or your measurement will be inaccurate.'

There was a general shuffling so that each could take a turn to stare through the stiles. The quartermaster moved to one side and the steersmen stepped back behind the wheel to make space.

'Mister Young, I noticed that you were fortunate enough

to take your turn at the critical moment. Pray tell us your measurement of the sun's azimuth at sunrise.'

'Nor'east-by-east a half east, sir,'

'Very good. Now what use is that information to us, Mister Young?'

Horace Young gazed abstractedly at the binnacle. He knew the answer but couldn't frame it concisely. He swayed back and forth as the master stared at him impatiently. Finally, it came out.

'As we know our position, and we know the date, we can calculate the true azimuth of the sun at sunrise. By comparing it with the observed azimuth we can determine the error in our compass, sir.'

The master continued to stare at him. Horace was aware that his answer was incomplete, incorrect even, but under the master's awful gaze his wits had left him.

'And what do we call that *error* as you are pleased to call it, Mister Young?' the master asked with a worrying emphasis on the word *error*.

Horace looked around desperately and his eyes lighted upon the quartermaster who was holding his two fingers against his face in a vee shape. It could have been that he was just scratching his nose, but a wink sealed it.

'Variation, sir,' Horace exclaimed in triumph, 'The difference between the true azimuth of the sun at sunrise and the observed azimuth is the magnetic variation.'

'Quite right, Mister Young, quite right. However, I object to the word *error* when applied to a compass in my ship, I object most strongly. It is a defamatory word and I'll thank you not to use it again. Perhaps you can redeem yourself by suggesting how an accurate understanding of the magnetic variation may be of benefit to us.'

There was a stunned silence. It was the sort of question that could be answered on many levels and in many ways, and almost anything Horace said would surely be wrong.

'Because, young man,' the master said after the silence had lasted for a few long seconds, 'it will mean that in two days' time we will sail smugly into the anchorage at Villa-Franca rather than blunder unhappily into the waiting arms of the French navy at Toulon! Now, gentlemen, the morning watch can remain on deck while those of you who were fortunate to stand the middle watch may join me in my cabin to consult the tables and determine the magnetic variation in this part of God's realm.'

The master ignored the audible groan from the four young men who were fated to lose another fifteen minutes of their rightful sleeping time. The quartermaster smiled grimly at them. He could sympathise but really, he knew that this was as it should be. No young gentleman had a right to sleep, and they would be more grateful for any sleep they did have if they were deprived from time to time.

*\*\**

From his vantage position on the poop deck Carlisle had seen the cluster of people around the binnacle, but his mind was elsewhere. The steady rise and fall of the ship went unnoticed as he swayed easily to the regular motion. The wind had backed in the past hour and now they were sailing two points free with their bows pointed squarely somewhat to the west of Villa-Franca, to allow for the ship's leeway. The last squall was over an hour ago and the Western Mediterranean appeared to have settled down now that the tramontana was subsiding.

Dawn had revealed an empty sea; there was no sign of the French seventy-four, nor of the corvette, and it certainly looked as though they would have an unmolested passage. He had received the casualty report, which always depressed him. It was modest by any standard, an able seaman had been killed outright by a thirty-two-pound ball that had entered through number five lower deck gunport, and three men were in the surgeon's hands with splinter wounds, all were expected to do well. That was hardly more than the usual casualty rate from illness and accident by this point in their voyage, and it would certainly excite no comment from the admiral or from their Lordships, but Carlisle knew that it could have been – it should have been – avoided. However, that wasn't his chief concern; the forefront of his mind was wholly occupied with his disastrous relations with his guest. By naval standards he'd been justified in confining him to his cabin, but nevertheless it was an unwise way to treat the King's envoy and the cousin of a belted earl to boot. The man had the power to do Carlisle great harm, and something must be done to retrieve the situation before they arrived at Villa-Franca when the balance of power would shift decisively in the envoy's favour.

'Mister Halsey. Be so kind as to pass the word for Mister Angelini. If he's turned in, I'll give him five minutes to appear properly dressed.'

Carlisle paced to and fro like a caged lion. The poop deck was one of the joys of a command of this size. He could be alone, away from the inquisitive eyes of his officers. Nobody had a need to linger on the poop deck when the ship was cruising, and only the midshipman of the watch appeared every half hour to cast the log. It was turning into a glorious spring day as the threatening squalls gave way to high, white clouds that marched down from the nor'west in stately procession. They'd be in Villa-Franca in two days' time and he should have been anticipating it eagerly. It was a short ride of an hour to Nice across the high ground of Mount Boron, and there he could be sure of a warm welcome in the elegant home of the Viscountess Angelini, his aunt by marriage. It was all spoiled, however, by the glowering presence of the envoy. They would only spend a day in Nice and then they would take a carriage to Turin, to the court of King Charles Emmanuel of Sardinia. At sea Carlisle carried authority, he had almost unlimited power, even over as august a person as the King's envoy, but ashore he knew that he would have to defer to him, in fact he had been specifically charged to do so. In Turin he would be dependent upon Mackenzie even for the roof over his head. With their present state of disharmony, it could only turn out badly for Carlisle.

'Sir?'

Enrico Angelini looked as spruce as any man can possibly look when he has been rudely shaken from his hammock after only a half hours' sleep. He had clearly shaved at some time in the last day and his uniform was immaculate. That would be the work of Black Rod, the mysterious Angelini family master of household. He had followed Chiara Angelini to the West Indies and Virginia, but the viscountess had summoned him back to Nice, and *Dartmouth's* deployment to the Mediterranean had been a convenient way of achieving that. Carlisle had his own servants at sea, and he had no doubt that Black Rod (for that was the only name that Carlisle knew him by) had attached himself to the only other member of the Angelini family at hand.

'Ah, Mister Angelini. You can do me a service if you would.'

Enrico waited in silence as Carlisle formed his words carefully.

'I had an unfortunate conversation with Mister Mackenzie before the engagement last night. On reflection, I may have been a little hasty in following the Frenchmen so far towards Mahon. However that may be, I find that I must eat a portion of humble pie to restore a working relationship, and I'm at a loss as to how to proceed…'

He tailed off indecisively. Enrico may be his cousin by marriage, but it was a hard thing to ask the advice of a master's mate in his own ship.

There was a sound behind them, a midshipman and a ship's boy were climbing the poop deck ladder carrying the logline and a half-hourglass. It must be nearly one bell in the morning watch. Carlisle dismissed them with a curt gesture. The cast of the log could be omitted this bell, the master would just have to make an estimate of the ship's speed.

'…I know you have some experience of diplomacy, which is why I am now asking your advice.'

It was true. Enrico had spent half his young life at Turin and the other half, until he came to sea, at the house in Nice where the affairs of ambassadors and envoys were a matter of daily concern. He barely paused before answering.

'I believe you are correct, sir. If you are to accompany Mister Mackenzie to Turin, you will need to be in perfect harmony with him. The French King has an envoy there, perhaps even an ambassador by now, as does the Empress, the King of Prussia and the King of Spain. They will all be testing the British envoy for any weakness that they can exploit, even the Prussian gentleman, your ally. They will sense any discord between you as a shark smells blood in the water.'

Carlisle gazed astern in silence. A small white seabird was picking titbits from the waves where the cook was emptying the inedible scraps from the beef joints for the day's dinner. As he watched a larger bird, darker in colour, swooped down and hustled the smaller bird away, taking the choice station astern of this great ship. A skua perhaps. Had it counted the crew? Had it calculated the volume of scraps that three hundred and fifty men produced?

'Then how should I proceed, Mister Angelini? Should I invite the envoy to dinner today?'

'I think not, sir. It could cause embarrassment if you were to disagree again. An abrupt departure from dinner is a very public statement.'

Carlisle noticed how confident Enrico had become now that he was discoursing on a subject that he was familiar with. He'd always been perfectly correct in his manner towards his captain with no hint of the familiarity that he may have been tempted towards.

'Perhaps coffee, sir, at least to start. Mister Mackenzie has a late breakfast, about seven o'clock. An invitation to take coffee at nine o'clock would give him time to digest his meal. If all goes well, you can then invite him to dinner.'

Carlisle watched the dark bird again. A skua, he was certain now. It had the reputation of eating the dung of other seabirds, but this one appeared happier robbing their food.

'Very well. Would you deliver an invitation, Mister Angelini? You know the correct form, I'm sure.'

'Certainly, sir. May I also suggest that Black Rod attend you on this occasion? He is much more discreet than any of your own servants.'

Carlisle nodded abstractedly.

'And may I observe, sir, that it may be the manner in which he was sent below that concerns him most. He isn't used to naval ways and perhaps relies too much on the prerogatives of his birth and station.'

'Well, I would find it hard to accept the way he attempted to give me direct orders on my own quarterdeck. I'm satisfied that I acted correctly in that regard, even under the severest of provocation. In fact, if an explanation is required, it is he who should be doing the explaining.'

Enrico bowed. He looked for a moment as though he had something more to say but he thought better of it and departed down the poop-deck ladder.

How curious, Carlisle thought, that Enrico should refer to the man as *Black Rod*. Surely Enrico knew his real name. But on reflection, he'd only heard him called by his title – master of household – and on *Dartmouth* he had no title.

*** 

'Begging your pardon, sir, but may I report the change of the watch?'

That was Halsey, his head bobbing above the level of the poop-deck, as though he would not disturb his captain's thoughts if only a portion of his body was seen. Halsey was the weak link in *Dartmouth's* corps of officers, the one in whom Carlisle had the least confidence.

'Come up and report correctly, Mister Halsey.'

Halsey stumbled up the last few steps. He knew all about his captain's low opinion of him, and it did his confidence no good at all. He avoided direct contact with Carlisle, but sometimes it was inescapable. This was one of those occasions, and he was conscious that he had already fallen short of the required standards. He stood stiffly in front of Carlisle and removed his hat.

'The watch has been relieved, sir, Mister Beazley has the forenoon. The wind is from the nor'west and the ship is under all plain sail steering nor'east-by-north for Villa-Franca, a point free on the larboard tack. There are no vessels in sight. The bilge has been pumped dry. I request permission to leave the deck, sir.'

'Very good, Mister Halsey, carry on.'

If it were any other of his officers Carlisle would have exchanged a few pleasantries, but with Halsey it always seemed to fall on stony ground. He watched the young man depart and then walked down onto the quarterdeck.

'All well, Mister Beazley?'

'Aye, all well sir. There's just one thing that the quartermaster has noticed, the steering feels a mite jumpy, it's probably nothing. The quartermaster of the morning felt it too, but then it stopped for a spell. It's back now.'

'What's the problem with the helm, Eli?'

'As Mister Beazley says, sir, it's probably nothing, but there's a sort of grating feel as we drop off the swell, as the pressure comes off the rudder.'

Carlisle walked to the wheel and took hold of the spokes. At first it felt normal, then *Dartmouth's* stern lifted and as the swell passed and the stern dropped, he felt it, a jarring sensation.

'You felt it, sir?' asked Eli.

'Yes, I believe so. Have you looked over the stern, Mister Beazley?'

The master nodded.

'Nothing to see, sir. It all looks normal. It's probably just a piece of junk caught between the rudder and the sternpost.'

'Well, ask the carpenter to look into it at Villa-Franca, would you? If necessary, you can shift the trim a little, we should be there for a week or two.'

Now wasn't that just like Halsey to avoid mentioning the rudder? Something would have to be done about that man.

*\*\*\**

# CHAPTER FIVE

## A Battle of Wills

*Wednesday, Twenty-Eighth of May 1760.*
*Dartmouth, at Sea. Cape Mola southwest-by-south 24 leagues.*

Robert Mackenzie walked stiffly into the captain's cabin. If Carlisle had hoped to see any sign of contrition, he was disappointed, the envoy was the embodiment of aristocratic arrogance. He glared angrily around the smaller cabin – he had the vacant flag quarters for his own use – and waited for Carlisle to make the first move.

'Welcome, sir, would you care to take a seat?'

'I would not, Captain Carlisle, I am come to hear what you have to say about last night's incident.'

This wasn't the start to the conversation that Carlisle had hoped for.

'A coffee perhaps?'

Carlisle was determined to play this through to the end. He beckoned to Black Rod who had donned his coat and breeches for the occasion and looked suitably magisterial. A small china cup of coffee was presented on a silver tray and the sheer force of Black Rod's size and bearing compelled Mackenzie to take it.

They stood either side of the small mahogany table with a fiddled top, their legs so accustomed to the sea that they didn't notice the gentle heel of the deck. The envoy doggedly avoided Carlisle's eye, staring haughtily at the furniture. Carlisle forced a smile and tried to look like a man bearing an olive branch. The ship lurched to starboard spilling some of the envoy's coffee and he slowly and deliberately placed it between the fiddles of the table.

'I find, sir, that I was a little hasty in pursuing the Frenchmen into Mahon, and I regret that I may have placed you and your mission in danger.'

The envoy turned his head slowly towards Carlisle and

stared straight at him.

'If you think I am concerned for my own safety you are sadly mistaken, Captain Carlisle, and I set aside, for now, the jeopardy that you placed upon my mission. The issue that should be addressed is the abrupt and insulting manner in which you required me to retire from the deck. I find it inconceivable that you should consider that to be acceptable behaviour to one of my station, and in front of common sailors.'

Centuries of patrician breeding lay behind Mackenzie's manner. There was no doubting his genuine anger, but Carlisle wasn't ready to concede any ground.

'Yet you must agree, sir, that your questioning of my conduct, on my own quarterdeck, was contrary to all norms of behaviour. It is directly addressed in the articles of war and makes no exception for supernumerary passengers...'

Carlisle bit his tongue. He would have retracted that last sentence if Mackenzie hadn't leapt upon it, his face discolouring into a high, bright crimson.

'Good God man, you surely don't class me as a supernumerary passenger! I happen to be His Majesty's representative to a foreign monarch with discretionary powers that you can only dream of. My responsibilities can hardly be imagined by a sea officer in command of a little, obsolete fourth rate. I remonstrated with Lord Anson when I heard that you were nothing more than a colonial, and my complaint should have been attended to. I find you wholly unfit for your commission, Captain Carlisle, and you can be sure that I will convey my displeasure to their Lordships at the earliest opportunity. It appears that I must endure your company in Turin for a few days and I am obliged by my duty to present you at court, God help me, otherwise I see no need that we should speak. Now good day to you, sir. I can find my own way to my cabin and I won't be disturbing your quarterdeck again.'

With that the envoy was gone, leaving Carlisle shaking in anger. How would they ever be able to work together in

Turin after that outburst? What rankled most was the casual insult about his birth in the Virginia colony. He had always felt an outsider in the navy and in British society, but never so far beyond the pale as he felt now. He sensed a rage coming over him, not unlike the fury he felt when boarding the enemy, although in that case it was more controlled. He raised his fist to smash it down upon the delicate fiddles of the table, then he saw Black Rod out of the corner of his eye, and shame overcame him. He stalked out to find the solitude of the poop deck.

\*\*\*

The tramontana died away in the forenoon watch to be replaced by a steady wind from the west-nor'west that speeded *Dartmouth* towards Villa-Franca. It should have been a happy time, with a quartering breeze, a warm sun and a sparkling sea, but the beauty of the day was lost on Carlisle as he paced the poop deck in a black humour. He saw nothing of the officers and seamen who came aft to tend the mizzen sheets, to cast the log and to attend to the myriad tasks that kept a ship of wood, canvas and cordage afloat on an unforgiving sea, and in their turn, they pretended not to see their captain. It was some mild consolation that his heavy tread – like a march of doom – would disturb the envoy's peace in the great cabin below. He recognised that nothing could be done to mend his relations with Mackenzie, but nevertheless, his orders compelled him to spend some days in Turin, and there he couldn't avoid the envoy's company. It was the logistics that concerned him now. If he couldn't rely upon the envoy's good offices, then he must shift for himself and find a means of travelling from Nice to Turin and a means of sustaining himself at the court of King Charles Emmanuel. He would have to turn to Enrico again, that much was clear.

It was a measure of how engrossed he had been by his own concerns that he genuinely didn't know who had the forenoon watch. It was a further confirmation that his first lieutenant was quite capable of managing the ship on a day-to-day basis without his interference. He leaned over the poop rail and looked down onto the quarterdeck. Wishart had the watch, and there was Enrico moving the pegs on the traverse board. He must be the mate of the watch. Probably he'd been on the poop deck half a dozen times in the last two hours without Carlisle noticing his presence.

'Mister Wishart. Can you spare Mister Angelini for a while? Then I would be glad to see him in my cabin.'

*\*\**

The glory of these fifty-gun fourth rates was that they were fitted out to take a flag officer – an admiral or a commodore – on distant stations. The great cabin under the poop deck was spacious in the extreme and when there was no flag embarked, or no illustrious guest – it was the envy of every captain not so blessed. However, when Mackenzie had joined the ship in Portsmouth, Carlisle had moved into the space designated for the captain, a much smaller and less convenient cabin on the starboard quarter of the upper gundeck. There was no great stern gallery such as the envoy was presumably enjoying, and no separate dining cabin.

'Well, Mister Angelini, I find I must ask your advice again. You may have gathered that my meeting with Mister Mackenzie didn't go too well; in fact, it made matters worse.'

Enrico inclined his head in acknowledgement but made no immediate reply. Carlisle studied him for a moment. He'd always rather taken his master's mate for granted, just another subordinate officer who happened to be his cousin. How old would he be? It had never occurred to Carlisle to ask about his age. The only relevance that age had to a master's mate or midshipman was in relation to his qualification to attend the lieutenant's examination, and as a Catholic, Enrico could never aspire to a commission in the British navy. Probably he was in his early twenties, a year or two younger than his friend Holbrooke who was now a post-captain. His demeanour was far too mature, too assured, for his station in *Dartmouth*. Carlisle guessed that he wouldn't remain much longer, perhaps he wouldn't sail with them when they left Villa-Franca. He'd be missed.

Carlisle waved to one of the only two chairs in the cabin and forced himself to sit in the other.

'Nevertheless, I still must travel to Turin and I had perhaps too readily assumed that he and I would travel together. I know nothing of the country beyond Nice and Villa-Franca; I am reliant upon your knowledge, Mister Angelini.'

Enrico smiled.

'It is the envoy who will find life difficult if he makes enemies of the Angelini family, sir. You have met the viscountess, of course.'

Carlisle had indeed met Viscountess Angelini and he had long ago resolved never to fall out with his wife's formidable aunt. She was Enrico's aunt too. Lacking her own children, she had more-or-less adopted those of her siblings as they passed away.

'I think you can expect no insult while you are in Nice and most certainly you will be able to stay at the family villa. As for travel to Turin, it's a long road, over a hundred miles. It's been improved since the days when it was a mule track for salt from the coast, yet it will still be a two-day journey, at least. The viscountess will surely make a carriage available.'

'There are facilities along the way, I gather.'

'Certainly. My family has an arrangement for fresh horses at Cuneo, where the road crosses the Tanaro River and at Carmagnola in the Po Valley. I'll see that a messenger is sent ahead of you. There are good lodgings at Savigliano, which is between the two and about halfway to Turin. I assure you, sir, that your journey will be arranged. Unless Mister Mackenzie has resources that we are unaware of, he cannot possibly have a swifter or more convenient journey than you.'

'And in Turin, will I be able to find lodgings?'

Enrico smiled again. His cousin still didn't fully comprehend the reach of the Angelini family in the

Sardinian King's domains.

'A distant cousin has a grand house in Turin close to the palace, and I'm sure you'll be welcome there.'

Carlisle digested this new information. He hadn't given any thought to the land journey, assuming, until today, that he and the envoy would travel together. He spoke quite reasonable French but only the few words of Italian that Chiara had taught him. Regardless of the arrangements, it would be difficult travelling alone. Enrico read his thoughts.

'May I suggest, sir, that you will need an aide for this journey. Perhaps I…'

'What an excellent idea, Mister Angelini,' Carlisle exclaimed, grasping at the half-formed offer and feeling some relief from his woes for the first time today, 'and I seem to remember you saying that your regiment is quartered in Turin.'

'That is correct sir. I've been given a lieutenant's commission into the Royal Piedmont Cavalry in my absence, and they're in Turin as far as I know. There's really nowhere else for them to be with my country so determined upon neutrality.'

Carlisle nodded in sympathy. The entire military establishment of the kingdom was furious at their King's fence-sitting.

'But it will be good to see them again, and my plain blue uniform won't look far out of place. They wear blue with red facings, you know. If I have time, I'll have a new uniform made; the yellow and red of my old cadet regiment will have to be set aside.'

***

The drawer above the desk's kneehole opened with a sharp click when Carlisle turned the key. His clerk kept all his papers except the few that he secreted away in this small space. Here he kept the letters from Chiara and his father – he didn't want either his intimate correspondence with his wife or the sordid details of his family's turbulent affairs to be known. In that same drawer he also kept the confidential orders that directed *Dartmouth's* movements.

Admiral Saunders had wasted little time over deciding which of his ships to detach on this peripheral duty, even without Pitt's advice he would have chosen *Dartmouth*. The Mediterranean Squadron's first task was to counter the still-powerful French squadron lying at Toulon, and that overriding mission largely determined which of his ships he could afford to send away. Only first, second and third rates could stand in the line of battle, and perhaps the larger sixty-gun fourth rates, but certainly not a fifty-gun ship such as *Dartmouth*. A frigate might have been suitable, but not to carry the Earl of Bute's cousin. King George's health was failing and his grandson who was to succeed him favoured the Scottish earl. It was widely rumoured that the death of George II would bring an end to the Newcastle Pitt ministry, in Bute's favour. A fourth rate was exactly right, it was at least *called* a ship-of-the-line and could carry the envoy in suitable dignity and yet it didn't significantly diminish the power of the Mediterranean Squadron.

Carlisle ruefully considered his own behaviour. He'd been warned, of course, but he hadn't given enough weight to the envoy's political and family connections. His dealings with Mackenzie had been reckless and it appeared that his efforts to remedy the situation had only made matters worse. What he would give for wise council, but neither Gresham nor Beazley had shown any inclination or indeed mental aptitude to consider the ship's employment beyond their own duties. Enrico had the breadth of education to advise him, but he couldn't consult a master's mate on matters regarding the ship's orders over the heads of his first lieutenant and sailing master, that would be too obvious a snub. He knew that he'd been sailing close to the wind in consulting Enrico about the situation in Turin, but at least he could justify that. There was his clerk Simmonds, but he'd never confided in him and didn't want to start now. David Chalmers, his sometime chaplain, would have been ideal, but he'd followed Holbrooke into the sloop *Kestrel* two-and-a-half years before. Good God, was it that long ago? Carlisle passed his hand wearily across his forehead. It was the one point where he feared he had failed in his profession, in not gathering and nurturing a large following of capable officers. Every time he had moved from ship to ship, his friends – all but a few – had melted away.

*You are to proceed with all dispatch to convey Mister Mackenzie to the King of Sardinia's realm at Nice or Villa-Franca, as the situation should appear most convenient.*

That was straightforward enough, but it was the next sentence that would hang him.

*You are to annoy the enemy's trade wherever you may find it without endangering the prompt arrival of Mister Mackenzie at Nice or Villa-Franca.*

That clause was loosely worded, but could he honestly say that he'd acted within the letter and spirit of it? Up to the point where he'd committed his ship to the Lair Passage, yes. Beyond that it was less certain. He was confident that he could defend his actions at a court-martial, but it wouldn't come to that, the mechanics of his downfall would be subtler by far. More importantly, how would his brush with the French at Mahon look to Lord Anson if it ever came to his attention? From almost any angle it looked like a shameless piece of prize-hunting conducted at the expense of his mission. Well, it was done now; his ship had suffered no harm and they had hardly been delayed an hour or two on their passage. Any protest from the envoy – if it were made – would lack real force. There was little to be feared, or so he told himself.

*Unless you judge that it would be dangerous to leave your ship, you are to accompany Mister Mackenzie to Turin, where you are to stay long enough to be presented at court, but you are to endeavour to be absent from your ship no longer than two weeks. In all cases you are to be guided by the advice of Mister Mackenzie.*

That was the awkward clause and it left little room for discretion. Saunders had expanded on the orders in Gibraltar, explaining how Pitt felt it important that King

Charles Emmanuel should understand the reach of British naval power. He could not, in all conscience, decline to follow the envoy to Turin unless there was an imminent threat to *Dartmouth*, and that was unlikely in the neutral, protected harbour of Villa-Franca. Unpleasant though it would be, he was committed to Turin and would just have to make the best of it.

His eyes strayed forward to the next paragraph, a much more congenial mission where his success or failure would owe nothing to prickly, aristocratic envoys.

*Having departed from Turin, you are to proceed to sea and cruise the Ligurian and Tyrrhenian Seas between Villa-Franca and the latitude of Cape Circeo, paying particular attention to the reports of ships-of-the-line being fitted out for the French navy in Genoese ports and other places on the Italian coast, and French privateers using ports along those coasts. If you discover any such ships you are to do all in your power to take, sink or burn them, while strictly observing the neutrality of the Republics of Genoa and Lucca, the Grand Duchy of Tuscany, the Papal States, the Kingdom of Naples and all other neutral states. As his Majesty's government does not recognise the Corsican Republic, you are strictly to avoid any action that could suggest acknowledgment of its legitimacy.*

The politics of these Italian states were enough to make a man's head spin. That paragraph contained sufficient ammunition to break a captain at a court martial if he should cause offence to any of them, without giving any indication of how he should *take, sink or burn* any French ships sheltering under their protection.

*If any of the aforementioned ships-of-the-line should elude you and make their way to sea, you are to immediately use your best endeavours to inform the commander-in-chief.*

Saunders had privately told him that he intended first to take his squadron to Toulon to ascertain the state of readiness of the French Mediterranean fleet. The time that he spent off Toulon would be determined by what he discovered when he looked into the outer road. If he could not be found off Toulon, then whatever British force he left there could advise Carlisle of his whereabouts.

There followed the usual instructions to rejoin the squadron off Toulon or at Gibraltar. If he could conclude his business at Turin quickly, he would have a whole three weeks for an independent cruise! He'd be free to harass French shipping along the whole of the coast, some hundred-and-twenty leagues, and it would be unusual if he couldn't gain some intelligence of these ships being built for the French.

But first, he had to suffer Mackenzie's company for a week or two.

\*\*\*

Sleep wouldn't come easily, and Carlisle tossed and turned in his cot as his over-active mind replayed the events of the day. Having Enrico with him on the journey to Turin would solve a host of problems and the certainty of transport and accommodation was very comforting. Yet it still left the problem of his relations with the envoy. Well, he would cross that bridge when he came to it. It was barely conceivable that the man would let his antagonism show at the court, in front of emissaries from a dozen countries, some of whom were at war with Britain. And he was concerned about leaving his precious ship in the hands of his second-in command. He'd be away for a week at least, possibly two, unless something unforeseen interrupted him. He had no doubt that Gresham could manage the ship in its day-to-day business but leaving a belligerent man-o'-war in a neutral harbour carried the potential for all kinds of problems. That French seventy-four's captain could guess where *Dartmouth* was heading and if he made an appearance off Sardinia's tiny seaboard, he wasn't at all certain that his first lieutenant was the right man to handle the diplomatic issues. That was partly why he'd chosen to anchor at Villa-Franca, because of its excellent protected harbour. Nice had nothing more than an open roadstead, and it offered a great temptation to anyone inclined to ignore the laws of neutrality. He hoped that General Paterson, the expatriate

Scotsman, was still the governor at Nice. He owed Carlisle a debt after his intervention in a previous incident that hinged upon the rights of belligerent nations in neutral waters and Carlisle was sure that he would do whatever he could to help.

That brought on pleasant memories of his first frigate command. He'd brought the old *Fury* into Villa-Franca just four years ago. How time had flown since then. His mind wandered to the fight with the French frigate *Vulcain* where he had first made his reputation, then on to marriage to his Italian beauty, to hurricanes in the West Indies, Dutch pirates, ice in the Saint Lawrence, and French fortresses in the frozen wastes of Canada. The gentle rhythmic motion of a well-found ship with a moderate quartering breeze finally had its effect and he fell asleep at last, as eight bells tolled the start of the graveyard watch.

***

# CHAPTER SIX

## His Excellency

*Friday, Thirtieth of May 1760.*
*Dartmouth, at Anchor. Villa-Franca.*

The Sardinian navy still clung to its antiquated row-galleys while their sailing navy boasted only a schooner or two, and those presently laid-up, so the spectacle of a two-decker sailing boldly into Villa-Franca under her tops'ls and jib brought the population out in force.

Gresham and Enrico had taken the longboat ashore at the earliest time that it could be assumed that the local commander would be breakfasted, and they had returned with the necessary assurance that *Dartmouth's* salute would be returned gun-for-gun. The navy never wasted its sacred gun salutes without being certain that the recipient would respond in kind. Mackenzie's secretary, a much more agreeable person than his master, had been landed at the same time to arrange for the envoy's reception.

As the anchor cable hissed through the hawsepipe, the first gun fired its salute, and the cliffs and hills burst into life as thousands upon thousands of seabirds took to the air in alarm, wheeling and soaring with their wings flashing white against the purest blue sky.

Carlisle left the business of anchoring to the master and first lieutenant while he studied the road to the left of the fort with his telescope. The road hugged the shoreline, rising and falling over the coastal undulations before disappearing around the seaward-facing skirts of Mount Boron. It was empty this early in the morning, not even the local farmers were abroad. Then a trail of dust appeared at the farthest point of the land, between the sea and the mountain slopes. A vehicle was hurrying from Nice towards the citadel at Villa-Franca. There had been enough time – just – for a horseman to have galloped to Nice, for General Paterson to have been informed of the arrival of a British ship, and for his carriage to have been summoned and set on the short drive to Villa-Franca.

'I do believe the general has missed the salute, Mister Angelini,' Carlisle said, taking a guess at the vehicle's identity.

'Yes, sir, that's his carriage,' Enrico replied confidently. 'There's not another like it in Nice. Those horses are being flogged unmercifully; look how fast it's travelling.'

Carlisle wiped the lenses of his telescope and looked again, with no better result. He stifled a sigh and nodded in agreement. It could have been a bullock-cart loaded with turnips for all he could tell but for its speed. However, there was no need for Enrico to know how far his eyesight had deteriorated.

'Well, I look forward to meeting him again.'

The carriage disappeared through the gates of the fort as the last gun of the returned salute echoed back from the hills.

'Is the longboat ready, Mister Gresham?'

'It is, sir, scrubbed and polished.'

'And the fort's commander understands that the gun salute that you'll fire for the envoy does not require a reply?'

'Yes, sir. Mister Angelini explained it most carefully in his own language. There can be no chance of misunderstanding.'

Gresham looked over his shoulder as the gunner raised his arm.

'The gun salute is ready, sir,' said Gresham removing his hat.

'Very well. Please inform Mister Mackenzie that his boat awaits.'

It was awkward but unavoidable; to have made their official calls separately would have advertised their disharmony. Carlisle just hoped that there would not be a scene on the deck of his ship, or worse still, in the boat. He clapped his hat upon his head and adjusted his sword.

'Keep a good lookout for me, Mister Gresham. I don't know how long I'll be, but if I'm delayed into the dogwatches, I'll send a message.'

'Aye-aye sir.' Gresham replaced his hat as Carlisle turned away.

Carlisle always regretted missing the exhibition of the *Microcosm* at Norfolk in Virginia back in 'fifty-five. He'd heard accounts of how each motion of its parts was started automatically by the preceding motion, the whole being powered by a clockwork mechanism. It must have been very much like the ceremony that was enacted each time he left the ship. The marine lieutenant watched carefully and at the instant that Gresham brought his hat to his head he gave the order that brought the muskets of the two files of marines from their shoulders to the salute. The assembled officers removed their hats and the bosun's mates raised their calls to their lips. The boys twitched their white sennet gloves, offering a startling contrast against the crimson baize that covered the side ropes.

There was no entry-port in these fourth rates and Carlisle had only to step down onto the gangway that ran above the waist on each side and pass through the space between the hammock cranes and the timber head. The steps had been scrubbed clean and sanded to prevent Carlisle's foot slipping, and four nimble boys held out the side ropes for him. He climbed carefully down and into the longboat, where his own coxswain, Jack Souter, was waiting to steady him. The last notes of the bosun's mates' calls died away as his feet touched the bottom-boards. He waited, covering his trepidation with a look of supreme indifference.

Carlisle shouldn't have been concerned. The envoy, for all his starchy aloofness, was a practiced professional and he could have smiled while dancing with the devil if it were required in the course of his diplomatic duties. And he was familiar with naval protocol. His secretary had announced his imminent arrival in enough time to allow Carlisle to be piped down into the longboat, for unlike the custom in carriages ashore, the senior person always entered the boat last. The envoy was handed carefully into the boat, and the first gun of his salute shattered the peace of Villa-Franca once more. The seabirds soared again, amazed and dismayed at two such disturbances in less than half an hour.

'A fine morning, Captain Carlisle,' the envoy said when he was settled in the stern sheets, as though never a cross word had passed between them. Carlisle could see that his mind was elsewhere, he was counting the guns, in case he had been short-changed. As the eleventh gun boomed, a brief smile showed that he was content. Carlisle had toyed with the idea giving him only nine, as the regulations allowed. Simmonds had pointed out the article to him: *other public ministers or persons of quality, eleven or less according to the degree of their quality.* But the calculated insult would have looked spiteful and could only have done further harm.

'I believe I saw General Paterson's carriage approaching the fort, sir.' Carlisle kept his voice neutral, not wishing to expose himself to a rebuff.

'Thank you, Captain Carlisle. I'm familiar with General Paterson, of course.'

The boat sped in silence towards the stone jetty that thrust from the fort's arched gate into the bay. The oarsmen knew the situation between their captain and the passenger, even if the strained atmosphere between them hadn't made it clear, and each man pulled his oar in stoic silence, concentrating on rowing dry and in perfect time with the stroke oar. The envoy showed no emotion at all; he could have been carved in stone for all the expression that his faced showed.

\*\*\*

Last in, first out, that was the rule in boats, and Carlisle followed Mackenzie onto the grey stones of the fort's jetty. The fort's commander met them and led them through a double line of soldiers in resplendent uniforms. Carlisle had the leisure to glance left and right as he walked a few steps behind the envoy; for once he wasn't the principal recipient of this ceremonial greeting.

'On behalf of His Majesty King Charles Emmanuel, I welcome you back to the Kingdom of Sardinia, Mister Mackenzie, and on my own behalf, I welcome you to the county of Nice.'

General Paterson bowed, a moderate bending of his lean body that was precisely measured to acknowledge the rank of his visitor but no further. Carlisle noticed that the general chose not to use the title *Excellency*. Of course, it was important in diplomatic affairs to maintain the difference between an ambassador and an envoy, and the governor of Nice – who himself was addressed as *Excellency* – could be expected to know the correct forms. Nevertheless, this was a side of the general that Carlisle hadn't seen when he had brought *Fury* into Villa-Franca all those years ago. Then the general had been dealing with a rather junior post-captain whom he could afford to treat almost as a younger relative. His dealings with the appointed representative of King George to his adopted country must necessarily be more formal in nature.

Mackenzie returned the bow, measured to within an inch of the courtesy that he had received.

'It is a pleasure to be back in the kingdom, your Excellency. I regret that I was unable to send a warning of my arrival, but this present war makes a sea passage necessarily more uncertain than in more peaceful times.'

Carlisle could see that time had taken its toll on General Paterson. He had visibly shrunk in height in the four years since Carlisle had last visited Nice, and no act of self-will could disguise the stoop in his shoulders. His voice, however, retained its youthful vigour and he had lost none of his North British accent. Of course, the general and the envoy were countrymen. Carlisle felt a stab of anger with himself for forgetting that fact; it could have a bearing on their relations while he was here.

Despite his advancing years, there was a gleam of

vitality in the general's eyes as he looked past the envoy to see who this sea officer was following him. Mackenzie spoke quickly to retain some control over the situation.

'I believe you know Captain Carlisle, General, he has been good enough to convey me from Gibraltar and he will accompany me to Turin, where I am bound as soon as I can arrange…'

'Captain Carlisle! What a pleasure to see you again!'

The general strode past Mackenzie and clasped Carlisle's hand, smiling with a genuine warmth that was noticeable for its contrast with the more formal greeting for the envoy.

'It must be four years since we last met, and here you are in command of a ship-of-the-line! I've heard everything about you, of course, but the last news was that you had lost your frigate – *Medina* I believe – at Quebec. You'll come to dinner, I trust, and tell me all about your exploits.'

Carlisle could see that the envoy wasn't pleased that this post-captain had upstaged his arrival in the country. Had their relations been more cordial, Mackenzie would have heard how close the general and Carlisle had been and would have been prepared for this reunion. In a flash of intuition, Carlisle realised that the envoy and the general had an uneasy relationship, despite both being Scottish, and this display of warmth brought it into sharp perspective. Carlisle felt himself caught up in events, unable to mitigate the further damage that was being done to his relations with the envoy.

Paterson saw the look on Carlisle's face and must have been aware of the delicacy of the situation, yet he plunged on as though Mackenzie wasn't there.

'You certainly won't be able to leave for Turin until tomorrow, and that will be the earliest. Dinner at two o'clock then? Four bells as you sailors say. The viscountess is in Turin, so she won't be able to claim you.'

Paterson turned belatedly to the envoy.

'You'll accept my hospitality while you are in Nice,

Mister Mackenzie? In which case I hope that you will also join me for dinner.'

Mackenzie bowed in response. It looked to Carlisle as though his anger was such that he didn't trust himself to speak.

*\*\**

Dinner had been less painful than Carlisle had feared. By the time they sat down, Mackenzie had recovered from his surprise at the warmth of the friendship between Paterson and Carlisle, and his innate diplomatic skills had returned. Paterson also had realised that he had treated the envoy with less respect than his rank demanded, and during the dinner he had worked hard to redress the balance. Now, however, the envoy had left them, and Paterson and Carlisle were alone on the patio of the general's house that overlooked the beautiful bay of Nice.

'I'm growing old, Carlisle. No, don't pretend that it's not obvious, although it's truly kind of you. I should retire but I have a certain sense of loyalty to King Charles Emmanuel, as well as to King George, and I'd like to see him safely through this present war. However much his generals and colonels may fume and bluster, his policy of neutrality is best for the country, although it's not an easy path to tread between England and France. If Spain should throw in its lot with King Louis, the pressure will increase, and I will need to help hold the line. I'll stay here at least for the present but then it's home for me and a well-earned rest. Perhaps not to Scotland, the climate would be too much of a shock after this,' he said sweeping his arm around the vista of blue sea and blue sky, 'but I have a hankering for Bath, for enlightened conversation and for the cure.'

Carlisle could think of nothing to say. The general's advancing age was written on his face and evident in the stick that had become less a fashionable accessory and more an essential support. How long would the war last? Another year, certainly, perhaps two, and if Spain should be foolish enough to take arms, then three or four years, at least. Perhaps fate would overtake the general's plans for retirement and his bones would be buried in this foreign country. It was a sombre thought.

'Is Lady Chiara well, and how has she taken to life in Virginia?'

That led to a more cheerful line of conversation. Carlisle told the general about his child, Joshua, fast approaching two years of age. He described the rather-too-grand house that they had bought during his visit to Williamsburg earlier that year, and how delighted Chiara was to be living just a few steps from the governor's palace. He passed over the obvious issue of how he, a sea officer in King George's navy at a time of global war, would be able to enjoy his family and his new house so far away from England, and the general was too polite to raise it.

'You know, if you have any letters that aren't of an official or sensitive nature, I can send them to England overland, and from there they can be in Virginia in three weeks. I can guess how difficult it must be for you to send letters home otherwise.'

That was something Carlisle hadn't considered. Any letter that he wrote to Chiara couldn't even leave the ship until he found a means of sending it to Gibraltar, and that probably meant waiting until he met the admiral, who had sloops at his disposal for just that kind of service. Then it would have to go to England unless he was incredibly lucky and there was a ship at Gibraltar bound across the Atlantic. It could take many months for a letter to reach his wife.

Paterson brought the conversation back to Nice.

'You'll find some changes at the Angelini house,' he said, cradling his brandy. 'The viscountess doesn't command the same level of influence at court that you may remember, and, if I may allude to it, the family's finances are not what they used to be.'

Only two good friends could possibly broach such subjects freely, as Carlisle well knew, and he valued this demonstration of their intimacy.

'Yes, some of it I know. Lady Chiara has a certain amount of news in letters from the viscountess, but you know, she has her own life, new friends and fresh interests. You can imagine how much she enjoys living just a few steps from the governor's palace. She's moved on from her old life in Nice, and I don't imagine that she hears all the news. The master of the household has been recalled, you know, and I brought him here from Virginia.'

'The man that Mister Holbrooke dubbed Black Rod? I'm not surprised she wants him back; perhaps he can bring some stability to the family's affairs. Incidentally, do you know his name? I've never heard it mentioned.'

'Not I,' Carlisle replied, shaking his head.

'Well, onto another subject. It's very odd that you should have arrived here at this moment as it has saved me a great deal of trouble. Tell me, is Enrico Angelini still with you?'

Carlisle looked warily at the general. He could guess what was coming, a summons for Enrico to return to the colours. He'd been away over three years and his colonel would certainly have thought that long enough for the young man to gain some experience. He'd be a rarity in his regiment, a subaltern who had experienced battle at sea and on land when far older and more senior officers had been forced to sit inactively while the world was in turmoil.

'Yes, he's a master's mate now and an accomplished petty officer. If he were English, he'd have passed for a lieutenant's commission long ago.'

'Well, I hope this will be good news for you. If he hadn't appeared at my doorstep, so to speak, I would have had to recall him…'

Paterson saw Carlisle's look of dismay and hurried on.

'…only temporarily and now it may not be necessary at all. He's to be offered a commission as a lieutenant in the soon-to-be reformed navy of the Kingdom of Sardinia, a navy that is moving away from galleys and sloops to frigates and in the fullness of time, ships-of-the-line.'

Carlisle's thought rapidly. It would mean losing his valuable master's mate and more importantly a man whom he was starting to rely upon as a confidant. On the other hand, it was an opportunity that Enrico mustn't reject. To be a lieutenant in this infant navy meant that he would be one of its most skilled sea officers. When the first frigate joined the fleet, he would be a candidate for command, a strong contender indeed with all his experience.

'I'll be sad to lose him, sir…'

'Not necessarily, Captain Carlisle, not necessarily.'

Paterson swirled the brandy in his glass, evidently selecting his words with care.

'I've been instructed to look into the possibility of Mister Angelini being seconded to a British ship-of-the-line to fill a lieutenant's billet for a year or two. It will take that time for the first ship of this new navy to be commissioned and then he can return to take his place, perhaps as a commander or post-captain by then.'

Paterson looked sideways at his guest, judging his reaction.

'I would have asked Admiral Saunders when he passes this way, but now it seems to me that Angelini may stay with you in *Dartmouth*. What do you think, Carlisle? Is it possible?'

Carlisle's heart pumped a little faster. He hadn't realised how much he would miss Enrico when he was gone, which seemed inevitable after this contact with his home country. He composed himself to answer with a level voice.

'Well, as far as I am concerned, I would welcome it although it will put me one lieutenant over my establishment. However, the regulations have something to say about this and they've been on my mind for some time.'

Carlisle stared out across the sea, bringing the relevant article to mind.

'It's article thirty-eight of the instructions to captains. I don't recall the exact wording, but in essence I need the approval of their Lordships to allow any foreign officers or gentlemen to serve in my ship. It's the same article that forbids me to carry women, yet my gunner's wife has sailed with him since he was awarded his warrant,' he added with a laugh.

'Nevertheless, I've been sailing close to the wind these past three years. Enrico is most evidently a gentleman although not an officer in the meaning of the regulations. My clerk pointed it out to me again only last month and I decided that if Enrico was still with me after this visit, then I would have to formalise his position.'

'Perhaps Mister Mackenzie could be prevailed upon to write to the first lord…'

'I think not, sir,' Carlisle replied flatly. Paterson had the tact to leave it there.

'Then if you had a written request from the minister of marine, could you take him on board as a supernumerary pending approval?'

Carlisle stared again at the sea. He didn't want to lose Enrico, that would be a personal disaster and furthermore Chiara wouldn't like it. Carlisle could just imagine the hurt that she would be unable to supress in the first letter after she discovered that her cousin had been left behind in Sardinia.

'Yes, I can do that,' he replied cautiously. 'I'll have to mark him discharged on the ship's books and re-enter him as my guest. He'll lose his pay, although I imagine he'll draw a salary from his own country. Admiral Saunders will see the merit in the proposal, and so long as Sardinia doesn't side with the French in this war, their Lordships will almost certainly approve it. It will take a few months, but I believe there is a strong chance that an exchange of letters can be achieved before the end of the summer.'

'And do you believe that Mister Angelini would welcome this? He will have heard nothing of it yet.'

Carlisle suppressed a smile. Unless the Angelini intelligence network had completely failed, Enrico would have heard of this on his first contact with the shore. A glance at the general confirmed that he knew it too.

'I believe he'll be delighted. I know he hasn't been looking forward to regimental duties in Turin after the service he's seen with me.'

'Ah yes. I heard about Cape François, and Louisbourg, and Quebec. He's seen some real fighting and profited by prize money also, I understand.'

'Fighting indeed. Did you know that he stood beside Wolfe on the Heights of Abraham? He was at the general's side when he fell. Wolfe had a great regard for him.'

'He stood beside Wolfe? Well, the more honour to him, I must get him to tell his story. He'd have found it all the harder to be relegated to escorting the King from the palace to the basilica on Sundays and holy days, for that's the present fate of the Royal Piedmont Cavalry. He must go back to sea with you, Carlisle, for his good and for the good of the Sardinian navy.'

\*\*\*

# CHAPTER SEVEN

## Intrigue at Court

*Monday, Second of June 1760.*
*Turin.*

Carlisle felt strangely calm and in control of himself. He had suffered Mackenzie for so long that had stopped noticing the man's conceit and unpleasantness. It had become like a toothache that he could do nothing about, and he cast the pain to the back of his mind.

The grand hall was the most ornate of the rooms that they had been led through and its gilded majesty was calculated to both impress and to oppress. Carlisle certainly appreciated the aesthetics of it, but if he was meant to be intimidated, then the ambience missed its mark. There were a dozen groups of men scattered around the vast floor, talking among themselves and all waiting for the arrival of the King's first minister. By sheer act of fate, he and Mackenzie had arrived in Turin the day before the audience for foreign envoys to present their credentials. Mackenzie evidently knew many of them but chose not to enlighten Carlisle. Nevertheless, he could identify the French party by the snatches of conversation that drifted towards him and a group of Spaniards made themselves conspicuous by their ruffles and feathers that had become unfashionable in the rest of Europe. Other groups must be from the multitude of smaller states that made up the Italian peninsula. Genoa would be there for sure and Tuscany, the Papal States, Naples and all the others. He spent the time studying the groups, but his eyes kept coming back to the four Frenchmen. One of them, a tall man in a black coat was surely the envoy, and a smaller man similarly dressed must be one of his staff, but the other two were more interesting. The French naval uniform wasn't as regularly prescribed as the British equivalent, but both of those men were wearing the blue and red, and both had that indefinable air of professional sailors. One of them, the older, caught Carlisle's eye and nodded briefly in his direction, an acknowledgement that fell short of a bow, Carlisle returned the compliment.

After the formal audience there would be an opportunity to speak to the other delegations and then Carlisle would discover their identities. Of course, it was impossible that he could be introduced to the French; as officers of belligerent nations, convention demanded that they ignored each other, much as men engaged to meet in a duel could not acknowledge each other before the event.

A gorgeously-dressed man – a chamberlain perhaps – brought his staff down twice on the floor with a double resounding crash. The double doors at the far end of the room were opened and the room came to a hushed silence. Carlisle wouldn't have been surprised to see King Charles Emmanuel himself walk through the doors, but the reality was more prosaic as a small, plainly dressed man made his way to the carpeted section at the centre of the room. The King's first minister was a business-like, brisk person whose manner was at odds with the elaborate ceremony that accompanied him.

Carlisle and Mackenzie were guided to their positions in a long line of people to be presented. This was a formal introduction for new envoys, those who had been away from the court for a length of time and any who wished for an audience with the King. The delegations were arranged in the order in which they had originally presented their credentials, and Carlisle and Mackenzie were close to the front with only a Florentine delegation between them and the French.

'Mister Mackenzie,' intoned a chamberlain in French. 'The envoy of his Majesty King George the Second of Great Britain and Ireland, Defender of the Faith.'

Carlisle was amused to note that an element of the King's title had been diplomatically omitted, the part that referred to his historical claim to the throne of France. But there was no time to ponder on archaic titles.

'Welcome back, Mister Mackenzie, I trust you had a fruitful time in England.'

The first minister was looking questioningly at Carlisle while replying to the envoy.

'I did, your Excellency, and Mister Pitt sends his best wishes to you. I have deposited a number of letters with your secretary.' He paused for a second and Carlisle was aware of the silence in the great room as a hundred pairs of ears strained to hear the introduction. 'May I present Captain Edward Carlisle of His Britannic Majesty's Ship *Dartmouth*?'

Carlisle stepped forward and made as elegant a bow as was possible while avoiding tripping over his sword. Nevertheless, he sensed that the French sea officers behind him had heard the name of his ship; the envoy had a loud voice and spoke superb French like most educated Scotsmen.

'You are very welcome to the kingdom, Captain Carlisle. Your ship is at Nice, perhaps?'

'At Villa-Franca, your Excellency,' Carlisle replied.

'And what rating is your ship, Captain?'

Carlisle had little to measure the tone of conversation against, but it sounded just a little impolite to be quizzing him so. He glanced sideways at Mackenzie whose face was an expressionless mask.

'*Dartmouth* is a fourth rate of fifty guns, your Excellency.'

'Of course, a ship-of-the-line to convey His Majesty's envoy, and a ship of appropriate force to sail so close to Toulon. General Paterson has undoubtedly made you aware of your rights and obligations as the commander of a ship belonging to a belligerent power, and we need say no more of it. I hope you will stay with us for at least a few days because I know my colleague the minister of the marine would like to meet you. Shall we say tomorrow at ten o'clock at his offices?'

Carlisle bowed in acknowledgement. With that the audience was over and Carlisle found himself ushered to the side of the room. He was too far away to hear the French officers being introduced, probably they were in diplomatic posts and had no ships to declare. He knew that there were no French ships at the only two substantial ports that the Kingdom of Sardinia owned; General Paterson would have told him if there were.

*\*\**

The viscountess was always formal in her dealings with Carlisle despite him being the husband of her niece. The tea was brought into the library by Black Rod, who had travelled with Carlisle and Enrico to Turin, and they received it in silence. The distant cousin's house – he was a second cousin of the viscountess – was a comfortable residence on a street that led to the grand square. The cousin himself was an old, old man, somewhat garrulous but sound in mind and body.

'Forgive me if I am prying…' Viscountess Angelini started.

You are, thought Carlisle, but I expected nothing less.

'…but would you be able to tell me what you learned at court today?'

Carlisle could see no reason not to tell her, there had been no state secrets and nothing that could compromise either himself or the envoy. However, it would be worth keeping something back to flush out any information that she may be holding.

'His Excellency the first minister welcomed me to the country and wanted to know the force of my ship and where she was anchored. I'm certain the French delegation heard what I said, but it's no secret.'

The cousin, who had also been at court that day, interrupted the viscountess.

'You are aware of where the French officers came from, Captain?'

'No, sir, I am not,' he said stretching his economy with

the truth to its limit.

He had heard the news from the Prussian delegation, that the Frenchmen came from Genoa, but the Prussians knew nothing more. Nevertheless, he leaned forward slightly. He knew that the cousin was extraordinarily well connected, as well connected as the viscountess, and it was useful to have a second source of information.

The viscountess looked irritated and gave Carlisle a look that said, really? You don't know? However, she knew her manners and deferred to the old gentleman.

'They are from the ships building in Genoa, Captain Carlisle. You will know more about this than I, but it appears that the French navy cannot build ships fast enough in Toulon and they have given a contract to a yard in Genoa for four ships of sixty-four guns each.'

Carlisle fought to keep his face from betraying his interest in this new information.

'I knew they were building ships somewhere in the republic, but I didn't know at which port. Then it's Genoa itself? The size of the ships – they're third rates it seems – is most interesting.'

'Then you would be further interested to learn the state of their completion, I imagine.'

The cousin was clearly enjoying being the source of this intelligence. It was all that Carlisle could do to prevent himself leaping to his feet and pacing the room. This was the information that he had been ordered to obtain. He had imagined it would take a week's cruising along the coast to discover what he was hearing now, and this came with no effort on his part. He didn't for a moment question the information; he knew enough about the Angelini family and its connections to be sure of its accuracy.

'The first two are in the water and being fitted out. Enough stores for a short voyage have been sent round from Toulon and some of their lighter guns, but they will take on the heavy guns at the arsenal. They have enough crew to sail the ship and man those guns that they have; what that number is I don't know. The remaining two will be fitted out in the next few weeks.'

Carlisle noticed, as he had before, that the viscountess was ill-at-ease when someone else had the limelight, but there was something more this time, some sense that she was annoyed that the cousin was so freely dispensing information.

The cousin was familiar with the technical terminology of shipbuilding and naval operations. There was none of that uncertain searching for the correct words that he heard from most people, and no hesitation in the delivery.

'Then those two gentlemen are the captains of the ships, perhaps?' Carlisle asked.

'One of them is, the other is a captain without a ship who was sent to oversee the building. But there's something more. The reason for their being here is to demonstrate the French navy's determination to dominate the Western Mediterranean. They hope to persuade the King to join the war on the side of France.'

The viscountess stared hard at her cousin, then at Carlisle.

'And they may succeed at that. King Charles Emmanuel is besieged by advisers who see only the power of the French. The British navy hasn't been seen in these waters since last year and then only a brief visit. From the vantage point of Turin,' he said with a hint of satisfaction, 'it appears that an alliance with the French would have few risks and many advantages.'

Carlisle returned his gaze unflinchingly. Perhaps this cousin was a useful path to get messages to those advisers of the King.

'I believe that if King Charles Emmanuel watches these seas over the summer, he will witness events that may convince him to remain neutral. I'm but the forerunner of a powerful battle squadron that is even now on its way from Gibraltar. It's commanded by Admiral Saunders who was so successful in bringing a great invasion force to take Quebec from the French last year.'

The cousin nodded his head thoughtfully.

'Well, it remains to be seen how far Admiral Saunders can influence the King. Meanwhile the French army is but a day's march from our borders and our own army is unblooded. You have heard about the King's plans for a navy, I imagine?'

'Yes, I have, but it will take a massive effort to build a sailing navy out of the galleys that the King presently owns. And it's not just the ships, the yards and the supplies, but the people to man those ships.'

Carlisle was deliberately leading the conversation on, to give the viscountess an opportunity to discuss Enrico, an opening to declare how much she knew.

'Indeed,' she said, 'and I understand that tomorrow the minister of the marine will formally ask you to take Enrico into your ship in the rank of lieutenant in the Sardinian navy. You are aware, of course, that he will make a similar request to the French.'

Carlisle couldn't help showing his surprise at that. Why hadn't General Paterson warned him?

'Then it's all the more important that an agreement can be reached. In any case I'll take him to sea on my own authority until I'm told that I shouldn't, and I don't anticipate that happening, particularly in light of this latest information.'

***

Signor Alessandro Lombardi had a small office some three hundred yards from the palace It was located on the third or fourth of the invisible circles of power that spread out from the royal residence, like ripples from a stone dropped in a pond. The ministry of war – with authority over the army – was firmly established in the first of those circles, which was an eloquent statement of the relative importance of the ministries.

'Of course, I rely entirely on your discretion in this

matter, Captain Carlisle. The Kingdom of Sardinia is strictly unaligned in this war between your country and France, and if it should be known that a Sardinian lieutenant is serving in a British ship, it could have grievous consequences for our ability to remain neutral.'

The minister was speaking in French, the common language of diplomacy, which allowed Carlisle to meet him in private without an interpreter.

'You'll be aware, Minister, that Mister Angelini has been serving in ships under my command for some three years now, in a non-commissioned capacity, and we have always managed to avoid making a public display of the arrangement.'

'Undoubtedly so, but that was a private agreement, deniable at a certain level and capable of being explained by your marriage to Lady Chiara Angelini. This is a quite different matter where the arrangement is formalised by an exchange of letters between your Admiralty and my Ministry. A new level of discretion is required.'

Carlisle considered whether to tell the minister what he already knew. This was a strange diplomatic dance, and he was certain that Mackenzie would be better at it than he was. But then the envoy had not been invited to this meeting and perhaps he would have declined to be involved if he were invited. To hell with it!

'I agree that there is a need for discretion, Minister, but perhaps not as much as you imagine. I know, you see, that a similar request is being made of the French officers that I saw at the palace yesterday, the gentlemen who are supervising the build of four ships-of-the-line at Genoa. As you are making an equivalent arrangement with both belligerent parties, then you can hardly be accused of favouring one over the other. Unless, of course, the arrangement with the French navy is of a different quality or scale to the arrangement with His Britannic Majesty's navy.'

Lombardi winced but recovered quickly.

'Well, be that as it may, I am not at liberty to disclose any agreement that I may have made with France, as I am sure you wouldn't want our agreement made public. But I see that your sources of information are better than I had imagined.'

The minister looked thoughtful for a moment, perhaps guessing who had told Carlisle about the French agreement.

'However, I take your point. Please be sensitive, nevertheless, to the need for discretion in this matter. I'm sure that you can see the benefits to King George in this arrangement, assuming that Mister Pitt still sees an advantage in Sardinian neutrality.'

Carlisle inclined his head slightly in acknowledgement that stopped short of actual agreement to the minister's statement. That was a step too far for a post-captain.

'I see that you have more diplomatic skill than most of your fellow land or sea officers, Captain Carlisle; I congratulate you. Now, perhaps you could assist me in the matter of the wording of this letter. I believe it is best addressed in the first place to Admiral Saunders so that he can make an immediate – albeit provisional – decision, but the letter to Mister Pitt will be sent overland, do you agree…?'

'That would be the best approach, yes, sir.'

'Very well. Now, I know you sea officers, always rushing to catch your tide, or the wind or the enemy and I know you could announce your imminent departure at any moment, isn't that so? I'll undertake to have the letter and Mister Angelini's commission ready at this office at this same hour tomorrow.'

\*\*\*

Carlisle would say this in favour of Mackenzie, he didn't let his personal disagreements get in the way of his bounden duty as a minister plenipotentiary of King George. He had summoned Carlisle to his home for what he described as an urgent discussion.

'It seems, Captain, that your fame has followed hard on your heels.'

Carlisle looked puzzled. He was wary of the envoy and suspicious of any form of compliment that came from that quarter.

'The French legation has heard about your brush with the seventy-four off Mahon.'

Mackenzie studied Carlisle's face, perhaps to gauge what effect the news had on him. Carlisle shrugged. There was nothing remotely to be ashamed of, the engagement had taken place within all the norms of warfare at sea.

'The French captain – the one who acts as a *de facto* commodore at Genoa – has concluded that neither you nor your ship are to be trifled with. Now, this came to me from the same sources. They had previously thought that your presence on the coast was an irrelevance. They are partly gunned and manned and felt that if you should be rash enough…'

The envoy paused for an eloquent second or two after invoking the word rash.

'…if you should be rash enough to attempt to engage them, they would merely brush you aside and continue on their way. The way you treated the seventy-four – *Le Bourbon*, I recall – has given them pause. Now they are planning to attempt to detain you in Villa Franca while they sail.'

Carlisle hid his interest behind a mask of indifference.

'Do you know under what article they plan to cause our detention, sir?'

'They have a small schooner at Genoa, a tender to one of the ships and the personal property of its captain. They intend to sail it into Villa-Franca and invoke the twenty-four-hour rule while the two sixty-fours slip past towards Toulon. Really, Captain Carlisle, you must keep your ear to the ground while you are in Turin. It's a hotbed of gossip, some which turns out to be real and valuable intelligence.

You would look singularly foolish if you were forced to watch your quarry slip past for want of a little easily-obtained knowledge.'

Carlisle was almost relieved to hear the envoy reverting to his familiar acerbic manner, and he had no doubt that Enrico or the viscountess would have the same information when he returned to their lodgings. But give the envoy his due, he was swallowing his personal animosity to further his country's cause.

*\*\*\**

'Mister Angelini! Congratulations on your commission which I understand is now merely a matter of a few words and a wax seal. However, we must be away, back to Villa-Franca. I will explain it all later, but *Dartmouth* must sail without delay. Pray make the arrangements to leave after we have called on the minister of marine tomorrow morning to collect an important letter and of course your aforesaid commission.'

My God, but news travels fast in these parts, Carlisle thought as he scribbled a list of everything that he must do before departing from Turin. He wondered what secrets of his own were known throughout the town. Probably the exact force of Saunders' squadron was common knowledge, and his orders to contain the French fleet, annoy their commerce and keep Spain and Sardinia out of the war. In that case he would need to be careful, because his every move would be known. Then he realised with a gulp that returning to Turin may not be so simple. What better way to neutralise *Dartmouth* than to waylay its captain on the long and lonely road to Villa-Franca!

'One more thing, Mister Angelini. Do you know any reliable and doughty fellows who may accompany us on the journey?'

Enrico smiled at that.

'I was going to obtain your approval, sir, but a friend of mine, a captain in the Piedmont Cavalry, has volunteered to bring a half-troop of horse as an escort. No doubt word of this will already have reached the French, so I don't anticipate any problems now, but still, it would be better to be safe.'

Carlisle laughed out loud.

'You'll go far, Lieutenant Angelini, far indeed!'

\*\*\*

Carlisle was alone at last. He had a pleasant room, light and airy if somewhat cramped, and it offered a view of the piazza that must have put an enormous premium on the value of the cousin's house. He reflected on how different these old European towns were from the newer American cities. In his own home of Williamsburg, he enjoyed endless space and his house stood alone without any adjoining dwellings. Here people lived on top of each other, often quite literally, and even the grandest dukes had barely enough space to swing a cat. But then this city had a splendour that the likes of Williamsburg would never attain. It was partly the people – who dressed in the most colourful fashion – but it was also the antiquity of the city and the system of hereditary privilege. To what extent was this vibrancy dependent upon the existence of dukes and duchesses, princes and princesses? Could any of it exist without the huge disparity of wealth that he saw at every hand? He'd always been suspicious of inherited rank and now, with his recent exposure to the likes of Mackenzie, his attitude was hardening. He sighed, longing for a time when he could live at peace in his Virginia home, even with the inevitable detrimental effect on his career in the British navy.

\*\*\*

# CHAPTER EIGHT

## The Carpenter's Mistake

*Thursday, Fifth of June 1760.*
*Dartmouth, at Anchor. Villa-Franca.*

The carriage rattled and shook as it sped along the road back to the sea. Carlisle fumed at each delay to change horses or snatch a hurried meal at a wayside inn; he begrudged each lost minute and hoarded the passing miles like a miser counting his coins. The had stopped for a few hours on the first night, but kept going through the second, merely slowing the pace to avoid accidents, and all the time their escort of Royal Piedmont Cavalry kept station ahead and behind. They crossed the pass in the Mercantour range with the first light of the new day at their backs. Now they were free of the Alps and the carriage plunged downhill, following the infant river Roya until it reached the coastal plain where carriage and riders veered off west towards Nice and Villa-Franca.

An urgent need drove them. Carlisle was determined to get *Dartmouth* to sea before this damned French schooner could arrive. He could guess at their ploy. They would anchor in a place where they could watch the British ship, and at the first sign of *Dartmouth* manning the capstan bars, they'd slip their cable and sail ahead of the ponderous two-decker, thus establishing the start of a twenty-four-hour prohibition on sailing from the port. It was a sensible rule, designed to allow a merchant ship of a belligerent nation the freedom to sail from a neutral port without the fear of a predatory privateer or man-o'-war following close on their heels. However, although the rule had been designed to protect merchantmen, it applied equally to King's ships. In this case it would allow the French sixty-fours a whole day and night to sail past Villa-Franca on their way to Toulon without risking a confrontation with this dangerous British fourth rate. He couldn't allow that to happen.

They stopped at a poor inn alongside the river where a rise in the ground offered a vista of the road that curved downwards until it was lost in the early morning mists. The brusque landlord, irritated at being woken so early, brought out bread and ham and cheese and the rough wine of the country folk. There were no fresh horses here and the driver pleaded urgently for a half-hour rest. Carlisle stared eagerly towards the south, imagining that he could detect the faint silver glow of the sun reflecting from the sea.

'How far to Villa-Franca from here, Enrico?' he asked, never taking his eyes from the road to the south.

'Perhaps ten leagues, sir, and the road is good now that we're free of the mountains.'

Carlisle didn't respond for a moment; he was apparently lost in thought.

'The French could have made Genoa by yesterday evening and it's only thirty-five leagues from there to Villa-Franca. A weatherly vessel – and the talk was of a schooner – could be off the harbour later today, even with this westerly wind. Much as he loves us, I have no doubt, no doubt at all, that General Paterson will enforce the twenty-four-hour rule. Whether he will allow the French to play the game twice… I'm not sure, but once certainly. I must get to sea before the schooner arrives. This coach is too slow, too slow by far, but I fear that I wouldn't be any faster on a horse, I've had little practice recently. Could you ride ahead and have the anchor hove short before I arrive?'

'Yes, sir. I could take one of the spare horses and two of the troopers.'

Enrico looked keenly to the south where the road and the river ran together until lost to sight.

'I could be three hours ahead of you, at least.'

'Then make it so and I'll urge this coach to make more speed. Tell Mister Gresham the situation, but in confidence, I don't want any of this to leak out ashore. Get the men aboard and be in all respects ready for sea by the time I arrive.'

Enrico hurried off to make the arrangements. He would ride on with the sergeant and one trooper while his friend and the rest of the half-troop would stay with the carriage. He was an excellent horseman, as was to be expected as an erstwhile ensign of cavalry, and the three men cantered off down the road, raising a thin plume of dust to mark their passing. Carlisle watched them go until they were out of sight. Something was nagging at his mind and he couldn't quite isolate it. He shook his head briskly to dispel the gloom and turned to urge on the harnessing of the horses. It was still a long way to Villa-Franca, a long way with many fords and rough country bridges as the road crossed the smaller tributaries of the river. There was no time to lose if he was to reach his ship with daylight left to take her to sea.

\*\*\*

The sun grew hotter as it arched towards its zenith over the faraway Alps and its heat faded only slowly as, in the late afternoon, it sank towards the nor'western horizon. The coachman, stimulated by the promise of a fat purse of silver, had at last become convinced of the need for haste and had flogged his horses cruelly for the last few miles. They had been following the main road to Nice, but now they branched off on a smaller road that led directly to Villa Franca. Only a few miles to go now and it was clear that they were going to make it, that *Dartmouth* would be able to sail on the first hint of a land breeze, if the schooner wasn't already there.

They crested a rise and suddenly the harbour of Villa-Franca was spread out before them. There was *Dartmouth* anchored in the centre with a few other vessels moored closer to the jetties or berthed alongside. Carlisle looked intently at them. They were the kind of vessels he would expect in a Western Mediterranean port. A few schooners, but they were all inshore of *Dartmouth*. If the French schooner was there, she would undoubtedly be anchored further to seaward. For it would be a race, and the first ship to leave the harbour would win, the second being imprisoned for the dreaded twenty-four hours. He scanned to seaward and away to the east but could see no sign of the schooner. He relaxed for the first time since he had heard the news of the French plans.

'Here comes Lieutenant Angelini, sir,' said the officer in charge of the escort, leaning perilously sideways from his trotting horse, 'and he's in haste, he's thrashing his horse up the hill.'

Carlisle could see the three horsemen now that they were pointed out, although he couldn't have said that it was Enrico and the troopers, not at that distance.

As they came closer, Carlisle saw that something was wrong. His lieutenant was in far too much haste for the circumstances. He pulled his horse's head around savagely as it came abreast the carriage.

'It's the rudder, sir,' gasped Enrico fighting for breath.

The rudder! In an instant Carlisle remembered what had been niggling in his mind. That scraping noise that they had heard with the wind abaft the beam, and old Eli's report that something was sticking as he turned the wheel. Carlisle had ordered the carpenter to look into it as soon as they were at anchor, although he had thought it was probably nothing more than some flotsam caught between the rudder and the stern post.

'Mister Gresham trimmed the ship by the head and the carpenter went down to look below the waterline,' Enrico continued when he had gulped in a few lungs of air. 'The lower two pintle straps were cracked through and they had to unship the rudder to come at them. They couldn't be repaired onboard, the armourer says his portable forge is too small, so they were sent ashore for repair. They've just come back and the carpenter's fitting them now.'

'How long before the ship's ready for sea?' Carlisle asked with a heavy heart. He knew it was days not hours. The rudder of a fourth rate was a ponderous great machine of thirty-five feet or so in height, crafted of many pieces of

timber and held together with heavy iron straps. Its head
projected into the wardroom, while its greater bulk by far
was suspended by a vertical row of pintles – seven if he
remembered correctly – that hinged on their partner
gudgeons which in turn were fastened to the stern post. It
must have been a heroic feat to unship it, and it would be
even more difficult to replace it.

'Chips says four days, but Mister Gresham swears it can
be done in two. He's trimming the bows down now and
rigging the sheers. Chips and the armourer were fitting the
new pintles as I left.'

Conversation was difficult between a trotting horseman
and a rattling carriage, but this was not the time to be
stopping for conversation. Carlisle had one more question.

'Does Mister Gresham understand the urgency, our
extreme need to get to sea as soon as possible?'

'He does, sir. I told him in private and he cut me off in
mid-sentence as he ran to get the people working.'

Think, think. The schooner was bound to arrive at
Villa-Franca before *Dartmouth* could sail, and that would
inevitably mean that the sixty-fours would escape. Perhaps
the schooner would suffer a mishap along the way,
perhaps it too had a rudder problem. But could it be
prevented from arriving? The germ of an idea was forming
in Carlisle's mind.

'Will your horse take you back at a gallop, Mister
Angelini?'

Enrico leaned forward and studied his horse's mouth.
It was flecked with foam and the beast's breathing was
coming in short gasps.

'You can take my horse, sir.'

That was the lieutenant of the escort, a contemporary
of Enrico's. They had served in the same cadet squadron,
but now, as a naval lieutenant, Enrico outranked him.

'Mister Angelini,' Carlisle, said, when the cavalrymen
couldn't hear him, 'tell the first lieutenant – listen carefully
now – he's to prepare the longboat and the yawl for sea

with full rig. The longboat is to have the boat gun and the yawl two swivels. Provisions for three days and pistols and cutlasses for the crews. I'll decide who is to command when I get to the ship. Have the cutter ready at the jetty to take me on board. Now go! Ride like the wind. Those boats must be ready to clear the harbour before dark.'

*** 

Dusk was gathering as Carlisle was rowed out to *Dartmouth*. He was met by a scene of intense but ordered activity and by a worried looking first lieutenant.

'I hope I did right, sir,' said Gresham when he came over the side. 'We couldn't have gone to sea with the rudder in that state and I didn't expect you to return for at least a week. I thought it would be all done and dusted.'

'We'll talk about it later, Mister Gresham,' he said severely, reserving his judgement until he knew the facts. 'Now, what's the situation?'

'Well, sir,' Gresham replied looking like a condemned man, 'the boats are alongside and the last of the provisions and water are being passed down. I've told Mister Towser to have a party of his marines ready in case you wanted to send them with the boats. It just needs your word as to who will command, and they can be away.'

'Very well, and the rudder?'

'The first pintle has been fitted and just needs to be sweated into place. The second one can be done by lamplight, but I wouldn't like to sway that great rudder over the side until daylight tomorrow. We've raised the stern by three feet, and we can get another two feet overnight, then if we work all hands, we can drop it onto the gudgeons before dark tomorrow. The critical thing is the movement of the ship; every time a bit of swell comes around the headland, we have to put a stopper on everything until she's settled again.'

Carlisle walked quickly over to where the work was going on in the waist. The carpenter and his mates had rigged a purchase to haul the iron bracket onto the oak of the rudder. It was a tight fit and required repeated attempts, interspersed by fine cuts of a sharp adze to create a satisfactory join.

'The workshop ashore did a decent job, sir,' explained the carpenter, 'but we couldn't get the whole rudder to them. They're up a narrow street and it just wouldn't fit, no way we looked at it, so we are having to do the fine work here.'

The sound of the adze was replaced by the harsh rasping of a coarse-cut file as the armourer removed excess metal from the bracket.

'Rightly I should have a day for each of the pintles, sir, but I understand this is a rush job, as you could say.'

'It is Chips. We must be at sea tomorrow night without fail. What do you think?'

The carpenter scratched his head with the butt end of his adze, while his mates ducked under the sweep of the razor-sharp blade.

'That's pushing it, sir. If there are no snags it may be possible, but if that second pintle strap fits worse than the first or if there's a swell tomorrow, we'll be in trouble. First Lieutenant gave me two days,' he added reproachfully.

'Two days for any ordinary carpenter Chips,' Carlisle replied, trying to sound cheerful, 'but I know you can do it in one. Now be certain to ask for anything you need, any men or materials; just ask and they're yours. I'll have the whole crew shifting stores all night if you need the stern raised any further.'

'Aye-aye sir,' the carpenter replied doubtfully.

'And keep me informed of progress,' said Carlisle as he walked carefully back to the quarterdeck through the clutter of timber, ropes and tools that were strewn around the waist.

\*\*\*

'Now, Mister Gresham. The first thing that I have to say is that you can rest easy. Without your decision to go ahead with the repairs, we would be a week away from sailing right now, not a day. However, we'll put all that aside for now and let's concentrate on getting those boats away. You will command, if you please, and Mister Wishart will take the yawl.'

'Thank you, sir.'

Gresham smiled for the first time since Carlisle had returned. He knew that he could easily be found culpable by an unscrupulous captain. It was even potentially a court-martial affair, and no court of post-captains would hesitate to find him guilty on any of several charges. After all, he'd rendered the ship unfit for sea, and that was a hard charge to talk away. Being placed in command of this expedition was an obvious and very public sign of Carlisle's approval.

'Thank you, sir, but what are the boats going to do?' he asked looking puzzled.

Carlisle was taken aback for a moment. He'd been thinking of nothing else since he heard of his ship's inability to sail, and he had forgotten that his first lieutenant hadn't been with him to follow his reasoning.

'You know about the twenty-four-hour rule and the French schooner?'

'Yes, sir, Angelini – I mean Lieutenant Angelini – told me. If we can't get to sea before the schooner drops anchor, then we may be detained for days.'

'That's true, Mister Gresham. But the schooner must get here for the French plan to work. Your task is to stop it from ever reaching Villa-Franca.'

Gresham looked as though a great light had dawned and he beamed a delighted smile. He'd imagined all kinds of missions for the boats, most of which involved complicated diplomatic entanglements. This straightforward job, to intercept and engage a schooner at sea, was much more to his liking.

'Now, our best information is that the schooner isn't armed for fighting, she's just a dispatch vessel for the French commodore in Genoa. She'll be fast and weatherly, but she'll have a small crew and probably no more than a pair of guns of no great weight. Four-pounders perhaps, like the longboat's gun. She won't be expecting her passage to be opposed, so if you spend the night at sea making your rig appear as close to some of the local fishing vessels as possible, she won't suspect you until it's too late. By all means take Lieutenant Towser and half a dozen marines, but no man is to wear a uniform, and that includes you. The wind is westerly, so she'll likely take short tacks along the coast. Lie off to seaward and then if she doesn't fancy fighting, she'll be forced ashore, and that will be as good as taking her. If you haven't seen her by the end of Saturday – that's two days from now – then meet me off Villa-Franca unless I can get away in time to run down to you.'

They spent a few more minutes in talking through the possibilities, the likely winds off the Ligurian coast and what the French would do when they realised that they were being hunted.

'You'd better go now, Mister Gresham. I want you underway within thirty minutes; that should give you enough time to clear Point Mala before twilight ends. Don't forget to take your commission, just in case, I don't want you being taken up for piracy. I shudder to think what General Paterson will say when he hears, but I'll work on that later.'

***

The little flotilla pushed off from *Dartmouth's* side and caught the infant land breeze that wafted them seawards. In five minutes they were indistinct shapes heading towards the easterly arm that enclosed the harbour, and in ten minutes they were gone. Carlisle looked over to the fort. There was no unusual activity, no hue and cry and no strange signalling. It seemed likely that their departure hadn't even been noticed. Most importantly, there was no official boat pushing off to deliver a protest. In fact, it was difficult to imagine what protest could be made. It was just possible for the general or the fort's commander to make a case that it was customary for a visiting man-o'-war to notify movements of its boats, but there was no actual rule to that effect.

Carlisle turned away with a sigh of satisfaction and surveyed the scene. The deck had tilted noticeably since he came on board and he could hear the shouted orders and the grunts of men shifting heavy loads below decks. From the shore the ship must look odd indeed, with the bows considerably lower in the water than the stern and the masts angled forward of the vertical. However, none of that should cause concern to the people in the fort; they had already been informed of *Dartmouth's* rudder problem and would expect this kind of activity. It occurred to Carlisle that word had probably leaked to the French in Genoa. That would give the sixty-fours more confidence in putting to sea. They would be reassured that *Dartmouth* was in no position to frustrate their plan to exploit the twenty-four-hour rule.

'Pass the word for the master and the bosun,' Carlisle said to Wishart, who had the deck. 'You may warn them that I want to discuss how we can expedite fitting the rudder tomorrow.'

It had been a long day, but for the crew of His Britannic Majesty's Ship *Dartmouth* it was by no means over, and most of them had a solid night of labour ahead of them.

***

# CHAPTER NINE

## Gresham's Day

*Friday, Sixth of June 1760.*
*Dartmouth's Longboat, at Sea. Off Cape Mele.*

The wind had continued westerly through the night and the longboat and yawl made a fast run to the east, keeping five miles offshore. At dawn they sighted Cape Mele, starkly silhouetted against the rising sun, and Gresham started to relax. For any vessel tacking down the coast from Genoa, Cape Mele would be their first landfall, the point where they passed out of the Gulf of Genoa and into the broader Ligurian Sea. The schooner would doubtlessly pass close to the cape to avoid the stronger, contrary winds further out to sea, and it was there that the trap would be sprung.

Gresham looked keenly around the horizon. He didn't expect to see much; the fishing boats only came out in the daytime and there had hardly been time for them to leave their tiny harbours. He had this stretch of sea to himself for now.

'Let's get that rig up then, Souter.'

'Aye-aye sir,' the coxswain replied grinning.

They'd spent the night working on the assortment of spars and bits of old sail that the bosun had thrown down into the boat, making them into something that could be taken for a local fisherman's rig. They had plenty of scope for their artistic talents as the boats in this region came in all shapes and sizes with a fantastic assortment of masts and sails that not even the most gnarled old seaman could name.

Up went a long oar at the stern, canted sharply aft, with a patched old boat's jib laced by its luff and tacked down to a makeshift bumkin rigged over the transom. The mainmast was angled forward by shortening the forestay and lengthening the backstays with cunningly wrought sheepshanks so that it could be quickly returned to its normal angle.

'There goes Mister Wishart's rig,' said Towser, pointing at the yawl where a similarly imaginative mizzen was being hoisted.

Gresham looked at the yawl critically. With its new rig it certainly didn't look like a man-o'-war's boat, and a willing mind could probably imagine that it was a fishing boat with just its mizzen hoisted to keep the bows into the wind and steady the boat while they worked their nets. There had been little time to make a plan, but by keeping in close company overnight he had been able to shout across to Wishart to tell him the outlines. He'd quickly decided that the boats needed to keep together. If the schooner had any guns at all, then they'd need all their force to overpower it, and in any case, he was confident of the course that the French captain would choose. In this crystal-clear weather he'd see the schooner in plenty of time to make his dispositions and the schooner would just see two fishing boats presumably with a net strung between them seeking out the shoals of sardines.

\*\*\*

The sun rose and one-by-one the little fishing boats started to nose out from the shore. Gresham realised that he had no need to be concerned at the authenticity of the boats' masts and sails, they blended in perfectly with the haphazard arrangements that he now saw. The two boats bobbed up and down in the light swell, their makeshift mizzens keeping their bows facing the westerly wind. They were within hailing range of each other, but there was nothing to be said now, they just had to wait. A couple of men had fishing lines over the side. There were always a few dedicated fishermen and there was no reason to deny them this simple pleasure. The canvas bucket started to fill with fat mackerel that had been duped by the scraps of coloured cloth attached to the fishhooks and the motion of the fishermen's arms as they rhythmically jigged the line was mesmeric.

'Do you see anything to the east?' Gresham called up to the lookout who was perched uncomfortably at the masthead.

They were taking thirty-minute turns at the masthead, any longer and the bones and muscles started to protest at the awkward attitudes they were forced to adopt.

'Just fishing boats, sir,' the lookout replied.

Gresham stood in the stern sheets and looked for himself. There were half a dozen boats well inshore of them and they were all sporting small mizzens, just like the longboat and whaler. It would be a strangely suspicious Frenchman who doubted the authenticity of these two that were further offshore than their fellows.

This was the kind of task that Gresham enjoyed. He had no illusions about his career; he wasn't likely to be promoted to commander, and certainly not to post-captain unless something very strange happened, and he had long ago come to terms with it. In fact, if he were prone to self-analysis, he would have quickly discovered that he didn't really want to be promoted. His was not a nature that craved responsibility beyond his natural capacity, and the rank of lieutenant, he had become convinced, was his limit. Let the likes of Captain Carlisle worry about diplomacy and the demands of admirals. A clearly defined set of orders was all that he wanted; that and the chance to make enough in prize money to be able to retire on half-pay. This present employment was ideal; either the schooner would come, or it wouldn't, and if the Frenchmen didn't arrive then nothing that he could do could make them appear. As for the probably bloody business of taking, sinking or burning, he was no coward and fighting was a natural part of his profession. He could be relied upon to press home an attack against any odds. He gazed again at the lazy sea, made himself comfortable and leaned back against the transom. The sun was hot by now, and slowly his eyes started to droop as his mind wandered to the cottage in the Sussex downs that he would buy when the war was over, the cottage and the neat wife…

'Sail ho! Sail on the starboard quarter.'

Gresham jerked upright; his drowsiness instantly forgotten. The lookout was only a few yards away from him, but he was perched at the highest point possible and commanded a view of the sea that stretched a mile or so further than anyone below him.

'I can just make out a scrap of sail, sir,' the lookout added. 'It's not a square topsail, I'm sure of that, but it could be the peak of a schooner's mainsail.'

The lookout knew their quarry, which encouraged him to make an intelligent assessment of what he was seeing. On the other hand, it carried the risk that he would see what he expected to see.

Gresham stood upright on the top edge of the transom with the crook of his elbow wrapped around the false mizzen to steady himself. He levelled his telescope towards the northeast. The cliffs of Cape Mele formed the left of the arc that he surveyed, and he started there and scanned slowly to the right. At the first pass he saw nothing except the sharply defined line of the horizon and the familiar fishing boats under the cape. At the second pass, he caught just a flash of white that broke the perfect line between sea and sky. He took out his handkerchief and carefully wiped the lenses of his telescope, then he looked again. It was astonishing how much more he could see after those few seconds. Yes, it could be the high peak of a gaff mainsail. Then again, it could be another lunatic fisherman with a rig designed to satisfy whatever strange whim came into his head. Every second brought more information. If it was a schooner, then it was on the starboard tack, hard on the wind to make an offing from the cape. There! A hair to the right was another flash of white. That was surely a schooner's foresail.

'I reckon we're in as good a position as we could be, sir,' Souter offered. 'He'll need to make an offing and when he tacks, he'll near-enough come into our arms.'

Gresham didn't reply. He had thought the same himself and he'd have had a sharp word if any other of the men had offered their thoughts on the subject. But Souter was the captain's coxswain, and a man of substance in the ship. It really hadn't been difficult to put the two boats in the way of the schooner, if that was what she was. Given the wind direction, the position of Cape Mele and the certainty that the schooner would be trying to make a fast passage, it had been easy to be in the right position. Now they just had to persuade the Frenchman that nothing was amiss.

The sail was coming clearer now, and Gresham was certain that he was looking at a small tops'l schooner beating hard to the sou'west under her for-and-aft sails. Of course, her square tops'ls would be a hindrance with the wind forrard of the beam.

'Get you marines under cover now, Mister Towser,' he said. 'You know what to do Souter.'

It had all been planned. The marines and half of the seamen would hide under the mainsail which was draped across the thwarts and the boat gun. From a distance it would look like a fishing boat with a heap of nets ready to be cast. The sardine boats needed a substantial crew to haul the nets when they were full, and half a dozen men wouldn't look unusual. Gresham looked across at the yawl and could see that Wishart was making similar arrangements; he only had seamen to concern himself with but there were still far more men in that boat than any fisherman would sail with.

'I'll bring the lookout down, sir,' Souter offered.

Gresham was about to agree, then he remembered how he had seen the larger sardine boats operate. They searched for the shoals of fish by sight, and only wetted their nets when they knew there were fish to be caught. They could often be seen with a man perched precariously atop the mast, scanning the water ahead for the tell-tale silvery sheen.

'Leave him up there, Souter.'

The schooner was coming closer now, she was no more than four miles distant and closing rapidly.

'She's a fine sailer, sir,' Souter commented, 'look how close she lies to the wind. She's in a tearing hurry, that's for sure.'

Gresham could see for himself how the lee gunwales kissed the sea, even under this moderate breeze. Souter was right, that schooner was wasting no time. Probably the French captain had heard about Captain Carlisle's hasty departure from Turin and was concerned that he would get his ship to sea before the schooner could arrive at Villa-Franca and enforce the twenty-four-hour rule. She was lying close indeed, but she could lie no closer and Gresham could see that the Frenchman was committed to his present course. There was no room to tack – Cape Mele loomed large on the schooner's weather bow – and to let her bow fall off to leeward would only waste time. No doubt the captain was preparing some choice words for the damned fisherman in his way, for he would pass close indeed.

'What do you think Souter,' Gresham asked, 'sails or oars?'

Souter eyed the fast-closing schooner. They had talked it through overnight and had determined that they would hoist the mainsail when the schooner was half a mile to leeward and run down upon her before her crew could react. It would mean a hard impact with the schooner as it tried to evade the two boats and the schooner's crew would have time to take up weapons, but it was more certain of success than rowing across half a mile of sea. The French crew would have to be asleep to allow a longboat under oars to approach them over that distance. However, the situation had changed and now it appeared that the schooner was coming right into their arms. On its present course it would pass no more than a hundred yards inshore of them.

Gresham could see that the same thoughts were going through Souter's mind as he judged the distances.

'Oars, I think, sir.'

Gresham nodded in agreement.

'Let the men know.'

There was another advantage to rowing; it meant that the boat gun could be brought into action more quickly.

'Send the quarter gunner aft, Souter.'

A young man struggled free of the mainsail and crawled across the thwarts, keeping below the level of the gunwale.

'I hope to get a shot into her at close range, Jones. Are you ready?'

'Aye sir; loaded with grape and two matches burning in the tub. I can have her run out in two shakes, when you give the word.'

Grape shot would be much more effective from a boat's gun. The only way of aiming it was to point the whole boat at the target, and in the rush to get the oars shipped it would be much better to have a spread of nine six-ounce balls than one four-pounder.

'Very well, I'll leave it to you to fire when your gun bears. You'll only get one shot unless we have to chase.'

Gresham had been studying the distances as he was giving his orders. There was a point in the sea where the schooner would be close enough for the trap to be sprung without giving her the chance to react. She was making a good speed on the wind, at least six knots, and that meant she would cover a cable – two hundred yards – in a minute. Four cables, Gresham decided. With the longboat moving towards the schooner, it would give his crew a little over two minutes. It was barely enough time for the oarsmen to ship their oars, for the quarter gunner to fire his piece and for the marines to scramble out from under the sail and level their muskets. Barely time, but any longer would allow the schooner to avoid the meeting. Once she'd paid off the wind there would be no stopping her, and she'd pass around the longboat and yawl and be back on her way to Villa-Franca.

'Schooner's pinching the wind, sir,' said Souter. 'She doesn't want to get between us and the yawl, she must be worried in case we have nets between us.'

Gresham nodded and smiled. Better and better, the

schooner could have paid off the wind to pass them, but she was clearly unwilling to waste any time. That suggested that the French captain was convinced of the innocence of the two boats that were now fine on his larboard bow. He would pass within twenty yards of them on this course. It also meant that she was slowing just a little, but every knot helped Gresham's plan. A mile now.

'Stand by Mister Towser.'

The marine lieutenant grinned from under the mainsail. It must be unbearably hot under there.

'Ready when you are, sir.'

\*\*\*

Closer and closer. The schooner was cleaving the blue water, throwing a white wave either side of her bow. Gresham waved to acknowledge that she'd had to alter course to avoid them, a normal friendly gesture.

'Now!' shouted Gresham. 'Man the oars. Marines stand to. Quarter gunner!'

The boat erupted into a frenzy of activity. Gresham spared a glance at the yawl and saw that Wishart was only a second or two behind them.

'Point your bow right at him, Souter.'

The oars were shipped in a flash and the oarsmen stretched to their tasks without waiting to shift the mainsail aside. God, she was coming on quickly. Now Gresham could see activity on the schooner's quarterdeck. Heads were craning forrard to see past the bows. He could hear the shouted orders and then, after what seemed like an age, the schooner's bows started to turn to windward. She was going to tack through the wind and run to the east rather than pay off to the south. She was too late, and with her bows not yet through the wind the two predatory boats were only fifty yards away.

Crash!

The whole boat jerked backwards as the four-pounder fired, throwing the bow oar off his stroke.

'Pull!' shouted Souter, setting the time with his body

arching forwards and backwards.

Gresham saw the splinters flying from the schooner's gunwales and at least one man fell from sight. That was a good shot, and now the quarter gunner and his mate were taking up their pistols ready for the assault.

'Aim for the main chains, Souter.'

The longboat's bows grazed the schooner's hull then smashed hard into the chains. The quarter gunner was ready with a grapnel and hooked it into the lanyards of the shrouds. Souter hurled a second grapnel from the stern which caught in the railing around the fo'c'sle. The oarsmen flung their oars into the boat and rushed to the side, eager to board, while the marines were firing at anyone who showed their face over the gunwale.

'Wait!' shouted Gresham.

So far there had been no sign of an organised resistance. The schooner was still turning to starboard, dragging the longboat around in its path. It looked like nobody was in control as the bows paid off on the larboard tack. Gresham realised she'd put her stern through the wind soon and then those two massive booms would sweep across the deck, adding to the confusion.

'Wait for my word!'

It was a curious feeling, being dragged backwards by the schooner as it continued its uncontrolled turn. Then there was a crash and a jolt as the stern passed through the wind. Gresham tensed himself for the masts going by the boards, but they stood the shock. Where was Wishart and his yawl?

'Mister Towser. Marines leading, up you go.'

Towser waved his sword and grasping the gunwale heaved himself up. His men followed, hurling themselves up the few feet of the schooner's side.

'Follow me!' shouted Gresham, and he launched himself onto the schooner's fo'c'sle, followed by the seamen, screaming like fiends.

Gresham knew that the Frenchmen wouldn't give up easily. The marines were gathered in a semi-circle on the waist their bayonets pointing outwards as they were assaulted from the quarterdeck and the other side of the waist. The fo'c'sle was empty but then Gresham saw Wishart's men hauling themselves over the starboard side. Somehow the yawl must have passed under the schooner's bow.

'Follow me, *Dartmouth*s,' Gresham shouted, and he vaulted the fo'c'sle rail into the teeming waist. He heard Sergeant Wilson's voice above the din of clashing steel and pistol shots, intoning the words of command as though he was on a parade ground.

'Marines face aft, present your bayonets, advance!'

He wasn't letting his men get out of control. He knew that a wild charge would risk fragmenting his small force, and a steady, inexorable advance towards the quarterdeck would be far more effective.

'Mister Wishart, get the headsails and the foresail down.'

Wishart looked confused for a moment, then realised what Gresham wanted. With the sails in the fore part of the ship down the schooner's head would seek the wind and lie more quietly.

Gresham angled across the waist to the starboard side. Now there was a solid body of men facing the French, spread across the width of the schooner. The enemy still held the quarterdeck, but it wasn't a raised deck, it was just the furthest aft part of the flush maindeck. The French were crowded together, unable to swing their weapons, and the schooner was careering madly to leeward, threatening another involuntary turn through the wind at any moment.

Gresham cut and slashed at the mass of humanity in front of him. There seemed to be more than he could ever have expected, an endless horde of people. And he could see why Wilson was commanding the marines, and not Towser. Now that they had moved further aft, he could see the marine lieutenant lying slumped against one of the schooner's guns, in a widening pool of his own blood. He took a step back. This would never do; he had to think. He was alongside the mainmast now with a small ship's boat behind his right shoulder. He could no longer feel the wind over the deck, so they must be running. That gave him an idea. He grabbed a seaman beside him who was hacking away with a boarding axe.

'The mainsail halyards! Cut the throat halyard first, then the peak,' he shouted and pushed the seaman in the right direction. He looked up at the tall mast. Yes, the halyard to larboard of the mast was the one he wanted. He pointed to it and the seaman swung his axe; once, twice and there was a jerk as the throat of the heavy gaff dropped and was arrested by the tension on the peak halyard.

'Now the peak!' he shouted again, but the seaman already knew what he wanted. Two mighty strokes of the axe severed the halyard and the gaff, retarded by the halyard's fourfold purchase, started to fall. Slowly at first, then it gathered pace and in less than a second it was hurtling towards the deck. The Frenchmen saw the danger but couldn't move and the massive spar crashed onto the quarterdeck narrowly missing the tiller but crushing half a dozen men who couldn't move for the crowd.

That was the end of the resistance. Everywhere the Frenchmen were throwing down their weapons and staring angrily at their captors.

Gresham pushed through the crowd.

'You surrender?' he asked the man who looked most likely to be the captain. Neither man spoke the other's language, but Gresham's meaning was obvious.

'*Oui, je me rends.*'

***

# CHAPTER TEN

## Belligerent Obligations

*Saturday, Seventh of June 1760.*
*Dartmouth, at Anchor. Villa-Franca.*

Carlisle was trying not to show his anxiety as he paced the poop deck, glancing quickly seaward each time he turned. He was in the way, he knew, and the bosun and carpenter were inhibited by his presence. Neither man was particularly profane, but fitting a fourth rate's rudder, even in a sheltered bay, was an occasion for a certain amount of verbal licence. They kept looking nervously over their shoulders, hoping that their captain wouldn't impose the sixpence fine for each instance of swearing, cursing or blasphemy – as the printed regulations required – and which he had been known to do on other occasions.

It was growing dark now, and soon the sun would be hidden behind the looming bulk of Mount Boron. He'd heard nothing from Gresham, and he was starting to become concerned. It had been in vain that the master had pointed out the persistent westerly wind. If the longboat and yawl had been forced far to the east, then it would be a long beat back to Villa-Franca. And that assumed that they'd been successful. The schooner may never have sailed. They may have missed it – almost certainly would have if it had chosen to take a long tack out to seaward instead of hugging the coast – but then the schooner should have appeared by now. They may have met the schooner and been defeated; it was hardly unlikely if the schooner was well-equipped with guns. Carlisle was torturing himself, he knew, and Gresham wouldn't bring the boats back in after dark, that would be a gross infringement of Sardinia's neutrality. Another few minutes…

'Captain, sir, I see the longboat, just creeping around the point!'

That was Able Seaman Whittle, a Virginian like Carlisle, who had followed his captain from ship to ship. He'd climbed to the main t'gallant truck to have the best view to seaward. With *Dartmouth* so far down by the bows, he could have dropped a biscuit onto the fo'c'sle, and now his report floated down from a point far towards the bow and high above the deck.

Carlisle looked out to the long point that enclosed the eastern side of the bay of Villa-Franca. Sure enough, there was the longboat hard on the wind and shaving the rocky promontory. A quick glance told Carlisle little, but at least it hadn't been destroyed or taken. As he watched the longboat struck its sails and the crew bent to their oars, for the land breeze had just started and it would have been a hard beat up the harbour. But where was the yawl?

'I'll be in my cabin, Mister Beazley,' he said as he walked steadily down the poop ladder.

He was tempted to add an order for Gresham to report to him as soon as he came on board, but that would have been unnecessary, and he was conscious that, for him, garrulousness was a symptom of anxiety.

'Break out a bottle of Madeira, Walker.'

Now there was a man he could usefully emulate. His servant never uttered an unnecessary word and now he did nothing more than bow and retreat towards the scullery. Carlisle settled himself into a chair as best he could, but it was awkward with the deck tilted so far forward. It wasn't even easy to see out of the stern windows and in any case the carpenter and his crew were crawling all over the stern galleries, guiding the rudder back into place.

'Come in,' Carlisle shouted as he heard a knock on the door. This couldn't possibly be Gresham, not yet.

'Beg pardon, sir,' said the carpenter touching his forehead where his hat should rightly be.

'Beg pardon, sir, but I need to rig a strongback across your window there, to get a good purchase on the rudder. I hope it's not inconvenient...'

Carlisle almost laughed. There was the carpenter, hatless and with his shirt open, in a state that he wouldn't have dreamed of approaching the captain's cabin under normal circumstances. Behind him were three of his crew carrying one of the skids for the yawl, and behind them was a bosun's mate loaded down with cordage and blocks. It was a ridiculous situation and of course there was no question of them being sent packing, but the aura surrounding a captain of a ship-of-the-line demanded that nothing be taken for granted.

'Very well, Chips, let your men in. How is it progressing?'

This was in fact a welcome distraction from the agony of waiting for Gresham to come aboard. He could decently ask for an update on the work without appearing to be concerned. Carlisle drew the carpenter aside as his crew manoeuvred the great timber through the door. He could see that the marine sentry had propped his musket against the cabin bulkhead and was helping get the gear into the cabin, which was an eloquent testimony to the unusual circumstances.

'We're well underway now, sir. I just need to get a line around the rudder,' he gestured out of the window where the ropes that suspended the rudder could be seen swaying gently as the ship moved at its anchor, 'and then we can control it as it drops onto the gudgeons. If it all goes well, we'll be done by sunrise. I hope we'll be able to start shifting the stores in the morning watch.'

Carlisle nodded. The carpenter's work may be over by sunrise, but it would take at least half a day to set the ship on its natural trim. A huge amount of gear had been shifted forrard to get the stern out of the water, and it all had to be replaced before they could sail.

'Good work, Chips. You and your crew have done well,' he said loudly enough to be heard by the men setting up the strongback. 'I'll leave you to your work.'

Evidently his day cabin would be untenable until this work was complete, and Carlisle nodded to Walker as he held open the door to his sleeping cabin.

\*\*\*

'We've taken the schooner, sir,' said Gresham without preamble. Not for the first time, Carlisle was struck by his first lieutenant's direct manner; there were no words wasted on niceties. 'She's lying four leagues offshore to the east with Mister Wishart in command and the marines to see that there's no trouble. I left the yawl and its crew with him.'

Carlisle nodded. That was a sensible decision. Wishart would need all the men that Gresham could spare to sail a prize with its previous owners still aboard. He could see that Gresham had something more to report.

'I regret that we lost Lieutenant Towser, sir. He fell on the deck of the schooner, hit by a pistol ball, sir.'

Gresham was unnaturally formal in this report, with no trace of a human reaction to the death of a messmate. No normal human reaction, but then he'd learned that Gresham dealt with success and failure in a different way to most people. Nevertheless, the strain was showing on his first lieutenant's face.

'No others killed, sir, but I've brought back three wounded. The French lost at least four and they have a dozen under their doctor's care. I left the schooner in good order and she doesn't need to be brought in.'

'Well done, Mister Gresham. Now excuse me for a moment.'

He pushed the door open against the tilt of the deck.

'Pass the word for Lieutenant Halsey, and you can bring in that Madeira.' Carlisle shouted.

He heard Walker passing the word to the marine sentry and the call being relayed across the deck.

'Good. I had a difficult interview with General Paterson yesterday. He wanted to be reassured that my boats weren't sailing on a belligerent expedition within Sardinian waters. He would certainly make a protest if we brought a captured

110

French schooner into the bay.'

'There's no need for that, sir. Mister Wishart has enough people to keep the French in order for a day or two. I see that the rudder is almost in place.'

'Yes, we'll sail tomorrow afternoon. I find that I must spare the time to call on the general and try to make my peace. It will be hard explaining away a missing yawl. Ah, Mister Halsey.'

Probably Halsey had been helping sway the rudder into place, which would excuse his dishevelled state. He looked more like a common seaman than a commissioned officer in King George's navy. Normally Carlisle would have some hard words to say, but today Halsey's evident zeal for the task had to be credited.

'Mister Halsey. It's imperative that there is no communication with the shore before we sail. No boat is to leave the ship and no boat from the shore is to be allowed alongside without my express approval.'

Halsey nodded cautiously.

Did he need to spell it out? Carlisle almost shook his head in despair.

'This is a diplomatic matter, Mister Halsey. If the authorities ashore hear about Mister Gresham's exploits, we may be detained in harbour, and I don't need to tell you how undesirable that would be.'

Privately, Carlisle was sure that Halsey did need it to be explained, word by word, but there was no time for that now, and in any case, it would probably dilute the message.

'Tell Mister Beazley and the bosun that you'll be taking no further part in rigging the rudder. I expect you to be dressed and on the quarterdeck in five minutes.'

Carlisle resisted to temptation to roll his eyes as Halsey left the cabin. Something would have to be done about him, but not today.

'Now, Mister Gresham. There's no hope of keeping the longboat's crew quiet, but there is a sensitivity that must be observed. By any standards we've trespassed upon Sardinian neutrality and of course Mister Angelini is an officer in the Sardinian navy. He can't help but be aware of your success, but we are all – you, I and the other officers – to avoid speaking of it to him. We must be sympathetic to his position.'

'Aye sir. Can I suggest that he's put to supervising the re-stowing of the hold? That will keep him busy until it's time to sail.'

'A grand idea, Mister Gresham. Now, describe the action for me. What of the French captain? How did the men perform?'

\*\*\*

# CHAPTER ELEVEN

## An Unexpected Ally

*Sunday, Eighth of June 1760.*
*Dartmouth, at Anchor. Villa-Franca.*

Carlisle looked back at his ship as he was rowed across the bay towards the fort. The rudder had been shipped and tested and he could see that the stern was already lower in the water. Three more hours, he estimated, and then they would be able to sail. He was confident that the French sixty-fours hadn't passed Villa-Franca yet. This persistent westerly wind would make it difficult for them to work out of the Gulf of Genoa, and in any case, they would have wanted to leave enough time for the schooner to do its work of detaining *Dartmouth* at Villa-Franca. Tonight, perhaps, or tomorrow. That was when he expected to see them.

However, the French sixty-fours were a problem for tomorrow. Today he had to satisfy General Paterson that he hadn't infringed the rules for using a neutral port. Strangely, when they last met, the general appeared more concerned that Enrico's position – as a Sardinian officer on secondment to the British navy – hadn't been compromised. He could have pressed Carlisle hard on what the two boats were doing, but he'd accepted the rather stiff response that they were engaged in *His Britannic Majesty's business outside Sardinian waters*, and their purpose in sailing was no business of the governor of Nice. Was it a recollection of the part that the general had played in saving the French frigate *Vulcain* from Carlisle back in 'fifty-six? Perhaps that and some sense of loyalty that Paterson had for his British home, that overlapped his purchased loyalty to Sardinia. In any case, Carlisle was conscious that he'd been excused a more-rigid questioning and that he'd been given a way out of what could have become a diplomatic incident. Today, however, it was a different case. Even if word of the schooner's capture hadn't reached the general – and Carlisle was by no means confident of that – the fact that two boats left the harbour without notifying the commander of the fort and two days later only a single boat returned, demanded an explanation. And General Paterson wasn't without the means to force the issue. It would be a bold move for *Dartmouth* to sail in defiance of a written injunction from the provincial governor. Yes, a bold move and a dangerous one, for *Dartmouth* lay under the guns of a powerful fort and two separate batteries, and the Sardinian rowing galleys lay only a few cables away. Then again, Paterson could insist that Enrico be landed, his secondment nullified as a forceful way of expressing the King's displeasure at Carlisle's actions.

Now he regretted leaving Enrico behind in *Dartmouth*. He'd done it out of a desire to shield the young man from the conflict of loyalties that he saw rising before him. Yet there was no doubt that he would have been a strong ally, and God knew, Carlisle needed an ally.

***

There was no guard of honour drawn up on the jetty today, no drums, no bugles, just a worried-looking aide who fussily ushered Carlisle towards the gate of the fort. It was an outrageous break with protocol on the part of the fort's governor, that a post-captain of a foreign power should be received by nothing more than a gilded lieutenant. In fact, it was the stimulus that Carlisle needed. Until then he'd felt that he was at a moral disadvantage, that the Kingdom of Sardinia was the wronged party in this matter. This off-hand reception – this affront to the King whom he served – straightened his backbone. He didn't even look at the aide but strode a few paces forward with a dangerous look on his face, then stopped to look around before he entered the fort's gate. He wasn't going to be rushed by anyone and in his new frame of mind he needed time to think. He noticed that a carriage was hurrying along the road from the north and it was turning aside from the gate towards the jetty. That couldn't be the general, he'd be coming from the south, around Mount Boron. The northerly road led straight to Turin; it was the road that he'd taken only a few days before.

'I have come to call on his Excellency the Governor,' he said in French without ever deigning to look at the lieutenant, 'is he in the fort?'

'His Excellency is at Nice as far as I am aware, sir,' the aide replied nervously. 'His excellency the commandant has asked for the favour of a meeting with you.'

Carlisle bit back the obvious retort, the demand to know why the commandant had sent a messenger rather than meet the captain of a British ship-of-the-line himself. He paused for a few moments. He pulled out his watch and studied it, then he replied in careful, very distinct tones.

'Please inform the commandant that my time is not my own to command, but I can spare him perhaps five minutes and then I would be grateful for a carriage to take me to meet General Paterson. Be sure to use those exact words, I wouldn't want any misunderstanding.'

Carlisle cursed the lack of a carriage that he could call his own. He was dependent upon the charity of the fort's commandant for his transport.

The young lieutenant gulped. Carlisle clearly saw his throat constrict as he contemplated delivering this calculated insult to his master.

That approaching carriage was in an awful hurry, Carlisle thought, as the lieutenant stood rooted to the spot. And he could see that it was heading directly for them. The aide was still swaying from foot to foot, looking from the fort back to Carlisle, hoping for some divine intervention. It came in a form that he could never have anticipated. The carriage drew to a halt as the driver reigned the horses in. At first, Carlisle could see nothing for the cloud of dust that the horses and the wheels had kicked up. Then to his astonishment, as the cloud subsided, the tall, erect, austere form of Mackenzie was handed down from the door. Carlisle just gaped in amazement as the lieutenant stood

115

appalled, wondering what fresh torment was to be visited upon him by these barbarous British.

***

'May I have a moment of your time, Captain Carlisle. Perhaps you would find a stroll along the jetty to be convenient?'

The envoy appeared unmoved by the drama of his arrival. Carlisle had recovered his equanimity enough to make an elegant bow in reply.

'I will attend on the commandant momentarily,' Carlisle said to the aide, knowing that whatever Mackenzie had to say to him would necessarily delay his meeting for a lot longer than the word *momentarily* implied.

The aide looked relieved and withdrew towards the gate of the fort, watching the two foreigners with ill-concealed apprehension. He made no move to deliver the message to his commandant, hoping that whatever occurred would relieve him of the need to do so.

They walked towards the centre of the jetty by mutual consent, to a spot that was equidistant between the walls of the fort, where the aide watched them cautiously, and the farthest end of the jetty where *Dartmouth's* longboat waited. Carlisle saw Souter starting to walk towards him but waved his coxswain back into the boat. He had no idea what news the envoy was bringing, but he had evidently hurried down the long road from Turin, so it must be important and not for the ears of either a foreign lieutenant or a British boat's crew.

'I regret the need for us to meet again, Captain Carlisle...' the envoy began.

Carlisle knew the man well enough to recognise that this was merely his thoroughly unpleasant way of making the other party ill-at-ease before the conversation started.

'...but I had a worrying report of a conversation between my French counterpart in Turin and the French commodore, before he left for Genoa. It persuaded me that His Majesty's business required me to follow you back to

Villa-Franca.'

'Indeed, sir?' Carlisle replied without committing himself.

'Yes, indeed. It concerns the French attempt to detain you in port under the rules of neutrality.'

'Ah, you may not know that my boats took a French schooner on Friday. The attempt to hold me under the twenty-four-hour rule has been nipped in the bud.'

'I know that, dammit,' Mackenzie replied, a flash of anger showing. 'Do you think I would hurry down here if the danger was over? I heard about the schooner when we stopped last night. The news is all over the country by now. There is no hope, no possible hope, that your hosts don't know about it. The danger now is perhaps even greater. The French have sent a diplomatic note to the minister of marine protesting that a British ship sent a belligerent expedition to sea while under the protection of King Charles Emmanuel. The minister of marine will certainly have to act on the note, and you can expect that a letter will reach General Paterson this afternoon. It is imperative, Captain, that you sail today, before you can be detained.'

Carlisle couldn't hide his shock. This was worse than he'd expected, and it posed a serious threat to him and his ship.

'Now, we cannot waste time talking to the commandant of the fort, however *excellent* he may be – we must make haste to Nice and obtain General Paterson's blessing for you to proceed before it's taken out of his hands.'

Carlisle noticed the emphasis on the word *excellent*. Mackenzie wasted no opportunity to obliquely complain at his not being addressed as *your Excellency*.

'You must tell that lieutenant that our business is with General Paterson and that his excellency the commandant is in no position to hinder the movements of an emissary of His Britannic Majesty. Tell him now, and let's be on our way to Nice.'

\*\*\*

Carlisle sat uneasily in the carriage. This proximity to man who he knew was intent on destroying his career was unnerving to say the least. At times like this he cursed his upbringing. He knew very well that nine post-captains out of ten would have dealt with Mackenzie – aye and the damned fort commandant – with infinitely more assurance. He thought of Augustus Hervey who he had known in these very waters in 'fifty-six. Now there was man who would have taken no insult without an immediate assertion of his own status. But then Hervey was the brother of the Earl of Bristol who at this very moment represented King George at the Escorial Palace, while Carlisle was the son of a failing Virginia planter.

'When will you be ready for sea, Captain?'

'Within the hour, sir. We had to fit a new rudder which entailed bringing her stern out of the water. The last of the stores are being shifted aft now.'

'And when do you expect the French to pass this way?'

'I expect they've sailed already but they have a long beat against this westerly wind, so probably tomorrow.'

'Then, as I said, it's imperative that *Dartmouth* leaves Villas-Franca today. In that case we must take a firm line with General Paterson and we must do so before the French delegation arrives.'

Carlisle nodded sagely. He could imagine that once a protest was made it could be days or weeks before the matter was resolved. On the other hand, if Paterson gave his agreement, he could be weighing his anchor before the French could make their case for his detention. As soon as *Dartmouth* was underway, he'd have won the first part of the battle.

Mackenzie sat in silent thought, staring straight ahead at Carlisle.

'I'm sure – almost sure – that the general will be inclined in our favour. He is after all a countryman of mine and I understand you know each other from a previous meeting. Is there any leverage that we can use?'

'It's old history now,' Carlisle said thoughtfully, 'but back in 'fifty-six the general intervened to stop me taking a French frigate in Sardinian waters. The Frenchman was the aggressor, he fired first, and the general, I know, feels that I had the moral right to the prize.'

'You're right, Carlisle, it's an old story, but we must use any leverage that we have. My French counterpart will undoubtedly have sent a note asking the general to detain your ship; we must persuade him that he can ignore that note at least until the delegation arrives.'

***

General Paterson received them in the same room that Carlisle remembered from their first meeting. Then, he had a British aide, but with King Charles Emmanuel so determined upon neutrality, Carstow had been returned to his regiment, and now a young Sardinian captain of cavalry attended upon him. The pleasantries were curtailed; all parties knew that time was short.

'Captain Carlisle finds that he must sail this afternoon, your Excellency, and we have come to thank you for your hospitality and bid our farewells.'

General Paterson looked uneasy and cast a sideways glance at a letter on his desk that was held down by a glass paperweight. The Sardinian captain looked severe, perhaps to hide his embarrassment. He was an old friend of Enrico's and well knew the power of the Angelini family.

'I wish you a prosperous voyage, Captain Carlisle,' the general replied. He hesitated before continuing.

'There is, however on matter – one objection – that must be clarified before you leave, it concerns your ship's status as a vessel of a belligerent power and Sardinia's status as a neutral haven.'

'Indeed, sir?' Mackenzie said, his face an immobile mask. 'I am surprised that the Kingdom of Sardinia should contemplate delaying one of His Britannic majesty's ships, particularly when there are no ships of a belligerent nation in sight. Perhaps you could state the nature of the

119

objection?'

'I have received a note,' Paterson replied, unable to stop his eyes straying towards his desk, 'from the French envoy at Turin. He is concerned that a schooner of the French navy that was sailing from Genoa to Villa-Franca has not arrived.'

'There are many reasons that could delay a schooner arriving at its destination, General. If it doesn't sail from Villa-Franca ahead of *Dartmouth* – and not being there in the first place makes that a practical impossibility – then there is no cause to impose the twenty-four-hour rule.'

Mackenzie held the general's eye. Both men knew more than they were saying but each was waiting for the other to reveal just how much they knew.

'It's not the twenty-four-hour rule that concerns me now,' said Paterson. 'As you have pointed out, there is no cause to impose that rule unless a French national vessel sails from Villa-Franca before *Dartmouth* does. It is a rather more serious matter that I must address. The French envoy at Turin alleges that the schooner was intercepted by boats from *Dartmouth*; boats that were dispatched from the ship while it enjoyed the protection of Villa-Franca.'

The room grew quiet as each of the men considered their next move. The general's statement was hardly a revelation to either Mackenzie or Carlisle, the question was, had the French offered any evidence?

'I am surprised, General, that you should be contemplating detaining a ship of a friendly nation with nothing more in the way of evidence than a note from a third party, a party with which the first is at war. If that became a general rule, it would lead to anarchy, with fleets being immobilised on nothing more than a vexatious accusation. I think you must agree that my French colleague must offer something more substantial before you take the serious step of preventing *Dartmouth* from sailing on her lawful occasions.'

There was another tense silence. The aide wrote a few

lines in a notebook and the general irritably motioned for him to stop.

This is where he asks why the longboat and the yawl put to sea without informing the fort, and why only one of them returned, Carlisle feared, but the question didn't come.

'And yet I find that I must…'

Mackenzie interrupted before the general could say the fateful words that would seal *Dartmouth's* fate.

'Sir, before you go any further, before you commit King Charles Emmanuel to an unwise course of action, I must remind you of your obligations as a neutral power. It is the word *neutral* that is so important in this case. It places an obligation upon you to treat each of the belligerent powers equally. I haven't raised it before because King George so values his friendship with the Kingdom of Sardinia, but there has been a previous occasion when the French have been favoured in these very waters.'

Paterson tried to give the impression that he didn't understand what Mackenzie was referring to, but it was quite clear that he knew very well. He couldn't possibly have forgotten the day when he intervened to save the *Vulcain* from Carlisle's frigate, *Fury*. By any sober assessment, the French had benefitted from that intervention, at the expense of the British. It was clear that Mackenzie was the better diplomat of the two, the most adept at manoeuvering his opponent into an indefensible position. Carlisle saw clearly that the envoy was a man of substantial parts. It was a pity that they had become such bitter enemies.

The general held the envoy's gaze for a few seconds then gave up the charade.

'That was an unfortunate episode that has no bearing on this matter.'

He looked sideways at the aide.

In another flash of clarity, Carlisle realised that this Sardinian captain must be charged with reporting back to Turin on the general's dealings with his home country. So that was what this was all about. That was why Paterson was walking so openly into all the traps that the envoy set. He needed an overwhelming mass of legitimate objections to his detention of *Dartmouth*. That was why he hadn't laid any great stress on the boats, and that was why he wasn't insisting that the note from the French delegation carried any legal or moral force.

'Can you assure me…'

'General, once again I regret having to interrupt you, but I am not obliged to assure you of anything. I am here to inform you of Captain Carlisle's intention to sail this very afternoon as soon as he returns to Villa-Franca. There is no legal reason to detain him, so I request that you send a note the commandant of the fort to prevent any misunderstanding.'

The envoy was relentless in the pressure that he was putting on the general. It really was a masterclass in assertion of belligerent rights and Carlisle was fascinated to hear it being delivered by such a maestro.

General Paterson turned to look out of the window at the beautiful bay of Nice, basking in the morning sunshine. Carlisle could see that the envoy had won. A glance at the aide revealed that he wasn't surprised by the outcome, he even looked relieved. Paterson turned back from the window.

'Very well, sir. I find there is no reason to detain Captain Carlisle's ship, and I will do as you ask regarding the note.'

He nodded at the aide who pulled out a chair and started writing the note.

'Three copies, if you please,' the general said. 'One for the fort, one for Mister Mackenzie and one file copy.'

Mackenzie bowed in acknowledgement.

'Now, I imagine that I cannot persuade you to stay for dinner, but at least accept a coffee while the notes are being prepared.'

\*\*\*

'A most satisfactory conclusion,' said Mackenzie as the carriage left the city wall, heading towards Villa-Franca.

'Indeed, sir. My congratulations on your success. I find that I had no contribution to make.'

Carlisle realised that this was his first civil conversation with the envoy. Perhaps he was a man who felt uneasy outside his natural environment. If so, then being confined to a ship at the whim of a man whom he considered his social inferior must have been deeply galling.

'Ah, but you did, Captain Carlisle, you did. The diplomatic arguments wouldn't have carried the day, of that I'm sure, but your mere presence reminded the general of his previous embarrassing intervention in the rights of warring nations, and your relationship with the Angelinis clearly terrified that appalling tale-bearer of a captain.'

Carlisle nodded. Perhaps something could be salvaged out of the wreckage of the disastrous cruise from Gibraltar to Villa-Franca.

There was a tap on the glass of the carriage and the whip twitched forward in the direction they were travelling. The driver was drawing their attention to something ahead. Carlisle leaned out of the window.

'It's just a carriage coming the other way.'

Mackenzie thrust his head out.

'Ha. That's the French envoy's carriage. He must have come past Villa-Franca to see if your ship was still there. He'll regret that delay.'

He pushed his head further out of the carriage.

'Driver,' he shouted in Italian, 'Don't give way. Whip up the horses, make him yield.'

The driver grinned down, his teeth showing white against his suntanned face, and he applied his whip with a will. The driver of the French carriage hadn't been so firmly instructed and at the last moment he veered off to the side of the road, as the envoy and Carlisle sped past in a cloud of dust. Carlisle had a fleeting glimpse of the furious face of the French envoy to King Charles Emmanuel shouting imprecations up at his driver.

'Most satisfactory,' the envoy repeated as he settled back

in the coach. 'General Paterson can be relied upon to keep him waiting for a couple of hours, even if he does bring evidence of your deeds. I suggest that a swift departure is in order, Captain. Don't stand on ceremony when we reach the jetty, I pray. I will deliver this most helpful note to the commandant of the fort, then I will have the greatest pleasure in seeing you sail before I return to Turin. I think that is a more useful place for me to be than Nice if there is any damage to be limited.'

***

# CHAPTER TWELVE

## The Rendezvous

*Monday, Ninth of June 1760.*
*Dartmouth, at Sea. Villa-Franca northwest 8 leagues.*

Carlisle breathed deep of the cleansing air of the sea. Only now were the cares of the land falling from his shoulders. He was trying to blot out the memory of his visit to Turin, the envoy's obstinate hatred, the intrigue and the falsehoods. Life was so much simpler at sea. Either he could achieve what he wanted within his own resources or he couldn't, and there was nothing to be gained by fretting over it. And he was his own master again! The great cabin was his and when he strolled on the poop deck, he didn't need to concern himself with disturbing a guest below. But all that paled into insignificance against the greatest of all gifts: he no longer had to put on a face before his own officers and crew. There was no need to pretend that he and the envoy hadn't fallen across each other's hawse. Not that anybody except the simplest of *Dartmouth's* people were fooled; the doings of the great were the staple gossip of the mess tables. But oh, the blissful freedom!

Carlisle studied Halsey carefully. Even now, at the last moment, he had misgivings about giving this task to his second lieutenant. Wishart had initially looked shocked that he would have to give up command of the schooner, but he soon realised that it meant a promotion for him – from third to second. And – with an engagement in prospect – a chance to further impress his captain. The longboat was alongside with the last of the crew to be transferred and Carlisle was impatient for the schooner to leave.

'Give Minorca a wide berth and keep well off the African coast. You should make Gibraltar in less than two weeks, even if this westerly persists. If you should fall in with the Spanish navy, hold your ground and insist on your rights.

Unless the Spanish have cast their lot in with the French since we had our last news, they're unlikely to detain you. It's more likely that you'll meet one of Admiral Saunders' ships than a Frenchman, but unless you're certain of its nationality, fly from everything!'

'Aye-aye sir,' Halsey replied.

'The sergeant is a capable man and I advise you to take his advice in all things in relation to the prisoners. They can stand confinement for two weeks without coming to any harm, and they have their own doctor.'

'I will, sir.'

Well, he looks confident enough, Carlisle thought. And yet it was no simple task that was being asked of him, sailing the prize with twenty-three French prisoners, half of them wounded, some eight hundred miles to Gibraltar. He would have to pass Minorca, which was still in French hands, and pass the Spanish islands and mainland where the authorities were increasingly anti-British.

It had been a hard decision to give Halsey the command of the prize. He hadn't been involved in taking the schooner and it would have been more normal to leave Wishart in command. In the end he had made the decision on selfish grounds. He had little faith in Halsey's capabilities and now that he had an extra lieutenant in the form of Enrico Angelini, he was looking for a way to move Halsey out of his ship. This was the perfect opportunity, but even now he had to be careful to avoid revealing his plan.

'Your orders are to rejoin *Dartmouth* in whatever British ship is most likely to find us; I'll leave that to your judgement. However, don't be surprised if the governor of Gibraltar has other ideas for the schooner. This letter,' Carlisle added handing over a separate packet, 'is my recommendation that you should continue to command the schooner in case the governor needs to employ it. You could even find yourself sailing for England, the governor is always short of dispatch vessels.'

Privately, Carlisle knew that there was a good chance

that the governor would send the schooner back to England, in fact he was counting on it. Then Halsey would almost certainly be appointed to another ship and he would have rid himself of that ineffective young man.

'Good luck then, Mister Halsey, and I expect we will meet again in a month or so.'

Carlisle resisted the temptation to cross his fingers behind his back. He had been remarkably lucky in the officers that had come over to him when he took command of *Dartmouth*. Gresham was the very dream of a first lieutenant: competent, energetic and brave and without an ambitious bone in his body. Wishart and Angelini were his longstanding followers and he had made them in his own image, and he had a good set of warrant officers led by the excellent Beazley. Wishart would become second, of course, and Angelini third, and that would solve the embarrassing problem of having a surplus lieutenant.

*Dartmouth* was blessed with a near-full complement of seamen and the loss of an eager young bosun's mate and half a dozen good seamen to man the schooner would hardly be felt. Perhaps he should have sent Sergeant Wilson instead of the second sergeant. Wilson would certainly have had no problem in keeping the French prisoners under control. However, having lost Towser in the fight to take the schooner, that would leave only the very inexperienced second lieutenant of marines to command the detachment, without the support of a strong sergeant. In any case, Carlisle was pleased to have a reason to keep Wilson by his side. The presence of that formidable man was a reassurance, and he'd promised his wife that he would never step into danger without Wilson by his side.

***

'Well, gentlemen, what do you think? Given this wind and what we know of these Genoa-built sixty-fours, are we waiting in the right place?'

Eight bells had just been rung and the forenoon watchmen were pouring onto the deck while their opposite numbers hurried below to their breakfast. Beazley looked up at the tops'ls and glanced at the compass.

'The wind's veered a point, sir, and I wouldn't be surprised to see it come from the nor'west before the day is over. They'll be reluctant to stand too far out to sea with the risk of a foul wind for Toulon. Unless they have all the time in the world, they'll take a departure from Cape Mele and the direct track to round the Hyeres Islands. Ten to one they'll pass close enough for us to sight them.'

'That still leaves a chance that we'll miss them if they do stand right out towards Corsica, sir,' said Gresham. 'We could be certain of them if we waited off the Hyeres Islands.'

Carlisle studied his two senior officers. Their characters showed in their commentary on his plans for intercepting the French. The sailing master was willing to accept a chance that they'd miss their prey, while the first lieutenant was willing to take more risks for an assurance of meeting them.

'I think not, Mister Gresham. The Hyeres islands are too close to Toulon. The French may not have much force ready for sea, but what they do have will be at anchor in the outer road and any fishing boat could bring news of our loitering off the islands. That damned great seventy-four could be there now, and they have a score to settle with us. No, I accept there is a slim chance of the sixty-fours evading us, but it is just that, a slim chance. We'll run a twenty-mile north-south patrol line centred here, but don't go far enough north for us to be seen from the shore, Mister Beazley.'

Gresham ginned. 'As soon as the men have all had their breakfast, I'll set them to drills at the guns, with your permission, sir.'

That was one of the best characteristics of his first lieutenant, Carlisle thought. He never took offence when his advice was discarded. It came with the man's complete lack of ambition, and it contributed to the features that made him a second-in-command to be cherished.

\*\*\*

*Dartmouth* was on her best point of sailing with the wind broad on her starboard beam as she headed out into the Mediterranean. Ten miles on this leg should take no longer than an hour-and-a-half and then they could wear ship and beat up to the north. Down on the main deck Carlisle could see the twelve-pounders being run in and out under Enrico's orders. The men seemed enthusiastic; they all knew that there was a fight in prospect, and it was good to see that they welcomed it. Down below on the lower gun deck Wishart would be similarly exercising the twenty-four pounders, taking Halsey's place. On the quarterdeck and fo'c'sle the six-pounders – dainty little pieces by comparison – were being put through their paces. The massive and reassuring frame of Gresham, his speaking-trumpet hanging by a loop from his wrist, orchestrated the whole. Was it his imagination, or did the drills run more smoothly than they had before? Could Halsey's absence have such an immediate effect? He watched Gresham with interest. In all previous exercises, and even in battle, Gresham had been like a jack-in-the-box, running down and up the ladder to the lower deck. Of course, he'd been checking on Halsey, but now with Wishart in charge of the great guns on the lower deck, he had time to perform his real task of orchestrating the whole of *Dartmouth's* armament. He looked a happy man.

Carlisle basked for a moment in the knowledge that at last he had a set of officers that he could rely upon. All he needed now was for Halsey to be sent back to England with dispatches. In a way, it would repay incompetence, because command of a schooner like that, however temporary, marked a young lieutenant as a possible future commander. He could even have the outrageous good fortune to be in action – to take a prize even – and then he would be known at the Admiralty. It was unfair of course, Wishart could have had that chance, but then *Dartmouth* would be stuck with a useless lieutenant for the foreseeable future.

Then Carlisle remembered. Towser was dead, he'd been buried at sea from the schooner, his body certainly couldn't have been kept on board for more than a day or two in a Mediterranean summer. It was easy to take the ship's marine detachment for granted, they were in many respects an independent unit within the ship's captain's overall command. They were liable to be moved from ship to ship at some unfathomable whim and they never identified with a particular ship in the same way that the sailors did. He had largely disregarded the marine second lieutenant – he even had difficulty remembering his name sometimes. Kemp, that was it. Francis Kemp. With an engagement in the offing – Carlisle touched the wood of the poop rail for luck – he would have to know the man better. He strode down the ladder to the quarterdeck, stepping wide of the larboard six pounder and its crew who were savagely running it in and out, determined to do everything faster than their competitors on the starboard side. He looked around for Kemp. He should be on the quarterdeck for these drills with his marines who were dutifully lining the gunwales going through the dumb show of loading and firing their muskets. Where was the man?

'Mister Young, Mister Young!'

It took a moment to gain the midshipman's attention, he was so engrossed in the gun drills, mouthing the words of command in time with the first lieutenant.

'Mister Young. My compliments to Lieutenant Kemp and I would be pleased to see him in my cabin.'

\*\*\*

Carlisle took a moment to study the man who was now responsible for his ship's military force. Francis Kemp had joined the ship at Portsmouth. He was short with what could generously be called a well-fed build, his hair was flame-red and not even the Mediterranean sun could darken his startlingly white skin. With that hair and that complexion, he would stand out from his shipmates under any circumstances. But now, in his red and white regimentals, it hurt the eye to look at him. He appeared to be about seventeen, perhaps eighteen, and his rank of second lieutenant gave him an equivalent status to the midshipmen, but only by courtesy of being embarked in a man-o'-war. On land he would rank with the lowliest volunteers, youngsters who were learning their business before being given any responsibility. Carlisle stifled a sigh.

So far Kemp had offered nothing more than a simple *sir* on entering the cabin, and then he had lapsed into a rigid silence, moving nothing other than his eyes that scanned from side-to-side. Carlisle realised that it was quite possibly the first time that he entered the great cabin and certainly the first time that he had been the sole object of the captain's attention. All the other officers had dined in the cabin and the midshipmen had occasionally breakfasted there when they had come off the morning watch. With no watchkeeping duties and no great status in the ship, Kemp had fallen through the gap. Well, this man's fortunes had a fresh start beginning today.

'Mister Kemp. Thank you for joining me. First, I must offer my condolences on the death of Lieutenant Towser. It is little comfort, I know, that he died honourably on the enemy's deck.'

Nothing. No reply from the wooden figure in front of him. Perhaps he needed a direct question.

'You're aware of the general situation, the possible action that we face in the next day or two?'

'I know that we are to intercept the French, sir…'

Kemp had managed to bring out at least a part of a sentence, but he had done so without any visible movement of his body. Carlisle realised that he was not making a connection.

'Sit down, Mister Kemp, I can see that we need to talk.'

Kemp looked around in apparent terror. There was a chair only a yard away, but his body was seemingly unable to relax sufficiently to make the transition from rigid uprightness to the bent posture that was normally required for sitting. He made an attempt at the chair without bending at the waist which almost ended in disaster, then he made an impetuous lunge at the seat and his posterior happily engaged with the cushioned surface without fracturing any bones. Carlisle had never seen anyone sitting at attention before; it was an unnerving sight.

'Now that you command *Dartmouth's* marines, it's important that you should understand how I plan to engage the enemy. You rank with my lieutenants now you know, with Mister Wishart and Mister Angelini.'

That fact, so bluntly delivered, seemed to petrify the young man. His eyes became larger and rounder as the peered out of his white face. He looked like a hunted hare in winter.

In a flash of intuition, Carlisle realised that Kemp had been an outsider in *Dartmouth*. Neither fish nor fowl. Being no seaman, he was disregarded in the midshipman's berth and his lowly rank excluded him from the society of the only other marine officer. Probably he barely knew what part of the world he was in and as for the nature of *Dartmouth's* mission, well, he was unlikely to be aware that the ship had a defined purpose beyond cruising the oceans looking for the enemy. He had to start learning.

'We're waiting for two enemy sixty-four-gun ships to come down from Genoa to Toulon. They must pass this way and we know to within a day or so when they left. I expect them today or tomorrow.'

The round eyes grew rounder still.

'You may perhaps be wondering what business a ship of fifty guns has in tackling two of sixty-four guns each?'

No response beyond a flush of colour starting to grow from the uniform stock, threatening to add an unhealthy crimson to make war with the reds of his coat and hair. Carlisle plunged on, determined to get some reaction.

'The two ships, we have heard, are partly manned and

missing half of their guns. They will have had no time to train their crews in either gunnery or seamanship. If that is true – and I repeat, if it is true – then we should be a good match for them. If I can take them both, I will; but in reality, we will need to board to subdue them, and one is highly likely to escape while we deal with the other. I take it that you have never boarded a ship, Mister Kemp?'

'No, sir,' the young man replied miserably. 'I had never been to sea before I joined you in Portsmouth.'

'Well, we all have to start somewhere.'

There was nothing to be gained in beating the man down. Carlisle needed his boarding party to be led with resolution, and boldness. Perhaps it was asking too much of such a young and horribly inexperienced officer, but there was a ray of hope.

'Now, you are fortunate in having a very experienced sergeant. This first time, I want you to follow what Wilson does and then next time you will be ready to lead yourself…'

'I've heard the stories about Sergeant Wilson, sir,' Kemp said, brightening for the first time since he had entered the cabin. 'Mister Towser told me that Wilson had been with you in the West Indies, and in North America.'

'He was indeed. In fact, Wilson has made a habit of saving me from my own folly. You will not go far wrong if you observe what he does when he boards the enemy. It's not pretty, you know. It's hard, close fighting, kill or be killed. If we meet the enemy – which I fervently hope – you will have tales of your own to tell.'

***

The master was waiting to wear the ship – turning its stern through the wind to place it on the larboard tack – and Carlisle stepped out onto the quarterdeck just before Beazley could wait no longer and had determined on calling him. He'd been reluctant to call the captain until the very last moment; like all the other officers, Beazley knew that Carlisle's meeting with Kemp would be difficult.

'Carry on, Mister Beazley,' Carlisle said without being asked.

It was quite clear what was afoot, with the hands spared from the guns to man the tacks and sheets. There was no need for Carlisle to supervise the manoeuvre. By now all his officers could handle the ship without his needing to do any more than agree to their requests. Only Halsey had needed watching, and Halsey was gone, hopefully for ever.

With the ship heading north, close hauled, the wind whipped across the deck in a way that had seemed impossible when she was on a broad reach on the previous leg of her patrol line. It was scarcely credible that this was the same wind, and that the ship was actually moving more slowly through the water than it had before. The air on the deck was incredibly refreshing. A sharp breeze and a warm sun and the feel of a live ship under his feet; these were the days that he would remember when he finally swallowed the anchor. There was no feeling like it on land.

The sea was their own for now, and there was nothing in sight, not even a fisherman. Carlisle looked away to starboard each time his pacing of the deck reached the taffrail at the aft end or the poop rail at the forrad end of his track. Any moment now the horizon could be pierced by the tops'ls of the French sixty-fours. He looked aloft where he could see the daring lookout at the very ultimate height of the masts. It was Whittle, of course, determined as always to be the first to sight the enemy.

Had he handled Kemp well? At least he hadn't done anything to destroy the man's confidence. The question now was whether he should speak to Sergeant Wilson. It was a delicate matter. On the one hand, Wilson could make or break Kemp and the more he knew of the situation the better. On the other hand, the whole ship's company would know if he spoke to the marine sergeant privately, and they would all know why. On balance it was better not to, and having made the decision, Carlisle knew it to be correct. Wilson would certainly know the character and experience of his officer and would naturally take the lead without any intervention from Carlisle; sergeants had been doing that for millennia.

\*\*\*

# CHAPTER THIRTEEN

## News Travels Fast

*Monday, Ninth of June 1760.*
*Dartmouth, at Sea. Villa-Franca northwest 8 leagues.*

*Dartmouth* ploughed the same furrow the rest of the day, with nothing to see except a few fishing boats that came out from Nice and Villa-Franca. They went about their business seemingly unafraid of the British man-o'-war, but then they'd become used to seeing her.

'Our presence off this coast will be no secret now,' said Gresham as he watched the nearest boat haul its nets. The sun reflected off the mass of fish that poured into the boat and the first lieutenant smacked his lips. He liked nothing more than a dish of grilled sardines.

'Our presence is well known in any case, sir,' Enrico replied, smiling wryly. 'We've been the talk of the region since we arrived and my people don't lack intelligence, you know. They've all heard about the ships being built for the French in Genoa; it's a matter of some importance to Sardinia. If the republic should throw its lot in with King Louis, then the little seaboard that Sardinia has becomes even more vulnerable. They all know that the ships must sail soon, if they haven't already, and with rumour of Saunders arriving off Toulon in the near future, they must make the passage soon, or they'll find Toulon blockaded. Nobody in Nice expects us to be anywhere other than where we are.'

'Then the word will have filtered through to Toulon, for sure.'

'Certainly. Toulon is closer than Turin, it's just down the road as you English say. What's known in Nice is known in Toulon. Whether the French navy will give any credit to reports from Nice is another matter entirely. There's a certain chauvinism you know, a feeling among the French that the people to the east of Cannes are simple country folk. My guess is that they'll want something more than tales from the Ligurian coast before they take any action.'

'Then the sooner we sight these sixty-fours the better.'

Gresham rubbed his hands at the prospect. A good fight and the prospect of prize money, what could be more agreeable? He'd seen how well the men had settled down after only a day at sea, he'd seen how much better the gun drills had been, and he knew the reason. With a friendly nod to Enrico, he turned away and left the deck to the Sardinian lieutenant.

***

The sun arced towards the north western horizon and the brilliant light started to fade. The fishing boats had all gone, stowing their nets and setting their sails for home; *Dartmouth* was alone again.

'We'll shorten sail, I believe, Mister Angelini, and beat up to the sou'west. Tops'ls and stays'ls should be enough. Pass the word for the master if you please.'

Carlisle had been pacing the poop deck for an hour or so, hoping for a glimpse of French tops'ls to the east. Now with darkness fast approaching he had to adopt a different tactic.

'Aye-aye sir,' Enrico replied, removing his hat.

'We'll follow the coast through the night so that they don't slip past us, then we can run down to the east again with the dawn.'

Enrico nodded. He didn't need to be told what Carlisle intended; it was an obvious way of reducing the risk of missing their quarry during the night.

'There's no need to call the hands. I'm sure you can get in the t'gallants and hand the mainsail and foresail on the watch.'

It may not be done quite as smartly on the watch, but there was no urgency and there was no admiral to criticise the speed of their sail handling. Carlisle was the only captain that Enrico had served under, but he had heard enough stories to know that he was more careful of his men's welfare than most. There was a good feeling in the ship today, a suppressed excitement at the coming action.

Beazley stood back and let Enrico give the orders. First the t'gallant yards were lowered and the sails furled; that was an easy task for the watch on deck. When that was complete, they moved to the lower yards and brought in the courses. Immediately the whole feel of the ship changed. She moved more easily over the water and the view forrard from the quarterdeck and poop deck opened to the lovely vista of a Mediterranean sunset. With the sails reduced, Enrico brought *Dartmouth* hard onto the wind and she plunged ahead into the darkening sea.

Carlisle gazed at the scene and nodded in satisfaction. Enrico was already a competent lieutenant and he'd grow fast with these new responsibilities. He could see a day when this young cousin of his would have his own ship in the reformed Sardinian navy, and then the opportunities would be endless. No other Sardinians would be able to claim the experience that he would have, not even the unknown officer who was being seconded to the French navy.

***

'Sail ho! Sail on the starboard bow!'

'Up you go, Mister Young. Let me know what you see.'

Enrico looked over his shoulder. Carlisle and Beazley were pointedly ignoring the hail, waiting for a report from the officer of the watch.

'Masthead lookout reports a sail, sir, on the starboard bow, inshore of us. It must be coasting down from the west.'

'Very well, Mister Angelini,' Carlisle replied. 'Let me know when you have identified her.'

'She's not a man-o'-war,' shouted Midshipman Young, from high up the main t'gallant mast. 'She could be a tartane. She's before the wind in any case.'

'Call the hands and bring us about, Mister Angelini. We can cut her off before she runs past us. There's a good chance that she's French. Set the t'gallants.'

Beazley looked doubtfully at the setting sun.

'We may just have time before we lose the light.'

The bosun's calls twittered and with a rush the watch below stampeded up the ladders. *Dartmouth's* bows came through the wind and soon she was settled on the larboard tack.

'I can see her from the deck now, sir,' Enrico reported. 'She's a tartane sure enough, heading up the coast with the wind on her beam.'

'Clear away the fo'c'sle six-pounders, Mister Gresham. She won't give us any trouble.'

'Ah, she's hauled her wind,' said Beazley. 'She's seen us. She's heading inshore now.'

Carlisle cursed silently. The tartane could easily find shelter under the Antibes peninsula before *Dartmouth* could come up with her. But at least she couldn't beat back towards Toulon and alert the French navy to his presence. There were French batteries on Antibes, and if the tartane should not choose to take their protection, the border with Sardinia lay only a few miles further east, and he didn't dare infringe their neutrality, not after yesterday's meeting with General Paterson.

'Keep her hard on the wind, Mister Angelini.'

It was always worth chasing for as long as the light held. There was no knowing what could happen, and they could yet take a prize. In fact, prize money was the last thing on Carlisle's mind. Of greater concern was the possibility that the tartane would head back southwest along the coast. She could be off Toulon tomorrow with definite news of a British man-o'-war off Nice. The French admiral would easily put two and two together and surmise that this was the same ship that had been in Villa-Franca. In which case it was a lone British fourth rate, and he could do something about that.

'There'll be no moon for another four hours, sir.'

'Thank you, Mister Beazley.'

The sailing master wasn't a pessimistic man, but he had

the irritating habit of stating the difficulties even when they were obvious.

There was a bustle around the binnacle as the mate of the watch checked the compass at sunset. Carlisle heard the report but ignored it. He was conscious of the greenish flash on the horizon as the very last rays of the sun spread out briefly, an effect of the refraction he assumed. It was a beautiful sight, made all the more exquisite by its brief life, a second or two and it was gone. He would normally have watched with pleasure, but this evening he was concentrating on the chase. The tartane's dark sails could still be seen, but it was clear that they would be lost to sight in twenty minutes.

'Ah-ha! She's come about, just as I feared,' said Beazley.

Carlisle could see for himself. The tartane was heading back from whence she had come. Whether that was in terror of this British predator, or with a sense of duty to report the sighting at Toulon, would never be known.

Everyone on the quarterdeck was watching Carlisle, waiting for orders, for some kind of a reaction.

'Bring in the t'gallants again, Mister Angelini, and lay her back on the starboard tack.'

Let them wonder! Yes, they'd missed a prize – there was no chasing the tartane into a hostile shore in the dark – but Carlisle knew that a report of his presence may be of benefit. The French could hardly send a ship of any force to the east before the sixty-fours came down from Genoa, and just possibly it would spur the admiral at Toulon to send a small squadron to deal with this lone British cruiser. Let him send the whole of his fleet! Admiral Saunders would be off Toulon in a few days, if he kept to his schedule, and he would no doubt be delighted to catch the French at sea.

*\*\*\**

Dawn revealed an empty sea. There was no sign of the Tartane – Carlisle would have been amazed if there had been – and the fishing boats had not yet set sail. *Dartmouth* was reaching back to her patrol line off Nice, still well out to sea, over the horizon and safe from prying eyes on the shore.

'God send us the French this day,' said Wishart as Enrico relieved him for the forenoon watch.

'They'll come today or not at all, David,' said Enrico, still watching the eastern horizon.

'I admire your certainty, Enrico, and I hope you're proved right, but what makes you so sure?'

'They must come now or not at all. Think about the French position. There have been no British ships of the line in these waters since last year. Now, suddenly, *Dartmouth* appears with the evident intention of intercepting the Genoa ships. It's known that a British fleet is in the Mediterranean, and what's more certain than that they'll look into Toulon, just to remind the French that they may not sail with impunity? With Saunders off Cape Sicié, the Genoa ships won't be able to get into Toulon, not without fighting their way in, and they're in no fit state for that. Time is running out for them and if they don't make Toulon in the next day or two, they won't dare to sail at all. Today is my mother's saint's day; we'll see them before the sun sets again!'

***

Ships at sea settle very quickly into a routine, and after less than two days out of Nice, *Dartmouth's* crew had already established a comfortable pattern to their watches. Once each watch they were called to handle the sails, the rest of the time was spent in routine maintenance of the rigging, spells as lookout and tricks on the wheel. In the forenoon they practiced handling the great guns, but no shots were fired to avoid alarming any ships within earshot. In this glorious weather none of these activities could be called a hardship, and there was a general feeling of wellbeing in the ship.

To Enrico it was still a novelty to stride the quarterdeck without the nagging feeling that he should be doing something. Even as a master's mate he'd been continually harried by the officer of the watch. There was always something that needed attention. Streaming the log, marking up the traverse board, stirring up the lookouts, there was never a peaceful moment. Now he had command, at least until the captain or the first lieutenant or the master came on deck. He could demand that the master's mate and the midshipmen look active, that they jump to his command, and he could take an Olympian detachment from the hurly-burly. Now the gun drills had ended, and everyone was looking forward to the change of the watch and dinner. Seven bells sounded and fifty heads turned aft to see that the glass was being promptly turned.

'Deck there!'

Enrico looked up. That was Whittle, high above the quarterdeck at the main t'gallant masthead.

'I can't be certain, sir, but as we rise on the swell, I can just see something to leeward. Not a sail, but perhaps a topmast or t'gallant.'

Whittle was the best lookout in the ship and Enrico wasn't going to ignore even this most speculative of reports, and in any case, it was about time.

'My compliments to the captain, Mister Young. The lookout reports a possible sail to leeward. Tell him that only a topmast is visible.'

But Midshipman Young was too late. Carlisle had heard the hail through his skylight and with a wave of his hand he dismissed the purser and his report of provisions and walked the few yards onto the quarterdeck.

'What d'you make of it, Whittle?' he shouted through the speaking trumpet.

'I'm certain there's something there, sir,' Whittle replied, his voice carrying easily to the quarterdeck. 'I can't see a sail yet, but it looks very much like the truck of a t'gallant mast.'

Carlisle looked thoughtful. This could be one of the French sixty-fours, but in that case why wasn't it setting its t'gallants? It was a long beat to Toulon, and the captain would certainly want to make it to safety as quickly as possible, and even hard on the wind he could make an extra knot with his highest sails set. Was he short-handed? The uncle in Turin had thought so and empirically it was quite likely. Probably the French admiral at Toulon had only spared enough seamen to bring the two ships the short distance along the coast to safety. He knew that guns had been sent to Genoa, although only half the number that the ships would usually carry. Then he'd be fighting undermanned, under gunned ships that had not yet shaken down at sea. His heart beat faster, this was a dream situation. Suddenly the prospect of engaging two sixty-fours didn't feel daunting at all.

'Mister Gresham. I want the watch below on deck as soon as they've finished their dinner. Let these men,' he swept his arm around the deck, 'have theirs and then you can beat to quarters.'

'Deck there! It's a ship under tops'ls, with her t'gallant masts sent up, and I think I can see a second one now.'

Carlisle was getting a feel for these ships already. T'gallant masts with no sails set? They'd been set up in the shipyard before they sailed, and the hands were too busy with the tops'ls and courses and stays'ls to worry about the t'gallant sails. Short-handed for certain.

'They're on a beam reach, sir, in line ahead with about five cables between them.'

Gresham and Beazley were watching him again, waiting for orders.

'We'll haul our wind, gentlemen, and lead them to the sou'west. I don't want to fight them off the Sardinian coast if I can help it, and there's plenty of time left in the day. Mister Angelini, bring her four points to windward.'

***

'The ship is cleared for action, sir, the hands are at quarters.'

Gresham looked eager for a fight; he was grinning broadly and casting frequent glances astern where the two

French ships were now clearly visible from the deck.

'Will you take them both, sir?'

It was a preposterous question; a fifty-gun ship to take on two sixty-fours? Nevertheless, Carlisle had been considering just that. Unless he had badly misread the situation, he felt confident that he could batter one of the sixty-fours into submission. That in itself would be a serious blow to the admiral in Toulon. The French fleet was short of ships, provisions and guns, but all of that paled into insignificance against their desperate shortage of trained seamen. It was unlikely that these two ships would carry less than two hundred each, and that was what would really hurt. If he could deprive the French Mediterranean fleet of two hundred trained seamen, he would have done his duty. He was very tempted to try for both ships. It could be done with a little luck, but a voice inside him urged caution. There was a danger that in trying to take both he would end up with neither.

'No, Mister Gresham, not unless fortune should favour us. We'll batter the first of the two until she strikes, I'd rather not risk our men in a boarding. If the other should come to her aid, then we'll see what can be done. I'll take it as a good day if we deprive the French of one of these ships that they've paid for.'

Gresham nodded. Dealing with two large prizes, even if they should be fortunate enough to take them both, would test *Dartmouth's* resources, and Gresham knew that much of the labour would fall on his shoulders.

'We'll lead them further down the coast until we're clear of Sardinia, then we'll bring the ship alongside the first of them.'

'The second will surely make for Toulon as fast as she can, sir. That would be the sensible thing to do.'

'It would, Mister Gresham, but we cannot look into the hearts of those French captains. I saw one of them in Turin, and he didn't look like a man to shirk a fight.'

Gresham looked at the wind, then at his pocket watch.

'Ten hours of daylight left sir. There's plenty of time to bring this affair to a conclusion.'

\*\*\*

# CHAPTER FOURTEEN

## A Hard Pounding

*Tuesday, Tenth of June 1760.*
*Dartmouth, at Sea. Villa-Franca northwest 8 leagues.*

'Cape Antibes is north at eight leagues, sir,' Beazley reported.

That would do. There was no chance of infringing Sardinian waters now, and it was senseless to leave the engagement any longer. Even now Carlisle could see that the crew was growing restless. The waiting was playing on their nerves.

'Very well, Mister Gresham, wear ship and put me alongside the lead of those two, our starboard to his larboard.'

This would be a straightforward slugging match, like two boxers fighting toe-to-toe. Carlisle had no interest in damaging the other ship's rigging, only the slaughter of her gun crews would cause her to strike, and that could best be achieved by a broadside-to-broadside contest.

'Now then, gentlemen,' he said to the officers still on the quarterdeck. 'We know that he has fewer guns than us and we believe he has fewer men, certainly her actions so far suggest that is the case.'

There were nods and growls of agreement all around him.

'We'll try his mettle; see how long he'll stand our broadsides. There's to be only round shot from the great guns, but the fo'c'sle and quarterdeck guns are to use canister and grape as they see fit, to clear her upper deck.'

More nods of approval. There really was nothing innovative about the plan, it relied upon superior weight of broadside and better trained gunners.

'To your stations then, gentlemen.'

*Dartmouth's* stern came through the wind and she settled on a course to intercept the enemy. Carlisle studied them carefully through his telescope. They were still eight miles away, but perfectly visible in this dazzling sunshine. They were making no attempt to reduce to fighting sail, their courses were still set, and they appeared intent on brushing past this lone British ship and making Toulon with as little delay as possible. Could it be that they didn't know their peril? Carlisle had a bad moment as he swept the horizon to the south and west. Nothing, not a sail marked the pristine blue of the sea. Then if they were expecting support it wasn't yet in sight.

They were closing fast now. Carlisle did a quick mental calculation; they'd be broadside-to-broadside in perhaps forty-five minutes. The time was passing frighteningly fast. He studied the lead ship, his chosen prey. It was flying a commodore's pennant; he could put a face to its captain. He remembered a tall aristocrat with a full powdered wig and a fashionable walking cane. They hadn't spoken, of course, but they had exchanged guarded nods of acknowledgement across the room. He hadn't looked like a man who would easily strike his colours or run from a fight. He was glad that he'd chosen the lead ship as his target because he was certain that this captain would come to the aid of the other if he was hard pressed, whereas he knew nothing of the second ship's captain.

Beazley was taking bearings of the approaching Frenchman.

'We should tack in five minutes, sir,' he said, over his shoulder as he kept his eye on the changing bearing.

Carlisle looked around the deck. The sail handlers were all in place and the starboard guns were manned. The larboard guns were attended by their gun captains but otherwise abandoned. There was Enrico, walking from gun to gun, checking the equipment and exchanging a few words with each crew.

'Very well, Mister Beazley. I'll leave it to you. Put me alongside that ship, at pistol-shot range.'

***

*Dartmouth* started the turn that would put her head through the wind and end with her laying alongside the Frenchman. Carlisle could see that Beazley had timed it perfectly. Slowly at first the bows moved to larboard, then the rate of turn increased. The orders were given, tacks were cast off and rigged on the opposite side, the sheets were handled, and the great ship-of-the-line tacked swiftly through the wind.

'Watch his bearing, Mister Beazley.'

'Aye sir. It'll be a slanting approach. I reckon we have about a knot on him.'

Carlisle nodded. *Dartmouth* would edge up to the Frenchman from her leeward side. Already they were within random shot of each other, but Carlisle had no intention of wasting his first carefully loaded broadside on long range firing. Battles were won by the massive impact of whole broadsides at close range, not unlike infantry engagements. Like the best of commanders on land he must hold his fire, accepting early casualties if necessary, so that the first shattering broadside could be delivered from a range where it would cause maximum damage. Ten minutes, that was his estimate of the time before they were close enough, and it was those ten minutes that would test his men.

The ship was close enough now to make out the individuals on her quarterdeck. He could see the captain and he could see other figures moving about behind her massive gunwales.

'She's tender, sir, look how she heels, even without t'gallants.'

Beazley was right. Carlisle could see right over her gunwales and the whole expanse of her upper deck and quarterdeck was open to his view. That was what Carlisle had counted on. The two ships only had to make the short voyage to Toulon and the French treasury would certainly not have seen fit to buy stores in Genoa when they would be issued from the arsenal of Toulon in only a few days. She was high in the water and heeling to even the lightest gusts.

'She's opening her ports, sir,' shouted Gresham.

Carlisle saw the long row of upper deck swing up and at each port the ugly, black muzzle of an eighteen-pound gun pointed towards him. There was something sinister about the way that the guns were run out, an unmistakable statement of intent. Carlisle shivered involuntarily.

'Ha. She hasn't shipped her thirty-two pounders!' Gresham came close to skipping in his excitement. It made a vast difference. It was now clear that *Dartmouth* had the greater weight of broadside.

'Mister Young. Jump up to the poop deck and watch the other ship carefully. If it looks like she's dropping down to leeward, you're to let me know immediately.'

That was one thing that Carlisle found difficult in the transition from commanding a frigate to a great ship-of-the line. He'd enjoyed an uninterrupted view all around from the quarterdeck of his frigate, while from *Dartmouth's* quarterdeck he had no view astern. The protection that the extra deck provided, and the higher, stouter gunwales, was comforting, for sure, but he didn't feel that he had as good a grasp of the situation. His plan had been based on the near certainty that the two ships wouldn't delay in their flight to the safety of Toulon. It wasn't a matter of cowardice; it was merely good strategic thinking. These ships were desperately needed to make up the losses that the French navy had suffered over four years of warfare. As part of a battle fleet their value was doubled or tripled, and even if they could take or destroy *Dartmouth*, it wasn't worth one iota of additional risk. Carlisle was convinced that the French commodore had ordered the second ship to ignore anything that happened to himself and make for Toulon. A single sixty-four arriving safely was worth more than two battered hulks, even when set against the loss to the British of a fourth rate.

Closer and closer they came. Now he could see the faces of the men as they crouched over their guns, waiting for the order to fire.

'He's steadier than most Frenchmen,' said Beazley.

'Yes, he's doing the same as us, waiting until we're close enough,' Carlisle replied.

Beazley bent to the compass and took a bearing of the Frenchman's mizzen.

'I fancy we're head-reaching on him, sir, just a touch.'

The disparity in speeds was greater than Carlisle had imagined. It was surprising; he'd expected they would be more evenly matched with the Frenchman so lightly burdened, even with *Dartmouth's* advantage of t'gallants.

'Then come a point more to starboard, if you please, and let's see whether he can resist a shot at our bow.'

That would close the distance faster, but it would mean exposing *Dartmouth's* bows to the Frenchman's full broadside.

Closer and closer. Now every detail of the French ship was clear. He saw the captain turn to another officer and give an emphatic order. The officer raised a whistle to his lips and blew a single blast. Before it had finished the Frenchman's broadside bellowed out. Carlisle heard the howling of chain shot as it swept through *Dartmouth's* rigging. He nodded appreciatively. That was exactly what his opponent should do, what he would have done in the same situation. The French captain was trying to disable *Dartmouth*, to cut away enough of his rigging and sails – perhaps even to bring down a mast – so that he could escape towards Toulon.

There was a tearing and ripping sound from aloft and the splinter nets bounced as blocks and halyards rained down from aloft. *Dartmouth* had been damaged, certainly, but a quick look showed that all the masts were still standing and all the sails still drawing.

'Hold your fire, Mister Gresham.'

Gresham nodded in agreement. He knew the value of that first broadside, and he could see that they weren't quite close enough yet.

Carlisle looked along the row of upper deck guns. The smoke from the enemy's first broadside was starting to drift down to them now, and already the details of his own ship were becoming obscured, but he could see that the men were still steady. The French officer in charge of those guns must have been very particular in seeing that they were all pointed as high as they could be to counteract the heel of the deck, and the result was that not a shot had swept *Dartmouth's* decks.

Carlisle noticed the bosun and his crew leaping up the mainmast to repair the damage. That would be an uncomfortable job with the French reloading for what would almost certainly be another broadside of chain shot. There was no protection aloft, and the men who would be knotting and splicing would be exposed to the full fury of the French eighteen pounders.

'Stand by Mister Gresham…'

Carlisle eyed the range carefully.

'Bring her two points to larboard, Mister Beazley, then keep her at this range.'

*Dartmouth's* bows swung quickly off the wind.

'Commence firing Mister Gresham.'

Gresham blew his whistle. At each of twenty-five guns spread across four decks, the gun captains shouted at their crews to stand clear then pressed the glowing slow match against the priming pan. The deep bellow of the twenty-four pounders on the lower deck was echoed by the sharper crack of the twelves on the upper deck. High up on the quarterdeck and fo'c'sle the six pounders spewed out their loads of grape against their opposite stations. Carlisle saw the great ship, now only thirty yards away, stagger under the impact. This was why he had waited; this was why the men had to endure the first broadside from the enemy. Every gun had been carefully pointed at the Frenchman's upper deck ports and the destruction was immense. A quarter of those guns would take no further part in the battle, and the crews of the remainder would be so shaken that their rate of fire would fall precipitously, and probably not one shot in ten would be properly aimed.

Carlisle knew that even his own crews could not repeat the destructive fire of that first broadside. The smoke, the heated guns, the shouted orders, the need for rapid reloading, all of these would relegate accuracy to nothing better than an afterthought. The officers could try their best to bring some order to the confusion, the midshipmen could harry and push, and the quarter gunners could run from gun to gun, shifting the aim and knocking at the quoins for elevation, but from now it would be a piecemeal affair. Each gun captain would fire as soon as his gun was loaded and run out, and even if he could see his target through the smoke, his aim would never achieve the perfection of that first broadside.

Gresham knew this as well as Carlisle. The only way to bring some order was to fire by divisions or by broadsides, waiting for all the guns to be loaded and ready. That meant that the rate of fire was reduced to that of the slowest gun, and even then, the accuracy would be lacking. No, better by far to accept that only one in four balls – one in four at the best – would be effective and trust in the rate of fire to carry the day.

Carlisle had nothing to do now. There were no orders to give, he just had to wait for the smashing effect of *Dartmouth's* fire to have its effect.

'The other ship's hauling her wind, sir. She's moving up to windward.'

Carlisle nodded at Midshipman Young. It was as he expected, the Frenchmen knew what they had to do, as unpalatable as it was. The second ship was leaving its leader to his fate and speeding ahead for Toulon. Well, there was nothing Carlisle could do to stop it.

The fire was continuous now as the best gun crews fired faster than the worst. The Frenchman's side was taking a battering and all along the upper deck gaps were starting to appear where two gunports were beaten into one. How long could they stand this sort of punishment? Carlisle looked aft at the French poop deck. There was the white of Bourbon France still streaming proudly from the ensign staff.

A splintering sound and a loud thud drew Carlisle's attention aloft. A chain shot must have parted the main t'gallant halyard and the yard had dropped down to the main topmast head. It wasn't shot through but still the starboard end of the yard swung in a drunken arc as *Dartmouth* moved to the westerly swell. That must be secured immediately because if it fell, no splinter net would stop it and it would create havoc among the gun crews below. He could see some of them looking nervously upwards. That would never do, he needed them to concentrate on loading and firing.

Carlisle turned to shout an order but the bosun was too quick, and already he was swarming up the ratlines followed by two of his mates.

With nothing more to do, Carlisle turned his attention back to the guns. There were casualties on his own deck now and he'd seen a few helped below, and at least two carried below by their mates. Probably the lower gun deck was unharmed as all the French guns were still aiming high at *Dartmouth's* rigging.

Another look at the Frenchman; it was only a matter of time now and already the second ship was surging past in its bid for Toulon.

'Sail ho!'

That was the bosun, perched at the main t'gallant head. He was pointing forrard, gesticulating wildly.

'Sail ho! It's a man-o'-war a point on the starboard bow, maybe five miles away!'

British or French? Carlisle desperately needed to know,

although a sinking feeling in his stomach foretold the worst.

'It's a third rate, sir,' shouted the bosun after a short pause. 'Could be that one we tangled with off Mahon.'

'Send a midshipman aloft, Mister Beazley. The bosun needs to secure that t'gallant yard.'

He looked quickly at Gresham. The first lieutenant had heard the bosun's hail but was ignoring it as though it had no bearing on his future. He was still directing his guns, still willing the Frenchman to strike.

In a gap in the smoke, Carlisle saw that the French captain had also seen the newcomer. That changed everything for him. There was no question of the British ship taking possession of his own in the twenty minutes that it would take for newcomer to reach them. Now the hunted could become the hunter.

Carlisle saw his opposite number giving rapid orders and he knew very well what they would be.

'Hard a-larboard, Quartermaster,' he shouted, bypassing the sailing master, 'put her before the wind.'

'Aye-aye sir, hard a-larboard it is.'

The quartermaster showed no surprise at this order. He'd spent a lifetime conning a ship at the whims of captains, lieutenants and sailing masters, and it was no concern of his that they were breaking off from what, until a few moments ago, had looked like a promising fight.

The last few chain shot howled overhead with unabated fury, then the French guns fell silent. The gun crews were being taken from their guns and given boarding axes, cutlasses and pikes, and the French ship's bows were swinging towards *Dartmouth* in a desperate attempt to grapple and board. That French captain knew his business. At any hazard he must pin his enemy in position until the larger ship came down upon them, and then the result could be foretold.

Through the smoke Carlisle saw the second Genoa ship following the first. They scented blood and were hunting as a pack now. If only *Dartmouth* could turn away fast enough and run away to the southeast. There was still a chance that he could escape.

Slowly, slowly, the bows swung away from the French ship. The smoke was clearing now that the guns had stopped – none of them would bear now, neither the French nor the British, and the long jib boom of the French sixty-four appeared as a great scythe, swinging towards *Dartmouth's* poop.

'Repel boarders!' Carlisle shouted. 'Mister Gresham, get the men onto the poop deck.'

He could see some daring Frenchmen crawling out on their own jib boom, ready to lash their ship to any part of *Dartmouth* that they should touch. It would be a close-run thing.

'Follow me, men,' Carlisle shouted as he leapt up the ladder onto the poop deck. He'd momentarily forgotten about the marines. In action the greater part of them were stationed on the poop deck, and that was where Kemp and Sergeant Wilson were now. While Wilson directed musket fire at the Frenchmen on the jib boom – he saw one man drop into the sea, his arms and legs windmilling as his doom rushed up to meet him – Kemp was waving his sword and shouting at a group of a dozen marines who were fixing bayonets and facing the menace that was fast approaching them.

Kemp appeared not to have seen him, and with another wave of his sword the childlike figure leapt upon the taffrail, grasping the ensign staff for support.

The jib boom swept closer. There was a man clinging to the luff of the jib as he balanced at the very end of the slender spar. Carlisle noticed the man's muscles, his intimidating physical presence. He held a grappling hook armed with a few fathoms of chain between the hook and the rope, and he swung it in his hand as he eyed the distance to *Dartmouth's* poop rail.

The danger was clear. If that grapnel could find a hold

on *Dartmouth's* poop deck, it would immediately be hauled taut and then the length of chain would prevent it being cut through. The two ships would be locked together and on the fo'c'sle there were another half dozen grapnels waiting to join the first. Carlisle rushed aft, pulling a pistol from his belt as he ran, but he knew he would be too late. As he rushed to the rail, Carlisle saw Kemp drop his sword, the loop slipping from his wrist as the valuable weapon fell into the sea. The marine officer pulled a pistol from his cross-belt where it had been held by a clip. He took hurried aim and fired. The grapnel wielding Frenchman's shirt blossomed red and with a despairing cry he fell from the jib boom to join his fellow in the deeps of the sea.

Kemp turned and shouted.

'Sergeant Wilson. Your men to the taffrail. Clear the enemy's fo'c'sle!'

\*\*\*

# CHAPTER FIFTEEN

## After The Battle

*Tuesday, Tenth of June 1760.*
*Dartmouth, at Sea. Villa-Franca northwest 10 leagues.*

'*Thank you, Mister Kemp.* That was all that I managed to say before I left him to it. By then the gap was opening and it was clear that we would live to fight another day. Perhaps it's wrong of me to say that I was astonished, but nothing in that young man's previous conduct had led me to believe him capable of an act such as that.'

Gresham chuckled deep in his throat. It was not often that his captain opened up to him in this manner, but it had been a trying day – to say the least – and now that the enemy ships had all disappeared over the western horizon, they could at last lower their guard and start attending to the damage.

'Well, I had no opinion of him at all, sir. He didn't mess with the sea officers and he lived entirely in poor James Towser's shadow. You know, you told me once that you believe that most men will surprise their peers when they are given responsibility. Well, so it seems with Mister Kemp. I have it in mind to invite him to join my mess, despite his rank, if you have no objections, sir.'

'Certainly, please do. I can think of no better way of marking such a heroic act. I hope that's one more of my concerns lifted, although I will still have to apply to Admiral Saunders for a new detachment commander when we meet the squadron.'

'Indeed, sir, he's far too inexperienced to command in a ship-of-the-line. I expect there are half a dozen better qualified men spread through the squadron, each just hoping for such an opportunity.'

Carlisle looked out of the stern windows at the setting sun. The ship was alive with the sound of hammering and every man who could splice a rope or sew a sail was busy making good the day's damage.

'It's taught me one lesson at least,' Carlisle said, still gazing astern, 'I should take more care of the marines in my ship. Had Kemp been the lowliest of the midshipman, or one of the volunteers even, I'd have known him ten times as well as I did. There's a tendency among captains to view the marines as a sort of tenant unit within the ship. I see now how wrong that is.'

Gresham nodded his agreement as he sipped Carlisle's Madeira.

'You and I both disregarded him, sir, I'm sorry to say. But do you know, Sergeant Wilson knew his worth. I spoke to him about Kemp two days ago and he said the boy would do well. He was right!'

There was a knock at the door and the unnaturally sombre face of Midshipman Young peered into the cabin. He removed his hat and took a hesitant step into the inner sanctum.

'Beg your pardon, sir... sir,' he said bowing first to Carlisle and then with an excruciating twist of his body, to the first lieutenant, 'Mister Wishart begs to inform you that the hands are mustered, and the bodies have been brought up.' He offered a black leather-bound book in quarto size. 'Mister Simmonds thought you may want to refresh your memory, sir.'

Carlisle noticed that the sounds of hammering had ceased. He took the book of common prayer from Young's hand.

'Thank you, Mister Young. Please inform Lieutenant Wishart that I will be on deck in five minutes.'

Young left the cabin, still wearing his funerary face, and Gresham made his excuses and left his captain alone.

Carlisle laid the book down. He had done this often enough to know the form of words and had no need to refresh his memory. Simmonds knew that very well; he was just tactfully offering his captain a few moments alone before such a solemn ceremony.

He thought of the men who had been killed, and the two or three whose wounds were such that they would inevitably follow their shipmates over the gunwale in the next day or so. Burials at sea always affected him, but somehow this time he felt a little easier in his mind. Gresham would never know how much he had helped his captain in those few minutes of conversation. Carlisle's wasn't a nature that allowed him to share intimacies with his officers, and it was only on the rarest occasion, after a hard fight for example, that he ever did so. It brought home to him how affected he was by the enforced solitude of the captain of a man-o'-war.

They buried their dead as the sun slanted swiftly towards the north-western horizon. Carlisle read the words of committal and the five shrouded figures slipped over the gunwale and disappeared into the deep Ligurian Sea. Only Carlisle knew how much he blamed himself for every death under his command. Only he knew how he tormented himself over his hubristic approach to a sea-fight. For want of a little more humility, five men whose mortal remains were drifting into the depths of the sea would be walking the deck now, swapping jests with their shipmates and looking forward to supper and a yarn.

\*\*\*

The wind had backed into the southwest and the clouds that had accompanied the earlier westerly breeze had dispersed with the setting of the sun. There would be no moon until late in the middle watch, and the starlight gave the scrubbed decks a spectral appearance, like the cover of a mother-of-pearl trinket box seen by candlelight. Carlisle was alone on the poop deck, walking backwards and forwards between the taffrail at one end and the poop deck rail at the other. He monitored the muted sounds of the watch on the quarterdeck with one part of his mind, and he sensed rather than saw the bosun and his crew still repairing the day's damage.

The new main t'gallant had been set up with a spare sail that had been produced like a rabbit out of a hat; spare t'gallants weren't normally carried but a good bosun ensured that the sailmaker made one before it was needed. Barring a few splices and a bit of cosmetic woodwork, his ship was ready for action again. There was no need to find a friendly port to refit, nor yet to flog all the way back to Gibraltar to surrender *Dartmouth* into the hands of the King's yard. Still, he was puzzled as to what to do next. His orders had been vague on the point of those two Genoa ships – deliberately vague, he suspected – and his meeting with Saunders before he detached from the squadron had led him to believe that little was expected of him. Should he now seek out Saunders and report his failure, or should he embark on the third part of his orders, the cruise along the Italian coast?

A muffled eight bells sounded. Enrico had stood the first watch and he must have ordered that humane practice, the wrapping of the bell's clapper in a piece of sailcloth. It emitted just enough sound to rouse the watch below from their hammocks without disturbing the idlers who had been working through the day to get the ship ready for whatever came next. The watch changed, a midshipman's head appeared above the poop deck ladder and immediately retreated. That would be at Enrico's orders, to ascertain whether his captain was still pacing the deck. A few more minutes passed and then Enrico himself appeared.

'I beg to report that the watch has changed, sir. The ship's steering sou'east, two points free under tops'ls, mizzen, jib and fore stays'l. The bilge is dry and the watch on the powder room has been relieved. There are no sails in sight, sir, and moonrise is at two o'clock. Mister Wishart has the middle watch.'

'Very good, Mister Angelini. I expect you are looking forward to your cot. Carry on if you please.'

'Aye-aye sir,' Enrico replied and replaced his hat. He had half turned for the ladder when his captain spoke again.

'Could you perhaps spare a few minutes to walk with me,

Mister Angelini?'

Enrico turned back and with a smile fell into step with Carlisle. For a few turns of the deck, Carlisle said nothing, he appeared to be marshalling his thoughts. They turned together at the taffrail, facing inwards as they did so, in the time-honoured, companionable way.

'Would you say. Mister Angelini, that we would be welcomed back in Villa-Franca or Nice, if I were to put in there tomorrow?'

They walked another two lengths of the deck as Enrico considered his reply. The starlight was so bright that the two men cast a discernible shadow on the pearly whiteness of the scrubbed planks.

'I think, sir… I think that you run the risk of embarrassing General Paterson, and by extension His Majesty King Charles Emmanuel,' Enrico replied carefully.

'Then we are *persona non grata* in Sardinia? That must place you in an interesting position.'

'Perhaps not, sir. It is all diplomatic manoeuvering. The minister of marine played a master stroke when he offered a lieutenant to the French as a counterpart to my secondment. You can be sure that without that, the French envoy would be making a noise about me being on board *Dartmouth*. As it stands, that argument has been nullified. I think we can discard my presence as a factor; it's more a question of how much information the French were able to lay before the general regarding the fate of that schooner, and how much of it he can shrug off as speculation. If there is incontrovertible evidence that the boats that left Villa Franca – the British boats – were on a premeditated mission to intercept the schooner, then the general will be forced to act when he sees you again. He may even find himself obliged to forcibly detain us.'

Carlisle hadn't told Enrico the full story of his last encounter with the general and the envoy, his lieutenant didn't know how close *Dartmouth* had come to being prevented from sailing from Villa-Franca two days before.

'He would take such a positive step? I'm surprised that the King would find such an action to be in his interests.'

Enrico paused again before answering. Carlisle had a moment of empathy with this young man. He'd spent the last few years in an extremely ambiguous position, as a foreign national of the wrong religion serving in a position of responsibility in a man-o'-war. All his colleagues were thirsting for promotion, yet he alone of them could never hope for a commission from King George. And he was also the captain's cousin by marriage. Now, by a stroke of the minister of marine's pen, he had been transformed into a lieutenant, but still serving in a foreign ship. Carlisle could only imagine how thin a line stood between appropriate and unwise friendship with his captain.

'Perhaps I'm being unfair, Mister Angelini. If you would rather not answer these questions, I'll think none the less of you.'

'Not at all, sir, I was just collecting my thoughts.'

A necessary untruth, but a lie, nevertheless.

'The King – *my* King that is – finds himself in a delicate position,' he paused as they turned again at the taffrail. 'Sardinia emerged from the last war on the winning side. Nevertheless, the peace left us with a great many unanswered questions, not only the question of our national identity, but also about the administration of the country. King Charles Emmanuel needs time: time to build a cohesive national identity, time to reform the army and create a modern navy, and time to institute the sort of reforms to the government that you in England take for granted.'

Carlisle let Enrico's slip pass; he didn't think of himself as English. British, perhaps but increasingly he found those national labels to be too constraining.

'He daren't cast his lot in with the British, because the French army is only a march away from his borders, and he's reluctant to side with the French because he fears what would happen in the next peace negotiations. In any case, he can't see how the French can win this war.'

Carlisle looked at Enrico quizzically.

'You heard all this during that brief visit?'

'Yes, sir, this is the common opinion in the country.'

'Then you used your time well.'

They walked on in silence.

'I have a choice to make, Mister Angelini. My orders allow me to take a cruise along the Italian coast, as far as Cape Circeo, to interrupt any French designs, particularly to disrupt any shipbuilding for the French navy. However, I had assumed that I would have time in Villa-Franca to gather information before the cruise. Having already had a brush with the French, there is an argument that says that I must abandon that part of my orders and seek out Admiral Saunders. In truth, there's little that I can say that will be of use to him. When he arrives off Toulon, he'll be able to see for himself that the two Genoese ships are already there. Still, that's my problem and you should turn in.'

'Perhaps I can be of more help, sir. If the cruise depends upon gathering intelligence before we start, then you could put me ashore in Genoa for a day or two. I have uncles and cousins there, of course.'

Carlisle's teeth flashed in the moonlight. The Angelini family connections were ubiquitous, and it came as no surprise to hear that there were branches of the family scattered all along the Ligurian shore, from Nice to Leghorn.

'Genoa of course favours the French, but they have not yet taken sides in this war, nor do I believe they will. I can walk the streets of Genoa in perfect freedom and if there's information to be had I'll have a good chance of gathering it.'

'Are you sure, Enrico? You'll be safe there?'

That was the first time that Carlisle had used his cousin's Christian name on the deck of his ship. To Enrico it demonstrated the filial concern that Carlisle kept so well hidden.

'I have no doubt of it, sir.'

'Then we'll take this fair wind to Genoa. We can spend tomorrow completing our repairs as we run down the coast.'

\*\*\*

Carlisle walked on through the middle watch, fourteen paces from rail to rail, ignoring his fatigue. At four bells a thin silver crescent of moon rose on the eastern horizon. Its light rather enhanced the starlight than outdid it, and now there was a point of reference on the larboard bow as its meagre glow cast a sparkling trail on the water.

Was he doing the right thing? His written orders certainly allowed him to head east, away from where he could find the rest of the squadron in a few days or a week's time. He glibly assumed that Admiral Saunders could see the Genoa ships for himself, and that was true if they were anchored in the outer road. But one of them was severely damaged, and the other had to be properly fitted out as a King's ship. Would they not be taken directly into the arsenal, in the inner road? In that case Saunders may never be aware of their presence. It was just that inability to see into the inner road that had motivated him to send Holbrooke in there at night, in a longboat, to see what war preparations the French were making. God, that was four years ago. Perhaps it was a sign of advancing years that the time seemed to pass so quickly.

Well, if Saunders objected, he'd deal with that problem when it came. For now, he had the prospect of an independent cruise along one of the most beautiful coasts in the world and if he didn't let his damned overconfidence get the better of him, it could be a profitable cruise. That would please Gresham, with his dreams of a cottage and a wife.

\*\*\*

# CHAPTER SIXTEEN

## Bitter-Sweet Memories

*Sunday, Fifteenth of June 1760.*
*Dartmouth, at Sea. Tyrrhenian Sea.*

'Pass the word for Mister Wishart,' Carlisle called down to the quarterdeck, 'and send Whittle up here, if you please.'

He reflected for a moment that it must be uncomfortable being the officer of the watch, with your captain an unseen presence on the deck above. At any moment he could lean over the poop deck rail and be a witness to any of the minor infringements of the standing orders. Enrico had the deck for the morning watch and Carlisle noticed that he had failed to move the pegs on the traverse board when seven bells was struck. It was nothing, really, and he'd remembered ten minutes later; Carlisle didn't choose to correct him.

'Good morning, sir,' said Wishart as he bounded up the last step of the ladder. He'd been on deck for the first watch, and Carlisle noticed that he'd shaved and probably had breakfast, so he'd had six or so uninterrupted hours in his cot. He looked fresh and rested, bursting with zeal and energy.

'Good morning, Mister Wishart. It's a fine day isn't it?'

The westerly breeze was on *Dartmouth's* starboard quarter, her best point of sailing, and it was pushing her along at eight knots, according to the last cast of the log. Summer had undeniably arrived in the Western Mediterranean and the sun was already hot.

'It is indeed, sir,' Wishart replied cautiously. This was a most odd conversation. What had he been called for? His captain didn't usually summon his lieutenants without some set purpose, and there was Whittle loitering at the mizzen bits, as though he'd also been called. That in itself wasn't so unusual; Whittle had grown up in Carlisle's hometown in

Virginia, and they occasionally spoke together. At least his captain was smiling, although there was something wistful in the turn of his mouth.

Carlisle turned slightly and pointed to windward where the mountains of Corsica broke the horizon and further south where the northern point of Sardinia could just be guessed at.

'A fine sight, sir,' Wishart ventured, thoroughly unsure of himself now.

'And yet it means nothing to you, Mister Wishart?'

'Begging your pardon, sir,' said Whittle, knuckling his forehead.

Carlisle motioned for the able seaman to stay quiet. He leaned over the poop rail.

'Eli,' he called to the quartermaster.

'Aye sir?'

'Do you remember this stretch of the ocean?'

'That I do, sir, this is where we fought that French frigate a few years back, in the old *Fury*.'

Carlisle turned back to Wishart with a wry smile on his face.

'Of course, sir,' Wishart replied looking abashed. 'It was just in this area, off the straits, but so much has happened since then…'

'That is just where we are, Mister Wishart, and we four are the only people on board who were there that day. You reported the warning signal from the barca-longa, Mister Wishart, and Whittle here identified the vessel as our old friend, *Vulcain*. Eli was quartermaster, as I recall, and yet he boarded the Frenchman with the rest of us.'

'That I did, sir,' Eli called up from the quarterdeck, 'though it weren't rightly my place to be waving a boarding pike around on the enemy's deck, not at my age!'

'I recall Mister Holbrooke's signal, sir,' said Wishart. 'We couldn't make out whether it was a black or a red flag – a merchantman or a frigate.'

'It was a dark cloth in the starboard leech of the fore

tops'l that gave her away,' added Whittle. 'I remember it right well; the rest of her sails were white as lilies.'

'It was a memorable day, for sure, a great day even, and one that we can be proud of. But let's not forget the fallen and perhaps we could spare a thought for Mister Keltie.'

Wishart flinched at that. His uncle had brought him to sea when his parents died and had looked after him like a father. He'd been shot by a French marksman in the very act of cutting away *Vulcain's* ensign. Wishart had tried to forget the moments that followed. How he'd grabbed the nearest seaman and together they had swarmed up the Frenchman's mizzen shrouds, intent on revenge. The hapless Frenchman had so very nearly reloaded when they burst onto the mizzen top. In desperation he'd swung his musket at the two figures, but Wishart, just sixteen and agile as a monkey, had ducked under the blow. The British seaman grabbed the musket's butt and pulled it towards him. Wishart had just time to haul out his hanger and thrust it forward, impaling his hated enemy. In their rage they'd hurled the still-breathing man into the sea, far below. It wasn't a pretty memory and Wishart wasn't particularly proud of his actions. However, the loss of the first lieutenant – his uncle – had led to a chain of promotions, and he'd been made master's mate. He always felt guilty at benefitting from his uncle's death, but he knew that the extra responsibility had prevented him falling into depression at the loss of the very last member of his family.

They stood for a moment in silence, watching the distant shore, and remembering.

'I wonder how Captain Holbrooke is enjoying his frigate,' said Wishart.

'And Mister Lynton,' Whittle added. 'He'll be in his little schooner, no doubt, somewhere in the American wilderness.'

'Well, wherever they are, I hope they have other things on their minds. Nathanial Whittle, if you'll drop in on Walker, he has a bottle of brandy for you and another for

Eli, with my compliments. I hope you'll share them with your mess, in honour of our passing this way.'

'Thankee, sir,' said Whittle, grinning.

He didn't like to point out that great quantities of illicit spirits had come aboard the ship in Villa-Franca, but then a bottle given freely by the captain would always taste better.

'Mister Wishart, I hope you will join me for dinner today.'

\*\*\*

Carlisle had enjoyed his dinner. He'd invited Gresham and Beazley to join him, and although they'd heard the story of the fight with *Vulcain* before, they'd never heard it from their captain. It was a dramatic tale, well told by two of the principles. *Dartmouth* had a holiday air about her. It was understood that the afternoon would be a make-and-mend, with no cleaning, no gun drills, no maintenance, and the men off-watch taking their ease and enjoying the Mediterranean weather.

*Dartmouth* was off the Bonifacio Straits for a good reason. The intelligence that Enrico had gleaned from his visit to Genoa had been discouraging; the only ships building for the French were the four sixty-fours, and two of them were in Toulon by now with the other two not ready for sea for a few weeks. Furthermore, trade from the west was drying up as news of *Dartmouth's* presence was passed around. From Toulon to Genoa and around to Leghorn, nothing was moving in French hulls and ancient vessels of the Italian states were being hastily caulked and launched to take up the slack. Carlisle was sure that for months to come any French merchantman would think twice before risking the Ligurian Sea.

But still, trade must go on. Normally, any traffic from France to Genoa and Leghorn – in fact, to any of the ports north of the Corsican Channel – would coast along past Nice. Trade to ports south of Elba would naturally come through the Bonifacio Straits. One way or another, olive oil, hides and corn from the Italian coast would be exchanged for manufactured goods – tools, furniture and clothes – from France. The Bonifacio Straits would be busy for the next few months.

The first lieutenant rubbed his hands in anticipation as he eagerly scanned the still-empty sea.

'We mustn't be over-zealous, Mister Gresham,' Carlisle warned, 'any French master with an eye to his own safety will be flying a flag from one of the neutral states. We'll need to be careful if we're not to be pursued by lawsuits for the next ten years.'

Gresham's expression could have been taken as agreement, or it could have expressed a qualified disagreement. If he couldn't see through a simple deception like that at his time of life, then he'd been a waste of a good naval education. Even he could tell the difference between French and Italian, although he spoke neither language. Still, the captain was right, and they mustn't detain a neutral ship. He knew of officers who were being hounded by lawyers long after they had retired from the sea.

'Mister Angelini could be invaluable, sir, he speaks the languages of this part of the world like a native, which I suppose he is.'

Carlisle had already considered that. Enrico wouldn't be fooled easily, and he could read a cargo manifest in whatever language it was written; a forgery would have to be exceptionally good to get past him. Nevertheless, he would be cautious about the situations that he sent Enrico into. His status on board *Dartmouth* was still subject to their Lordships' agreement, and the last thing he wanted was to raise any more diplomatic dust than he had already. If the chase was clearly a merchantman, then Enrico may well be the right officer for the job, but not if there was any doubt. He could always send a prize into Leghorn under a master's mate, if it proved to be French, and avoid any more entanglements with Sardinia or Genoa.

*Dartmouth* stood on towards the straights. With this wind he could just make it through without tacking and then they could run back to the east during the night.

\*\*\*

'Sail ho! Sail on the larboard bow.'

'Up you go, Mister Torrance,' said Beazley to the midshipman who was hopping excitedly beside him. 'And you can take the youngster with you,' he added gesturing at the tiny person – one of the ship's young gentlemen, not yet old enough to be rated midshipman – who was Torrance's perpetual shadow. 'Let me know what you see.'

Beazley looked again at the masthead pennant, then glanced at the compass. The wind – a lively breeze with the occasional veering gust that made him wonder about his t'gallants – had settled into the sou'-sou'west. Whatever the lookout had sighted would be hard pressed to turn back now. The straights were only four miles wide at their narrowest point, and *Dartmouth* would be upon them before they had made a single tack to the west.

*Dartmouth* sailed on unperturbed. Beazley knew that not one in ten vessels coming through the straits would be French, and everything else would be a neutral, but still…

'Deck there, she's a brig,' shouted Torrance after a minute or two. 'I can see some high land just beyond her, it looks like she's just to the north of it.'

A brig! Now that was an unusual vessel to find on the Italian coast. Brigs and snows – close cousins separated only by the arrangement for the luff of their mainsail – were much favoured by Atlantic seafarers, but here in the Mediterranean they were rare. The French used brigs, as did the British and all the other northern countries, but for the Italians they were almost unknown.

Carlisle had been watching from the poop. There was a definite danger in reacting too quickly to every sail, raising the expectations of the crew, interrupting their meals and their sleep. On this cruise they would sight many merchantmen, and he had to remember that in this part of the Mediterranean, all the coastal nations were neutral.

'Bear away and close her, Mister Beazley.'

Carlisle had been taking a stroll to clear his head after dinner. It had seemed disrespectful to stint on the wine, given the reason for his guests being there, and now he was regretting it. He'd let the sailing master handle this in the hope that a few more minutes in the fresh air would restore his wits.

A brig she was, of about a hundred and fifty tons and with a distinctly French look to her, whatever she tried to pretend by flying the flag of the Papal States. Enrico had spent a bare half hour on board before the yawl came racing back towards *Dartmouth*. The grins of the yawl's crew said it all and the answering smiles and calls from the ship's company said that they understood what was afoot.

'She's a Frenchman without a doubt,' said Enrico. '*Dauphin*, she's called.'

'That's a little pretentious, don't you think? For such a small vessel.'

Enrico smiled in reply; it was good to see Carlisle so relaxed.

'Her master knows it's all up and he's inclined to be helpful in the hope that we'll put him and his crew ashore. He has an exceedingly small interest in the vessel and none whatsoever in the cargo, and it's all insured. He sailed from Marseilles three days ago bound for Genoa, then southwards to half a dozen other ports, ending at Rome. He heard about *Dartmouth* when he was off the Hyeres Islands, and decided to take the straits rather than risk the direct route to Genoa.'

Carlisle grinned in satisfaction. It had been absurdly easy to guess how his presence off Nice would affect the traffic patterns.

'What's her cargo, Mister Angelini?'

'It's all crated and casked, sir, and consigned to merchants in each port. Furniture, clothes, cheeses, brandy, all properly documented on the manifest, and there's been no attempt at forgery that I could see. Then there's the curiosity: eight six-pounders on sea carriages, with sponges, rammers, worms and handspikes. They're consigned to a merchant with a French name in Cecina.'

'Cecina? I don't know it.'

'It's a small place, sir, in the Grand Duchy of Tuscany, about twenty miles south of Livorno… Leghorn that is.'

Carlisle smiled at that. Livorno had been called Leghorn by British seamen for so long that it had become the normal name; even the Admiralty referred to it as Leghorn. It was perhaps too much to ask Enrico to remember to use the British name for a place that was so familiar to him.

'Why would eight naval six-pounders be shipped to Cecina when France is embroiled in a war, I wonder?' Carlisle asked. 'What do you know about the place, Mister Angelini?'

'I've never been there, sir, but I know that it's a tiny port that has languished under the shadow of Leghorn. There's a river and a few wharves where it hasn't silted too badly. They build small vessels there, nothing more than twenty tons or so. I'd be surprised if they can build anything large enough to need those guns.'

'And the master has no idea what they are to be used for?'

'None that he's saying, sir, but I get the feeling he's holding something back, some information to trade for his freedom when he's pressed, perhaps.'

Carlisle thought for a moment. It could be nothing at all, but on the other hand…

'Ask Mister Beazley to step down here for a moment, would you?'

While he waited, Carlisle gazed out of the stern window. *Dartmouth* was lying-to with the brig under its lee. It looked like the wind was still in the sou'-sou'west giving them some shelter under the bulk of the island of Sardinia to windward.

'Ah, Mister Beazley. I have it in mind to row over to that brig. Are we safe to lie here for a while?'

'Safe as houses, sir. There're twenty-five leagues of sea under our lee before we fetch up on Elba, and we're sheltered by the islands the whole way. You can take all the time you like, sir.'

'Very well, then I'll take the yawl and Mister Angelini.'

\*\*\*

The brig's master was all nervous smiles and forced affability when he saw the captain of that great ship in the yawl's stern sheets. He handed Carlisle over the gunwale and ushered him down to the cabin.

'Well, Captain, you are a fair prize, I see. I can only hope for a speedy end to this war so that you can rejoin your family without too much delay.'

Carlisle's French wasn't perfect, but it was more than adequate to convey his meaning. The Frenchman's face fell; his earlier discussions with Enrico had given him hope that he and his crew would be released at one of the nearby ports.

Carlisle affected indifference to the man's distress. It was a heart-wrenching spectacle as he wrung his hands, started to say something then thought better of it. He looked at Enrico but found no help there.

'Surely, sir, surely something could be arranged. Parole perhaps…'

'You know as well as I do that no parole is binding on merchantmen once they are put ashore. You could all be serving in King's ships in a few weeks. No, I regret it, but I must detain you until we reach Gibraltar.' Carlisle ignored the Frenchman's disjointed pleading. 'Now, perhaps we can talk through this manifest.'

A sly look came over the master's face. Was this Englishman planning to appropriate some of his cargo, to spirit it away into his ship before a prize court could assess it? He licked his dry lips as he saw his chance.

'It's a valuable cargo, sir, I saw some of it before it was placed in its crates. Now, I could help you to select the choicest items…'

'If you please, Captain, and if I have your full co-operation, we may be able to find a way – on strictly humanitarian grounds – of easing the burden of captivity.'

He had the Frenchman's interest now. He was evidently convinced of Carlisle's larcenous intent, and he expounded on the intrinsic and aesthetic values of each item on the manifest. In time, they came to the cannons, about five lines from the end of the list. The master was inclined to pass over them without comment.

'Are these of no value?' Carlisle asked.

'Pah! They are just iron cannons for the little ships fitting out at Cecina. They have no value to a man such as yourself. Now, this escritoire here, that would grace a duke's drawing room.'

The Frenchman had warmed to his task and it took some determination to bring him back to the cannons. But gradually the story came out. There were three privateers fitting out at the old customs wharf in Cecina. The Frenchman knew it well, he had frequently brought stores for them. They were the property of a shipping company in Marseilles and sailed under a letter of marque from the French Minister of Marine. Gradually it started to dawn on the master that this was what really interested Carlisle, perhaps the real reason for him coming over in person. The floodgates were open now and Carlisle and Enrico could barely keep up with the volume of information. By the time they had finished, they knew the tonnages and armaments of the ships, the depth of water over the bar and at the wharves, and the precautions – none whatsoever, as they heard – that the privateers took against surprise.

'Is that all that you know?' Carlisle asked, looking severe, 'there is nothing that you are withholding?'

'Nothing, sir, I've told you everything.'

The man was thinking hard, for anything else he could add. Odd snippets of information came out at random.

'I carry beef and bread for the privateers sometimes, but only guns on this voyage. If I cannot get into the river – the bar you understand, it is dangerous sometimes – I go north to Vada, but I have to sail around the reef. Never to Livorno, it's too official and the privateers try to remain discreet.'

The Frenchman babbled on although Carlisle was barely listening to him now. He knew that he too often let his heart rule his head, but he felt a real repugnance at sentencing these innocent merchant sailors to months – more likely years – of incarceration. Enemy seamen were supposed to be sent back to England, to be consigned to the prison hulks until the war's end. But prisoners on board a ship-of-war were a damnable nuisance; they had to be fed and sheltered and eventually space must be found for them in a homeward bound ship. In the face of these inconveniences, commanders-in-chief generally didn't ask questions about the disposal of a French merchantman's crew when a fair prize had been taken. The Admiralty could fume as much as it liked and send letters to all and sundry about the need to starve the French navy of seamen, but in practice no action was ever taken against officers who took the practical and humane measure of releasing them.

'I can have my men bring up whatever you need from the hold, sir. And please, sir, please, I have a personal store of wines in my cabin, they are not part of the manifest…'

He still clung to the idea that Carlisle was intent on personal plunder. It was an idea much closer to his own way of thinking than worrying about the location of a handful of privateers.

'Oh, hold your tongue,' Carlisle snapped in exasperation. He'd made up his mind.

The Frenchman looked crestfallen as he contemplated the British hulks in Portsmouth Harbour. He'd spent eighteen months there in the last war and was appalled at the prospect of another indefinite spell.

'You may take your wine ashore with you.'

The Frenchman looked puzzled then his face brightened as he realised the meaning of those few words.

'Now, I'm sure you are aware of the need to keep our conversation between ourselves. There is the matter of treason that an unfeeling official in Toulon may raise…'

'Oh, oh, of course, sir,' the master replied, wringing his hands and smiling ingratiatingly.

'Then I think, if you give your parole for the voyage, you can be put ashore at whatever port that I send you to. Good day to you, sir.'

***

# CHAPTER SEVENTEEN

## Message in a Bottle

*Sunday, Fifteenth of June 1760.*
*Dartmouth, at Sea. Tyrrhenian Sea.*

Back in *Dartmouth's* great cabin, Carlisle studied the chart of the Italian coast. He wanted to be rid of the brig as swiftly as possible now that he had the prospect of action against the enemy. Sending a prize into a port where she had been expecting to land some of her cargo was always a sensitive matter, and the local magistrate's view of the law regarding prizes might be quite different to his.

'Is there anything consigned to Leghorn, Mister Angelini?'

'Leghorn? No, sir, after Genoa the next port of call for the brig was to be Cecina.'

'Very well, then Leghorn it will be. I'll need to send in an officer to deal with the consul, so it had better be Mister Wishart. Pass the word if you please.'

Wishart had been waiting on the quarterdeck in anticipation of a call, and he came into the cabin almost before the sentry had repeated the order.

'You're to take this brig – *Dauphin* – into Leghorn, Mister Wishart, you'll be there tomorrow evening if this wind holds. Perhaps you recall Mister Mann, the consul, from when we were last there? No? Well, I'll send a letter in with you.'

Of course, Wishart was nothing more than a midshipman four years ago, more concerned with where his next meal was coming from than the name of the British representative in the port that they happened to be visiting. A meal could fill his belly while a consul had no bearing at all on his comfort.

'The brig's crew have given their parole for the voyage and you can put them ashore as soon as you land. I don't anticipate any problems. They know that we'll be cruising offshore and our retribution will be swift if they misbehave; a petty officer and half a dozen men should be sufficient. We'll follow you but we'll stay well offshore. Take the yawl on deck, rigged for sailing. As soon as Miser Mann has signed for the brig, we'll meet at sea. If there are any questions about your destination you can discretely point out that the yawl is perfectly able to sail the length and breadth of the Tyrrhenian Sea, and you should hint that your rendezvous with *Dartmouth* is far away to the south. Now, Mister Angelini, what would be a suitable place to meet, away from prying eyes but within a short sail of Leghorn?'

Enrico leaned over the chart and without hesitation pointed at a small island that lay in the channel between Leghorn and Corsica.

'The island of Gorgona, sir. It was held by the Carthusian order in antiquity, but it's been abandoned for three hundred years.'

'Is there a landing place?'

'I believe so, sir, on the east side, and there's an old tower on the west coast. It's only about a mile across, but quite steep.'

'You won't mind a few hills, Mister Wishart. That will be our rendezvous. Hoist a jack on the tower when you arrive, and we'll look in every day until we see you. It's six leagues further offshore than the Meloria Shoal that you may remember we visited back in 'fifty-six, so don't go to the wrong place!'

\*\*\*

The decidedly westerly wind had a different feel to it now, and it brought a low, wet sky with nasty squalls. The brig was labouring under reefed tops'ls and *Dartmouth* had to spill her wind to avoid head-reaching on her prize. After the glorious weather of the past week, it came as a nasty reminder that the Mediterranean could never be taken for granted, not even at the height of summer.

'I think we'll retreat to my cabin, gentlemen,' Carlisle said. 'Bring the chart, would you, master?'

He led the way past the quartermaster and steersmen into his apartments at the aft end of the quarterdeck, shaking the drops of moisture from his coat.

'Coffee would revive us, I believe, Walker.'

Carlisle's servant, silent as always, edged out of the door to beg a pot of boiling water from the cook.

'Now, here's the conundrum,' he said when the first lieutenant and master had taken their seats. 'How do we persuade these privateers to leave Cecina?'

'Can't we go in and get 'em, sir, with the boats? It's a clear breach of Tuscany's neutrality to allow the enemy's ships to use their harbour as a base for operations.'

'Rather like we did when we took the schooner, Mister Gresham? I fear we've set ourselves at a moral disadvantage already; we need to be whiter than white for a while, to make amends. Anyway, my orders forbid me to do anything that could infringe on the rights of the Italian states. No, we must find a way of meeting them at sea.'

'Well, we have their brig. Perhaps that would tempt them to come out.'

'I've been considering that, but it's such a routine thing for him to run into the river, berth at one of the wharves and discharge his cargo, that they would be bound to be suspicious if the brig hung around outside.'

'Aye, it's a quite simple place to get into, except for the bar which is just four fathoms,' Beazley added.

There was a knock at the door. A bedraggled midshipman removed his hat, sending a cascade of drops onto the deck.

'Mister Angelini's compliments, sir,' he said. 'The wind's getting up and it's starting to rain. He'd like to take a reef in the tops'ls.'

Carlisle glanced at the sailing master who nodded in agreement.

'It'll need all hands, sir, I'll go on deck if you don't mind.'

'Very well, Mister Beazley. I'll send your coffee out to you. Leave the chart behind if you please.'

Carlisle and Gresham studied the chart. It had a small cut-out showing the port of Cecina. There was the bar, with some tiny pen marks that showed a depth of four fathoms, barely enough for light privateers or the brig if the wind kicked up a swell. And presumably that was the reef that the Frenchman was so desperate to tell him about. It thrust out three or four miles from the shore and would be an effective shelter for Cecina in any wind from north to west.

The door opened again, and a rather wet sailing master came in.

'Mister Angelini has it in hand, sir. He'll cut a rare fine figure in his own navy when he goes back there; he's quite the seaman, you know.'

Carlisle nodded. He was more concerned with how to tempt the privateers to leave their haven than he was with the abilities of his cousin, which he knew well without Beazley having to tell him.

'It'll get worse before it gets any better,' Beazley added. 'The wind's backing towards the sou'west again and you can bet it'll blow for a day or two, at least.'

'Well, I'm sure we'll survive, and the brig can get into Leghorn in almost any weather. They'll be safe as you like once they round-to behind the mole.'

'Aye, it's a good harbour. Not like this here Cecina. I wouldn't like to attempt to cross that bar for the next two days.'

They were all absently gazing at the line of soundings that stretched across the river. It was a seaman's interest; the bar was not unlike Salcombe's or any number of the other ports on the southwest coast of England. Many a ship's bottom had been ripped out trying to cross those bars when a swell was running.

Gradually Carlisle's interest in the bar became less academic. There was something there, something that was starting to form into an idea.

'Mister Beazley. Could that brig cross the bar in this weather?' he asked cautiously.

Beazley took out a magnifying glass and studied the soundings carefully.

'It's a good chart, Mister Angelini picked it up for me in Villa-Franca and those sounding are said to have been taken less than a year ago. Look, the sea shelves quite steeply from a hundred fathoms not five miles offshore.'

He straightened up from the chart.

'I wouldn't try it, sir. One touch on that bar and the brig would be finished. She draws nigh on three fathoms, there's four over the bar, and this wind will easily kick up a six-foot swell.'

Carlisle stared again at the chart. Cecina was a perilous place in a sou'westerly. It would be easy to become embayed between the coast that trended away to the south and the reef that thrust westwards into the Ligurian Sea. No merchant brig would dare to cross it under those conditions. What was it the French master had said? If he couldn't get into Cecina he sailed north to Vada. Ah, there! Just north of the reef and wonderfully sheltered on a day like today. And there was a road between the two ports! Three or four miles perhaps. He could guess what the arrangement would be. If the brig had to go to Vada, it would send a message around to Cecina and the cargo would be carted between the two ports. But the brig couldn't go to Vada; it wouldn't stand inspection for five minutes before it was discovered that its crew were all prisoners, and a British lieutenant was commanding. And in any case, that wouldn't bring out the privateers, not when there was a good road available.

'What would you do, say you were the captain of the privateer waiting for those guns, if the brig showed itself off the bar and then beat out to sea, around the reef?'

'I'd leave it a few hours then take my cart around to Vada,' Gresham replied, clearly puzzled, 'but I can't see how that would help us, the privateers still wouldn't come out.'

'I'd be worried,' said Beazley. 'Look how this reef lies.

The brig will have a hard beat to weather it, with a fair chance of not making it around. If I were waiting for those cannons before my next cruise, I'd be deeply concerned when the brig was lost to sight.'

'And if it didn't arrive at Vada, what then?'

'As soon as the weather abated, I'd put to sea to find her…'

'Exactly!' said Carlisle, thumping his fist on the table.

Gradually the light dawned on Beazley and Gresham, and they stared at their captain in wonder. Perhaps there was a way after all.

From nothing, in barely two minutes, the plan had formed in Carlisle's mind.

'The weather's too bad for boatwork, don't you think, Mister Gresham?'

'Aye, it is, sir.' He replied. 'If you're thinking of calling Mister Wishart here, then I'd say it's not worth the risk.'

'I agree. Then it'll be a heaving line and a bottle. Pass the word for the bosun and for Simmonds.'

***

The bosun took ten minutes to reach the cabin; he'd been high aloft securing the ship for the expected blow. By the time he arrived, wetter and more windblown than was strictly right for the captain's cabin, Carlisle was well into dictating the letter that was to be sent to Wishart.

'Good evening, Mister Hewlett. When this letter is ready it needs to be delivered to the brig. I have in mind to send it over on a heaving line. What do you think?'

Hewlett had served in *Dartmouth* for many years; he was one of the ship's standing officers and he'd stayed with her through her spell in ordinary, and through the previous captain's time. He was becoming used to Carlisle's ways, but even he wasn't expecting this.

'It's a right dirty old day out there, sir, and it'll be dark in an hour. I don't know…'

'Come, Mister Hewlett, a man of your abilities, I'm sure you can heave a line to leeward over thirty yards or so.'

'That I can, sir, but can you hold us so close to the brig?'

'Leave that to Mister Beazley, Bosun. Now, a heaving line you think?'

'With a belaying pin seized to the end…'

'Very well, I'll leave it to you, thank you.'

The bosun departed, shaking his head.

'Now, Mister Simmonds. Where were we? The brig is to show itself off Cecina for a short spell then beat out to sea again, taking care not to become embayed. Mister Wishart is to take the advice of the French master on the extent of the reef and he is to rendezvous with *Dartmouth* to the south of Gorgona. Make it quite clear that he is not to make for Leghorn until ordered.'

***

The wind had backed into the south by the time the letter was ready.

'Seal it into the bottle, Mister Simmonds. Use plenty of wax. Ah, Mister Hewlett, is all prepared?'

'It is, sir. I would just ask Mister Simmonds to push this note into the bottle along with your letter.'

'The note's for Mister Wishart?'

'It is, sir,' the bosun replied, clearly unwilling to disclose its content.

'And may I know what you have said to Mister Wishart?'

'It's nothing really, sir, just reminding him that the heaving line and the belaying pin are on my chit, and he's to remember not to leave them in the brig.'

Carlisle smiled at that. Even when a tricky piece of seamanship was being planned, the ship's warrant officers had to be careful to account for their stores. Hewlett knew very well that the navy board clerks would spot the missing items in a heartbeat and no vague talk of their being expended in the service of the country would prevent them deducting their value from his pay.

***

The wind was strong on the fo'c'sle, tugging at the men's shirts and blowing their hair to leeward in streamers.

Hewlett had passed a line around his middle and made it fast to the foremast bits.

'Do you want to make a signal to the brig, sir?' the first lieutenant asked.

'I think not, Mister Gresham. We only need the brig to hold its course, and there's no signal for that. If we try to explain our intentions with the flags that we have available, it will most likely confuse Lieutenant Wishart.'

Better by far, Carlisle thought, that he should see the great ship coming up on his windward quarter and deduce that he needed to stand on. Nevertheless, it was an interesting problem, to bring that vast two-decker to a point from where the heaving line could be thrown with some hope of it reaching the brig. Thirty yards, he had decided. It was a monumental distance but with the wind at the bosun's back it could be done.

'I've readied three lines, sir, just in case. There's a net seized to the inboard end of each so that the bottle can be quickly dropped in when we know they've caught the line. My mate's standing by with the bottle and a hank of marline.'

Carlisle examined one of the nets. It was a good job and done very quickly. A small net, just large enough to take the bottle, with a drawstring to pull the mouth closed. He thought through what would happen. When the line was caught, the bosun's mate would have just a few seconds to secure the bottle before the ships started drifting apart again. If the line should drop short, then it would be left to trail astern while the second heaving line was thrust into the bosun's hand. Carlisle looked at the bosun. He was a powerful man, not quite in his prime, but he certainly looked confident. His mate was equally well-muscled and perhaps ten years younger.

'Very well. Then we'll make the approach, Mister Hewlett.'

'Young Wishart knows something's up,' said Gresham, studying the brig through his telescope. 'He's been watching us this quarter hour.'

'Show him the line, Bosun.'

Hewlett held up the heaving line and Wishart raised his hat to show that he understood.

That would be a relief to Wishart, Carlisle thought. It must be disconcerting having *Dartmouth* so close on his windward quarter. Now, as long as he had the sense to stand on…

Carlisle walked steadily back to the poop deck; this was no time to be setting a bad example by running.

Beazley was standing on the poop where he could best feel the wind and watch the sea. He was spilling wind from the mainsail and foresail to keep station a cable on the brig's larboard quarter. Even then, with every gust, *Dartmouth* surged ahead. The reefed tops'ls were drawing well and it was clear that they alone could have held the fourth rate in station on the brig.

'How does she feel, Eli?'

The quartermaster was directly below Beazley. He nudged the steersman aside and felt the wheel in his hands.

'A mite of weather helm,' he replied after half a minute.

'That's as it should be,' Beazley muttered.

'Shake out the fores'l brails,' he shouted.

The foresail filled with a crash and *Dartmouth* gradually started to pick up speed.

'She's steering like a dream now,' said Eli, 'hardly griping at all.'

The distance between the ships was closing slowly. It looked like Wishart had spread all his available men along the windward rail to catch the heaving line wherever it fell.

Carlisle had considered handling the ship himself for this difficult manoeuvre, but now he could see that he'd made the right decision. Beazley was a better seaman than he would ever be. He looked competent and confident as he stood feet apart gently swaying with the ship's motion. He was hatless – a most remarkable occurrence – and a ship's boy lurked behind the mizzen clutching his tricorn.

Were they coming up too fast?

'Ease the foresheet,' Beazley called to the men in the waist.

There was an ugly rattling as the leach of the sail flapped unhappily, but Carlisle could feel the ship's speed easing.

Now *Dartmouth* was less than half a cable from the brig. The temptation to hurl orders at the master and the bosun was almost overpowering, but Carlisle knew that it would be counterproductive. He couldn't handle the ship better than Beazley and he certainly couldn't throw a weighted heaving line better than Hewlett. He gripped the poop rail and held his peace.

Fifty yards now, and it was becoming clear that *Dartmouth's* leeway would be the limiting factor. There would be time for only one try before *Dartmouth* would have to break off and make a fresh approach.

'Brail the foresail!'

Beazley's voice was cracking with the strain. *Dartmouth's* jib boom was thrusting as far as the brig's fo'c'sle now, but still Hewlett made no move.

'Stand by the tops'l sheets,' Beazley shouted.

Then Hewlett threw. It was a mighty heave that carried the tight coils in a high arc. The belaying pin actually reached the brig, striking the main chains before bouncing off into the sea.

'Let fly the fore tops'l,' Beazley shouted. 'Bring her two points to windward, Eli.'

Relieved of the pressure forrard, *Dartmouth's* bows started to swing away from the brig. At the same time, her speed noticeable dropped. Even so, it was a close-run thing as the vast two-decker sagged away to leeward, her jib boom barely missing the brig's backstays.

\*\*\*

Carlisle realised that he was gripping the poop rail with manic ferocity. He nodded to the master who brought the ship's head back to windward and started the process of clawing up on the brig's quarter again. He would need to be closer if this was to work. Again, *Dartmouth* crept up on the brig's larboard quarter, balancing the forward movement of the bigger ship against the prodigious leeway that it made when the wind was spilled. Closer and closer again. Carlisle resisted the temptation to go forrard to the fo'c'sle; the first lieutenant and the bosun were quite capable of choosing the right time to heave the line. He watched as the jib boom moved steadily past the brig's quarterdeck. Was the master taking it just a little closer? Probably, he decided.

The bosun gathered all his energy and threw. Again, the belaying pin carried the heaving line aloft. This time it didn't even reach the brig but fell cleanly into the sea a few yards short.

'I daren't go any closer, sir,' said Beazley, as he again brought *Dartmouth* up on the brig's quarter. 'One contrary gust of wind and we could lose our jib boom.'

'Take her in as before, Mister Beazley, I'm going forrard.'

The sailing master nodded, relieved to be able to handle the ship without his captain looking over his shoulder.

The atmosphere on the fo'c'sle was tense. The bosun looked dogged, defiantly swinging a new heaving line in his massive fist. The two wet lines lay the other side of the mast and a seaman was feverishly making up a fourth line from dry rope.

'Wouldn't the wet lines give you more weight, Mister Hewlett?' Carlisle asked.

Hewlett shook his head.

'It'll be in the wrong place, sir. I need all the weight forrard and the belaying pin's fine.'

Hewlett was breathing hard. The exertion and the mental pressure were clearly getting to him. He looked around as if seeking inspiration and his eyes lit upon his mate. No words were exchanged but the mate took the heaving line out of the bosun's hands. He hefted the belaying pin as though it were made of wood rather than solid iron and stared grimly at the brig.

Carlisle turned a questioning eye upon the first lieutenant, who nodded reassuringly.

The bosun's mate beckoned to two seamen and then he climbed up onto the gunwale, his legs pinioned by the men. He looked a spectacular sight with the last rays of the setting sun striking his muscular torso. Carlisle remembered that this bosun's mate hadn't been selected to wield the cat on any of the few occasions that it had been used. Every time the bosun had winked and said that he was being reserved until a serious criminal was brought to the grating. He could see why now.

*Dartmouth* was moving up again. The perspective from the fo'c'sle was quite different to that from the quarterdeck. The brig was horribly close, and the massive arrangement of *Dartmouth's* bowsprit and jib boom dwarfed the little vessel's slender masts and yards. Wishart waved from the quarterdeck. There were seamen in the most precarious positions, ready to catch the belaying pin; some lashed into the chains, some outboard of the gunwale, there was even a man on the end of the main yard. Wishart was leaving nothing to chance.

Carlisle felt that he could reach across and touch the brig, they were so close. Each time a wave hit the smaller vessel it rebounded onto the steep leeward sides of *Dartmouth* and sent a spout of water soaring into the air. He could see that everyone on the deck of the brig was soaked through. There was the French master, watching dispassionately from the waist; this was no business of his, and if the brig were to be damaged, well, he would be none the poorer.

Time stood still in a breathless pause as *Dartmouth* reached her optimum position. No orders were given, it was entirely the bosun's mate's decision when to throw. Carlisle realised that his heart was racing.

Then the giant of a man drew back his arm, caught his balance and heaved. This time the line shot out almost horizontally and the belaying pin nearly took off the head of the man waiting in the main chains. His mate on the deck behind caught it and took a quick turn around the pin rail.

Simmonds jumped forward clasping the precious bottle. He dropped it into the basket and the bosun made it fast with a quick hitch around the net's neck. Just in time, because Beazley could hold *Dartmouth* in position no longer and the basket was ripped out of the bosun's hands as they two ships moved apart.

Carlisle watched as the line was hauled in. He saw Wishart remove the cork from the bottle and read the letter. He read it a second time, then waved the French master towards him. They exchanged a few words, probably to clarify the position of the places that Carlisle had mentioned. Then, in the very last of the daylight, Wishart raised his arm in a gesture of understanding.

***

# CHAPTER EIGHTEEN

## A Lee Shore

*Monday, Sixteenth of June 1760.*
*Brig Dauphin, at Sea. Ligurian Sea.*

Wishart hadn't slept at all. It would have been difficult, irresponsible even, to rest with a scratch crew in an unfamiliar brig, outnumbered by Frenchmen. However, it wasn't the brig – he was quite capable of handling it – or the prisoners that kept Wishart awake; it was the sketch that the French master had made for him. *Dauphin*, despite her preposterously grand name, carried no real charts beside a large-scale ornamental map of the Western Mediterranean that hung from the cabin bulkhead. The master relied upon his knowledge of the ports that they planned to touch at, and if he was bound for somewhere unfamiliar, well, he would take a pilot.

The master knew Cecina well, and he knew the Vada Shoal, that nasty, vicious reef of compacted sand and old rocks that lay close under the surface. It guarded Cecina's northern approach and sheltered it from the mistral and tramontana, but it was the graveyard of many an unwary trader. Oh, in fine weather, he assured Wishart, he would sail across it with impunity, but in a *libeccio* like this, when the wind was set in the sou'west? Certainly not.

'You are surely not going into Cecina in this weather, Captain,' the Frenchman asked aghast. 'Why? Why? when Livorno is only six leagues up the coast?'

'I'm ordered to look into the place,' Wishart said, with as much lofty disdain for his captive as he could manage.

The Frenchman shook his head in horror.

'You see the way the Vada Shoal lies? It makes a natural gulf with Cecina as deeply embayed as can be. With the wind in this quarter, we will be lucky to escape with our lives.'

'The wind is backing, and I expect it to be nearly

southerly by dawn.'

'Perhaps, and perhaps not,' the master said, waving his arms to express his disquiet. 'And what if it should veer while you are running in? The bar at Cecina will rip the bottom out of us and there's nowhere else to go except across the rocks of the Vada Shoal. You may be lucky and hit upon one of the deep channels, but I couldn't guide you, not in this weather. Our lives will hang by a thread. I implore you, sir!'

There was much of the same for the next hour before Wishart sent the master down to join his fellows. He only endured it for the sake of the information, and he had to say that he had some sympathy with the Frenchman's point of view.

Wishart sat down and poured a glass of good French brandy while he studied the sketch. There was an odd, rhythmic graunching sound that happened each time the brig slid down a wave. It was difficult to isolate it, but it could be transmitted by the mainmast that ran through the forrard end of the cabin. He'd ask Rodgers to check it out.

It was easy to see why the brig wouldn't attempt to get up the Cecina river in a sou'westerly or southerly blow. It didn't take much intellect to see that the contours of the bottom would generate a steep swell that would break on the beaches all along this coast. The flow of the river would certainly bring down sediments that would be impeded by that swell, and over the years would build into a dangerous bar. Perhaps a local fisherman would know the deeper parts, but evidently his guide did not, and in any case they weren't bound for Cecina. He only had to get close enough to be certain that *Dauphin* would be seen and recognised. Probably the brig had been expected a day or so before, on the assumption that she had taken the direct route from Marseilles, north of Corsica.

Wishart stepped off the distances again. Three miles, that should do it, and it would keep him clear of those rocks that lay off the river's mouth. He shivered slightly as he looked at the Vada Shoal. A landsman may see the soundings and conclude that there was a good passage across the shoal for a brig such as this, something like two miles wide. But a seaman would know the danger. The swell that this libeccio was already raising would move the brig through a vertical range of two or three fathoms and rip her bottom out if she touched ground. He knew the danger, and Carlisle had given him the option to abandon the enterprise if it looked too dangerous, but that he would not do unless it looked utterly hopeless.

\*\*\*

The sun burst out from the Italian mountains and a new day dawned over this far corner of the Ligurian Sea. The wind had indeed shifted a little into the south and it revealed a sky that was scoured clean, polished to a shade of blue that no artist could hope to capture. Yet the wind was still strong, powerful enough to have reduced the little brig to its foresail and gaff driver, and even then, it was pressed over by each gust so that the sea churned into the scuppers and ran freely across the deck. For the wind was unpredictable, as the master had warned, and occasionally it blew hot from the south, as though it were the start of a sirocco.

*Dartmouth* had left them during the night, steering for the Corsica Channel while *Dauphin* skirted around Elba and headed nor'east-by-north for Cecina. He wouldn't see his ship again until this was over. *Dartmouth* would lurk offshore, far enough to be unseen by coastal watchers yet close enough to see a small privateer rounding the Vada Shoal. Meanwhile, *Dauphin*, her work done, would steer out sea to meet *Dartmouth*. Leghorn could wait.

'The master wants to speak to you, sir, I told him to go to the devil.'

Rogers was a good petty officer and he'd heard much of the conversation the previous evening. If Mister Wishart wanted to speak to the Frenchman, he'd ask. Until then he wasn't going to let him or any of the others on deck.

'Quite right, Rogers. Keep them away until this is over.'

'There's that grinding again, sir. It's the jaws of that gaff, I reckon. If we get some decent weather, I'll get up there and look at it.'

Wishart looked aloft. He could see that the gaff swung jerkily against the main mast. Well, this wasn't the time to be carrying out maintenance on a brig that would soon be the responsibility of the prize agent in Leghorn. He'd told Rogers the plan, and steady seaman that he was, Rogers just nodded and went on his way to make the brig ready for some fancy tacking – as he put it – in case the wind should shift.

Dawn revealed the land ahead; on his starboard bow and all along the coast he could see the surf breaking on the sand. If he looked over his starboard quarter, he could see Elba receding in the distance and over on the larboard quarter the peak of Capraia broke the horizon. None of this concerned him, his whole attention was on the brig's bow. He could guess where the Cecina river flowed into the sea, but fine on the larboard bow there was no doubt of what awaited him. There the sea broke on some unseen submerged feature, and even from six miles he could see it writhing in torment, the water leaping into the air in great spouts as though a first rate ship-of-the-line was cannonading the sea. That was the Vada Shoal in a southerly blow, and the French master had hardly exaggerated its terrible aspect.

'Bring her two points to starboard,' Wishart said to the man at the helm.

Rogers grunted his agreement. The brig was almost directly before the wind; it had been uncomfortable further out to sea but now that the swell was growing steeper, it carried a risk to the driver. This would put the wind on their starboard quarter.

Five miles, Wishart estimated. They only had to stand on two more miles and then he could safely assume that they would have been seen.

'Beg pardon, sir, but the wind's veering a touch.'

The steersman was finding it difficult as the wind chased their stern around to the sou'west.

Wishart looked up at the dog-vane on the backstay. He was right, the wind was veering, as the master had suggested it might. That was the most dangerous thing that could happen, and it was becoming clear that every yard that he moved further towards Cecina made it more likely that he wouldn't be able to weather the Vada Shoal. One more mile, then he'd veer the brig and claw his way to seaward.

He heard a hammering on the hatch. That would be the Frenchmen who could guess what was happening. If they struck, the French prisoners were dead men unless someone knocked out the battens on the hatch. Well, he'd worry about that if it happened.

Now the mouth of the Cecina River was in sight, and he could see the waves smashing on the bar. Beyond he could see some tall buildings that looked like masonry warehouses and he could just make out the masts of a few vessels in the river. Those must be the privateers, one of which was waiting anxiously for its cannons to be delivered.

'Stand by to veer!'

Wishart's voice carried the length of the brig and must have been heard by the prisoners because they stopped their banging to hear better.

'Up helm!'

The brig's stern swung through the wind, the gaff driver lurched across to the starboard side, and the job was done. Cecina was astern now and the open sea ahead, but the Vada Shoal was desperately close under their lee.

The prospect was truly daunting, and Wishart realised that in his eagerness to do his captain's bidding, he'd stood on too long. The brig was never a weatherly craft, and now with a point of reference he could see the extraordinary amount of leeway she was making. The seaward end of the Vada Shoal was marked by a shallow, rocky patch that was easily visible as the sea broke upon it. He could tell without the need to take compass bearings that they wouldn't weather it.

'We'll tack, Rogers,' he shouted, 'and make our way to the south.'

'Aye-aye sir,' Rogers replied, looking sceptical. They would only have a mile or two until the land would force them to tack again, and it was hardly likely that they'd make any ground to windward. That was the peril of becoming embayed, they were sentenced to tack and tack again, gradually being set deeper and deeper into the bay until the wind shifted or they were driven ashore.

'Down helm.'

The brig's bow started to move into the wind, then there was a loud crack from aloft and the jaws of the gaff split into two parts, letting the throat of the gaff dangle down towards the deck. The brig immediately started to pay off from the wind. The steersman fought her, and Rogers ran forrard to douse the jib, but it was too late, and in an instant they were driving hard before the wind, directly towards the Vada Shoal.

***

'She'll strike, sir!' Rodgers shouted.

'Get the tops'ls in,' Wishart replied, 'there's just time.'

Rodgers turned to give the orders, but it was no good. The men could see the end coming and none of them were keen to be aloft when the brig struck the ground. It wasn't that they refused the orders, they just looked every way but at the officer and the petty officer. They moved about the deck, finding bits of lashing for themselves, with sullen, dogged faces.

Wishart looked wildly about him. The broken water was close ahead now and it stretched far away on both bows.

'Then let everything fly,' he shouted in exasperation.

The men brightened at that. It was an order that they could obey without putting themselves in any greater danger than they were already. Off came the sheets and tacks and the tops'ls and fores'l flew horizontally from their yards.

The stays'l was hauled down and the jib sheets slipped. The useless driver came down, thankfully under control.

'Does she answer,'

'Aye sir, she answers,' said the steersman. 'Sluggish-like, but she answers.'

Wishart strained to find a gap in the white water ahead, but there was nothing to be seen.

'The prisoners, sir?' asked Rogers, standing beside the main hatch with a heavy belaying pin in his hand.

Wishart felt a wave of shame. He hadn't thought about the Frenchmen since the gaff jaws parted. They must be released!

'Let them out, Rogers, but before you do that get all the men aft in case there's any trouble.'

The seamen knew what was afoot and they could see the danger. They'd brought the Frenchmen to this pass and it was not unlikely that they'd try to take their revenge. There were more French than English in the brig; Wishart's men had weapons – cutlasses and pistols – but it was best to be prepared.

Rogers knocked out the wedges and the battens sprang free as the men pushed from below. The French captain was the first out of the hold and he took in the situation in an instant.

'Mother of God!' He exclaimed as he saw the brig's position. He looked up at the flying tops'ls and aft at the wrecked driver.

In a few strides the captain was on the quarterdeck and wrestling the tiller from the seaman. Rodgers was on him in an instant, his cutlass raised. The Frenchman covered his head with his arms but didn't back down. He looked towards Wishart, half pleading, half furious, and gestured off the larboard bow.

'You'll kill us all,' he shouted in French. 'You must steer more to the west, there's a deeper channel close to the rocks at the end of the shoal.'

Wishart looked but could see nothing different in the

direction that the Frenchman was pointing, just the same wall of white water that was now so close that it seemed to form a crescent around the doomed brig. Yet the man was obviously sincere, and Wishart had no better plan. He held up his hand to stop the petty officer striking down the French captain.

The Frenchman grabbed again at the tiller and pushed it hard to starboard. There was enough canvas still aloft, even though it was flying free from its sheets, for the brig to respond to the helm. Slowly, reluctantly the bows started to move to larboard.

Wishart moved close to the French captain.

'You are sure?' he asked, his sword in hand. He still didn't trust the man.

'It's our only chance,' the Frenchman said as he leaned hard on the tiller. 'The shoal runs right out from the shore, but there's a deeper channel just before the rocks at the western end. If I can find that we may perhaps yet save the brig.'

The wind had increased and was now firmly in the sou'west. The brig rolled horribly as the swell caught her quarter, and now she was starting to pitch and heave as she dropped into the troughs. They must be on the Vada Shoal already.

The French crew were all gathered in the waist and the fo'c'sle, held back by the prize crew with naked cutlasses.

'There!' one of them shouted, flinging out his hand about four points off the bow.

Wishart looked; at first, he saw nothing but the wild, white water and the monstrous steep swell. Then he saw it, a column of spray much taller than all the rest.

'Those are the rocks at the end of the shoal,' said the French captain, 'we must steer as close as we can, there's a five-fathom channel.'

Wishart stared hard, wanting desperately to see a gap in the leaping waves, but he still could see nothing. He resigned himself to the skills and knowledge of the Frenchman. The brig was making about five knots, he decided, an outrageous speed with no sails drawing, and if they struck the shoal – when they struck the shoal – the masts would certainly go by the board.

'Get everyone aft, Rodgers, the Frenchman and all.'

Rodgers could see the danger as well as Wishart could and he didn't fear any trouble from the French seamen, who all looked cold, wet and demoralised.

There was that column of spray again. It was much closer now, and it looked like it would pass two cables down their larboard side. The swell had become waves now, a sure sign that they were in shallow water. They were short, incredibly steep waves that sent showers of spray to leeward as their crests broke. The brig was bucking now, its bows riding high on each wave as its stern dug deep into the trough below. Then, as the wave passed on, the bow dropped liked a stone and the stern was flung skywards on the following wave. It was a scene from hell as the fragile brig drove hard towards its certain destruction.

'If we don't strike in the next five minutes, we'll be through,' the Frenchman shouted as he forced the tiller to starboard to counteract the tendency of the stern to seek the wind.

'What's he saying, sir?' Rogers asked, still clutching his cutlass and warily watching the Frenchmen now herded against the taffrail.

'He's trying to run through a deep passage. If he's found it, we'll be through in a few moments.'

Wishart could see the scepticism on Rogers' face, and he could see it echoed in the rest of his crew. And he could see why. There was no horizon to be seen and all about them was white water and viciously steep seas. The sky could only be guessed at in small flashes of blue through the flying spray. It didn't take a seaman to know that they were in dangerous shoal water.

And then they were through. With one monumental last plummet into the trough of a wave, which Wishart thought must surely end in the brig's bottom being stove in on the Vada Shoal, they were past the broken water and into the relative calm in its lee. The wind still howled, and the waves still crashed, and the little brig still pitched and rolled as though it was determined to send its masts overboard, but they were through!

The French captain looked drained. He handed the tiller back to the steersman and staggered to the lee rail where he vomited yesterday's supper into the white water.

Wishart looked astern. The sight was truly terrifying, and it seemed nothing short of miraculous that the brig had made it through. In a wide arc, there was nothing to see but ferocious waves and flying spume, but ahead and to larboard the horizon was now visible, and a pale sun was trying to reassert itself.

*** 

'We should anchor, sir,' the French captain said weakly as he clung to the lee rail.

The brig was still on a northerly course, still steering at the whim of the wind and waves, with no sails properly drawing and the wreckage of the gaff driver cluttering the quarterdeck.

'We should anchor here, in the lee of the Vada Shoal. We must repair the gaff otherwise she won't point to windward.'

Wishart looked around. There was one small vessel anchored a mile to the east, off the tiny port of Vada, and he could see that this anchorage would be safe so long as the wind didn't veer any further to the west or nor'west. His problem was that the brief letter from Carlisle didn't give enough information on his captain's plans to allow him to make a sensible decision now that the brig desperately needed repair. He'd carried out the first part of the orders at least. Anyone watching from Cecina would have seen the brig disappear into the maelstrom of the Vada Shoal and if he put his head seaward now, it was unlikely that anyone in Vada would see him. The natural conclusion would be that either the brig had been lost or it was anchoring under the lee of the shoal until the wind had moderated. What would the privateers in Cecina do? Wishart tried to imagine, wishing he'd been in *Dartmouth's* great cabin to hear Carlisle's plan.

First, someone would ride around to Vada – it was only three or four miles according to the French master – then, if the brig wasn't at the anchorage, they would send one of the privateers to search for it. In that case it was imperative that he get the brig out of sight of the land.

'Put her before the wind,' he said to the steersman, pointing out to sea. 'Rodgers, put the men below immediately, but leave the captain on deck.'

There was a howl of protest from the Frenchmen who didn't relish being under battened hatches with this insane Englishman in command of the brig. There was no knowing what danger he would find. But Rodgers had cut his teeth on moving unwilling bodies of men about a deck. The threat of his pistol and the flat of his cutlass, together with the rest of the prize crew crowding around him, persuaded the men to get below, where the hatch was again laid, and the battens wedged in.

'Let's get those tops'ls sheeted home,' Wishart shouted. 'We'll try the stays'l but hand the jib and stow it, and we may be able to point a little to windward.'

That was the problem. Now that the wind had veered into the sou'west again, it would be no simple matter to claw off this horrible Tuscan coast. Like the much smaller Cecina just six leagues to the south, Leghorn was protected from northerly winds by a shoal ground that stretched five or six miles out to sea. Wishart could visualise the chart that he'd studied in *Dartmouth's* great cabin before taking command of the prize, and he knew that without the gaff driver they'd never lie close enough to the wind to weather that shoal, not if the wind veered, and in any case, he shouldn't let the brig be seen from the shore.

'Can you lash the jaws of the gaff together, Rodgers, just

as a temporary fix?'

They both considered the broken gaff as it lay in ruin on the deck.

'I wouldn't like to answer for it if you were to veer the brig sharply, sir, not with all that pressure as the gaff swings over!'

'Then we'll tack, and tack only,' Wishart said, 'but sea room I must have, and Captain Carlisle expects us to stay out of sight now we've done our business. Get the men to work, Rodgers, it'll be a long day.'

***

# CHAPTER NINETEEN

## Wishart's Redemption

*Monday, Sixteenth of June 1760.*
*Dartmouth, at Sea. Gorgona Island, northwest by north, 4 leagues.*

'You are sure you were close enough to Cecina to be seen and recognised?'

'Oh, yes, sir. There's no question of that. If anyone at all was looking to seaward, they would have seen us.'

Wishart was nervous. He knew that he'd hazarded the brig in taking it so close into a lee shore. He'd re-read Carlisle's orders, and they were quite specific in their insistence that Wishart abandon the enterprise if it looked likely that *Dauphin* would become embayed; there was no room for equivocation. He knew that his desire to impress his captain had led him to put at peril the valuable prize and the lives of its crews, both English and French. If he hadn't confessed to the captain, the disordered and jury-rigged state of the brig would have given him away, and in any case his crew would certainly have talked about their hair-raising escape. He'd deemed it better by far to confess to his error of judgement, and now that was all over. He was just waiting for the inevitable reprimand.

'This Vada Shoal, could a privateer cross it?'

'In clear weather and a calm sea, yes, it could, but not in this.'

Both men glanced out of the stern windows where the libeccio was still blowing hard, turning the whole of the Tuscan coast into a dangerous lee shore, best avoided until the wind and sea had subsided.

'If he can cross the Cecina Bar, can he then cross the shoal?'

These were difficult questions, unfair even as Wishart had only glimpsed Cecina and had not gone close enough to get anything more than an impression of a furious sea beating on the bar. He thought for a moment before answering.

'The French master claims that the bar is passable before it's possible to navigate the shoal, but I'm not entirely sure he can be trusted. I believe he's guessed your plan and will lay a false trail if he can. He didn't tell me about the channel across the Vada Shoal until his own life was in danger.'

'I suppose it's only natural and what you or I would do under similar circumstances.'

Carlisle turned back to face Wishart.

'Well, I should send the prize in to Leghorn, it can do us no good now, but you must wait a day to let the wind drop a little. Once you're behind the mole you'll be safe, but it's no place to be relying on a broken gaff when you have but half a cable to round-to. You can stay in company until at least tomorrow.'

'Aye-aye sir.'

Wishart thought it best to say no more, to be out of the cabin and back to the brig as soon as possible. Perhaps he would get away scot-free after all.

'However, Mister Wishart, I must clearly state my disappointment in the way you handled the business.'

Here it comes. Wishart drew himself straight to receive the blast.

'But for the timely intervention of the French master – a man who had no obligation to help at all – you and the prize crew would be drowned or beaten to death on the rocks. That's a dozen valuable men that were nearly lost to the King's service. I was most particular in ordering you to withdraw if the weather wasn't suitable, I even pointed out the danger of a veering wind, yet you chose to ignore me.'

Wishart couldn't look Carlisle in the eye. He knew he was in the wrong and he knew that he'd let down the man who had brought him to his present position. With no family left in the world, Carlisle's good opinion meant everything to him. He felt his cheeks redden and hoped that he wouldn't betray himself with a tear.

'Well, as I said, I'm disappointed in you, but for now I have other concerns, not least how to bring our privateer to action when he has his home port under his lee, not forgetting the Vada Shoal where we cannot possibly follow. Now, stay under my lee until I signal you to depart for Leghorn, Mister Wishart.'

Wishart was dismissed without a smile. He walked stiffly towards the door, then paused, one foot on the threshold and the other still in the great cabin.

'Well, Mister Wishart? Would you like me to expand further upon my feelings regarding your recent action?'

'Oh no, sir, if you please, sir, but something has just come to me, a way of preventing the privateer escaping.'

'I do hope you don't intend to waste my time Mister Wishart…'

Carlisle bit his tongue. He'd made his point and he could see that his lieutenant had taken it all in, there was no point in wantonly destroying his confidence.

'…well, let's hear no more of that. Now tell me what's on your mind.'

***

The libeccio blew strong and steady for the rest of that day, while Wishart paced the tiny quarterdeck of *Dauphin*, chewing over the bitter ashes of his captain's words until they were etched into his memory. There was boldness, he knew, and then there was foolhardiness, and he had been left in no doubt as to which of the two had been the driving force that led him to the near loss of the brig. However, he'd been given a chance for redemption, or rather he had pleaded for the chance. When he had outlined his plan to Carlisle, he could tell for certain that his captain was inclined to relieve him of command of the *Dauphin*, probably shifting the first lieutenant into the brig. That would have been intolerable, and Wishart had decided to throw in his claim before Carlisle could make the fateful decision. He'd pleaded his now intimate knowledge of the brig, his hard-won familiarity with Cecina and the Vada Shoal, and finally, and most personally, his burning desire to redeem himself in his captain's eyes. It had worked, and here he was back in the brig with the French crew all transferred to *Dartmouth* and with thirty British seamen and twenty marines under his command. He looked aloft to where the gaff had been expertly repaired by *Dartmouth's* carpenter. It would grind no more as the ship worked in a seaway, and as Chips had said, it was good for another twenty years.

It was a long night for Wishart, but as dawn crept stealthily over the Tuscan mountains, the wind dropped and veered into the nor'west. The scene was set for the trap: *Dauphin* was to be the bait – aye, and the jaws – while *Dartmouth* was to be the keeper to administer the *coup-de-gras*.

\*\*\*

'It will be damned unpleasant in that hold,' said Kemp as he watched the dawn lighten the land, the sea and the sky to the northeast.

'Yet that's where you're bound, Mister Kemp. I can't have more than half a dozen men on the deck, and they all need to be seamen. Your coat would give you away at two miles.'

Kemp nodded. He knew all about Wishart's dreadful interview with Captain Carlisle – the whole ship knew – and he'd heard wild speculation that the lieutenant would be put ashore at the next port of call, perhaps after being keelhauled and tarred and feathered, but that was all just talk. Certainly, the lieutenant didn't seem like a man awaiting execution, and if the counter rumours were to be given any credence, he was the architect of this latest plan to annoy the enemy. He hoped that Wishart would survive this setback; he was one of the few officers who had noticed him before Towser's death, and he was still the one that he could speak to most easily.

'Well, I'll be able to see what's happening through the holes that Chips bored in the hold.'

'Yes, and remember; when the hatch is thrown off, you're to come out yelling like fiends!'

'Oh, we'll do that, sir, we'll do that.'

Kemp lovingly stroked his particular charge, his favourite weapon, for in the brig's waist, hidden between the boat and the foremast, sat a short, squat twelve-pound coehorn mortar, the least and ugliest of its unattractive tribe. Carlisle had begged it from the ordnance yard in Portsmouth, and Kemp and one of his corporals had spent a week at Woolwich arsenal learning how to use it. The gunner had looked upon it with deep scepticism and shook his head in a knowing way. Towser had hated it on sight; he was an infantryman first and foremost and distrusted any kind of artillery. It had been a point of contention between him and Kemp from the start of the commission, but Kemp secretly loved it. Carlisle had been close about his purpose in carrying the coehorn all the way from Portsmouth, but those who had served with him in his previous ship – the frigate *Medina* – told strange stories of using coehorns as a means of signalling at the siege of Louisbourg. And that was its purpose today. Kemp had only eight shells and eight charges. The shells were fused for three seconds so that at maximum elevation they would burst high in the air and the puff of smoke would be seen by *Dartmouth* out in the Corsica Channel. Wishart was not to order the coehorn's use until the trap had been sprung – it would otherwise mark the brig as something other than what she purported to be – and then a shell burst would indicate that it was time for *Dartmouth* to run down and seal the privateer's fate.

\*\*\*

Kemp gave the touchhole of the coehorn a last rub with his handkerchief and then disappeared down the main hatch. Wishart watched the hatch cover being laid and looked around the deck. No privateer would be able to guess that anything was amiss; his crew were dressed just like French seamen and he had stowed his uniform coat under the binnacle. There wasn't even any need to sail under false colours. No Marseilles brig would fly an unnecessary flag, not when she was well known along the coast and bunting so expensive with the Toulon fleet refitting and refreshing its flag lockers.

They were running down from the north with the wind on their starboard quarter, for all the world as though they'd been blown up the coast by the storm and were now taking advantage of this fair wind to make their way back to Cecina. Far away the western horizon was an unbroken line ruled between sea and sky, except that a keen observer would notice a solitary break in the line. That was the Corsica Channel and without a doubt that would be one of the first merchantmen to sail after the weather abated, probably southward-bound into the Tyrrhenian Sea. That would be the conclusion of any reasonable observer, but high on *Dauphin's* mainmast perched a lookout whose sole focus was that tiny mast that broke the horizon. From there, if the observer knew what he was looking for, it was possible to identify it as the main t'gallant mast of a man-o'-war, innocent of any yard or sail, and with the main and mizzen topmasts struck. And it had its own lookout, staring fixedly to the east. *Dartmouth* was twelve miles to the west, waiting for the coehorn's signal, and over to the east, running down close to the land under her lugsail, was the longboat, with Lieutenant Angelini commanding. The trap was set.

\*\*\*

# CHAPTER TWENTY

## The Trap Sprung

*Tuesday, Seventeenth of June 1760.*
*Brig Dauphin, at Sea. Off the Vada shoal.*

The Vada Shoal looked like a different stretch of water now that the wind had veered and subsided. It was only the rock at the western end that made it a hazard to navigation; the ridge of hard sand between it and the shore was covered by enough water for the coasting traffic to cross it with impunity. It looked blue, calm and safe, unlike the wild white maelstrom of the day before.

'Now Rodgers, just shave the tail of that blasted Vada Shoal as close as you like and keep a lookout to larboard.'

'Aye-aye sir, I'll give her a bit of wide berth, with your permission, because I don't quite like this rig,' he added gesturing aloft.

It hadn't been difficult to make the brig look like it needed assistance. The leach cloths of the tops'ls had parted company with their bolt ropes in yesterday's blow and with a few slack halyards she looked the picture of a vessel in distress. Rogers was right though, there was no saying what would part next and it was best to steer clear of those wicked rocks at the western end of the shoal.

There were so many things that could go wrong, Wishart thought, as *Dauphin* rolled its way past the Vada Shoal. The French privateers may be utterly disinterested in the fate of the brig and may at this moment be having a leisurely breakfast and wondering mildly why their cannons had not been delivered. They may not have seen the brig the previous day, they may not be ready for sea, or may not care to risk it without the eight guns that still lay snugly in *Dauphin's* hold. Then, if they did come out, they may grow suspicious. Perhaps they would see that pole on the horizon for what it was and retreat behind the bar. In any of those situations, the elaborate plan would come to nought. Carlisle would just shrug it off and *Dartmouth* would continue her cruise down the coast, looking for other ways to annoy the enemy; it wouldn't even be a footnote in the report that he would write to the admiral. But for Wishart, it would be an opportunity lost. It was his first chance to redeem himself after yesterday's fiasco, and he desperately wanted the plan to work.

'Do you see anything up against the land on the larboard bow,' he shouted up at the lookout.

It was a few seconds before he heard the reply as the lookout was quite properly concentrating his attention to seaward.

'Nothing on the bow sir. I can see the longboat on the larboard quarter.'

Wishart paced nervously. The brig would be visible from Cecina soon, and he didn't want that to happen. If the privateers could see them, they would have no need to venture out to sea. He'd put the brig before the wind in ten minutes.

Two more minutes. If nothing showed he'd have to tack, otherwise he'd be visible from Cecina. He glanced up at the lookout and could see that he was sweeping the whole horizon now, taking in *Dartmouth's* t'gallant mast, the longboat and the Cecina River estuary.

'Stand by tacks and sheets,' he shouted, 'ready about.' There was really no need to raise his voice on this tiny deck, but he did so out of a sense of what was right and proper.

'Helm a-lee.'

'Deck there. I see a sail close into the land on the larboard bow!'

'Helm amidships,' Wishart roared, stopping the manoeuvre before it had properly started.

'Rodgers, you have the deck, I'm going aloft.'

Wishart ran up the ratlines with ease; he scrambled around the maintop and shinned up the topmast. It really was quite precarious with two grown men up there, but the lookout gave him a bowline to support his knee and with one arm around the mast he was able to steady his telescope. At first it was difficult to see anything, there was a mist over the river estuary that hid the low land behind it. He rubbed the telescope's lens and looked again. Ah! There! Tops'ls, two of them. Then the privateer must have passed the bar and be already at sea, he'd certainly have had to be towed out of the river with this nor'westerly wind.

A glance over to starboard showed *Dartmouth's* t'gallant mast. He even fancied that he could see a figure clinging to the very top of the mast, but perhaps that was his imagination. The privateer was six miles further away from *Dartmouth* and would be lucky to see anything at all and it would take a very suspicious man to identify that tiny speck as a man-o'-war.

'You go down to the maintop now,' Wishart said to the lookout. 'I don't expect a French lookout would trouble himself to perch up here.'

The lookout grinned and slid down the t'gallant mast to a much more comfortable position on the solid floor of the maintop.

Wishart looked searchingly at the brig from this new perspective. Nothing must be allowed that would suggest that *Dauphin* was a prize and now the property of the officers and men of *Dartmouth*. The sails looked ragged, the coehorn was out of sight and the seamen on the deck were all wearing the distinctive French caps that they had appropriated from the erstwhile crew of the brig. Satisfied, he made his way back to the deck.

'Has he seen us yet, sir?' Rodgers asked.

'I'm sure he has, and now that he's over the bar I hope that he'll think it worth coming out to see whether we're going to make it to Cecina, or whether we'll founder on the way in.'

Rodgers chuckled; he was enjoying this role-playing.

'You can see the longboat from the deck now, sir,' he said with a jerk of his head to larboard.

Sure enough, there was the lugsail showing clear against the misty land. Enrico would be bringing it across the Vada Shoal to cut off the privateer's escape.

'Thaaar she blows!' cried Rodgers as a spout of water was flung skywards by the rocks a mile on their larboard bow.

Had Rodgers been a whaler before he'd come into *Dartmouth*? It was unlikely as whalers were well paid and had exemptions; they had no incentive to volunteer and couldn't be pressed. Wishart decided to ask at another time; he'd like to hear an account of a whaling expedition.

'The privateer's setting her stays'ls now, sir,' shouted the lookout. 'She's hard on the wind, steering to the sou'west.'

That meant little. Assuming they hadn't been seen from Vada, the last that anyone on shore knew of the brig was that she was running fast for the shoal ground and probable destruction. They would know about the deeper channel and hope that *Dauphin* had found it, but in either case she would be north of the shoal, and that was the direction that the privateer must start his search. The western end of the Vada Shoal was directly to windward of the privateer and it was natural that he would take a board to seaward before tacking to weather the shoal.

Wishart's greatest fear was that he'd misunderstood how usual it was for a small boat to cross the Vada Shoal. The longboat with her lug rig looked sufficiently like a local trading boat to escape notice; they had no need to look like a fisherman as they did off Cape Mele, where they had needed to loiter rather than sail purposefully in one direction. However, if the French master had lied to him, if the Vada Shoal was considered too dangerous even for a thirty-foot open boat, then the privateer's suspicions must surely be aroused. There were no other boats in sight, except far to the north where the early traffic would already have left Leghorn.

Wishart could see the privateer clearly now and he ordered the lookout down from the maintop. She was a brig also but designed for a vastly different purpose to the one that he temporarily commanded. Whereas *Dauphin* was built for cargo carrying, wide in the buttocks and deep in the keel, with conservatively proportioned masts and yards, the privateer was long and low in the water with tall masts raked aft. She looked every inch the predator and her black topsides picked out in white around the gunports added to the air of latent menace.

It was like watching the moves on a chess board, but from the perspective of one of the pieces, the bishop perhaps, while Enrico in the longboat was a knight and *Dartmouth* was the queen. Wishart swept his eyes from one piece to another, assessing their movement in relation to the land and the shoal, the pawns that blocked their free movement.

The longboat was moving fast now with the wind on her starboard quarter. She was less than a mile from the land and would soon be in the shoal water. Even now, a day after the blow, the swell still piled up on the Vada Shoal and the water was broken and confused. The longboat's bows lifted on each wave and crashed down into the trough. It would be uncomfortable for Enrico and his crew, but at least they didn't have to row.

'I reckon they've seen us now, sir,' said Rodgers. 'They're putting a short tack in.'

So they were. The privateer had come about long before the point that would allow her to weather the Vada Shoal. Her captain must have seen the brig and was expecting that she'd swing her stern through the wind once she was clear of the danger. Damn! That would never do, he must lure his prey further out to sea!

'Let the gaff fall, Rodgers, just like it did yesterday, then let it look as though we can't keep her stern off the wind. Run down as though you're going to strike on the shoal.'

'Aye-aye sir,' Rodgers replied grinning hugely and winking at the steersman. 'There's plenty of water to the south of those rocks, I reckon, but that privateer won't know that we're going to clear them, not from where he's looking. He'll have to come up to us.'

'That's right, we mustn't let him loiter in the bay, we've got to bring him out.'

Wishart couldn't have explained why he was so freely discussing his manoeuvres with Rodgers, but just then he needed someone to test his ideas against, and Rodgers seemed an intelligent and able man.

'There he goes, he's tacked again. He's trying to get to us before we're cast ashore.'

Wishart looked aloft. It really was a shocking sight with the tattered tops'ls, the mainsail not properly sheeted and the gaff hanging drunkenly from its peak halyard.

The longboat was at the heart of the shoal now and Enrico was heading a little more to starboard, to move into a position between the privateer and her haven. Did it look suspicious? Perhaps, but then the privateer's attention would surely be upon the stricken brig.

'Your coehorn is ready, Corporal?'

Wishart was answered with a muffled reply from under the tarpaulin that covered mortar, ammunition and corporal. He could see the faintest of smoke trails where the three lengths of slow match burned quietly in their individual tubs. There must be no delay once the trap was sprung, and a slow match failing at the last moment could mean that *Dartmouth* came too late; he thoroughly approved of two spares.

One more look to seaward. There were two sails visible now – apart from *Dartmouth's* bare t'gallant mast – and both were making their way south. There was no danger that the privateer would notice *Dartmouth's* mast now, and if it he did it would just appear like another innocent merchantman. As he looked, he saw a square of white blossom where *Dartmouth's* pole mast had been. Evidently Captain Carlisle had decided that there was enough traffic in the channel for him to blend in.

Wishart looked back again at the privateer. God, but she

had come up fast! In a few minutes they'd be able to make out individuals on the brig's deck. A quick glance showed that all was well.

'You can get that gaff down now, Rodgers.'

'Aye sir, that'll look realistic. That's what we should be doing now if we were who we claim to be.'

The chess pieces were converging fast now. The attacking knight was hemmed in by the pawns that made up the Vada Shoal and still didn't see the danger from the opposing knight or the queen.

'Tell Mister Kemp to stand by, Rodgers. We'll be alongside in five minutes.'

Rodgers lifted a corner of the main hatch and passed the message. Wishart was glad he was on deck rather than waiting below, not really knowing what was going on. Kemp would see little from his spyholes, despite his optimism. They were bored through two-inch timber and would naturally have a narrow field of view.

'Are you ready, Rodgers?'

'Ready, aye, ready,' Rodgers replied, still urging the men in their sham attempt to get the brig under control.

***

'She's heaving to, I reckon, sir.'

The Frenchman was shouting across the narrowing gap and sure enough her bows were coming into the wind and her jib and stays'l were flat aback. A few men were jumping down into a small jollyboat. Wishart could see that they weren't armed.

'Hoist the driver! Helm hard a-larboard! Haul aft those sheets!'

A dozen hands grasped their allotted ropes and in a moment the brig was transformed from a drifting wreck into a living, vibrant, animate vessel. The French officer in the boat stared in amazement as the brig bore down on him, riding the little boat aside on its bow wave.

Out of the corner of his eye, Wishart saw Rodgers grab the tiller and push the steersman away. That was in good hands, and he leaped for the main hatch and started to pull it aside with brute force. He had hardly moved it when it burst from his hands as a dozen shoulders pushing from below lifted it clean off the deck. Kemp led the marines onto the deck, screaming like madmen, and the sailors that had also been below followed them, adding their own voices to the cacophony.

'Fire the coehorn!' Wishart shouted.

He'd made sure that the mortar was aimed outboard to avoid removing the heads of his own sailors. It really didn't matter whether it was fired to starboard or larboard but as luck would have it the mortar was pointing right over the enemy's deck. There was a loud bang as the shell left the short barrel. There was no danger of it hitting the other vessel – that wasn't its purpose at all – but the sound of a shell passing overhead added to the surprise of the privateers. A glimpse – a glimpse only – of the shell exploding high in the air to seaward: that should bring *Dartmouth* down to them. About an hour and a half, that was how long they'd decided he would need to hold on. He must pin the privateer in place until *Dartmouth* could come down to them.

Thirty yards to go and another shattering crash as Kemp's marines delivered a volley at short range. Wishart saw men bowled over on the deck as others looked for shelter. The marines and the seamen of the boarding party were screaming across the fast-closing gap.

There had been one great unknown in the planning: how many men would the privateer have on board? A brig like that could easily take a hundred to sea, although the French master thought it was only eighty. Wishart and Enrico had only a few less men than that, but they had the definite advantage of surprise.

Crash! The brig's bows smashed into the privateer alongside her larboard waist and slid aft, destroying shroud lanyards, chain wales and port lids as it went.

'Boarders away!' Wishart shouted, but it was all in vain,

because Kemp was already on the enemy's deck and his marines and sailors were following him in an unstoppable wave of fighting fury.

Wishart hauled his jacket on – the mark of his command – and vaulted over the rail to follow them. He looked wildly around for someone to fight, but the decks were clear except for a few bodies, wounded or dead he didn't yet know, that lay groaning or rolled lifelessly in the scuppers.

The ensign! He should strike the ensign, but there was no ensign. Of course, the privateer wasn't expecting to fight and would be cautious about showing French colours when sailing from a neutral port.

He felt a jolt and heard another wild yell as the longboat smashed into the privateer's starboard side and Enrico led his men onto the deck. They looked around, confused to find that the fighting was all over.

Wishart's heart was racing. He fought to gain control of himself. Was it all over? It had been far too easy, but he could see Kemp and half a dozen marines stabbing at hands that thrust upwards from the hold as the main hatch was dragged into place. He seemed to be redundant. He looked quickly out to the west to see *Dartmouth* under full sail running down towards them. She was almost hull-up already, but it looked very much like she wasn't needed. Over the side he saw a quick commotion as two men jumped overboard and struck out towards the jolly boat that was already pulling for the shore. He saw a marine level his musket and was just in time to knock it up before the ball flew harmlessly into the air. The marine looked at him reproachfully, but he knew he'd done the right thing; the navy didn't make war on men in the water. The sea was their common foe and surviving its deadly embrace was quite difficult enough without being shot at.

'Beg pardon, sir,' said Rodgers, 'but I took this here sword off an officer before I booted him down the hatch. I reckon you should have it.'

\*\*\*

# CHAPTER TWENTY-ONE

## End of the Cruise

*Tuesday, Seventeenth of June 1760.*
*Dartmouth, at Sea. Off Leghorn.*

The sharp wind of two days before was but a distant memory as *Dartmouth* lay hove-to off Gorgona, barely moving as the tiny breeze from the west played upon her backed fore-tops'l. The water overside was of the deepest blue and even the most experienced topman had a touch of vertigo as he gazed down into its translucent depths.

Carlisle shed his coat with relief and mopped his face with his handkerchief as he walked into the great cabin, followed by the first lieutenant.

'Well, Mister Gresham, we won't be sending our prizes into Leghorn.'

Gresham nodded impassively. He had expected nothing else.

'It seems that an unreasonable number of the great and good of the city profited from the activities of the Cecina privateers, and the news of the loss of one of them has preceded us. Mister Mann was horrified when I suggested that we may send *Fraicheur* and *Dauphin* in to be condemned. He had already paid out of his own pocket – so he assured me – for a guard on his home and office. I can only agree with him; I felt the hostility from the moment that I set foot ashore, a hostility that certainly didn't exist the last time that I was in Leghorn.'

'Then I imagine it must be Gibraltar, sir,' Gresham said. 'I can't believe we'll be any more welcome anywhere else on this coast once the word is passed.'

'Well, perhaps, but I'm reluctant to send those two valuable ships the length of the Western Mediterranean without some sort of protection, not with all those privateersmen on board. Pass the word for Mister Beazley, if you please, and Mister Angelini. The mate can have the deck for half an hour.'

\*\*\*

The charts lay in a disordered heap on the cabin table, and Carlisle looked thoroughly dissatisfied. He jabbed his finger at Cape Circeo, the legal limit of their cruising ground and rounded on Enrico.

'Tell me again why I shouldn't send the prizes into any of the ports along this coast, Mister Angelini.'

Enrico stifled a sigh. He'd already told his captain half a dozen times, and his explanation wouldn't change this time.

'Genoa won't have us,' he said, sweeping his hand around the northern coast of the Ligurian Sea, 'not after we set about those French sixty-fours…'

'That much is plain,' Carlisle interrupted with heavy sarcasm, 'and in any case they seem to be almost a vassal state of France now.'

'Just so, sir,' said Enrico, 'and now Tuscany is outraged against us.'

'That, I believe, is a personal outrage against *Dartmouth*, against me. I don't imagine it is a policy as Genoa's seems to be.'

Enrico bowed. He had accompanied Carlisle on his call on the consul in Leghorn and had seen the mood for himself. However, Tuscany had much closer historical trading links with Britain than Genoa had, and it would take more than the capture of a French privateer to change the Duchy's foreign policy. In any case, they would strenuously deny having offered a safe haven to French corsairs. No, the citizens of Leghorn knew who to blame for their loss, but they wouldn't let that affect their favourable trading position.

'Lucca is neither here nor there; King George has no representative in Viareggio so we can't dispose of our prizes there,' Carlisle said thoughtfully. 'Now, the Papal States, what do you know of them?'

Enrico raised his hands, palm upwards, a gesture that

secretly infuriated Carlisle. In fairness, he couldn't expect Enrico to know the politics of the whole of the western Italian coast. Nice was a long way from the borders of the Papal States and he'd never travelled that far, and for the past three years, until a few days ago, he'd been cut off from the general gossip in his home city.

Carlisle looked stern. He was angry with himself for not learning more about this southern part of his cruising ground. In his defence, he'd had no access to any sources of information since he received his orders. He could have asked Mackenzie, if their relationship had been better, and he could have inquired in Turin, if his time there hadn't been cut short by the need to prevent his ship being detained in port. Nevertheless, he felt that he'd fallen below his own standards.

'Very well, then we'll work our way to the west in case the squadron is already off Toulon. If they are not there, then I'll consider whether to make for Gibraltar. In any case, it seems our cruise is over.'

Beazley and Gresham were unmoved by this news. It was the inevitable way that most successful cruises ended, when so many prizes had been taken that there were not enough men to make up the prize crews. It was a long way to Gibraltar; a long way with contrary winds at this time of year, and the two prize brigs would need substantial crews to man them and to guard the prisoners.

'The privateers must certainly go to Gibraltar, but the crew of the brig, they were almost promised their freedom and I'm reluctant to go back on my word. Where do you suggest we should land them, Mister Angelini?'

Enrico thought for a moment. With the whole coast against them, it was difficult to see where the Frenchmen could best be landed without creating greater ferment.

'I believe, sir, that Nice would be the best place. It's not a defended harbour like Villa-Franca and you can either anchor or lie-to while the prisoners are sent ashore in the longboat. It will also be the most convenient for them as the

French border is no great distance from the city, and they may not wish to trust their freedom to another sea passage with Admiral Saunders' squadron ranging the sea.'

Carlisle thought for a moment, watching the sparkling sea through the stern windows. If he couldn't pace the deck, then staring out of the wide sweep of windows in the great cabin was the next best way of stimulating his mind. Enrico was probably right; landing the Frenchmen anywhere along this coast risked a confrontation. While it would certainly be unwise for *Dartmouth* to pay a visit to the Kingdom of Sardinia until the diplomatic storm subsided, lying off Nice while a boat was sent in would hardly be likely to provoke a diplomatic incident.

***

# CHAPTER TWENTY-TWO

## Altered Loyalties

*Friday, Twentieth of June 1760.*
*Dartmouth, at Sea. Off Nice.*

Even the most beautiful Mediterranean summer weather can become burdensome when the wind comes light and fickle from dead on the ship's bow. *Dartmouth* spent three frustrating days beating across the Ligurian Sea towards Nice, looking for every fluke in the wind and tacking incessantly so that the watch below had no sooner swung into their hammocks than they were roused with the dreaded cry of *all hands on deck, all hands on deck to tack ship*. As if it wasn't bad enough working a great two-decker to windward in those conditions, *Dartmouth* had to keep the two prizes in company. The privateer wasn't so difficult because it was built for speed, but the fat tub of a merchant brig would hardly point to windward at all. Carlisle wondered whether it was all worthwhile just to land his prisoners in Nice, whether he shouldn't have put the Frenchmen ashore on Gorgona island with a cask of water and bid them go to the devil.

The last few miles were if anything more trying than the previous hundred as the wind was killed by the mountains, the south-western tail of the Alps that stretched in a great arc across the top of Italy, from Vienna to Nice. And there was no respite when they finally came close enough to send the boats inshore. Carlisle had chosen not to anchor as that gave an impression of a visit with all the formality that would entail, while lying-to would have meant a gradual drift to leeward, losing precious miles that had been hard won over the last three days. *Dartmouth* and her prizes were sentenced to beat backwards and forwards off the bay of Nice, while Enrico took the longboat and yawl inshore, loaded down with its cargo of weary Frenchmen.

The great cabin offered scant relief from the heat, but it was a better place to meet his officers than on deck, where a hundred sets of ears would be eager to hear what was afoot. Enrico was dressed in the new blue uniform that came with his rank of lieutenant in the Sardinian navy. His boots were gleaming, his hat was brushed, and his sword was hitched just so. He listened patiently to his captain.

'I've given the French captain some coins to keep them in food and lodgings until they should find a passage west. In exchange he has promised not to make a noise in Nice. Whether he will keep that promise is anyone's guess.'

Enrico shifted his sword self-consciously. Its attachment was quite different to the sabre that he had last used in the uniform of a cavalryman, while a midshipman in the British navy could wear any sidearm that he wished without any kind of formality, and he'd become used to that comfortable arrangement.

'I'll have to declare their landing, of course, but as we haven't been to any port to the south, I don't expect there to be any question of quarantine.'

'Indeed, I hope it will all pass without incident.'

Carlisle moped his face and shifted uncomfortably in his tight breeches.

'You should take the opportunity to speak to General Paterson, if he is in Nice,' Carlisle continued, 'and find out whether the disturbance that we caused has died down yet. And any news of the other two ships in Genoa, of course. You may find that the general chooses to ignore your presence, and that may be all to the good also.'

Carlisle had chosen Enrico to take the boats in exactly because he was an officer in the Sardinian navy. It was at least conceivable that a British officer would be detained upon some confected pretence. The general's standing in Nice wasn't what it was four years ago, and his status as a foreigner was coming under suspicion as Sardinia trod the narrow path between the two warring nations. He remembered that young captain who seemed to make a mental note – aye, and sometimes a written note – of every word that the general addressed to his British visitors.

'Don't let the men stray from the boats, Mister Angelini. Souter will be coxswain of the longboat so you shouldn't have any trouble.'

Carlisle had often noted how well the Sardinian aristocrat and the British seaman of no known family worked together. Visions of the Saint Lawrence river at Quebec passed through his mind, where Enrico and Souter made such a reliable team in the boats.

'I'll expect you back by the first dogwatch, but you may take all day, if your time is being used profitably. Keep a watch for my signals and send a boat out if it looks likely that you'll be delayed.'

'Aye-aye sir,' Enrico replied, and turned to leave.

'Oh, and don't take any nonsense from those Frenchmen, Mister Angelini. They've been well treated and should be grateful that they're not on their way to the hulks in Portsmouth Harbour. You may mention that to them, if necessary, and point out how likely we are to meet again unless they give up the sea for the plough.'

\*\*\*

After a few words with an official of the customs office and a hurried message sent to General Paterson, the Frenchmen departed without any fuss, trooping off to find a tavern that would take them while they sought a passage to Marseilles. The French captain was last heard explaining to his men that if they found the cheapest possible lodgings – the floor of a stable if necessary – they would have enough money to keep them in food and wine for at least a week. For his men that was the difference between misery and happiness, and they brightened considerably at the news. They even had a cheerful wave for their British captors.

'Did your man deliver my message?' Enrico asked the customs officer.

'He did, sir,' he replied bowing, 'and the general is sending a carriage for you.'

In Nice, a member of the Angelini family was to be treated with respect, regardless of what bizarre guise he came in. The officer blessed the moment he decided to hear Enrico out before pronouncing quarantine for him and his cargo of Frenchmen.

'Then the larger of my boats – the longboat – will return to my ship and the yawl will wait for me. Is it convenient if it lies here?'

'Oh yes, sir. I control this berth, for customs purposes, you see, and while the yawl is here your men may use the customs house, with my compliments.'

Enrico turned to find Souter. The coxswain had heard the conversation but understood nothing of the language. Enrico explained it to him, and in a few moments the boat crews had been re-organised so that the steadiest men stayed with Souter while the remainder set the lugsail for the easy run back to *Dartmouth*.

'Here's some coin, Souter. The customs officer will send out for some food and wine for the boat's crew. Just don't allow any man to become drunk.'

Enrico knew the British sailor well by now and knew how unlike his own countrymen they were when wine was freely available. A native of these parts would drink sufficient and no more, where every sailor he knew would drink hard and fast and given enough scope would soon become unconscious or fighting drunk. He'd told the officer how much wine to provide, a pint per man and no more.

\*\*\*

'There's your carriage, if I'm not mistaken, sir.'

That was the general's carriage, certainly, and it was being driven with elaborate care as though it already held an important passenger. The footman leaped down as the carriage drew to a halt and opened the door. A head emerged – a familiar head – and a beckoning hand. Mystified, Enrico climbed in.

The general gave the roof of the carriage a smart double tap with his cane.

'How pleasant to see you, lieutenant,' he said as they started moving.

'The pleasure is all mine, your Excellency,' Enrico replied politely but cautiously.

He squinted out of the carriage into the bright light outside. They weren't heading up the hill to the general's house, nor to his official quarters, but they were following the harbour wall eastwards, away from the town.

'I trust you don't mind, Enrico,' he said, with the familiar terms that he had used when Enrico was just an ensign in the cadet squadron of the cavalry, 'I find that I need to speak to you privately, and that cannot be done anywhere in this town. You must trust me, if you please.'

The carriage soon left the paved roads but kept close to the sea. Enrico knew this road well; it led around to Villa Franca. That would be hardly less public than Nice, so they couldn't be heading there.

After ten minutes the town was left behind and Mount Boron loomed above them on their left. The carriage swung off the main road and headed down a smaller track. Enrico remembered this path, it led to a rocky promontory overlooking the sea. It was an ideal place for a private discussion.

The carriage drew to a halt where a turning place had been flattened and spread with graded stones. The door opened and the general climbed down. Enrico noticed for the first time how old he had become. His stick was now a permanent prop whenever he stood or walked. The footman brought two folding campaign chairs and they sat together looking out onto the blue Mediterranean. Over to the left the scene was dominated by *Dartmouth*, her stern towards them as she moved slowly seawards. The two brigs followed close astern and there was the longboat, closing on the two-decker. She'd be alongside in ten minutes. Enrico felt a surge of pride as he gazed at the scene. If he had chosen to stay in Sardinia, none of his adventures would ever have happened. None of his old friends could boast the experience of war that he had, and the sight of two French prizes sailing obediently behind *Dartmouth*, like ducklings following their mother, proved it.

\*\*\*

'You know, I shall retire soon,' the general said thoughtfully when they had taken in the beautiful scene in front of them. 'As I told Captain Carlisle, I'll see this war through and do my best to help the King maintain his neutrality. I hope – I believe – that I have given loyal and valuable service to King Charles Emmanuel, and I intend to continue doing so.'

He stopped there as though lost for his next words. Enrico broke the silence.

'I hope that I will serve a foreign master as well as you have, sir. It's not always an easy or straight path, I find.'

'Indeed not,' the general replied, as though he'd been waiting for some confirmation of a shared perspective. 'It requires nuanced shades of conduct; it's not always black and white, but if you behave with integrity in the interests of your present master without prejudicing your heritage, you can't go far wrong. The problem occurs in other people's perceptions; they are too often shaped by their jealousies.'

Enrico nodded, wondering where the conversation was going.

'I find myself treading a more delicate path than I have for many years. Sardinia's neutrality stands on a knife-edge; the French are extremely active in Turin and the King is assailed from all quarters by advisers who whisper of the advantages of siding with them. Corsica is mentioned, Genoa and Tuscany, even, when they speak of the spoils to be divided at the peace. These men see the situation so locally; they point to the absence of the British from the Mediterranean, to the advances that the French have made in Germany, and the Empress in Silesia. His Majesty takes a wider view, and he can see the grand strategic picture. However powerful the French may look from the perspective of a small Mediterranean kingdom, he can see that the French empire beyond Europe is crumbling, and any gains that may be made in Germany will have to be exchanged for the sugar islands that provide the gold for its treasury.'

He paused again, staring out to sea at the beautiful two-decker.

'I can tell you this because you are a subject of King Charles Emmanuel: the offer of a lieutenant on secondment was made first to the French, and only to the British to maintain a semblance of even-handedness.'

Enrico wondered how to respond. He didn't yet know where this conversation would lead and was cautious about being too candid.

'I rather expected as much, sir,' he replied. 'The mood in Turin is very much in favour of the French.'

'It certainly is. That attempt to detain *Dartmouth* would never have been allowed to develop as far as it did if it were the British requesting a French ship be detained. It's understandable, of course. King Louis has it in his power to do great and immediate damage to the kingdom. You know the size of our army; if the French marched from Provence we'd lose Nice and Villa-Franca in a few days, and they'd be in Turin in a week.'

Enrico was aware of these sobering truths. Since leaving his home three years ago he'd seen much of the world, and he'd witnessed warfare in all its mechanical brutality. He carried a mental image of what would happen to the brave Sardinian army when it came up against the battle-hardened French infantry, and more particularly against the hugely experienced French generals. It would be all over in a few wild, glorious cavalry charges, and then his country would be wide open to the invader. That was the stick, but the carrot was territorial expansion. The kingdom was awkwardly shaped with its wealth concentrated in its mainland possessions but much of its territory on the island of Sardinia. Only the two fragile ports of Nice and Villa-

Franca gave the mainland access to the Mediterranean and the links with the island possessions. Acquisition of part of Genoa, the Finale coast, would transform the cohesion of the kingdom. That was what the French envoy was whispering into the ears of the King's ministers. It was no wonder that so many in Turin heeded the siren calls of their western neighbour.

'I see that you understand, Enrico. Now, I believe that Captain Carlisle recognizes the realities of the situation here in Sardinia is as well as you do.'

The general looked searchingly at Enrico.

'I believe he does, sir,' Enrico replied, 'and he understands your difficult position.'

'Difficult indeed, and I'm grateful that he didn't bring *Dartmouth* into Villa Franca, nor yet come to anchor off Nice. I wouldn't have detained him, of course, but I would be wantonly spending much of my political capital in resisting those who would say that I should. Perhaps you could find a way of relaying my thoughts on the matter to your captain?'

'I can certainly do that, although I don't think anything that you've said will come as a surprise to him.'

'No, perhaps not, and that will make it all the easier.'

The general gazed out to sea as they sat quietly together.

'You know, this is what I'll miss when I retire to cold and wet England – oh, I won't be settling back in Scotland, Bath is more likely, somewhere with at least the pretence of a mild climate, where I can recruit my health and extend my span on earth for a few more years.'

Enrico shivered involuntarily. He'd been in England in the winter and he could think of few places less likely to preserve the life of a man who had become used to a Mediterranean climate. Sure, Bath was warmer than Scotland, and it had a hugely attractive social and cultural life, but still…

'However,' the general said abruptly, cutting into Enrico's thoughts, 'that's not the principal reason that I've brought you to this place, away from wagging ears. It's a much more delicate issue, and I hardly know where to start, so forgive me if I leap in where even angels may fear to tread.'

Now what? Enrico wondered. What could be more delicate than discussion of loyalty to one's King and employer?

'It concerns your family; I regret to say.'

Enrico frowned. He'd been brought up to regard the Angelini family as something set apart, a special institution with a manifest destiny to be a power in the land. He wasn't accustomed to having outsiders refer to his family at all, and certainly not in a way that it appeared the general was about to attempt. He knew something wasn't quite right, of course. There were fewer servants and in Turin the viscountess didn't seem to be accorded quite the same degree of deferential treatment that he remembered from before. Nevertheless, for all the general's rank as the provisional governor, he was somewhat looked down upon by the senior Angelinis. He was tolerated in their society, but only for as long as he held his position from the King, and only for as long as he understood the wide chasm between his lineage and that of one of the oldest families in this part of the world. He was treading on dangerous ground.

'I understand, Enrico, why you may not want to hear this from me, but it's important that you're told, and I doubt whether anyone else will do you that service.'

Enrico nodded guardedly. He'd hear the general out, to a point.

'Your family's financial position is not what it was – you must have noticed – and there's been a certain amount of… restructuring, I think that's the best word. The country estates are being sold off quietly and the viscountess is consolidating what remains of her wealth in Nice and Turin.'

Enrico tried not to look shocked. Nobody had seen fit

to mention this to him. It must have been an organised silence, otherwise someone would have said something. He hadn't even heard of this from his old regiment which was normally a hotbed of gossip when it came to the dealings of the nobility. Of course, that could have been out of a certain sense of delicacy, but he thought not. Then this information was held close within his family and – it appeared – General Paterson.

'Now, that is no business of mine,' the general continued, 'but I've come to suspect that the viscountess has chosen a dangerous means of recovering the family fortunes.'

Paterson looked again at Enrico, perhaps trying to judge how the young man was taking this news and whether he should proceed. Enrico had a dogged, sullen look that didn't fit well on his usually cheerful face, but he nodded slightly and the general decided he could continue. Did Enrico know what was coming? Had he guessed?

'I have good, solid information that the viscountess has thrown her lot in with the French.'

Enrico turned sharply and stared at the general. He'd had three years away from the family, but all that breeding couldn't be denied, and the hauteur of his gaze made the general wonder whether he had gone too far.

'Your sources are reliable, General? For this is a profoundly serious allegation that the viscountess would resent most deeply.'

'Oh, I assure you of its accuracy. I am after all the governor of this province and there is little that's hidden from me…'

Enrico came close to smiling at that. If the general knew how much happened *sub rosa*, he'd be forced to re-evaluate where the real power in the kingdom lay.

'…It is however new information and I've only known for certain for the past week, although hints of the matter have been surfacing for some time. The viscountess,' Paterson was too much in awe to refer to Enrico's aunt as *she*, 'has become an advocate for an alliance with the French, one could almost say an agent. This may distress you, Enrico, given your formal secondment to the British navy, but the viscountess is actively advancing the French case. In fact, I have good cause to believe that the viscountess was the moving force behind the attempt to detain *Dartmouth* in Villa-Franca.'

Enrico's jaw dropped open. He'd been ready for almost any kind of revelation; a marital scandal, smuggling – which in any case was endemic all along the coast – corruption, but not this. The curious thing was that he didn't doubt the general; certainly not his honesty, nor his credibility; in that case there must be some truth in what he said.

'Then how…?'

'You wonder perhaps how the viscountess could act against the interests of both her nephew and her niece's husband?'

Enrico nodded, not trusting himself to speak.

'The viscountess is a great lady from a noble house and is childless as you well know. Now all that energy, all the hopes for the continuation of the lineage lie in the family name. The viscountess knows Chiara too well to imagine that she will ever leave Captain Carlisle and return to Sardinia. In fact, the viscountess dreads that happening because the dowry and the legal fees to marry her appropriately in Sardinia – she would of course require a *decree absolute* – would break the family's fragile finances. Chiara is lost to the family; the viscountess knows that and is not prepared to compromise her recovery plans by considering the impact on Captain Carlisle's career.'

So great an insight into the workings of the Angelini family! Enrico hadn't dreamed that anyone outside the family could so well understand its machinations.

'As for you my dear Enrico, as far as I can tell, the viscountess is gambling that you will be recalled when King Charles Emmanuel takes the French side in this war.'

'What does the viscountess hope to gain from this advocacy, General? I can only imagine the extent of the family's financial losses, but it doesn't seem likely that the French would pay enough to mend them; it would take an enormous sum of money.'

The general smiled grimly. It was hard to imagine the viscountess discussing an amount of money – a bribe it could almost be called – that would persuade her to act in secrecy within the kingdom's government. He knew that and most certainly so did Enrico.

'Can you not imagine? The King's reward for taking sides would be a portion of territory along the Finale, perhaps as far as Sanremo, Albenga or even Savona – a Ligurian Duchy, a tributary to the kingdom with all the access to the sea that His Majesty could desire. Great lordships would be displaced, and the viscountess would be in a position to acquire some of those estates. You think it's incredible? I can assure you that from the Angelini household it is seen as the only way to save the family's fortunes.'

Enrico didn't think it incredible at all. The look on his face that the general had taken for incredulity was actually shock, deep moral outrage that this could be perpetrated in the Angelini family name. He stared out to sea for a moment, seeing nothing through a mist of tears in his eyes.

'Why…why are you telling me this General?' he asked in a quiet voice.

'So that you can warn Captain Carlisle in any way that you see fit, and so that you can take whatever personal measures you deem necessary.'

The general had a faraway look in his eyes and he poked with his stick at a stone in front of him.

'I have no children, Enrico. In that respect I can sympathise with your aunt, so I am permitted to be jealous of the welfare of those who I regard as my proxy children. Captain Carlisle and you are my most treasured acquaintances. Oh, I have nephews and nieces – grand nephews and nieces for all I know – and a more useless, idle gaggle of geese you have never met. They don't bear comparison with you two naval people. I know I cannot see you often, but I can do whatever is in my power to preserve you both.'

Enrico stood and took a few paces on the hard ground. He turned back to the general.

'I thank you, sir, for these confidences. I see that I must take a position, and it may not be to the liking of my family.'

'Then I'll leave you with this prediction, Mister Angelini. If King Charles Emmanuel should take the French side in this war, it will end badly for him. His advisors see only this theatre, and the French ascendancy on land, but it's on the trade routes of the globe that this conflict will be decided. The world is changing and it's no longer about feudal power, it's the great mercantile nations that will inherit the earth, and for the present Britain is the principal of them. Even if Spain should join the conflict, it won't change the outcome and it will be one more nation to weep at the peace settlement. I will do my best to keep Sardinia out of it, but if I fail, I'll be out of office as fast as a horse can gallop from Turin to Nice. Take heed and decide where your loyalties lie; the interests of the kingdom and the interests of the Angelini family are no longer the same!'

***

They drove back to Nice in silence, the General bound for his home and Enrico bound for the Angelini house – his own home when all was said and done. He wondered how he should feel knowing what he now knew. One thing was certain; he would have to keep the information to himself. He had no real confidants in the family, and he was increasingly seen as an outsider. Well, that may be for the good.

The short, mute drive had achieved one thing. He was certain that he knew the general's source of information, quite certain indeed. It was the casually released admission that the general had only known for sure for about a week.

Yes, the timing was precise and there could be no other source. How interesting!

*\*\**

# CHAPTER TWENTY-THREE

## The Viscountess

*Friday, Twentieth of June 1760.*
*The Angelini House, Nice.*

The viscountess had expressed no surprise at Enrico arriving unannounced, just thirty minutes before the dinner hour, and her greeting was as warm as it always was. Enrico wondered whether the general had been correct, or whether in fact there was nothing in this story of the viscountess siding with the French.

They were dining alone on the terrace overlooking the sea. Perhaps it was the sight of *Dartmouth* and her two prizes tacking backwards and forwards, or perhaps the viscountess' head was still a-buzz with the hot-house atmosphere of the court, but she was more talkative than Enrico remembered, more decided in her opinions and less welcoming of dissenting views.

'Will you try some of the fish, Enrico? I don't eat meat at this time of day, I find that it lies heavily upon me for the rest of the afternoon.'

'If you please, ma'am,' Enrico replied.

Black Rod – even Enrico thought of him by his seagoing name now – was in attendance as he had always been before he had been sent to minister to Lady Chiara. Enrico wondered vaguely how the viscountess had managed without him for three years. He seemed to have resumed his old position effortlessly and looked as though he had never been away. He deftly picked up one of the soles between the silver fish serving pieces and placed it precisely in the centre of Enrico's plate.

'I regret that we haven't had much chance to speak since you returned, and my time is so taken up by the court that the family must fend for itself to some degree. Chiara sends me the news from Virginia. It appears that she is making a new home for herself there; they have bought a house I understand.'

Enrico swallowed a piece of the sole. It was particularly good, baked in a cream and lemon sauce with garlic and herbs and served cold. He thought ruefully of the food in *Dartmouth*. It was better now that he was a member of the wardroom mess, but it still had a long way to go to meet the standards of the Angelini house.

'It's an exceptionally fine house, ma'am, in the centre of the colonial capital and just a few yards from the governor's palace. I imagine that Cousin Chiara is a regular visitor there.'

The viscountess sniffed her disdain. Enrico imagined that she classified the governor of Virginia along with the governor of Nice, to be heeded as a temporary irritant in the knowledge that all things ignoble must pass, but not to be given any equivalence to a great family such as hers.

'And does Captain Carlisle have the means to support a household in the colonial capital? I'm surprised that a post-captain's pay can stretch that far.'

Enrico noticed the implied sneer on the word pay, and he was aware that he was probably the first Angelini in centuries to rely upon a vulgar salary for his living. That attitude seemed foreign to Enrico after three years at sea. With only a few exceptions, his messmates – the men that he knew and respected – relied upon their pay and prize money. Few sea officers had a private income and those that were so fortunate didn't stay long in the wardroom but were soon wafted up to be captains of ships. Of course, only three years ago he had shared the viscountess' perspective. When he looked back at his old life, he saw a different person, having only a passing resemblance to the Lieutenant Angelini who strode the decks of a ship-of-the-line.

'Captain Carlisle has been remarkably successful in this war, ma'am. His fortune is sufficient, I understand.'

'There is a plantation, I believe, that his father owns.'

'There is ma'am, but he has an older brother who will

inherit.'

He didn't add that Carlisle wanted nothing to do with that frightful plantation. He remembered his one visit there and the barely concealed hatred of his brother and his father. Things had changed since then, and the father had made his peace with his second son, but the brother was intransigent in his antipathy towards Carlisle, Chiara and the infant Joshua.

'I wish, I wish that she would come home,' the viscountess said.

Enrico was shocked. He had never seen his aunt display such a human reaction before. The viscountess appeared to take the same view - perhaps she thought of the expense, as the general had suggested — and quickly recovered her accustomed hauteur.

'And as for your future, Enrico, I understand you will be with Captain Carlisle for some time to come.'

'Yes ma'am, probably a few years, until the minister of marine has acquired a few men-o'-war. There's no place for me in the galleys and I'll be of much more use to the King with all this experience that I'm gaining.'

The viscountess took a sip of wine and sat silently for a few moments, as though she was marshalling her thoughts, or considering whether her next words were quite wise.

'You know, Enrico, that I could have you transferred to a French secondment. It would be more convenient in many ways and we could arrange for you to join a Toulon ship, then you would be always close to home rather than roaming the seas.'

Enrico froze with his fork hovering over his plate. It hadn't occurred to him that his aunt may interfere in his career, but that just showed how far he had become detached from the family. His aunt always interfered; he had just forgotten that fact. He'd also forgotten how easily she put people at a disadvantage. She had cultivated the art of veering the conversation into a new direction where she controlled the agenda.

'I…I'm perfectly content…'

'I feared that would be your reaction, Enrico,' she said, cutting off his sentence, 'so let's speak no more of it.'

She paused for a moment, then continued.

'I'll say no more of it, but there is one point that I must make, I feel it is my duty to the family.'

Enrico stared at his plate, wondering what was coming. The viscountess looked swiftly around to see that they were alone. Black Rod had withdrawn to the kitchen, perhaps sensing that the viscountess wanted privacy.

'The British are here and gone; they have no permanent presence in the middle sea since they lost Minorca, and in the autumn this Admiral Saunders will also be gone. The French navy, on the other hand, is just seventy miles away and will have an influence on this country long after this present war is over. Nobody can tell what countries, dukedoms and republics will fall at the peace, but if Sardinia is to profit, it will be from the French, not the British.'

The viscountess stopped abruptly, as though she had said too much. Enrico pretended that her words carried no particular significance and adopted his most dutiful expression as he waited for her to continue.

'Well, that's high politics and not for the likes of me.'

Enrico bit his lip at such a preposterous statement.

'However, a Sardinian sea officer with connections in Toulon will have the ear of the King, without a doubt. I cannot say that for one who only knows the British navy.'

The silence lay heavy upon the terrace. Out of the corner of his eye, Enrico saw Black Rod at the wine table. He hadn't been there a moment ago, how much had he heard? He was sure that the viscountess hadn't seen her head of household, so intensely had her gaze been focussed on her nephew.

Was this the general's source of information? The timing was right. Enrico again marvelled at how little he knew about Black Rod. He had always been an enigmatic figure and not only because nobody knew his name or where he had come from before he took service with the viscountess. That was long before Enrico was born, and before the memory of anyone who was prepared to hark back to those distant times.

'I see that you are determined. Then I wish you well. Now, I imagine you must get back to your ship. Captain Carlisle's impatience can be felt from here. Where are you bound now? Back to the Ligurian Sea, to Toulon or in search of your admiral?'

'I really don't know, ma'am,' Enrico replied with a straight face. 'Captain Carlisle hasn't yet informed me.'

*** 

Enrico lingered a while in the house, pretending to sort through a trunk of his clothes and some books that he hadn't thought about for three years. He knew very well that Carlisle was waiting anxiously for his return, but he felt that he had unfinished business. He made a show of disturbing the contents of the trunk. There was nothing there that he could possibly want, and it would all be an intolerable nuisance on board *Dartmouth*. There was a coat, a few pairs of breeches and some shirts that had no place in a sea officer's cabin. Six books, all from a different life, on subjects that seemed childish to him now. He had the feeling that he was walking away from his old life, and he hadn't felt at all like that three years ago when he took passage for England and Antigua. It was foolish, of course, because when the frigates were ready the minister of marine would send for him. He'd probably be made post-captain, and for all his aunt's dire predictions, he would be a man of consequence in the kingdom. Perhaps this house would one day be his; there was no other obvious inheritor after the viscountess.

The door creaked softly as it was pushed open from the corridor outside.

'You will be leaving soon, sir?'

Black Rod stood tall and straight-backed in the doorway, not fully entering the room and looking unsure of himself.

This was a day of surprises for Enrico. Never, in all the time that he had known the Angelini head of household – and that was all his life – had he ever seen the slightest hint of uneasiness in the man. It was one of the fixed points in his recollection: the tall, faintly mysterious man who, when Enrico had been a child, had always terrified him.

Enrico stuffed the few clothes and books back into the trunk.

'I'll dispose of those for you, sir,' Black Rod said without moving further into the room.

'I have to return to *Dartmouth* immediately,' Enrico replied. 'Captain Carlisle has been good enough to wait for me, but the ship must be away without delay.'

Black Rod looked swiftly over his shoulder, as though he was confirming that they weren't being overheard. In a flash of insight, Enrico realised that this was what happened to a household that was divided within itself – Matthew's gospel had something to say about it, he half remembered – a household where the mistress had her secrets, and the servants had theirs.

'Would you please give this letter to Captain Carlisle, with my compliments,' he said, offering a slim folded paper.

Enrico took it uncertainly, handling as though it may explode at any moment. He turned it over and saw that it was taped and sealed so that no prying eyes would see it before its intended recipient.

'It is important and for the captain's eyes only,' Black Rod continued with another cautious glance over his shoulder.

'Certainly,' Enrico replied, watching Black Rod's face carefully.

He thrust the envelope out of sight inside his uniform waistcoat, patting it down so that no bulge showed. That was the measure of the fall of the House of Angelini, he thought, it had come to the point where he had to assume that anyone seeing him with an unexplained envelope would suspect him of subterfuge.

'Then I wish you good fortune, sir,' Black Rod said, 'and if I may say, sir, you are making a wise choice.'

*A house divided against itself, cannot stand.* The biblical passage came to Enrico in a flash, and he turned away so that Black Rod could not see his face.

\*\*\*

Enrico noticed the first sign of the weather changing before the longboat reached *Dartmouth*. The few clouds that had been in the sky vanished towards the east and the visibility became so sharp that the peaks of the mountains behind Nice looked as though you could reach out and touch them. The wind veered abruptly into the nor'west and strengthened to a fine tops'l breeze and the air became distinctly cooler. Enrico knew what that meant. Nobody who had lived on that coast could possibly mistake the mistral, even in its rare summer appearance. Over to the west in Provence and far out to sea towards Minorca it would blow hard for a couple of days and people would stay indoors hugging their blankets around their shoulders and pulling their woollen caps over their ears. Here off Nice they caught only the edge of the wind and in midsummer it brought a welcome relief from the hot, humid weather.

\*\*\*

# CHAPTER TWENTY-FOUR

## The Mediterranean Squadron

*Sunday, Twenty-Second of June 1760.*
*Dartmouth, at Sea. Off Minorca.*

'Well, this is fine sailing, I must say. Now, if we didn't have that slug of a brig in company – begging your pardon, Mister Wishart – we'd be flying along.'

Wishart bowed, being the only response that his usually quick wit could find to his captain begging his pardon. It was true that he had become attached to the brig and the other officers ribbed him for it, but he hadn't realised that the captain had also spotted his preference.

Carlisle looked briefly at the two prizes – the privateer and the merchantman – that were sailing under their lee quarter. The privateer was under reduced sail like *Dartmouth*, while the merchantman had set every stitch that it possessed in an effort to keep station.

'I'm afraid we'll have to furl the fore t'gallant,' he said, 'otherwise we'll lose *Dauphin* before dinner.'

'Aye-aye sir,' Wishart replied and turned to give the orders. They had already furled the main and fore courses but even with only tops'ls and t'gallants, stays'ls and jib, *Dartmouth* kept creeping ahead. Still, with the lower sails furled, the officer of the watch had an excellent view of the sea ahead. Minorca had been in sight since dawn and now the Lair of Minorca where they had chased the French corvette and merchantman – was it only a month ago? – was in sight.

'Sail ho! Sail a point on the starboard bow! It looks like a t'gallant, sir, a man-o'-war.'

'The squadron for a guinea,' said Beazley.

'You won't have my money that easily,' Gresham replied. 'The French are all tucked up in Toulon, who else could it be?'

Beazley shrugged and reached for his telescope. This keen mistral, almost far enough aft to be on their quarter, would be right on the squadron's beam until they rounded the eastern tip of Minorca. The closing speed would be twelve knots at least, and he would get the first glimpse from the deck in less than ten minutes.

'Nevertheless, gentlemen,' Carlisle said, studying the compass, 'we haven't survived this long without being ready for the unexpected. It's an hour to the change of the watch, so we'll beat to quarters I think, Mister Gresham. The cooks may continue their business and the watch below can be dismissed to their breakfast as soon as you've reported.'

The drummer beat his urgent tattoo and the sleepy watch below poured up onto the deck. In just a few minutes the apparent chaos was over, and every gun was manned with the sea lashings cast off. Carlisle noted with approval that the midshipmen had checked each gun's equipment and the powder boys were poised below the hatch with the first of the deadly paper-wrapped cartridges in their wooden carrying-cases clutched to their chests.

Probably – almost certainly – Beazley was right. Only the Mediterranean Squadron could sensibly be sighted here and the reports from the masthead tended to confirm that. As the number of ships in sight grew and grew, it became a certainty; that was Admiral Saunders, just where they could have most expected to meet him.

The final confirmation came from Whittle who had been sent to join the lookout at the masthead.

'That's *Neptune* leading the line. She's flying blue at the fore, sir; a vice-admiral.'

*** 

The whole squadron was lying to the nor'westerly wind as Carlisle stood before Saunders in *Neptune's* great cabin. These three-decked second rates were true flagships, built to accommodate a senior admiral on an overseas station, and the cabin was immense. First rates almost never left home waters; they were the flagships of the channel fleet.

With their hundred guns and massive forty-two pounders on the lower deck, they were the hammers that would smash a hole in the enemy's line when an invasion of Britain was threatened. Thus, the second rates spent their time deployed to distant stations and Carlisle was quite familiar with *Neptune* having been aboard her often during last year's Quebec campaign.

'Then the Genoa ships got into Toulon,' Saunders said, a slight frown drawing his eyebrows down.

'Two of them, yes,' Carlisle admitted. 'The other two are still fitting out and aren't expected to sea for a few weeks at least.'

'And it was *Le Bourbon* that brought them in,' Saunders added, fingering Carlisle's report. 'She's one of their new seventy-fours. I'm not surprised that you found those three too much to handle, even though the sixty-fours were under-gunned. I'd dearly love to send one of those as a present to Lord Anson.'

Carlisle made no comment. Not the most demanding admiral in the world could fairly criticise him for failing to prevent three ships of their force from escaping. It was a minor miracle that *Dartmouth* had survived at all. Only one graduation of the rating system separated a seventy-four and a fifty-gun ship, but they were in no way comparable in force or in their ability to withstand blows.

'This business with the Sardinians makes me uneasy. That they should even have contemplated detaining you is a sign of the times. Mackenzie believes a show of force off Nice would be a timely reminder to them of the consequences if they were to be foolish enough to join the French cause. I believe I may cruise past there after I've looked into Toulon, although I don't plan to go ashore, not if the Toulon fleet shows any signs of stirring.'

'If I may say, sir, General Paterson finds himself in a delicate position. Showing your squadron off Nice may support his party in its attempt to keep the kingdom neutral but making a visit without diplomatic preparation may inflame things.'

Saunders looked up from the report. He knew that Carlisle had connections in Nice, but he had never taken him for a deep thinker.

'Just so, Captain, just so. Now, about these prizes. We met your schooner off Cartagena, and she's gone into Gibraltar. These other two must also go to Gibraltar but I'll take the privateer – *Fraicheur* is it? – into the service. My secretary and sailing master will go over there and survey her. They'll make a preliminary valuation, for your approval, of course.'

For Carlisle's approval! An eighth of the value of the privateer belonged to the admiral so it was hardly likely that his secretary would under-value it. This was the best of news because it circumvented the vice-admiralty court and brought the payment of the prize money forward by months if not years. Gresham's cottage in the country was coming closer.

'I'll give *Fraicheur* to one of my lieutenants and he'll escort the brig to Gibraltar. *Dauphin*! where do these merchants get such inflated opinions of themselves?'

Saunders shook his head in despair.

'Then he'll sail for home with dispatches. Lord Anson won't thank me for making commanders on station, so he'll stay a lieutenant for now. If you have any letters, then you'd better get them over here quickly because I want to be away to Toulon.'

Then his next fear had come to nothing. It would have been quite usual for Saunders to make Gresham an acting Master and Commander and send him away in command of the prize brig; in fact, it would have been a compliment to Carlisle. If it were any other lieutenant, he would have been disappointed, but Carlisle knew very well that Gresham didn't lust after command like most sea officers, and he didn't want to lose him. With Halsey gone and Enrico installed as third, he had as good a set of officers as he could desire, and he didn't want to disturb that comfortable arrangement.

Carlisle was satisfied with the meeting so far, but there was one issue that hung over his head like Damocles' sword. He'd been waiting for the storm to break ever since he'd had handed over Mackenzie's letters. He was sure that the vindictive envoy would have made a complaint against him and he'd rehearsed his defence over and over. Could it be that the man had relented? It was almost too much to hope.

'Your Sardinian lieutenant, Mister Angelini, may stay with you, it's an excellent idea. I've heard his name before, you know; General Wolfe thought highly of him, he told me so the night before the battle. If it wasn't for his religion, I'd have made him an acting lieutenant, in compliment to Wolfe, but of course, he could never take the oath. I'll send a letter to the minister of marine to regularise it when we're off Nice. He can replace your Lieutenant who's taken the schooner home.'

Saunders gave Carlisle an old-fashioned look. It was clear to the admiral that Halsey had been sent back with the schooner in the hope that he'd never be seen again in *Dartmouth*. He'd used those stratagems himself, to circumvent the Admiralty's inflexible system of allocating officers to ships.

'Lieutenant Angelini is a sort-of cousin of yours, is that correct?'

'By marriage, sir. He's my wife's cousin.'

Saunders nodded silently. Lady Chiara had been something of a celebrity in Jamaica, a titled Sardinian aristocrat with extraordinary beauty and grace. The whole navy knew about Carlisle's amazing luck.

'Now, I find myself in the extraordinary position of having a battle fleet that's adequate to my needs, so I can spare you again, Captain Carlisle. I'm concerned about those other two Genoa ships. I can't take my squadron into the Ligurian Sea, it's too far to leeward of Toulon, so I'm sending *Dartmouth*. I want you to patrol off Genoa for a month or so; I'll send a message when I want you back. You seem to understand the sensibilities of the people on that coast, so I'll leave it to you to decide whether to go ashore. Don't put yourself in a position where you can be detained, of course, but make it quite clear that those ships won't go to sea unopposed, and of course you may annoy the French trade whenever you get an opportunity. Take your place in the line for now and I'll detach you when we sight the Hyeres Islands.'

Carlisle breathed easily again; there had been no mention of Mackenzie's antipathy; not yet in any case. Perhaps the admiral hadn't yet read the envoy's letter. Or perhaps the envoy had relented.

***

It had been a harrowing first day, getting used to sailing in rigid line ahead when for the last month they had been enjoying an independent cruise. Now, at last, night was falling, and nobody would notice this smallest unit of the Mediterranean Squadron at the very rear of the line. If they surged ahead or lagged astern, sagged to leeward or luffed to windward, only the ship ahead would know, and its captain was junior to Carlisle. There was no danger from that quarter.

Carlisle smoothed out the letter from Black Rod. He'd read it a dozen times but was still unclear what he should do about it. He'd been trying to decide whether he should discuss it with Enrico, after all it concerned his family, but he was afraid of crossing some invisible line on Angelini family affairs. How much did Enrico know already? He'd reported the general's concern that King Charles Emmanuel was being unduly influenced by a French-leaning faction at his court, but he felt there was something that Enrico was holding back. Could they both have the same information from different sources?

'Pass the word for Lieutenant Angelini,' he shouted to the sentry, suddenly clear as to how he should proceed.

Enrico appeared very quickly, properly dressed, as though he had been waiting to be called. The bell on the fo'c'sle struck seven. Of course, Enrico had the middle watch and he'd probably been playing cards or reading before he went on deck.

'Take a seat, Mister Angelini,' he said, as he paced the cabin, trying not to show his discomfort. 'I haven't discussed with you the contents of the letter from your head of household, principally because I didn't want to put you in an invidious position. However, now that we're returning to the Ligurian Sea, I find that it is necessary.'

Enrico showed no sign of emotion, he just sat mutely, looking respectfully at his captain.

'Dammit, Enrico. Just read the blasted letter,' he said in frustration, pushing it across the desk towards his cousin. He continued pacing, looking like the caged lion that he'd seen at the Tower of London, he imagined.

Enrico read the letter through twice then put it back on the table, still without any sign of emotion. Ten seconds; it was Carlisle whose nerve broke first.

'Well?' he demanded.

What Carlisle didn't know was that Enrico had accurately guessed the content of the letter and was prepared for this meeting, he'd been prepared since they left Nice more than two days before, but he had also been undecided. On the one hand, Carlisle was only loosely a member of the family and not entitled to the inner secrets. On the other hand, he was Enrico's commanding officer and it now appeared that the doings of the viscountess had a bearing on *Dartmouth's* mission.

'This letter confirms what I heard from General Paterson, in a private aside, that the viscountess is actively working towards bringing the kingdom into an alliance with the French.'

Carlisle considered pointing out that Enrico should have told him that earlier, but then his newest lieutenant would have assumed that the letter from Black Rod told him everything. Among the Angelini family, he had come to realise, there was a sense of their uniqueness, their distance from the motivations that guided the rest of humanity. He also had to consider that Enrico was now a commissioned officer in a foreign service. Yes, he was Carlisle's third lieutenant, but he couldn't be treated the same as he treated Wishart. It would do no good and possibly some harm to press the point.

'What intrigues me, Mister Angelini, is that Black Rod should be sending this information to me. I thought his loyalty to the viscountess was absolute.'

'So did I, sir, but in the three years that we have been away from Nice, he seems to have transferred his allegiance to Chiara. I've been thinking about this, piecing together incidents and scraps of conversation, and I'm beginning to believe that Black Rod's loyalty has always been to Chiara first and to the viscountess and the wider family second. I never knew my uncle, but from what I have been told he was the sort of man who would make provision for his daughter's welfare. I believe that he left some instructions with Black Rod; he was my uncle's manservant before he became the head of the household, you know. It's only now that the viscountess has taken the French side, and when Lady Chiara is becoming so decidedly English, that his loyalty is being tested.'

Enrico had never been so candid about his family's affairs. Perhaps it was his commission and his new position of responsibility in *Dartmouth* that had made the change. Carlisle's mind was whirling as he pieced together clues from the incidents of 'fifty-six.

'Then some of the questions that I had long ago despaired of, may yet be answered,' Carlisle said. 'I have always wondered how Chiara's godfather knew about her movements. After all, it must have been dangerous for a Tunisian merchant to ask questions about so powerful a family. If Chiara's father could make such a strange choice of godfather, then he sounds just like the sort of man who would leave his daughter's care as a secret bequest to his manservant.'

Enrico looked disturbed for the first time since he had entered the cabin.

'Then Black Rod had been in contact with Ben Yunis right up to 'fifty-six?'

'That's my belief,' Carlisle replied. 'He's been carrying out his dead master's wishes all this time, and now he's found that he cannot do that and serve the Angelini family in the way that he did before. I pity him, he has a dark and difficult road to follow.'

They sat quietly, each lost in his own thoughts. Carlisle had never wanted to get involved with the Angelini family intrigues, but he felt as though he couldn't stand on the sidelines any longer. Probably Chiara would never again be a real part of that family, but she still had ties of blood to Sardinia, and possibly a legacy when the viscountess should pass away.

'There is one thing that I don't understand,' Carlisle said and looked strangely at Enrico. 'Why on earth would the viscountess favour the French?'

'Ah, now that I can answer,' said Enrico. 'First, you should know that she is deep in debt.'

Carlisle looked shocked. Nothing about the viscountess hinted at poverty.

'Family estates have been sold to keep the core holdings in Nice and Turin afloat. From where she sits, the French look the most likely to be the power brokers all along this coast, and she has an arrangement to step into the lands to the east. The French whisper of toppling Genoa, Tuscany and Lucca, and the opportunities could be immense. It is a simple matter of assessing where she sees the greatest advantage to the Angelini family, and she's chosen the French. I believe she's discounted Chiara and I from the family calculation.'

\*\*\*

All through the middle watch, as the squadron beat its way northeast towards Toulon, Enrico was aware of Carlisle pacing the poop deck over his head. At one bell, Walker had come silently from the cabin bringing Carlisle's cloak and at four bells he'd brought coffee for the captain and a surreptitious cup for the officer of the watch. Enrico could guess what was keeping Carlisle from his cot, and much the same thoughts occupied his mind in the brief moments that he could spare from keeping in station with the next ship ahead.

To Enrico, it came as no surprise that his family's affairs should impinge upon the strategies of France and Britain; he'd been brought up to expect it, and in some measure, he was educated to take his part in grand affairs. That his aunt should make a cold-blooded calculation of advantages and decide that her best interests lay with the French was also unsurprising. What did give him pause for wonder was the way that she seemed to have discarded Chiara and himself. He knew for certain that his aunt had always loved her niece – he'd been jealous of it when they were younger – so it came as a surprise to him. Perhaps in her hard-edged scheming she'd realised that Chiara would never come back to Sardinia and that she was in fact lost to the family. His own expulsion, however, was not nearly so easy to rationalise. He'd be an important man in the new Sardinian navy in a year or two, an asset to the family that was so short of male members. Did the viscountess believe that he also was lost to the kingdom? It came as a shock to acknowledge that she had good reason to believe so. He must have appeared as a foreigner when they met in Turin and Nice. He tried to put himself in her position. He'd been full – too full perhaps – of tales of his adventures on the high seas and the coasts and rivers of North America. He must have given the impression that he had moved away from Sardinia, both physically and in his outlook on life. And perhaps, he realised, she was correct. The narrow confines of that old and crumbling kingdom perched uncomfortably on the borders of the mighty France may no longer hold much attraction for him.

When Enrico was relieved by the master, Carlisle was

still pacing the poop deck. He went below to his tiny cabin off the quarterdeck and tried to sleep. He should have been exhausted but the tangled web of Sardinian politics, family intrigues and his naval duty kept him tossing and turning for an hour. He finally slipped into a fitful sleep at three bells, with the dawn brightening his cabin, and with little resolved in his troubled mind.

***

# CHAPTER TWENTY-FIVE

## A Rotten Republic

*Thursday, Twenty-Sixth of June 1760.*
*Dartmouth, at Sea. Off Genoa.*

Carlisle had thought long and hard about whether he should anchor off Genoa, and if he did whether it was politic to go ashore. Undoubtedly the people of the republic would be at best equivocal about this British captain who had so nearly captured at least one of the ships that they had built for the French, even though they'd been paid for and strictly were no longer their concern. Certainly, they didn't want the same thing to happen to the two that now lay alongside.

Long and hard he thought, and in the end, it was the dignity of his master, King George, that tipped the balance. It would never do for the people of this out-of-the-way republic to believe that a servant of King George hesitated to step ashore wherever he chose.

He'd sent Gresham and Enrico ahead before he'd come to anchor, to be certain that his salute would be returned gun for gun. They had brought the British consul back to the ship, a stout, business-like man named James Hollford who traded in wool from England and wine from wherever he could find it.

'Oh, they'll be civil enough, Captain, you can be sure of that, and if they say they'll return the salute they will. However, you should have no illusions; they don't love the British at present and they're incensed at the way you dealt with that schooner and the sixty-fours, even though they owned none of them. I'll be frank, Captain, and tell you that my trade has suffered. Nobody wants to do business with an Englishman anymore. I just live on what I've accumulated and hope for better times.'

Carlisle looked covertly at Hollford whose massive girth filled the cabin. He didn't look like a man who'd fallen on lean times. His position as the British consul in Genoa was no reliable guide to the man's integrity or his allegiance. At least he was British, which was not always the case, but most consuls had lived in their adopted country for many years, and it wasn't surprising that some had forgotten where their loyalties should lie.

'What news of the second pair of ships, Mister Hollford, when will they be ready for sea?'

'Well, you can see for yourself, we'll have to drive right past them if you're to call on the secretary. Their masts are stepped, and their yards are crossed; they just want their running rigging. A week ago, I'd have said that they wouldn't move for a month, but now I'm not so sure. As soon as word passed around that you'd sailed from Nice, apparently bound for Gibraltar, the traffic from Toulon started up again and a flood – a positive deluge – of stores came around. Like the others they're short of guns and they're only manned for a short cruise and stored for two weeks. They only need an escort and they'll be ready to sail next week.'

'An escort? They won't sail without one?'

'After the way you roughed-up the first two? No, the word is that a seventy-four will come and bring them to Toulon.'

Carlisle nodded. He didn't know how much he should reveal to Hollford, but Saunders would be off Toulon by now and no seventy-four would get past the Mediterranean Squadron. Unless it was already at sea it could only come to Genoa by fighting its way out of Toulon or slipping out when the squadron was blown off station.

'By the way,' Hollford added, 'the secretary is a man of some consequence in the republic, although perhaps not as much as he imagines. He's a member of the great council; an offspring of a cadet branch of one of the noble families that have provided Doges by the dozen.'

\*\*\*

They anchored off the lighthouse at the end of the New Mole, close enough for an easy pull into the city wharves but not within the embrace of the two moles. Carlisle didn't want anything to hinder him if he decided that he needed to sail, and with this persistent westerly – the mistral had died away as quickly as it had come – he could cast the ship to the south and be at sea in an hour.

The longboat had been scrubbed and re-painted since they left the Vada Shoal. The crew in their matching blue and white clothes fresh from the slop store rowed slow and dry, barely raising a ripple in the sheltered waters of the harbour and never letting a drop of water reach their captain in the stern sheets.

'You see them now, Captain?' said Hollford, pointing over to starboard where the two French ships lay alongside the fitting-out wharf.

Carlisle wished that the consul wouldn't point so. Clearly any British officer would be interested in two enemy ships, but he didn't feel that it sat well with his dignity to make it obvious. He tried his hardest to look at them less obtrusively. They certainly looked as though they could venture to sea at any moment. True, they were riding a little high but that was to be expected if they didn't have all their guns and were stored and provisioned for only a few weeks. Their captains would be reluctant to take on extra ballast for the short beat to Toulon – perhaps three or four days at sea – in the height of a glorious summer. They'd be crank and perhaps slow in stays but otherwise they were fit for the Mediterranean at this season.

'Toss your oars,' called Souter in a soft voice.

The oarsmen lifted their heavy blades vertically, handling them with effortless ease as though they weighed nothing at all. The bowman jumped ashore as the rope fender on the bows kissed the masonry of the wharf and he took a turn on a bollard with the painter. Souter had judged it to perfection and with the tiller pushed hard to starboard the last of the longboat's momentum swung the stern in so that he was able to drop his painter over a bollard without letting go of the tiller.

'There's my carriage, sir,' said Hollford with evident pride.

It was a smart two-horse affair with a driver but no footman. Carlisle looked at it appraisingly; Hollford's cries of poverty were looking less and less credible.

'Now sir, if you'll take a seat, we'll call on the harbour master first, then the ministry. I don't doubt that we'll be invited for dinner at some point; that won't be disagreeable to you, I trust. I'm sure it won't be to me,' and he laughed and patted his belly.

Carlisle felt that he wouldn't want to be the man who stood between the consul and his dinner.

Hollford said something in Italian to the driver and with a crack of the whip they set off along the cobbled streets, leaving Souter and the longboat crew to row back to *Dartmouth*.

'I've told him to swing by the French ships and to take it slow as we pass.'

Carlisle nodded. He hoped with all his heart that Hollford wouldn't start pointing again.

***

At close quarters Carlisle could see that there was still a significant amount of work to do before the ships were ready for sea. Although the lower masts had been stepped and the main yards crossed, the courses hadn't been bent on, the topmasts were still on deck and a quick look suggested that the halyards hadn't yet been rigged. There was a great heap of canvas on the nearest ship – the only one that Carlisle could see clearly – that covered the fo'c'sle, impeding movement from the waist to the head of the ship.

'What do you think, Captain?' Hollford asked.

'If they were in a King's yard, I'd say a week, but here I would have to say two,' Carlisle replied reluctantly.

He didn't like being quizzed, but he needed the consul's

good offices during this visit.

'Ha! That's just what the harbour master said when I spoke to him yesterday. Let's see if he's changed his mind.'

\*\*\*

The harbour master may well have changed his mind, but it was clear that he wasn't going to tell Carlisle if he had. He handled the visiting captain of this British man-o'-war like a hot coal and he was visibly relieved when Hollford suggested that it was time to pass on to the ministry.

'If Admiral Saunders had come here, the Doge himself would have met him, but I fear that we'll only see the secretary of foreign affairs,' Hollford said, 'although the secretary is an important person in the Republic,' he added quickly, seeing Carlisle's frown. 'He has an office in the Doge's palace.'

The carriage swept into a large piazza flanked by tall buildings, gleaming in the sunshine. The Doge's palace was at the head of the piazza and Carlisle had a brief impression of a wide sweep of tall colonnaded windows reaching up for at least three stories to a roofline punctuated by statues. It was a grand building indeed, but it gave the impression of watchful vigilance, as though it saw and recorded the doings of all its citizens. Carlisle shuddered involuntarily. The Republic of Genoa was going through hard times since its invasion by the Austrians fourteen years before. Their maritime interests had been in decline for centuries and their banking business was failing. They had lost their last colony – Tarbaka – to the Bey of Tunis and it looked like Corsican independence would be a reality before long. Carlisle agreed with Gibbon; states in decline tended to turn in upon themselves, to become obsessed with controlling their own people, and that was the impression that Genoa gave. Tarbaka! Of course, that was where Chiara had been born. It was where her father had settled and thrived and where her godfather now lived, when he wasn't at sea. Then Chiara had been born Genoese; he must have known that, but it had never seemed relevant. He'd had this feeling before, and it was even stronger now: this corner of the world was claustrophobic. It was concerned only with itself and managing its own decline. Yet like it or not, Carlisle was now bound to these parts by the strong bonds of marriage.

\*\*\*

The secretary of foreign affairs had donned his robes of office for Carlisle's call. He was adorned in crimson silk and ermine, the trappings of a senior official of a great and once glorious republic. The reason for the harbour master's reticence quickly became evident; he'd been warned to say nothing to this British captain and to leave it all to the secretary. The secretary quickly passed through the preliminaries and the coffee, and his line of conversation revealed his concerns.

'Will you be staying long in Genoa, Captain?'

'No, sir, I sail this evening. I have only come to present Admiral Saunders' compliments and his hope that he may be soon able to visit you in person.'

'Ah, I see. Admiral Saunders is the new commander-in-chief I take it. I seem to have heard his name recently.'

'He commanded the naval forces at Quebec last year, sir,' Carlisle replied. 'I had the honour to command a frigate on that occasion.'

The secretary nodded thoughtfully.

'Would it be impertinent to ask where you plan to sail from here, Captain?'

Yes, it certainly would be impertinent, damn you, Carlisle thought.

'I regret that I cannot comment on the movements of His Majesty's ships in time of war, sir. I am sure you understand.'

'Yes, of course, Captain.'

The secretary was an accomplished diplomat and even this stark rebuff didn't worry him.

'I am merely concerned for your own safety. I betray no confidence in telling you that a powerful ship of the French navy is expected in these waters within days, and I wouldn't want there to be any more unfortunate incidents.'

Carlisle bowed but didn't reply.

'No doubt you will have seen the two ships-of-the-line being fitted out in the harbour. They belong to the republic still, and when they sail, they won't be subject to the laws that govern the movement of belligerent ships in times of war.'

So that was it. The secretary thought that Carlisle was here to impose the twenty-four-hour rule. He must have been speaking to the French commodore and they had jointly concocted that casual lie about the ownership of the vessels.

'Naturally, sir.' Carlisle replied.

'Good, then is there anything that I can offer you? Do you require provisions? wood or water?'

'You are exceedingly kind, sir, but none of that will be necessary; my ship is perfectly well found in all respects.'

'Then perhaps you would care to see the Hall of Paintings. We have some of the greatest works of art in the world, particularly in maritime art. You may find some of the representations of archaic vessels most illuminating.'

Carlisle was growing sick of this diplomatic fencing. He glanced sideways at Hollford and rose to make his apologies. There was nothing more to be gained here.

'It's just occurred to me Captain, where I have heard your name before. Unless I am mistaken you are connected to the Angelini family. You married Lady Chiara, did you not?'

Damn your impertinence, Carlisle thought, but he had learned the hard way to control himself in these situations.

'I have that honour, sir,' he replied bowing.

'Then you must be familiar with the viscountess. The Angelinis are an old Genoa family, you know. They settled in Nice after we gave up Tarbaka. It's all one on the Ligurian coast you see, the old families barely recognise the borders.'

Carlisle bowed again. He knew when he was being warned off. The secretary was telling him that he was in contact with the viscountess and that he may not find operating off this coast as easy as he hoped. Well, to the devil with them all. He'd put their ancient, decayed city under a blockade so tight that not a French cockboat would get through.

\*\*\*

Carlisle settled into the carriage as Hollford gave vent to his feelings at the cold reception that they had suffered, and without a hint of an invitation to dinner. The carriage started moving and the cobblestones immediately made themselves felt, despite the carriage's strapped suspension. A movement at a door at the far end of the palace caught Carlisle's eye: a man was watching the carriage intently and talking rapidly to someone else concealed in the shadows. Carlisle recognised him immediately. It was the French commodore, the same that he had seen in Turin. He must have delivered the first two ships to Toulon and come swiftly back to Genoa. Well, if he hadn't got all his stores from the French navy's arsenal yet, he wasn't going to get any while *Dartmouth* cruised the Ligurian Sea.

\*\*\*

# CHAPTER TWENTY-SIX

## Blockade

*Wednesday, Second of July 1760.*
*Dartmouth, at Sea. Off Genoa.*

The mild westerly wind persisted for the next week, sometimes veering into the northwest and sometimes backing towards the south but always, always bringing to mind the lee shore that awaited the unwary mariner not many leagues to the east. Each morning a brief sea breeze reminded *Dartmouth's* people just how enclosed was this Gulf of Genoa, the most northern part of the Ligurian Sea, as it threatened to embay them. Then, most evenings brought a longer but fitful land breeze that allowed them to relax their vigilance.

From the main topmast head the masts of the two French ships could be clearly seen when *Dartmouth* stood cautiously into the highest reaches of the gulf. They watched as the topmasts were sent up, as the higher yards were crossed and eventually saw the sails being bent onto the yards. Day by day the ships' readiness for sea moved forward, yet every day the French commodore must be aware of *Dartmouth's* ceaseless patrol. He would recall how close he had come to disaster only three weeks before when he had brought the first two ships to sea in the teeth of the British ship's blockade.

There was little for *Dartmouth* to do but watch the two ships in Genoa and keep a close lookout for any French ships coming along the coast from Toulon or beating up through the Corsica Channel. Nothing; no sign of a French ship at all, although they boarded half a dozen vessels that turned out to be neutrals, and none were carrying contraband cargoes. Their activities did not go unnoticed in Genoa and a note from Hollford, sent out in a hired fishing boat, warned him of the heightened feelings in the republic.

The French commodore was withholding payment for the ships until they should be able to safely clear the harbour, and the shipyard owners were at their wits' ends as they saw their profits melting away in interest charges.

Carlisle knew all this, and he also knew that, weakened as it was, Genoa alone could do nothing about it. *Dartmouth* was acting within the law as it applied to belligerent's rights and so long as he didn't overstep the mark and detain an innocent trader, he was untouchable.

Yet, he didn't really believe the two sixty-fours would come out to fight, not without support from a powerful unit of the French fleet: a fully manned ship-of-the-line with its proper complement of guns. With Saunders blockading Toulon that sounded unlikely, so all he could do was wait and maintain his blockade.

***

'Mister Beazley's respects, sir,' said the midshipman at the cabin door, 'the wind's veered again into the nor'west and it's freshening. He asks whether he may take a reef in the tops'ls.'

Carlisle looked out of the window. He'd been so caught up in the bosun's tangled accounts that he hadn't noticed the change. Now that he looked, he could see that the previously untroubled blue sea was flecked with white horses where the keener wind was blowing the crests of the waves away to leeward.

'I'll come on deck,' he said, rising stiffly and leaving Simmonds to make some sense of the books. He had a lingering suspicion that the bosun was engaged in a little free trading, that he'd disposed of some of his more obscure stores in Gibraltar for cash. He hoped not, and if it were true, he prayed that it would be a small enough amount that he could explain it away. Well, if anyone could find his way through it, Simmonds could, and being a messmate of the bosun he had an incentive to find a solution.

'I don't doubt that we're catching the edge of a mistral again, sir, although rightly speaking we're too far east for that and it's unusual to have two summer mistrals so close together.'

Carlisle looked up at the tops'ls. The master was right, of course, they should be reefed and the sooner the better.

'Carry on and take in a reef then, Mister Beazley.'

Carlisle climbed up to the poop deck while the business of sail handling was conducted. *Dartmouth* was steering south so he had a grand view of the Ligurian coast from the taffrail. It was a daunting prospect for a square-rigged ship; from forrard of the starboard beam right around to the larboard quarter they were hemmed in by the land, with the coastal hills giving way to small mountains that marched away to the east and the west until they faded into the distance. The air was clear and cool – most certainly they were experiencing a mistral – and the details of the land stood out starkly.

He walked forrard and shouted down from the poop rail.

'Mister Beazley, send up my telescope, would you?'

Now he could see Genoa more clearly than he had for days. They were as close as they had been since he had gone ashore and with this clear air the detail that he could pick out was astonishing. Yet he could do better. A nor'west wind meant that there was little danger from a lee shore as the eastern coastline trended away to the southeast. He could dare to go closer to Genoa.

'Mister Beazley, as soon as the tops'ls are reefed, put her about, if you please, and close Genoa.'

The hands were already on deck, so it was a simple matter to tack. When she'd steadied on her new course, Carlisle climbed steadily up the larboard main shrouds to the maintop. He stopped to catch his breath then continued to the main topmast head, where the lookout offered his hand to help him onto the crosstrees.

From there he had a fine view ahead. He was higher than the fore tops'l yard and so could see the whole panorama of sea, sky and land without any obstructions.

*Dartmouth* was moving fast now, two points free on the

larboard tack, and they advanced towards the great port city at a steady pace. There was the new mole to the west, and the old mole lying further back on the other side of the harbour. He could see the lighthouses on the end of each mole and could even make out the figures of people walking along the stone paths atop the moles. He shifted the telescope a little to the right to where the main part of the walled city lay. The topmasts of the two sixty-fours came immediately into view. They soared above the other vessels and only the towers and spires of the grander churches reached higher.

He could see the tops'l yards resting on the tops, each with its neat roll of shining new canvas bent on. Every moment as *Dartmouth* drew closer a new detail emerged. He could see the very halyards now, and the tops'l stays and shrouds. He looked down to see the master staring up at him, a look of concern on his face. True, he didn't often go aloft, but really…

'Mister Beazley, put the ship about, we've come close enough.'

'Aye-aye sir. Will you be coming down?'

'No, Mister Beazley. Carry on.'

It was a long time since he'd been to the main topmast head and even longer since he'd been aloft when the ship was being layed upon the other tack. He'd forgotten how disconcerting it was to be staring down at the sea on the starboard side at one moment then, after a brief half minute of dizzy turning, to be far above the sea on the larboard side of the ship. The lookout who had shinned a few yards up the t'gallant mast wondered whether he would have to steady his captain who was showing all the signs of disorientation. But Carlisle recovered, shifted his seat on the crosstrees and looked now astern through the telescope.

It was the same scene except that now they were retreating from it, heading back out to sea before they could be fairly accused of breaching Genoa's sovereign waters. Nothing had changed in the few minutes since he gave the order to tack. He took one last look at the ships. Something was moving on the main topmast of the nearer ship. He could just make out a black dot climbing up and up. Another minute and he would have been too far away to see it. The lookout saw nothing; he didn't have a telescope. Carlisle saw the dot reach the masthead and blossom into a long streamer. A commissioning pennant. Then he saw another smaller flag break at the fore topmast. He couldn't make it out, but he was certain that it would be a commodore's pennant. Another long pennant broke out at the masthead of the further ship. He had just witnessed the exact moment that the last two Genoa ships became the property of King Louis. Now, was that coincidence? Had it been planned that the ships should be turned over to French ownership at exactly this moment, as *Dartmouth*, coincidentally, was the closest that she'd been since she visited a week ago? Or was it mere bravado, a gesture of defiance? Carlisle instinctively swept the horizon from shoreline to shoreline. Nothing; no sign of the French man-o'-war that he both hoped for and feared in equal measure.

***

'Something's happening, sir,' said Gresham. 'No sea officer hoists a commissioning pennant, let alone a commodore's pennant, without he means it. They're coming out, as sure as anything.'

'Would you come out and face us, Mister Gresham? With untrained crews and without your full number of guns? That commodore came close to disaster the last time we met, and it was only the arrival of *Le Bourbon* that saved him.'

'Perhaps he's had word of an escort on its way, sir.'

'Perhaps. Or is he looking at this wind, this edge of the mistral, and thinking how much stronger it will be blowing off Toulon? Saunders won't want to wear out his squadron so early in the season and you can be sure that he won't waste cordage and canvas on a close blockade in this weather. I think we could be in for a visitor, Mister

Gresham. If it's blowing this strongly here then Toulon will have been under a right, roaring mistral since yesterday evening, at least. With the wind in this quarter an escort could reach Genoa at any moment, or by this evening at least.'

Gresham looked at the chart and stepped off the distance from Toulon to Genoa. He gazed out of the window, imagining this wind howling across Provence and down to the French fleet at anchor in Toulon's outer road. It would be easy for one or two ships to weigh anchor and run out to sea. If one of Saunders' frigates saw them, well, it would take a superhuman effort for the squadron to beat back to the north to intercept them. It was a desperate gamble, for sure, but these were the perfect conditions for the Genoa ships to make a break for Toulon. All they needed was to get past *Dartmouth*, and for that they needed help.

Carlisle looked at the chart. If he was to fight, he needed sea-room. This Gulf of Genoa was no place to be, not with the wind likely to back into the west again at any moment. He could feel the baleful presence of the coastline that would be under his lee.

'Tell the master to bring the ship onto the wind, as close as she can go. Let's make some sea-room to the west while we can.'

\*\*\*

*Dartmouth* lay over to the nor'westerly wind and her stem bit into the short, steep waves, with her bows crashing down into each trough, sending a scintillating shower of spray aft along the waist. There was a new sense of urgency about the ship, a feeling that they had a definite purpose, as though a chase were in sight. But the horizon ahead stayed resolutely innocent of sails all through the afternoon and dog watches. No fisherman who valued his skin put to sea in this weather and *Dartmouth's* known presence had stifled the trade all along this coast. They had the sea to themselves as they steadily ate up the miles westward.

Carlisle knew very well that he was taking a gamble. His orders were to cruise off Genoa, not race away westward on what may be – probably was – a wild goose chase. Any of his guesses could be wrong, and then he was guilty of leaving his post. Saunders may be holding his squadron tight up to Toulon – risking grave damage to maintain a close blockade – in which case no Frenchman would come out. The French commodore may have been hanging his flags out to dry. Or at this moment, the French ships could be hurrying south to take the Bonifacio Straits, having seen *Dartmouth* disappear to the west. Any of those cases would leave him in the wrong, at best looking foolish and at worst standing before a court martial. Yet he had learned to trust his intuition and in this case his instincts told him that his enemy was nigh and that he must be met to windward.

Eight bells rang from the fo'c'sle, the end of the first dogwatch.

'Sunset at three bells, sir,' Wishart reported when he took the watch.

Already the day was fading as the sun hurried towards the mountains just forrard of *Dartmouth's* starboard beam. The peaks and ridges were outlined in gold and the valleys were already in shadow. Carlisle paced restlessly on the poop deck. He'd made the right decision to come to the west, he was sure. However, if they saw nothing by the time darkness fell, then he'd run back along the coast towards Genoa and repeat the process tomorrow. He knew in his bones that something was about to happen, and he was torn between his proper station in the Gulf of Genoa, and this westward leg that covered the approach of a relief force.

The exercise of striding across a sloping deck stimulated his mind. He'd thought all he could about the tactical situation and his mind drifted to the last letter he'd received from Chiara, handed to him in a large bundle by Admiral Saunders' secretary.

It was letter full of joy and hope. Spring had come to Williamsburg when Chiara had sat down to write, their son was growing fast, and their family affairs were prospering. He realised how much he missed being with his wife and son, and it could be years before he saw them again. He was the captain of a ship-of-the-line on active service and he wasn't even permitted to sleep ashore without the admiral's permission, much less abandon his command and take passage to Virginia. He knew that he'd been lucky to be stationed in the Americas for the past couple of years, and even luckier to be given convoys up and down the coast, where it had been easy to find a reason to put into Hampton and take the short road trip to Williamsburg, but so long as he was with the Mediterranean Squadron that was impossible. He did worry about Chiara on her own in Williamsburg. It had been easier when Black Rod had been with her; he would have trusted that stalwart to lay down his own life for his mistress. But Black Rod was in Nice now, and Chiara had only his own aged to father and his cousin's husband to defend her cause. He thought about his brother who was so hostile to him and his family. Much of his poison had been drawn by his father's changed attitude, but still his antipathy worried Carlisle. He paced on and on as the sun sank lower towards the mountains, his feet growing sore with the repetition of his steps. He turned at the taffrail, determined to go below and wait until darkness and his already-made decision to turn back to the east.

'Sail ho! Sail right ahead!'

Carlisle sprang for the quarterdeck. With this reaching wind *Dartmouth* and the strange sail would close very fast indeed. In half an hour they could be exchanging broadsides if he'd guessed correctly.

'Up you go with a telescope, Mister Young. Let me know what you see.'

The midshipman ran for the main shrouds, dodging through the gathering crowds of men who had come pouring onto the deck at the hail from the masthead.

'Mister Gresham. Beat to quarters.'

Carlisle was easy in his mind now. He was sure that the

ship ahead of him was a Frenchman or a frigate from the squadron. In either case he was in the right place and preparing for action was certainly an appropriate response.

'Deck there!' shouted Young. 'She's a man-o'-war under reefed tops'ls. Looks like a Frenchman to me.'

'We'll see, we'll see,' said Carlisle to the quarterdeck at large. He knew how easy it was for a youngster like Horace Young to see what he expected and hoped to see.

Down on the waist the sea lashings were being cast off and the crews were hauling the massive guns into their places in front of the ports. It was a scene of intense, ordered activity, and one by one the gun captains raised their hands to declare that their crew was ready.

'She's French, for sure,' shouted Young.

Now the tops'l was visible from the deck. Carlisle trained his telescope at the tiny square of white and stared at it for a few heartbeats. He lowered the glass and nodded to Gresham.

'*Le Bourbon*,' he said quietly.

Gresham smiled savagely and Beazley nodded briefly in reply, his face an unreadable mask.

'Deck there, she's the French seventy-four that we met before, sir. I'd recognise her anywhere.'

'Thank you, Mister Young, you may come on deck now and return to your station.'

The quarterdeck was silent now as everyone – the first lieutenant, the sailing master, the mate, the quartermaster, the steersmen – waited for Carlisle to give his orders. He looked up at the tops'ls, over the side at the waves being flung aside by *Dartmouth's* blunt bows, and away to the northwest at the sun sinking towards the far mountains.

'Steady as she goes, Mister Beazley, keep her right on our stem. You can furl the main and fores'l and shake out the reefs from the t'gallants.'

\*\*\*

# CHAPTER TWENTY-SEVEN

## Night Engagement

*Wednesday, Second of July 1760.*
*Dartmouth, at Sea. Off Cape Mele.*

'A word with you, if you please, First Lieutenant.'

Carlisle led the way up the ladder to the poop deck and aft to the taffrail where they could speak without being overheard. He took a moment to stare at the mountains to the nor'west, the tail end of the mighty Alps that even as they diminished towards the sea had a sublime grandeur that was only enhanced by the sun that hung a hand's breadth above them.

'This will be a hard fight, sir,' said Gresham, grinning as he rubbed his hands together.

Carlisle was always amazed at Gresham's lust for a fight. He'd felt it himself in the heat of a battle, but never in anticipation of one. For all Gresham's protestations that he wanted nothing more than to retire to his cottage in the country, he would miss this feeling of imminent action. And it wasn't just the prize money that drove Gresham on, for this encounter held little prospect of that. It was the fight itself. Carlisle shook his head in wonderment.

'It will, Mister Gresham, that's for sure, and we can't expect any help from the admiral. He won't be straying far from Toulon, and when the mistral fades, he'll be right up to Cape Sicié again. That gentleman,' he pointed forrard to where the seventy-four was now visible past the jib boom, 'must try to brush us aside and bring those two ships out of Genoa before the wind changes. He has perhaps two days at the most, so he has no time to waste. If I were the captain of *Le Bourbon*, I would be using chain shot to disable us, and I wouldn't stand on ceremony. If I could get past us, I'd be away to Genoa without delay.'

Gresham scratched his head. He never really thought in

those terms. To him a fight was a fight and all he was concerned about was pummelling the enemy to soften them up before boarding them in the powder smoke. He just didn't consider what the enemy's mission might be, it was enough for him that the opponent was in sight.

'You don't think he'll want to settle a score then, sir?'

'No,' Carlisle replied positively. 'He didn't the last time we met, he stuck to his mission to bring the first two ships home. Nothing has changed, he still has to show himself off Genoa so that the second two can sail and join the fleet.'

'Still, to refuse a battle with a fifty-gun ship…'

Gresham looked wistfully ahead at the fast-closing Frenchman.

Carlisle could see that he'd get nothing sensible on the subject from his first lieutenant. Any moment now Gresham would conclude that he must double-shot the guns and lay *Dartmouth* alongside at pistol shot.

'He won't want to board us unless he's certain that he can do it without losing too many of his men, and I have no intention of boarding him. I'll not pit our three-hundred-and-fifty against his six or seven hundred, not in a man-to-man fight. Chain shot for the upper deck guns, bar shot for the lower deck and grape for the six-pounders,' Carlisle said firmly. 'We'll keep him at arm's length and cut up his top-hamper so badly that he'll need to turn back for Toulon. Our only aim here, Mister Gresham, is to prevent him from making Genoa.'

Carlisle took another look around from the poop deck. He could guess where Cape Mele was, on the starboard beam, but it was already in darkness under the shadow of the mountains. *Dartmouth* must be just a little to seaward of where Gresham took the schooner a month ago; a good omen if one believed in that kind of thing. Apart from the two ships-of-the-line hurtling towards each other, the sea was innocent of traffic. Not a sail showed on the deep, deep blue of the ocean, a blue that was turning to purple as the sun sunk lower and lower towards the mountains. Its bottom limb was already kissing a high ridge and, in an hour, or an hour-and-a-half, it would be quite dark. The waning, sinister, gibbous moon wouldn't rise until an hour later. That was something worth knowing; he had to immobilise his foe before the last of the sun's glow disappeared. After that the Frenchman would surely escape to the east and then he'd have the whole thing to do again the next day, but then he'd have to contend with three ships.

***

'He's hauled his wind a point or two, sir,' said Beazley.

'He's offering us the opportunity to refuse the engagement,' Carlisle said. 'If we keep this course, we'll reach past each other out of cannon-shot.'

'Indeed, we could just continue on our lawful, peaceful occasions,' Beazley said, chuckling at the thought.

Carlisle watched the enemy carefully. It was a little thing, but it showed that he was right; *probably right*, he corrected himself. This man would avoid fighting if he possibly could. He'd seen *Dartmouth's* reluctance to engage with him on two separate occasions and now he was offering a third. It made sense; it was no business of a fifty-gun ship to engage a seventy-four. Yet today – tonight – it was most certainly Carlisle's business. His duty was quite clear. With Saunders blown off station – *Le Bourbon's* presence here made that almost certain – and likely to be so for a couple of days, only *Dartmouth* stood in the way of the French navy taking delivery of two additional ships of the line, and only by preventing *Le Bourbon* reaching Genoa could he achieve that.

He remembered the frown that had crossed Saunders' face when he heard that the first two had made it to Toulon. There had been no criticism, just that one frowning glance. It would look bad if it happened a second time. Carlisle could just imagine the sneers behind his back. There would be whispers about his colonial upbringing, suggestions that he had not made the transition from command of a frigate to a ship-of-the-line, perhaps even crude jests about his foreign wife. His face was a rigid mask when he turned back to the master.

'Bear up two points, Mister Beazley. Keep him three point on your larboard bow.'

That should make his intention clear to the Frenchman. He carefully watched the luff of the fore tops'l. Was it lifting? No, but he couldn't come any further to windward. If the Frenchman was faster than he imagined, then he'd have to tack.

'Thus and no higher, Master, I want to cross his bows on this tack. Watch the bearing if you please. Mister Gresham! Run out the larboard guns.'

*Le Bourbon* had elected to pass to windward of *Dartmouth*. The weather gage had its advantages but in Carlisle's opinion they were exaggerated, and too many sea officers clung to it as though keeping to windward of the enemy was some sort of empirical tenet of naval faith. Now the Frenchman was pinned against the coast and his scope for manoeuvre was curtailed. If he'd put up his helm and gone to the south, he'd have taken longer to reach his objective but his superior speed – those long French seventy-fours were famously fast – would have allowed him to stay clear of *Dartmouth* while the light lasted and then he would certainly lose her in the dark. Carlisle slapped the quarterdeck rail with the palm of his hand. Got him!

The rumble of the trucks on the oak decks brought back floods of memories. It was the inevitable precursor to action, and nobody who had been in a sea fight could ever forget it. The deep bass tones and the shouts of the gun captains were followed by a dead silence as the crews laid back on the train tackles keeping the guns hard up against the ports.

Gresham and Beazley exchanged glances as each, in their own time, followed Carlisle's thoughts at a more pedestrian pace.

Night was falling fast now and down in the waist the battle lanterns were being distributed among the guns. The same would be happening on the lower deck and a glance towards the fo'c'sle showed the six-pounder crews were doing the same. That was the great advantage of a well worked-up crew, and the blessing of having officers who had served with him for a year; he had no need to either give instructions for routine precautions such as battle lanterns or check that they were being carried out. His standing orders were sufficient and the hours and hours of practice in all conditions that had punctuated the days at sea had ingrained them into the routines.

'Bearing's drawing a mite left now, sir,' said Beazley, stooped over the binnacle, 'we'd be stiffer without the guns run out.'

*Dartmouth* was winning the race, even though the weight of twenty-five guns run out to leeward was pressing her over in this sharp breeze. She was undoubtedly the slower ship but that wasn't the point. She would reach that spot in the ocean where the two ships tracks would converge a few cables ahead of *Le Bourbon*.

'Keep her steady on this course, Mister Beazley, we can bear away later if we need to.'

In a race, don't give away an inch to leeward if you don't need to. That was what Carlisle had been taught from his first days at sea and it was as true in *Dartmouth* in the Ligurian Sea as it had been when he was a midshipman in the old brig-sloop *Wolf* in the Caribbean. Every minute sailing large took at least four minutes sailing hard on the wind to recover.

The fittings of the French ship were becoming indistinct now as the gloom spread seaward like a giant hand, erasing all the fine detail and turning everything into shades of grey.

Silence on the deck. The gun crews crouched tensed around their monstrous charges. The marines stood immobile along the poop deck and the fo'c'sle and the swivel guns that dotted the gunwales were all pointed at the fast-closing enemy.

\*\*\*

'Bear away two points, Master.'

Carlisle was going to shave the Frenchman's jib boom. But first *Dartmouth* had to endure the opening broadsides from her foe. It was clear that *Le Bourbon* wasn't going to interrupt her eastward flight if it could possibly be avoided. Her captain must be gambling on surviving *Dartmouth's* broadside and then rushing past. Perhaps he thought *Dartmouth* would be firing ball, as every British captain preferred to do under normal circumstance. But today wasn't normal, today – this evening – Carlisle had nothing more in mind than disabling his opponent. Once *Le Bourbon* broke free to the east of the British ship, there was nothing to stop her being off Genoa at first light, and then the two sixty-fours would come out to join him. This damned Englishman had already been seen off by a combination of the seventy-four and two under-gunned sixty-fours and he'd do it again. It was a good plan, Carlisle conceded, but it relied upon him obliging the Frenchman by battering away at the ship's hull rather than clawing at her masts and sails.

Carlisle saw the Frenchman's starboard side erupt in flame and smoke. He had an instant to notice how bright the flashes were in the deepening darkness of the twilight before *Dartmouth* was hit. He'd been right; the Frenchman was aiming high with chain and bar shot. He had no intention of fighting, he just wanted to get past to the east.

The howling of the shot overhead was swiftly followed by the sounds of splintering wood as the iron spheres and chains and bars smashed through masts and yards, sails and cordage. The splinter nets sagged and bounced as an assortment of blocks and cordage and chunks of timber rained down from above.

Carlisle looked aloft. The fore tops'l was holed in half a dozen places and each of the sails was rent in at least one place. There were loose halyards aplenty and the forrard part of the mizzen top was shot away with its swivel gun hanging by its mounting. There was no sign of the two men who served that gun.

'Stand by; not yet!' Carlisle said, as Gresham fingered his silver whistle.

Gresham nodded. He knew that he must reserve this first broadside for the moment that they crossed the Frenchman's bow.

Closer and closer. The master was cutting it fine indeed and for a mad moment Carlisle wondered whether he wouldn't do better to run his bow into the Frenchman and have done with it. At this speed they'd be irrevocably bound together and then it would be a question of hand-to-hand fighting on the deck. He cast that idea away as soon as it was formed, the odds were too highly stacked against the smaller ship with the smaller crew. The Frenchman would win and then there would be nothing to stand between the Genoa ships and Toulon.

*Le Bourbon* emerged from her own smoke like some sort of phantasmagorical figure, a crowd-pleasing trick at a show, to be followed by fireworks and rum punch. Carlisle could dimly see the guns being reloaded and he saw the calm, steady uniformed figures on her quarterdeck.

'You may fire when you're ready, Mister Gresham.'

Gresham nodded again without taking his eyes from his prey. Any moment now…

A single blast on his whistle was followed by the vast roar of the larboard battery. Carlisle staggered as *Dartmouth* was pushed bodily to starboard by the force of the recoil. Why, oh why do the French always allow that to happen? Why do they let me deliver the first raking broadside? Carlisle knew the answer; it was a result of their determination to fulfil their mission rather than engage in a kind of personal knightly contest. *Le Bourbon* had to get to the east – that was necessary for her mission – and whatever damage she took along the way was incidental. In this case, however, Carlisle intended that the damage should be far more than that.

Gresham's broadside – his twenty-four, twelve and six-pounders loaded with an assortment of disabling shot –

smashed through *Le Bourbon's* head rig, carrying away the jib boom and the spritsail yard and leaving the jib flying uselessly to leeward. It was a shrewd hit indeed, but it wasn't fatal, not by any means. The great seventy-four staggered under the blow and her head came up a point, then the steersman regained control and the behemoth continued eastwards, her tops'ls drawing her on at six knots despite their shot holes.

'Now! Master. Bring her about!'

The sail trimmers were at their stations and Beazley ordered the helm put down. *Dartmouth* responded quickly, her bows swinging to starboard towards the wind. She was quick in stays but not quick enough to avoid the inevitable consequence of having the first raking advantage.

The Frenchman's larboard battery spat fire and powder smoke, catching *Dartmouth's* exposed stern as she was in the act of turning into the wind. It was chain shot again – Carlisle knew that banshee howling – and it ripped across the poop deck and tore through the mizzen rigging. He looked aloft to see the mizzen yard hanging drunkenly in its slings.

Beazley raised his speaking trumpet.

'She's through the wind, sir, never fear…'

Carlisle waited for the shout to let go and haul, but nothing came. He whipped around. Beazley would give no more orders that day; he lay sprawled on the quarterdeck, one arm locked into the binnacle as though he was still taking bearings. It must have been one of the French swivel guns or a musketeer firing blind into the near complete darkness.

Old Eli was conning the ship as though nothing had happened, and he stepped delicately over the sailing master but otherwise took no notice. Carlisle scooped up the speaking trumpet and bellowed the instructions that brought order out of the incipient chaos.

He heard the whistle again and the starboard battery fired, throwing him off his balance just as the larboard battery had. Gresham, quite unperturbed by the damage was fighting his guns as though he was at drill. Chain and bar again, as he had ordered, and now in the light of the flashes he could see real damage being done to the French ship. Her fore topmast had been shot way and her sails were in tatters. She'd lost her speed advantage and given away the weather gage. Now it was merely a matter of not losing her in the dark and firing as fast as the crews could reload.

*Dartmouth's* deck was like a scene from the Inferno. In the dim light of the battle lanterns, and the intermittent flashes of the guns, half-naked men were caught in suspended animation. Some leaned outboard with spongers in hand while others strained to run up the guns or leapt back to stand clear of the recoil. Powder boys ran here and there, dodging the bellowing guns to deliver the cartridges that they clutched to their chests, and the midshipmen strode from gun to gun, encouraging and lending a hand where it was needed. Above all, Carlisle could hear the popping of the marines' muskets as they added their slight weight of metal to the fight. And all the time, the wreckage from aloft poured down onto the splinter nets, making them droop lower and lower. The master had been hauled away below and there were mercifully few other casualties, so far.

\*\*\*

With the still-strong wind on their beams the two ships raced east, pounding away at each other's masts and sails. *Le Bourbon* had been hit harder than *Dartmouth* and the loss of her fore topmast had stripped her of her speed advantage. Both ships were firing their guns as soon as they were reloaded now, without waiting for the slowest crews. The gun flashes were almost continuous and the dark of the night was no more as each ship was illuminated, again and again. Now was the time that the British superiority in the rate of fire should start to tell, but Carlisle could see no sign of it. What he could see was the greater weight of the French shot; thirty-two pounders on the lower deck and eighteen pounders on the upper. He shrugged. If this were a normal engagement where they aimed to smash each other's hulls, to overturn the guns and kill the crews, then the Frenchman's greater guns and here massive scantlings would prove fatal to *Dartmouth*, but in this battle for mobility, the size of the guns and the strength of the hull mattered less. A twenty-four pounder's chain shot would hardly do less damage aloft than a thirty-two pounder's.

A crash from overhead told Carlisle that the mizzen yard had at last come down. The heel of the great spar lay over his head, and it had ripped through the splinter nets, letting a heap of wreckage fall onto the deck. It hardly mattered, and the bosun and his crew were already hacking away at the tangle of cordage, while the carpenter and his men were dragging the yard bodily onto the poop deck. Through all that the guns had kept firing and that was the only thing that mattered. In the flashes he could glimpse the damage to the French seventy-four. Another hour of this and she'd be a mastless wreck. So would *Dartmouth* come to that. The fight had degenerated into a slugging match between two equal wild beasts, each intent on damaging the other while no longer caring about their own wounds.

And still the two ships continued eastwards. Their speed was down to less than two knots and from the deck up they looked like floating wrecks, but neither ship had yet been severely damaged in the hull.

'Mister Gresham!' Carlisle had to shout again to get the first lieutenant's attention. 'Load with ball now, I want to bring her masts down so pass the word to aim low at the base of her mainmast.'

Gresham grinned, his teeth showing white against his blackened face. He didn't immediately reply but started shouting orders down to Enrico in the waist. A midshipman ran to the lower deck to relay the order to Wishart.

'That's good, sir, we're starting to run out of chain and bar shot.'

One by one, as the new ammunition was brought up, the guns started firing round shot. It gave them a deeper voice than the specialised ammunition. It wasn't nearly as good at cutting up sails and rigging, but it was a much surer way of damaging the massive lower masts or the topmasts of a ship-of-the-line. *Le Bourbon's* masts would already have been hit several times by the lighter ammunition, and indeed her main t'gallant had been brought down, but it would take the punch of a twenty-four or eighteen-pound ball to bring down the lower masts.

There was another crash from aloft and Carlisle saw that his fore topmast had been shot through above the foretop. There was a rush of men up the shrouds – the bosun and the carpenter again – to cut away the wreckage.

'Hot work, sir,' said Gresham.

'Aye, hot work but we must keep at it,' Carlisle replied.

Gresham nodded. Carlisle noticed that he had a bandage under his hat and a trail of dried blood ran down to his shirt. He must have been hit by some solid piece of wreckage from aloft.

Down in the waist Enrico was running from gun to gun, making sure that each was aimed well. He knew that the crews, exhausted by the physically demanding work of loading the guns and running them out, could hardly be relied upon to aim them properly. He pushed and cajoled until each gun was pointed at the enemy's mainmast before it was fired. He could imagine that Wishart was doing the same on the lower gun deck.

It was impossible to see where the shot was impacting on their enemy, but the gunwales beside the mainmast had been largely shot away and at least one gun had been dismounted. The French were still firing for *Dartmouth's* rigging, sticking rigidly to the tactic that would best support their mission. And it was working. The Frenchman was starting to draw ahead of *Dartmouth*.

'The main topmast and the headsails are drawing, sir, but little else.'

The bosun looked exhausted as he wearily swung a boarding axe in his huge fist.

'Can you set the fores'l?' Carlisle asked.

'Aye sir, that I can. There'll be a few holes in it, no doubt, but it'll set alright. I'll need to take a dozen hands from the guns, sir.'

'Mister Gresham! A dozen hands for the bosun.'

Carlisle could see that the French ship was drawing ahead fast, and now her quarterdeck was abreast *Dartmouth's* waist. Soon it would be a stern chase, and then he would have failed. Even now, the after-most guns couldn't bear, and there were ample spare hands to send aloft.

***

With the foresail set – Carlisle didn't want to set the main in case it interfered with the guns in the waist – *Dartmouth* started to catch *Le Bourbon*. Still the chain shot howled overhead with the occasional poorly aimed shot crashing into *Dartmouth's* hull or screaming at man-height across the deck. There were casualties now and a steady stream of broken men were being guided or carried below.

'There she goes, sir!' shouted Gresham, pointing across at *Le Bourbon*.

In the intermittent orange light from the gun flashes – for it was fully dark now – Carlisle saw his adversary's fore topmast fall drunkenly to larboard. Deprived of all her forrard sails and with the wreckage dragging her head around, the great seventy-four-gun ship slewed to windward. Looking at his own deck he had a brief image of Enrico clapping his hands delightedly at this evidence of his handiwork.

'Hard a-starboard!' shouted Carlisle. 'Stand by the larboard battery.'

Gresham could see what Carlisle intended. He was going to cross the Frenchman's stern and deliver a devastating blow that would rake the ship from stern to stem. The larboard battery was loaded with ball and the guns were all run out.

'Man the larboard battery!' he shouted. 'Mister Angelini, get your men over to the other side!'

Enrico looked up and saw the situation. He took up the shout and ran among the starboard guns, thrusting stupefied men across the deck to where the spare gun captains waited.

'When you are ready, Mister Gresham.'

*Le Bourbon* was helpless as *Dartmouth's* bows swung to starboard, her jib boom missing the larger ship's taffrail by a matter of a few feet.

Crash! The forrard guns of the larboard battery spoke in thunder and flame. Then as *Dartmouth* moved slowly across the Frenchman's stern, the rest of the larboard guns fired in turn as they passed.

Gresham was almost dancing with excitement, Carlisle noticed. Surely this was the end of the fight, surely *Le Bourbon* couldn't recover from this.

Then Carlisle felt the deck move unnaturally below his feet. He felt instantly dizzy. He looked forrard and to his horror he saw that his mainmast was shot through above the partners. An unlucky ball from the Frenchman's last shots must have crossed the deck and hit the mast squarely. The larboard gun nearest to the mast was over, he noticed, and there were half a dozen figures writhing on the deck or lying still. With a mighty crash that shook the ship, the fractured higher part of the mainmast slipped off the lower part and came to rest on the deck. The mainmast was still standing, held up by the intricate but fragile network of stays, shrouds and backstays, but its heel was unsupported, and any movement of the deck would send it skidding towards the gunwale. Probably it would smash through and slip over the side, bringing the whole main and main topmast down on deck.

'Bosun! Secure the heel of the mainmast!'

It was a ridiculous order to give in the heat of an action, barely possible to be obeyed. The mainmast was two-and-a half feet in diameter and every movement of the ship sent it skidding a foot or two across the deck. It would take massive ropes to restrain it.

Carlisle looked around. The Frenchman had stopped

firing now and was drifting – it wouldn't be right to say that she was sailing – away to the southeast. Without the flashes of her guns to focus the eyes, she would soon be lost in the darkness.

'Cease firing, Mister Gresham. Let's get all hands to work on the damage. I want to be underway and after her by dawn.'

Gresham looked at him uncomprehendingly. *Dartmouth* was a floating wreck; it would take a miracle to save her from being cast ashore at the first land that they should find as they drifted to leeward. Resuming the action was a fantastic dream.

***

# CHAPTER TWENTY-EIGHT

## In the Nick of Time

*Thursday, Third of July 1760.*
*Dartmouth, at Sea. Off Cape Mele.*

Carlisle didn't leave the deck all night. The moon rose at five bells in the first watch, a ghastly left-handed three quarters moon, and cast its deathly pallor over the sea. The wind was still kicking up a lively sea although it was losing its earlier force, and the only vessel in sight was *Le Bourbon* three or four miles to leeward. Carlisle had to look twice to check how she lay; her missing fore topmast gave her an odd appearance that disguised the bow from the stern in the moonlight.

The work was moving forward apace on *Dartmouth's* deck. The jagged heel of the mainmast had been restrained and although it wasn't in the right place it could no longer scrape in circles across the deck as the ship rolled, and it was far less likely to break through the upper deck and spear down through the ship's bottom, sending them all to an early and watery grave. The carpenter was hard at work with bowsaw, ripsaw and adze making the head of the lower part of the fractured mast ready to receive the stump of the upper part. The first lieutenant and bosun were rigging sheer legs from the spare yards. With the help of a cat's cradle of purchases led to the fore and mizzen masts, they would be used to heave the mainmast bodily aloft to be lowered onto the stump. Even with all that highly skilled work to be done, the sailmaker had been able to fashion a trysail from the wreckage of the lateen sail and hoist it on the mizzen mast. *Dartmouth* had headsails, a foresail and a mizzen of sorts. She was no beauty, but she could at least save herself from foundering.

'Upper deck guns are all ready, sir,' said Enrico. He'd lost his hat in the battle and looked strangely lost without it. 'I've lashed number six gun to the gunwale until Chips can be spared to repair its carriage.'

'Very well, Mister Angelini. How are the crews?'

'Tired, sir. I've lost four dead and six are below with the surgeon. I've sent those that are fit to help Mister Gresham now that the guns are in order.'

'Very well. Go below and see how Mister Wishart is doing with the lower deck guns.'

There was a line of people waiting to see him, but the first lieutenant waved them all aside.

'The mast's ready to be raised, sir. If all goes well it'll be done by dawn and then we can see about our friend over there,' he added with a jerk of his head towards *Le Bourbon*.

'Very well, let's have a look.'

Carlisle followed Gresham down to the waist. The situation was plain; the ship couldn't stand any kind of violent motion with the mainmast in that state, there was just too much chance that it would fall through the deck. The bosun had passed heavy lashings around the mast and taken them forrard and aft to the other masts and athwartships to the gunwales. Yet however tight the lashings, each time the ship moved the broken end of the mainmast shifted an inch or two across the deck with a fearful screeching sound.

'Either we set it up on its stump, sir, or we salvage what we can and send what's left of the lower mast over the side. We can make a jury rig with the topmast, which will at least give us some balance.'

Gresham grimaced at the prospect of shifting that ponderous weight with a sea running.

'How long to set it up on the stump?'

'Two hours, sir,' he glanced at the bosun who nodded, 'we're ready to start in thirty minutes, at your word, sir. Chips has everything he needs to fish it as soon as it's set up; it should see us back to Gib.'

Carlisle looked around the deck. The main part of the lifting would be done by the immense tackle that was rigged from the sheer legs. The hauling part of the tackle was passed around the capstan and the marines were resting on the bars, waiting for their effort to be called for. He slapped the nearest leg of the sheers; it seemed solid enough, but he had to remember that it would be called upon to raise about four-fifths of the weight of the mainmast, a job that was normally done by specialist equipment in a yard. In a yard and without this sea running. He was tempted to put it over the side and have done with it. He glanced at the topmast that had been stowed on the fo'c'sle.

With the mainmast set up and the topmast sent aloft he could resume the fight. If he sent the mainmast over the side, then all he could do was limp back to Gibraltar.

'Lower deck guns are all ready, sir,' Wishart reported, breaking in on his thoughts.

'What's that?' he asked in irritation.

Wishart winced but delivered his report again.

'The lower deck guns are set up and run out sir, all ready if you need them.'

Carlisle shook his head as though waking from a dream. What had he been thinking of? His duty hadn't changed, he still had to stop *Le Bourbon* from reaching Genoa and bringing out the two sixty-fours. Saunders would almost certainly not regain his station for a day or two and by that time, with this wind, the French Mediterranean squadron would be the stronger by two ships-of-the-line.

'Then carry on and set up the mainmast, Mister Gresham. I'll be on the quarterdeck keeping the ship as steady as possible. I believe she'll lie-to under this rig.'

\*\*\*

It was well into the middle watch before the delicate operation started. Carlisle left it to Gresham while he shielded the first lieutenant from the dozens of people who came looking for orders. The surgeon needed help in the cockpit. Could the cook serve out bread and beef to the men? The gunner wanted to know how many cartridges to make up, and the purser – for want of a chaplain – requested

Carlisle's intentions for burying the dead. Through all this, Carlisle watched *Le Bourbon* and made minute adjustments to the helm and the sheets to keep *Dartmouth's* head off the wind. How he missed Beazley, but his sailing master was hovering between life and death after the surgeon removed a musket ball from his shoulder.

Down in the waist the lashings were checked, the guys for the sheerlegs were bowsed down tight and the unnamed lines that would take the place of stays and shrouds were grasped by tired hands. Gresham walked around and inspected it all, checking everything one last time.

'Ready to proceed, sir,' he reported simply. 'I'll direct things from here,' he added, standing at the quarterdeck rail. From there he had a grandstand view and could almost reach out and touch the mainmast.

'Carry on, Mister Gresham.'

Gresham took a deep breath and started. Everything had to work in harmony. As the mast was raised a foot, so the heel lashings had to be slackened and the substitute stays and shrouds must be taken in to prevent the top of the mast swaying.

'Heave on the capstan!'

Gradually, foot by foot, the great mainmast rose vertically upwards. Carlisle tried to calculate its weight, probably three or four tons, but it was more of a guess than a computation. In any case, a preposterous weight to be dealing with in a moving ship at sea.

Gresham was concentrating on the mainmast and it was Carlisle who saw the dangerous sequence of waves approaching.

'Hold her there, Mister Gresham,' he said pointing over the larboard bow.

'Avast!' Gresham roared.

A hundred men leant back on their ropes, holding them just so, without either hauling them in or veering them an inch.

*Dartmouth's* bow rose to the waves, dropped into the

trough and rose again. The mainmast swayed dangerously and rotated on its long axis. Then the danger was past. Carlisle and Gresham exchanged relieved glances.

With one last heave the mainmast rose above its stump. The carpenter risked the loss of a limb by checking for fit with his arm under the heel, feeling the rebate that he had fashioned to stop the mast from twisting once it was in place. He waved to Gresham without lifting his face from the stump.

'Take up the slack,' Gresham shouted to the master's mate at the capstan. The marines took up the weight, one step, a second step, and with a sharp click the pawl sprang free.

'Veer away! Handsomely there, handsomely!'

The mast dropped towards the stump inch by inch. The carpenter leaned close, waving to the men at the heel tackles. He lowered his hand and with a slight but definite thump the mainmast dropped into its step.

'Avast! Hold at that!' shouted Gresham as he ran to inspect.

The mast was there or thereabouts, perhaps two inches out of line, no more, but it was close enough.

'Bosun, you may set up the stays and shrouds and the backstays and belay all. Chips. Get those fish-pieces in place, then the bosun can set up the woolding. We'll have a mainmast to be the envy of Portsmouth Yard!'

*** 

Carlisle studied the Frenchman through his telescope. The loom of the sun was already brightening the northeaster horizon; it would be daylight in half an hour. He looked at his mainmast. The fish-pieces were woolded with turns of three-inch hawser and even now the bosun was tightening them with a Spanish windlass. The apparatus of twisted cords being slowly tightened by the turning of an iron bar reminded Carlisle of the garotte that he had been shown in Saint Augustine a couple of years before; he shuddered at the memory.

In half an hour, he judged, he'd be ready to continue the fight. A quick look told him that *Le Bourbon* had been busy overnight too, and although she lacked half her headsails and she had botched her attempt to jury-rig a main topmast, she was in no worse state than *Dartmouth*. It would be a long hard fight to the finish unless the Frenchman gave up and set sail to the west.

'She's as ready as she'll ever be, sir,' the bosun said grinning with the satisfaction of a job that he knew to have been well done. 'She won't win any prizes in point of beauty, but she'll hold the wind and she'll tack and wear should you wish.'

Carlisle looked up at the foreshortened mainmast. Apart from the ugly woolding, it looked as it had always done. True, the lanyards were at two-blocks, and still the shrouds were a little slack, but that couldn't be helped today. The topmast had been sent up and the trysail on the mizzen was doing its duty. He knew that this was his last opportunity to refuse to fight; to do the rational thing and put the wind on his starboard quarter and sail away in search of the squadron. Possibly – probably, even – *Le Bourbon* would decide that she was in no fit state to escort the Genoa ships to Toulon. By so wounding his enemy, he may already have done his duty. A fight now would be a fight to the finish, that was certain. It would be like two enormous, wounded beasts, still dangerous and locked in combat, and in that case the heavier weight of the Frenchman's broadside had a good chance of deciding the contest. He thought of the men who had already died; he had not even considered his sailing master since he had been carried below. He thought of his wife and son and his new house in Williamsburg. But that was just weakness; his duty was still clear. While there was a chance of the Genoa ships making their way to Toulon, he must fight on with the last breath in his body. Strangely, having come to that conclusion, all his doubts fled, and he felt at least some ease of mind.

'Beat to quarters, Mister Gresham.'

The drum rolled and the answering cheer from the crew was deafening. Carlisle raised his hat in acknowledgement to his brave men. He thought of the gladiator's creed: *we who are about to die salute you!*

\*\*\*

*Dartmouth's* head paid off slowly as she gathered way. Carlisle looked aloft again; the sails were all drawing well. Given more time he'd have bent on the spare sails, but these tattered old rags would have to do for today. *Le Bourbon* was underway too, with her head to the east, and still missing a fore tops'l and with only a staysail at her head; this time *Dartmouth* was the faster ship.

'We'll try to rake her stern again, Mister Gresham,' he shouted.

He'd try, but he didn't believe the Frenchman would easily allow that. Most likely he'd bear away as *Dartmouth* came closer and force a broadside-to-broadside battle.

This was where Carlisle missed his sailing master. Now he had to both handle the ship and fight her, and it was almost more than one person could manage.

'Larboard battery, I believe, Mister Gresham.'

'There she goes, sir,' Gresham replied.

Sure enough, the Frenchman had put up his helm and now *Le Bourbon* was running free, inviting *Dartmouth* to draw up alongside for the heavyweight slugging match.

'Then you know what to do, Mister Gresham. I'll lay us alongside as close as I dare, you just keep the guns firing.'

Carlisle looked one last time at the bright blue sky and the deeper blue of the sea. If this was to be his last sight, then it was a good one.

'Sail ho!'

Carlisle snapped out of his reverie.

'Where away?' he shouted back to the masthead.

'A point abaft the starboard beam, sir, it's a British ship-of-the line, sir, looks like a third rate, on a broad reach towards us.'

Carlisle bit off the instinctive harsh words. The lookout

had clearly been watching the Frenchman rather than the horizon all around. Carlisle could see the ship plainly and it must have been in sight from the masthead for the last twenty minutes. The lookout's loquaciousness was explained; he urgently needed to atone for the sin of letting a sail approach so close without being reported.

*Le Bourbon* would surely strike her colours to this overwhelming force. Now he wouldn't have to die, and he wouldn't have to sentence his crew to death or mutilation or captivity. He was disorientated for a moment in this bright, hopeful new world. Gresham, however, had a different perspective.

'That's *Hercules*,' he exclaimed in disgust, putting enough venom in naming the ship to poison every man and boy on board her. He snapped his telescope closed and stamped his foot on the deck, 'a great, overblown, pretentious, high-and-mighty seventy-four. Damn him for muscling in on our prize.'

***

# CHAPTER TWENTY-NINE

## Rodrigo Black

*Saturday, Fifth of July 1760.*
*Dartmouth, at Sea. Cape Mele north by east 8 leagues.*

The mistral had ended as mysteriously as it had started, and normal business had resumed in this western part of the Ligurian Sea. The three ships bobbed gently as they lay to the gentle ponente wind with their tops'ls backed and their courses furled. Carlisle loved the sound of the Mediterranean winds and used them whenever he could in preference to the harsh mathematical cyphers of the boxed compass. The winds had been named back in antiquity and they had been adapted and changed to suit every civilisation that had come and gone in the middle sea; whole mythologies had grown up around them. *Tramontana, Grecale, Levante, Sirocco, Ostro, Libeccio, Ponente, Mistral*; the words rolled off the tongue in honeyed waves of sensual pleasure.

Carlisle studied his own ship from the stern windows of *Hercules*. There was no doubting her odd appearance. The strangely proportioned mainmast was only apparent to an informed observer, but the complete absence of a mizzen yard was immediately obvious and offended the naval eye. However, it was marvellous what a new suit of sails did for a ship, and *Dartmouth's* crew had worked day and night to bend on the spares that she had carried all the way from Portsmouth. The sailmaker had cut down the old mizzen and made the trysail a semi-permanent fixture, for there was no fishing the shot-through yard, it just wouldn't stand any kind of blow.

*Le Bourbon* had an equally cottage-made look about her. *Hercules'* bosun had managed to send up a spare topmast and most of her sails had been replaced, but naught could be done for her jib boom and she would carry nothing more than a staysail at her head until she could be taken in hand by a regular yard.

'Well, that's settled then,' said Jervis Porter, who enjoyed a full eight years of seniority over Carlisle. 'When your longboat returns from Villa-Franca, you'll take *Le Bourbon* under your wing and beat back to Toulon to find the admiral. Your first lieutenant looks competent and perhaps their lordships will take notice of him when he brings a prize seventy-four in. I don't doubt that the admiral will send you back to Gib, but God alone knows what they'll make of you. You'll be for Portsmouth, I expect. I'll take up your station off Genoa and carry out your orders until Mister Saunders tells me otherwise.'

Porter was clearly delighted with the turn of events. He'd take his share of the prize money for *Le Bourbon* after doing nothing more than firing a single gun to leeward, just for form's sake, at which the Frenchman had promptly struck his colours. Fair enough, Carlisle thought, if *Hercules* hadn't appeared it was a better than even chance that *Dartmouth* would be a French prize now. For that fortuitous arrival and the expenditure of a single ball and charge, the crew of *Hercules* would share equally with the *Dartmouths* and Porter would take half the captain's share; one eighth of the value of the prize, as the admiral would still have his whole eighth. Even that wasn't the sum of Porter's good fortune. He'd been sent east to warn Carlisle of *Le Bourbon's* escape from Toulon and as those orders were issued verbally across a wide, mistral-tossed sea, they had been necessarily vague. He felt justified in taking this opportunity to fill Carlisle's place watching the Genoa ships, and he hoped – his whole ship's company hoped – that he would have as much luck in taking French merchantmen and privateers as Carlisle had. Yes, Porter was happy – ecstatic even – with the way things had turned out.

'You're sure that this foreign lieutenant of yours will have no difficulty ashore, Carlisle? From what you've told me it's a delicate political situation with Sardinia. What will they make of us taking a French third rate almost off their coast?'

Carlisle composed his thoughts. Although *Hercules* and *Dartmouth* had both been at Quiberon Bay last November, he had met Porter for the first time at Gibraltar, at dinner in the flagship before he'd been detached. He knew little about him except that he wasn't renowned as the most deep-thinking captain in the squadron. His reputation was as a fighter and a seaman, and since he'd been posted he'd been in one battle squadron after another. He'd never had the sort of independent command that required any diplomatic skills. Well, he'd have to learn fast.

'Lieutenant Angelini grew up in these parts; he's a cousin of mine by marriage, you know. Nobody will dare interfere with him and he'll be in Villa Franca where they stand on less ceremony than Nice. He has orders to deliver the letter to the fort's commander for dispatch directly to Mister Mackenzie at Turin. There will be no difficulty.'

Porter knew that Carlisle wasn't British born – he was known as the *Colonial Post-Captain* throughout the fleet – and he also knew about his exotic foreign wife. He sniffed dismissively; he'd rather not know too much about colonials and foreigners, and he was inclined to disregard Carlisle in consequence. He turned over his copy of the letter to the envoy.

'This was necessary, was it?' he asked.

Carlisle stifled a sigh. He'd explained the necessity of informing the British envoy to Sardinia of the action off the coast before he heard it from other sources, so that he could prepare his defence against the inevitable French protests.

'It is, sir,' he replied simply. 'Now, I fear I should return to my ship. I thank you for the excellent dinner and in case we don't meet again, I wish you the best of fortune in the Ligurian Sea.'

'Very well, Carlisle. Unless Mister...' he looked quickly at a note on his desk, '...unless Mister Angelini brings any news that I should hear, you may proceed with *Le Bourbon* as soon as your longboat returns. Goodbye and good luck to you also.'

***

The longboat was hailed within minutes of Carlisle returning to *Dartmouth*. She was running fast before the westerly wind and there was only an hour or so between her first sighting and her lying alongside. Carlisle was in his cabin. He had realised that in all the excitement of the past few weeks, he'd slipped in his resolution to be more detached from the ship's daily routine, and he was trying to regain a sort of Olympian detachment by waiting for Enrico with apparent unconcern. His self-enforced solitude wasn't made any easier by the inept ministrations of one of the lesser of his servants, Walker having suffered a blow to the head from a falling block while attempting to offer a cup of cold coffee to Carlisle at the heat of the battle.

'Come,' he said in reply to the knock on the door.

It was Enrico, as he had expected, looking remarkably spruce for a man who'd spent two days in an open boat, most of the time beating hard to windward. But that was Enrico's upbringing showing through. He would have taken clothes brushes and shaving kit in the boat and wouldn't have cared a fig for the amused looks of the crew as he made himself presentable before going ashore or meeting his captain.

'The letters have been delivered, sir. I gave one copy to the fort's commander and saw it galloped away up the Turin road by a trooper from my old regiment. It will arrive safely, I'm certain. I was bringing the second one back and was just about to depart when General Paterson's coach drew up, and he offered to deliver any letters to Turin, where he was immediately bound, so I gave him the duplicate.'

'Thank you, Mister Angelini. Then we can be sure of their timely arrival without any interference.'

That had been Carlisle's chief concern, that someone

other than the envoy should open one of the letters. It was not impossible in a country that was grappling with the question of neutrality. However, Enrico knew the situation better than he did, and he knew who could be trusted.

'Then it all passed off without incident, I gather?' Carlisle asked.

Enrico gave him a curious, furtive look.

'Ah, not quite, sir.'

Carlisle raised an eyebrow, ready to hear the worst. Had Enrico committed some sort of diplomatic breach? Had he been accosted by the viscountess?

'Perhaps I can best explain by bringing a visitor in, sir?'

Carlisle hesitated, then nodded cautiously.

Enrico stepped to the door and pulled it open. Carlisle saw a tall figure framed in the cabin doorway and took a moment to recognise the man.

'Sir, it is a pleasure to meet you again,' said Black Rod.

Carlisle stood open-mouthed for a span of a few seconds, then he recovered himself and composed his face into one of official disapproval.

'I assume there is a good explanation for your being here,' Carlisle said.

*** 

The story, when it was told, had all the drama of one of the modern novels that Carlisle's wife so enjoyed. Black Rod had only been back in Nice a few days when he learned of the viscountess' arrangement with the French envoy – of her preference for France over England – and her consequent casting-off of her niece and nephew. For her part, the viscountess started to suspect that her head of household's allegiance had shifted from her own person to that of Chiara. No words had been spoken, and she hadn't directly accused him of passing information to Carlisle, but it was clear that the viscountess suspected him of disloyalty, and she started excluding Black Rod from discussions on the family's business.

When he heard that *Dartmouth's* longboat had returned,

he fled the Angelini house without a moment's thought, and started walking the few miles to Villa-Franca. He'd been overtaken on the road by the general, who had not wished to hear his story – so that he could later deny any knowledge – but had willingly carried him the rest of the way.

In Black Rod's own words, his loyalty was to Lady Chiara now, not to the rotten rump of the once-great Angelini family, and he would be much obliged if Captain Carlisle would give him passage to anywhere from where he could make his way back to Virginia. He was happy to be put ashore on any coast, but the further from Sardinia the better, because he feared the viscountess' retribution when she realised that he had fled. He would gladly act as the captain's servant in the meantime, as he understood that Walker would take some weeks to recover from his wounds.

'Well, if your loyalty is to Lady Chiara then you're welcome of course,' said Carlisle, 'but you came from Virginia as a supernumerary passenger. If you're to be my servant then we must think about how you're victualled, it could be a long voyage as I suspect we are bound eventually for Portsmouth.'

'If I may suggest,' Enrico interjected, 'we're short of complement now with our battle losses, so you could enter him as one of your servants.'

Carlisle thought for a moment. It was an excellent idea in many ways. It meant that he wouldn't have to suffer the fool who had replaced Walker, and Black Rod would have both victuals and pay. Better still, being one of the captain's allowance of servants, he could be discharged without any formality.

'Then you may be entered in the books as a landsman,' he said. 'You will, of course, need to give a name, and I'll leave it to you to decide what that should be.'

'We've already discussed that, sir,' Enrico said, looking sideways at Black Rod.

'Rodrigo Black, your honour, that will be my name in my new life. It's neither Genoan nor Sardinian but I had an uncle who lived in Seville for many years and he styled himself Rodrigo. It will do for me.'

Carlisle looked in wonderment at his new servant; it was almost the first time that he'd seen him smile.

*\*\**

# CHAPTER THIRTY

## An Admiral's Favour

*Monday, Seventh of July 1760.*
*Dartmouth, at Sea. Off Cape Sicié.*

They found the squadron newly returned to the watch on Toulon. The ships looked storm-tossed as well they might having been driven before a summer mistral with the consequent long beat back to station. Yet still the squadron looked formidable and Carlisle could only marvel at what the French thought of such a strong enemy force cruising with impunity off their principal Mediterranean naval base.

*Dartmouth* was barely over the horizon before the signal was hung out in the flagship for him to come aboard. He was rowed over in his yawl, conscious of the telescopes of the entire squadron alternately trained on *Le Bourbon* and on him. This was the squadron's first success and although they might guess that *Hercules* had been involved, it was *Dartmouth*, the lowly fourth rate, that was bringing in the prize.

*\*\*\**

'Well congratulations, Captain Carlisle, she's a fine prize.'

Saunders gazed across the blue water at *Le Bourbon* with the utmost satisfaction. Apart from the reduction of the French force by one formidable seventy-four, he was now a richer man by a few thousands thanks to the sacrifice of *Dartmouth's* crew. There was no doubt that she'd be bought into the service; Anson was crying out for captured French seventy-fours to join his fleet. Even though the design had been brazenly copied after Anson himself captured the French *Invincible* in the last war, most sea officers agreed that the French-built ships were superior to those that came from the British yards.

'Gibraltar, of course, and without delay before that

mainmast plunges through your decks and brings an abrupt end to your concerns. You'll escort *Le Bourbon,* and your first lieutenant can command her at least until she's safely in the yard's hands. I'll give you some marines to help with the prisoners.'

Saunders pivoted in his chair to look out of the wide cabin windows. He had a grand view centred on Toulon's outer road with Cape Sicié to the west and the Hyeres Islands to the east. It was a familiar scene to Carlisle; he'd cruised these waters back in 'fifty-six watching the French fleet's opening moves in this war.

'The French show no signs of coming out, Carlisle. It appears that the four Genoa sixty-fours were more important to them than we'd thought and with one badly mauled and the other two unable to make Toulon, they're short of ships for a battle. Lord Anson has already guessed that there'll be no fleet action this year. This latest letter that *Weazel* brought informs me that I may send my hospital ship to Antigua along with four of my storeships, if I don't need them. Pitt is contemplating action against the French sugar islands and what with the sickness and the enemy they'll need a hospital ship.'

Carlisle froze. He could hardly dare to hope that he'd be sent to escort this group across the Atlantic. Antigua was barely any distance from Virginia in seagoing terms and if he were in the Leeward Islands Squadron, there was a good chance of taking a convoy north up the American coast.

'I regret that I shall have to lose you, Carlisle,' the admiral said, grimacing. 'I have great need of all my frigates, and I don't care to lose a third rate. *Dartmouth* is the ideal ship for the job. You won't mind the Leeward Islands for a spell? Commodore Moore is commanding there but I understand he's coming home this year; he may already have hauled down his pennant. I don't know who his successor is.'

It was a testament to their remoteness that the

commander-in-chief should be unaware of the latest
movements of station commanders. The Mediterranean
often spent months in isolation from the news in
Whitehall.

'You may be there for years, you know, and you'll have
to brave the hurricane season for your passage across, but
I believe you've done that before.'

Carlisle nodded but said nothing. Was it possible that
the admiral didn't know that he was doing Carlisle a
favour? It was the best of news.

'Now, you'll have difficulty with those scoundrels at the
Gibraltar yard. They won't want to deal with *Dartmouth*,
but they'll positively salivate at the sight of *Le Bourbon*.
They've been short of work recently and your prize will
keep half the yard at work for the next six months. I'll
write a most strongly worded letter to the commissioner to
the effect that you're to have priority. I want you to sail
from Gibraltar no later than the eleventh of August. With
these westerlies and those old tubs of stores ships you'll
take two weeks to reach Gibraltar, so I'll give them three
weeks to refit you. I know they have spare masts and yards
for all the rates.'

Carlisle had taken a walk through the yard when the
squadron had called at Gibraltar on its voyage to the
Mediterranean. He'd seen the mast pond with the long
rows of lower masts, ordered by ship's rate, and he'd
noticed two mainmasts that matched a fourth rate fifty-
gun ship's establishment.

'The hospital ship, sir, where is she?'

'That's the silliness of the whole thing, Carlisle. *Jersey*
only left Portsmouth at the end of May. She's at Gibraltar
now, so *Weazel* tells me, you can pick her up there. Andrew
Wilkinson has had her since last year. He was posted in
'fifty-seven,' Saunders added with a significant look.

That was of the utmost importance. Wilkinson was
junior to Carlisle on the post-captain's list and there would
be no embarrassing questions – no sordid wrangling –

about who commanded.

Carlisle could hardly keep his mind on the rest of the details, he was too busy digesting the wonderful news that he was heading back across the Atlantic. With an effort he brought his mind back to the present. They discussed the details of transferring additional marines to *Le Bourbon* to keep the French prisoners under control, and the state of the sixty-fours in Genoa. Then Saunders grew more sombre.

'I'm sorry for Mister Beazley's injury; I hope it's only temporary. I understand he wants nothing to do with the hospital ship and is determined to stay in *Dartmouth*, so you may keep him on your books until he recovers. Although by the sound of his injury you'll have to make do with one of his mates until you reach Antigua, at least.'

Carlisle nodded; it was what he had expected. No squadron carried spare sailing masters.

The sombre – severe even – expression remained.

'Now, where's that letter?' Saunders asked his secretary.

The secretary was a grave man who brought a folded letter and presented it as though it were a patent of nobility. He then withdrew to a desk in the corner of the cabin and dipped his pen into his ink pot, ready to record a conversation, it seemed to Carlisle.

'I regret to say, Captain Carlisle, that I've received a complaint about your conduct from Mister Mackenzie.'

Carlisle felt as though he'd been hit by a sledgehammer. He'd hoped that after their last meeting the envoy would have relented in his determination to punish him. Apparently, he wasn't a man to forgive or forget, and Carlisle knew that he shouldn't be surprised.

The admiral passed the letter for Carlisle to read. It was much as he feared; a not entirely unjustified tirade at the way that Carlisle had delayed the envoys arrival at Nice – put the voyage at risk even – for the sake of taking prizes. There was more about the lack of respect that Carlisle showed for the envoy's rank, but that was inconsequential, it merely embellished the main clause. Carlisle read the letter then looked up, there was nothing to say; in its essentials the letter was correct. Carlisle thought about defending himself – telling the admiral about Mackenzie's high-handed attitude – but he knew it would be useless, even damaging.

'A copy has been sent directly to Lord Anson, so I cannot follow my initial instinct to ignore it,' he looked sharply at his secretary, 'don't record that if you please.'

'I don't need to lecture you on the necessity of maintaining good relations with the diplomats in this theatre, Carlisle, so I'll leave the homilies alone. I'll have it recorded,' he nodded to the secretary, 'that I've admonished you for your conduct.'

Carlisle opened his mouth to remonstrate then closed it with a snap. Really, Saunders was doing him a favour – a second favour. With a good will, Anson could note the admonishment and with the passage of months and years it was quite possible that he'd take no further action. Carlisle bowed gratefully.

'Thank you, sir, and I have taken your advice to heart.'

'Good, then that's over and I hope to hear no more of it. Have a good passage, Captain, I believe you may see your family long before I see mine.'

***

A long, slow passage to Gibraltar. The summer westerlies blew with infuriating steadiness and the storeships refused to keep the wind, sagging to leeward at the slightest provocation, while the French prize laboured under the dreadful mauling that *Dartmouth* had given her. The carpenter barely left the waist; he watched the fished mast with deepening concern and tightened the woolding with an obsession that bordered on the religious. He looked like a wizened old ascetic keeping a lonely vigil at the shrine of some wooden god of the forest.

At Gibraltar, the master attendant shook his head and vowed that *Dartmouth* should be sent to Portsmouth for repair, and that the yard would be better employed in the thorough refitting of *Le Bourbon*. He was adamant on the point, until he had an abrupt change of heart after a harsh interview with the commissioner. It was wonderful to see the zeal with which *Dartmouth* was taken in hand after that meeting. The sheer hulk was alongside before dinner and by the following day the old mainmast had been drawn like the stump of a rotten tooth. The carpenter slept soundly for the first time in two weeks.

The little convoy sailed from Gibraltar on the eighth of August, three days ahead of the admiral's schedule, and was soon reaching to the southwest to pass between Madeira and the Canaries where they found the blessed trade winds. For over three thousand miles they barely touched a sheet as the steady sou'easterlies, and the invisible but oh-so-helpful current, wafted them across the Atlantic towards Antigua. They saw no French ships, neither man-o'-war nor merchantman, which was an eloquent testament to Britannia's growing ownership of the oceans.

\*\*\*

# CHAPTER THIRTY-ONE

## Fair Winds

*Friday, Fifth of September 1760.*
*Dartmouth, at Sea. Off English Harbour.*

'I wonder what's in store for us at English Harbour,' Carlisle mused as he strolled with Gresham on the poop deck, enjoying the first warming rays of the sun.

'We'll find out this evening, sir,' Gresham replied. 'I'll just be glad to stretch my legs on *terra firma*, and to taste some real, fresh fruit. Our orders can wait for another day as far as I'm concerned.'

'You know, it's one of the joys of these old fifty-gun ships, you never know what's coming next. If we had a sixty or a third rate, we'd be in line ahead with the battle squadron, and we may yet be, but we may equally be given some more interesting employment.'

'Aye, that we may, sir. Perhaps something where there's the chance of a prize or two.'

Carlisle let that pass; it wasn't prizes that he was thinking of.

'Sail ho! Sail on the larboard bow.'

Carlisle looked up sharply. They hadn't sighted another sail for the past two weeks, but with Antigua so close under their lee, Whittle's hail was hardly surprising.

'I'll go up and take a look, with your permission, sir,' Gresham said, reaching for his telescope.

Within minutes the single sail had become half a dozen, then a dozen.

'It's the squadron, sir, it looks like they're exercising,' Gresham shouted down. 'I can see *Stirling Castle* in the lead flying a pennant.'

Now that was odd. The Leeward Islands Squadron barely stirred from English Harbour in the hurricane season, preferring to reduce the risk by lying at anchor unless they had a definite need to be at sea.

***

Carlisle knew Sir James Douglas from the Quebec campaign where he'd commanded *Alcide*; in fact, he'd been knighted for his part in the capture of the city. He'd been a post-captain then and that was still his substantive rank; he was only a commodore while he held this post. Nevertheless, he was a commander-in-chief now and held Carlisle's immediate future in the palm of his hand. He was new to the station, which explained why he was so keen to see his squadron at its drills, but he was keeping English Harbour comfortably under his lee in case he had to run for shelter.

'Glad to see you, Carlisle, and *Jersey's* a welcome sight; I believe we'll be glad of her next year if we have a go at Martinique or Dominica. Now, is *Dartmouth* fit to keep the sea?'

'Yes, sir, as good as new. The Gibraltar yard did a fine job and I'm stored for another two months.'

'You were badly mauled, I suppose? Hardly unlikely if you will take on a French seventy-four. Still, it was well done.'

Carlisle wondered what that question was about: *could Dartmouth keep the sea?* He didn't have to wait long.

'I regret that the delights of English Harbour will have to wait for another time, Carlisle. I can allow you a day for wood and water and to take on fresh provisions, then I have a convoy for you. The ships that brought down my stores from the Chesapeake – hogs and grain mostly – need to return. There are still French privateers around and I don't quite trust the Spaniards... what the devil is it man?'

Carlisle just couldn't keep the grin from his face. In ten days, two weeks perhaps, before September was out in any case, he'd be home with his family!

***

# HISTORICAL EPILOGUE

## New France

After a fearful winter in Quebec, the British army was defeated at the battle of Sainte-Foy in April 1760, just a short walk from where Wolfe had beaten Montcalm in the previous year. However, the French commander at Sainte-Foy, the Chevalier de Lévis, was unable to follow up his success and when in May a British navy squadron sailed up the Saint Lawrence as the ice melted, it was all over for New France. The promised French squadron failed to materialise after the terrible defeats that the French navy suffered at Lagos Bay and Quiberon Bay, and the supply ships were sunk at the Battle of Restigouche. Lacking men, provisions and even a clear means of communication with France, and with British armies closing in on three sides, Montreal surrendered in September. By the end of 1760, the long dream of New France was over.

## Europe

Broken at Lagos Bay and Quiberon Bay in 1759, and after losing a third of its ships trying to maintain New France, the French navy at the end of 1760 was in no state to contest the mastery of the oceans and had largely abandoned any plans for an invasion of England. Versailles now accepted that it was only by diverting its resources to the army in Germany that anything could be salvaged from this ruinous war. Assaulted by large and vigorous French armies, the allied forces could only hold the line in Hanover.

## *Spain*

The powerful squadron that Admiral Saunders took into the Mediterranean in 1760 was calculated not only to pin down the French in Toulon, but to make it clear to the King of Spain what awaited him if he should join the war on France's side. Without Spain, France could not see a way to end the war with its colonies – and its honour – intact, yet Spain couldn't afford to enter the war. The bloody stalemate had a few years yet to run.

## *Where Fact Meets Fiction*

*Ligurian Mission* is a work of fiction. Nevertheless, its background – the scene against which it is set – is true to the historical narrative.

After a period when Britain largely ignored the Mediterranean theatre, Admiral Saunders took a squadron through the Straits of Gibraltar in May 1760 to blockade Toulon and to demonstrate to Spain the consequences to its trade and to its navy if it should join France.

Spain wasn't Pitt's only concern. All the small states that bordered the Italian coast, from Sardinia to Naples, were being urged by France to enter the war. Sardinia was in the most unenviable position, with a short seaboard, few useful ports and little strategic depth to absorb a French invasion. However, King Charles Emmanuel was a seasoned statesman by now and he was determined to remain neutral despite the Machiavellian manoeuvering within his government and army. Many of the other states, while formally retaining their neutrality, were unable or unwilling to prevent French privateers using their ports.

It may sound odd that France should commission its ships to be built in Genoa, but that is in fact what happened. The French navy couldn't build ships fast enough to redress its recent losses and sought foreign shipbuilders to assist. Genoa was only too happy to oblige and built four sixty-four-gun ships-of-the-line for the Toulon Squadron. Carlisle was well placed to interfere with their delivery.

# OTHER BOOKS IN THE SERIES

## Book 1: The Colonial Post-Captain

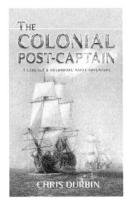

Captain Carlisle of His Britannic Majesty's frigate *Fury* hails from Virginia, a loyal colony of the British Crown. In 1756, as the clouds of war gather in Europe, *Fury* is ordered to Toulon to investigate a French naval and military build-up.

While battling the winter weather, Carlisle must also juggle with delicate diplomatic issues in this period of phoney war and contend with an increasingly belligerent French frigate.

And then there is the beautiful Chiara Angelini, pursued across the Mediterranean by a Tunisian corsair who appears determined to abduct her, yet strangely reluctant to shed blood.

Carlisle and his young master's mate, George Holbrooke, are witnesses to the inconclusive sea-battle that leads to the loss of Minorca. They engage in a thrilling and bloody encounter with the French frigate and a final confrontation with the enigmatic corsair.

# Book 2: The Leeward Islands Squadron

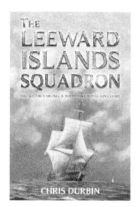

In late 1756, as the British government collapses in the aftermath of the loss of Minorca and the country and navy are thrown into political chaos, a small force of ships is sent to the West Indies to reinforce the Leeward Islands Squadron.

Captain Edward Carlisle, a native of Virginia, and his first lieutenant George Holbrooke are fresh from the Mediterranean and their capture of a powerful French man-of-war. Their new frigate *Medina* has orders to join a squadron commanded by a terminally ill commodore. Their mission: a near-suicidal assault on a strong Caribbean island fortress. Carlisle must confront the challenges of higher command as he leads the squadron back into battle to accomplish the Admiralty's orders.

Join Carlisle and Holbrooke as they attack shore fortifications, engage in ship-on-ship duels and deal with mutiny in the West Indies.

## Book 3: The Jamaica Station

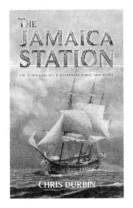

It is 1757, and the British navy is regrouping from a slow start to the seven years war.

A Spanish colonial governor and his family are pursued through the Caribbean by a pair of mysterious ships from the Dutch island of St. Eustatius. The British frigate *Medina* rescues the governor from his hurricane-wrecked ship, leading Captain Edward Carlisle and his first lieutenant George Holbrooke into a web of intrigue and half-truths. Are the Dutchmen operating under a letter of marque or are they pirates, and why are they hunting the Spaniard? Only the diplomatic skills of Carlisle's aristocratic wife, Lady Chiara, can solve the puzzle.

When Carlisle is injured, the young Holbrooke must grow up quickly. Under his leadership, *Medina* takes part in a one-sided battle with the French that will influence a young Horatio Nelson to choose the navy as a career.

# Book 4: Holbrooke's Tide

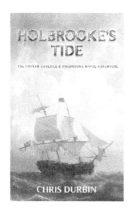

It is 1758, and the Seven Years War is at its height. The Duke of Cumberland's Hanoverian army has been pushed back to the River Elbe while the French are using the medieval fortified city of Emden to resupply their army and to anchor its left flank.

George Holbrooke has recently returned from the Jamaica Station in command of a sloop-of-war. He is under orders to survey and blockade the approaches to Emden in advance of the arrival of a British squadron. The French garrison and their Austrian allies are nervous. With their supply lines cut, they are in danger of being isolated when the French army is forced to retreat in the face of the new Prussian-led army that is gathering on the Elbe. Can the French be bluffed out of Emden? Is this Holbrooke's flood tide that will lead to his next promotion?

Holbrooke's Tide is the fourth of the Carlisle & Holbrooke naval adventures. The series follows the exploits of the two men through the Seven Years War and into the period of turbulent relations between Britain and her American colonies in the 1760s.

## Book 5: The Cursed Fortress

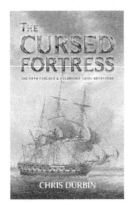

The French called it *La Forteresse Maudite*, the Cursed Fortress.

Louisbourg stood at the mouth of the Gulf of Saint Lawrence, massive and impregnable, a permanent provocation to the British colonies. It was Canada's first line of defence, guarding the approaches to Quebec, from where all New France lay open to invasion. It had to fall before a British fleet could be sent up the Saint Lawrence. Otherwise, there would be no resupply and no line of retreat; Canada would become the graveyard of George II's navy.

A failed attempt on Louisbourg in 1757 had only stiffened the government's resolve; the Cursed Fortress must fall in 1758.

Captain Carlisle's frigate joins the blockade of Louisbourg before winter's icy grip has eased. Battling fog, hail, rain, frost and snow, suffering scurvy and fevers, and with a constant worry about the wife he left behind in Virginia, Carlisle will face his greatest test of leadership and character yet.

The Cursed Fortress is the fifth of the Carlisle & Holbrooke naval adventures. The series follows the two men through the Seven Years War and into the period of turbulent relations between Britain and her American colonies in the 1760s.

## Book 6: Perilous Shore

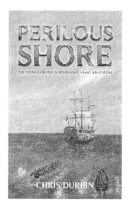

Amphibious warfare was in its infancy in the mid-eighteenth century – it was the poor relation of the great fleet actions that the navy so loved.

That all changed in 1758 when the British government demanded a campaign of raids on the French Channel ports. Command arrangements were hastily devised, and a whole new class of vessels was produced at breakneck speed: flatboats, the ancestors of the landing craft that put the allied forces ashore on D-Day.

Commander George Holbrooke's sloop *Kestrel* is in the thick of the action: scouting landing beaches, duelling with shore batteries and battling the French Navy.

In a twist of fate, Holbrooke finds himself unexpectedly committed to this new style of amphibious warfare as he is ordered to lead a division of flatboats onto the beaches of Normandy and Brittany. He meets his greatest test yet when a weary and beaten British army retreats from a second failed attempt at Saint Malo with the French close on their heels.

Perilous Shore is the sixth of the Carlisle & Holbrooke naval adventures. The series follows Holbrooke and his mentor, Captain Carlisle, through the Seven Years War and into the period of turbulent relations between Britain and her American colonies in the 1760s.

## Book 7: Rocks and Shoals

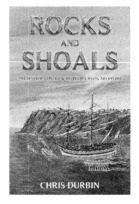

With the fall of Louisbourg in 1758 the French in North America were firmly on the back foot. Pitt's grand strategy for 1759 was to launch a three-pronged attack on Canada. One army would move north from Lake Champlain while another smaller force would strike across the wilderness to Lake Ontario and French-held Fort Niagara. A third, under Admiral Saunders and General Wolfe, would sail up the Saint Lawrence, where no battle fleet had ever been, and capture Quebec.

Captain Edward Carlisle sails ahead of the battle fleet to find a way through the legendary dangers of the Saint Lawrence River. An unknown sailing master assists him; James Cook has a talent for surveying and cartography and will achieve immortality in later years.

There are rocks and shoals aplenty before Carlisle and his frigate *Medina* are caught up in the near-fatal indecision of the summer when General Wolfe tastes the bitterness of early setbacks.

Rocks and Shoals is the seventh of the Carlisle & Holbrooke naval adventures. The series follows Carlisle and his protégé George Holbrooke, through the Seven Years War and into the period of turbulent relations between Britain and her American colonies in the 1760s.

## Book 8: Niagara Squadron

Fort Niagara is the key to the American continent. Whoever owns that lonely outpost at the edge of civilisation controls the entire Great Lakes region.

Pitt's grand strategy for 1759 is to launch a three-pronged attack on Canada. One army would move north from Lake Champlain, a second would sail up the Saint Lawrence to capture Quebec, and a third force would strike across the wilderness to Lake Ontario and French-held Fort Niagara.

Commander George Holbrooke is seconded to command the six hundred boats to carry the army through the rivers and across Lake Ontario. That's the easy part; he also must deal with two powerful brigs that guarantee French naval superiority on the lake.

Holbrooke knows time is running out to be posted as captain before the war ends and promotions dry up; his rank is the stumbling block to his marriage to Ann, waiting for him in his hometown of Wickham Hampshire.

Niagara Squadron is the eighth Carlisle and Holbrooke novel. The series follows Carlisle and his protégé Holbrooke through the Seven Years War and into the period of turbulent relations between Britain and her American colonies in the 1760's.

# BIBLIOGRAPHY

The following is a selection of the many books that I consulted in researching the Carlisle & Holbrooke series:

## Definitive Text

Sir Julian Corbett wrote the original, definitive text on the Seven Years War. Most later writers use his work as a steppingstone to launch their own.

Corbett, LLM., Sir Julian Stafford. *England in the Seven Years War – Vol. I: A Study in Combined Strategy.* Normandy Press. Kindle Edition.

## Strategy and Naval Operations

Three very accessible modern books cover the strategic context and naval operations of the Seven Years War. Daniel Baugh addresses the whole war on land and sea, while Martin Robson concentrates on maritime activities. Jonathan Dull has produced a very readable account from the French perspective.

Baugh, Daniel. *The Global Seven Years War 1754-1763.* Pearson Education, 2011. Print.
Robson, Martin. *A History of the Royal Navy, The Seven Years War.* I.B. Taurus, 2016. Print.
Dull, Jonathan, R. *The French Navy and the Seven Years' War.* University of Nebraska Press, 2005. Print.

## Sea Officers

For an interesting perspective on the life of sea officers of the mid-eighteenth century, I'd read Augustus Hervey's Journal, with the cautionary note that while Hervey was by no means typical of the breed, he's very entertaining and devastatingly honest. For a more balanced view, I'd read British Naval Captains of the Seven Years War.

Erskine, David (editor). *Augustus Hervey's Journal, The Adventures Afloat and Ashore of a Naval Casanova*. Chatham Publishing, 2002. Print.

McLeod, A.B. *British Naval Captains of the Seven Years War, The View from the Quarterdeck*. The Boydell Press, 2012. Print.

## Life at Sea

I recommend The Wooden World for an overview of shipboard life and administration during the Seven Years War.

N.A.M Rodger. *The Wooden World, An Anatomy of the Georgian Navy*. Fontana Press, 1986. Print.

# THE AUTHOR

Chris Durbin grew up in the seaside town of Porthcawl in South Wales. His first experience of sailing was as a sea cadet in the treacherous tideway of the Bristol Channel, and at the age of sixteen, he spent a week in a tops'l schooner in the Southwest Approaches. He was a crew member on the Porthcawl lifeboat before joining the navy.

Chris spent twenty-four years as a warfare officer in the Royal Navy, serving in all classes of ships from aircraft carriers through destroyers and frigates to the smallest minesweepers. He took part in operational campaigns in the Falkland Islands, the Middle East and the Adriatic and he spent two years teaching tactics at a US Navy training centre in San Diego.

On his retirement from the Royal Navy, Chris joined a large American company and spent eighteen years in the aerospace, defence and security industry, including two years on the design team for the Queen Elizabeth class aircraft carriers.

Chris is a graduate of the Britannia Royal Naval College at *Dartmouth*, the British Army Command and Staff College, the United States Navy War College (where he gained a postgraduate diploma in national security decision-making) and Cambridge University (where he was awarded an MPhil in International Relations).

With a lifelong interest in naval history and a long-standing ambition to write historical fiction, Chris has completed the first nine novels in the Carlisle & Holbrooke series, in which a colonial Virginian commands a British navy frigate during the middle years of the eighteenth century.

The series will follow its principal characters through the Seven Years War and into the period of turbulent relations between Britain and her American Colonies in the 1760s. They'll negotiate some thought-provoking loyalty issues when British policy and colonial restlessness lead inexorably to the American Revolution.

Chris lives on the south coast of England, surrounded by hundreds of years of naval history. His three children are all busy growing their own families and careers while Chris and his wife (US Navy, retired) of thirty-nine years enjoy sailing on the south coast.

## Fun Fact:

Chris shares his garden with a tortoise named Aubrey. If you've read Patrick O'Brian's *HMS Surprise*, or have seen the 2003 film *Master and Commander: The Far Side of the World*, you'll recognise the modest act of homage that Chris has paid to that great writer. Rest assured that Aubrey has not yet grown to the gigantic proportions of *Testudo Aubreii*.

# FEEDBACK

If you've enjoyed *Niagara Squadron*, please consider leaving a review on Amazon.

This is the latest of a series of books that will follow Carlisle and Holbrooke through the Seven Years War and into the 1760s when relations between Britain and her restless American Colonies are tested to breaking point.

Look out for the tenth in the Carlisle & Holbrooke series, coming soon.

You can follow my blog at:

www.chris-durbin.com

Made in the USA
Las Vegas, NV
13 March 2021